Praise for *UNDER SILKWOOD*

'Rich in atmospheric detail, *Under Silkwood* – set among the brooding cane fields of 1980s Far North Queensland – hums with humid, sticky tension, sexual longing, and long-held resentments. Drawn with genuine humanity and warmth, Bourke's cast of characters, outsiders and insiders alike, make this an unforgettable tale of Far North treachery, betrayal, love and revenge.' —*Melanie Myers, author*

'It is so important to tell the stories of Queensland's diverse community, including our Italian communities, to the rest of the world. Bourke's characters spring to life fully formed and engaging in this immersive and sensual tale. His compelling narrative unfolds with great effect against a backdrop of the vivid, colourful landscape of the North.' —*David Hinchliffe, artist, writer, and former Brisbane Deputy Mayor*

'A wonderful, engaging story combining the majesty and malevolence of Queensland's northern frontier in the 1980s.'
—*John Vandeleur, reviewer, former FNQ resident*

'Equal parts gripping, salacious, and beautiful, *Under Silkwood* dives deep into the tensions between desire, duty, and family expectation. Set against the intoxicating backdrop of Far North Queensland's Sicilian community, this is a story of forbidden romance, and the strength of a mother's love. A bold debut that leaves your mind lingering in the steamy tropics long after the final page.'
—*Rebecca Barkman, reviewer*

'I was gripped from the first page, drawn by the characters, landscape, and the storyline which enthrals and surprises. The story provides a great testament to the character and resilience of farming communities of Far North Queensland, mixed with Italian passion and fury.'
—*Josie Caltabiano, reviewer, with Sicilian and FNQ ancestry*

Praise for *UNDER SILKWOOD*

With exceptional characterisation, the story takes unexpected and rewarding twists and turns, leading the reader onwards to a shocking, brilliant finale. Wonderfully written, this novel has converted me to Australian fiction. —*Robyn Fellowes, author*

As a former Silkwood resident and female, I was immediately taken back to my childhood growing up within a Sicilian immigrant family, bound by tradition, religion, protective parents, food, and feasting. The description of the landscape, cane farming and expectations of women is picture perfect. A thoroughly enjoyable and entertaining read and I was gripped until the end. —*Lorna White (nee Nucifora), former Silkwood resident*

UNDER SILKWOOD

Greg Bourke

HAWKEYE

PUBLISHING

First published in Australia in 2025 by Hawkeye Publishing.

Cover Design by Vikki Vaughan
Cover photo by Alison Jones Photography

This novel is entirely a work of fiction. The names, characters and incidents portrayed in it are the work of the author's imagination. Any resemblance to events or actual persons, living or dead, is entirely coincidental.

Hawkeye Publishing recognises the Traditional Custodians of the lands where we live and work. We pay our respects to Elders past and present and extend that respect to all Aboriginal and Torres Strait Islander peoples. We celebrate more than 60,000 years of storytelling, art, and culture that continue to shape and enrich our world.

A catalogue record of this book is available from the National Library of Australia.

ISBN 9781923105584

Proudly printed in Australia.

www.hawkeyebooks.com.au

To Mum
(1943-2023)

Thank you for the gift of literacy and expression.
I hope this story reaches you, wherever you are.

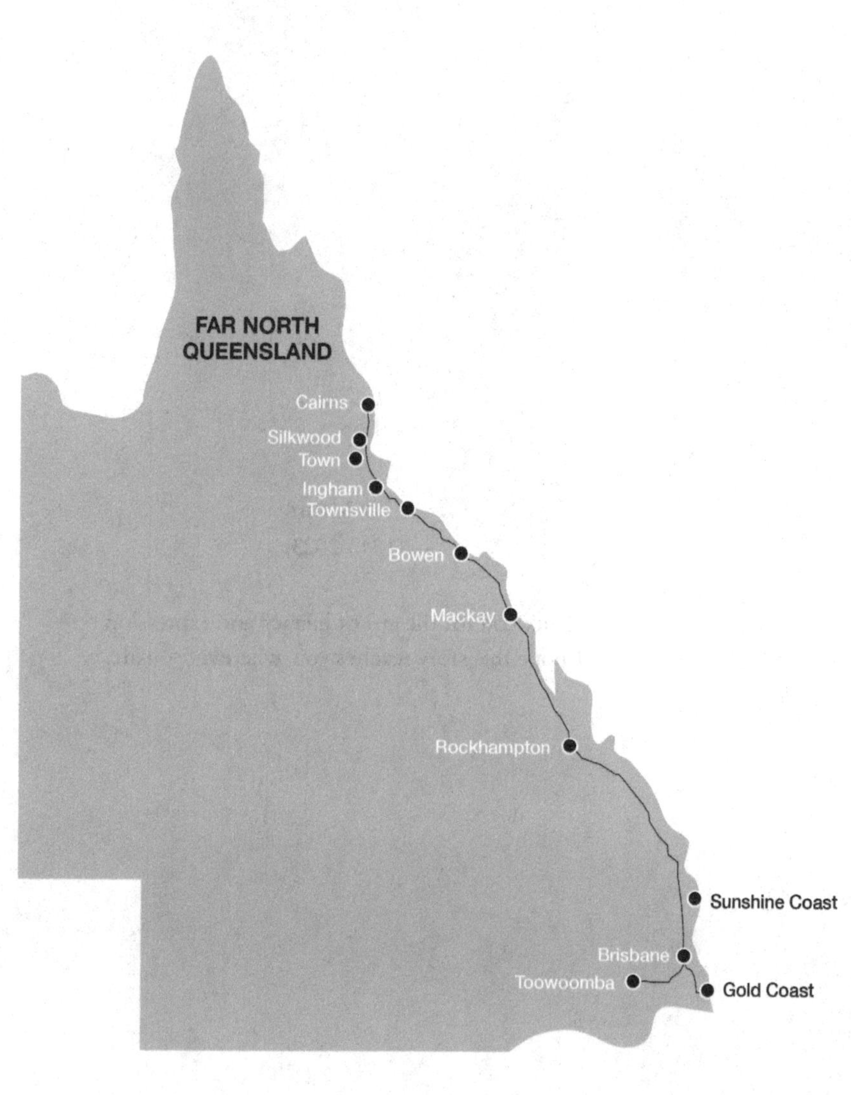

FAR NORTH
QUEENSLAND
Cairns
Silkwood
Town
Ingham
Townsville
Bowen
Mackay
Rockhampton
Sunshine Coast
Brisbane
Toowoomba
Gold Coast

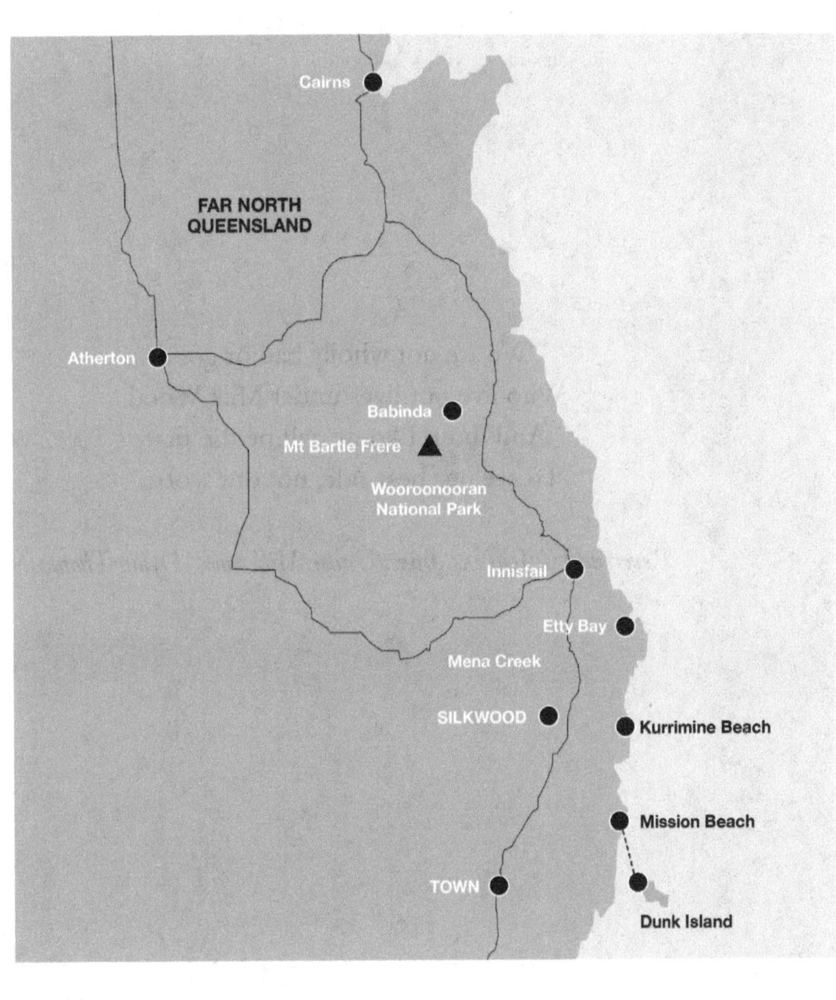

Cairns
FAR NORTH QUEENSLAND
Atherton
Babinda
Mt Bartle Frere
Wooroonooran National Park
Innisfail
Etty Bay
Mena Creek
SILKWOOD
Kurrimine Beach
Mission Beach
TOWN
Dunk Island

'We are not wholly bad or good
Who live our lives under Milk Wood
And thou, I know wilt be the first
To see our best side, not our worst.'

Reverend Eli Jenkins, from 'Under Milkwood' Dylan Thomas.

1

April 1985.

ON Good Friday, three women trudged into a neat field of small stone beds and tablets set within glossy green grass. Dressed in black, flowers in hand, they joined other Far North Queensland Sicilian families to involve their deceased ancestors in Holy Week. Isabella Russo, the youngest, walked with her mother, Frances, who pressed a tissue from eye to eye. Her older sister, Bianca, shuffled behind, grumbling.

'C'mon, Bianca,' Isabella whispered, tugging her older sister's arm. 'For Mamma.'

Dark clouds crowded overhead as the women climbed the slope to the top of the cemetery hill. The deceased Italians had the best view, looking over the town. The Sicilian section was the highest. Isabella glanced ahead at the mausoleums: miniature, church-like homes. Beside them, Sicilian graves bedded together, shoulder to shoulder. Sicilian immigrants always kept close company, thought Isabella, whether dead or alive. Ceramic photos of her relatives embedded in the mausoleum granite reminded her that real people dwelled within, not just stale, chalky remains. She shivered at the thought. At eighteen, she could not remember the relatives who stared unblinkingly for eternity, although she could identify her grandparents by name.

Sicilian boys paused from weeding and polishing family graves to stare at beautiful Bianca. One boy stood and whistled.

'Really?' Isabella hissed, for even in supposed reverence, the town boys were always gawking at her sister. Bianca stopped grumbling, lifted her head and smiled at a tall, dark-eyed boy.

'Oh, Bianca,' Isabella whispered. *'Per favore*, we're here for Mamma.'

When they reached their family mausoleum, her mamma slumped to her knees, sobbing prayers in Italian. Her mamma's head rested by her parents' mute photos. The photo of Isabella's grandfather – her Nonno, who she'd never met – was bronzed as if embalmed. In front of his photo, the grass looked stomped on by boots, as if her grandfather still farmed. Neat, combed grass lay in front of her grandmother's memorial plaque, as orderly as a starched tablecloth ready for a traditional Sicilian family lunch. Isabella cocked her ear to listen to her mamma but heard only jerky fragments.

'I shamed you. It wasn't all my fault, but I accept God's will.'

Her mother's guilt was always the confusing part of their annual visit. *What could her kind and devout mother have done?* She made them sit in the front row of the church every Sunday, uncomfortably close to the staring altar boys. Her mamma knelt, praying, long after mass had finished. Isabella trembled, hearing louder sobs. This morbid place also had the power to weaken. Her mamma was tough. She once drove their sugar cane harvester with a sprained wrist while Papa rested in front of the television nursing a bruised finger. Mamma shot their wounded and dying pets, not Papa, despite his love of guns.

Isabella knelt, resting her head on her mamma's shoulder.

'Mamma, it's okay. I'm sure they can feel your love.'

Isabella glanced at the dates etched into the mausoleum granite. Her grandparents had both died around the time her sister was born, over twenty years ago. It seemed like a long time to remain sad and sorry. Isabella gripped her mamma's hand, realising she didn't appreciate genuine sorrow. But this year, she was more curious.

'What is it, Mamma? What is the shame?'

'Don't worry.' Tears streaked her mamma's beautiful olive-skinned face. 'Easter makes me reflect on my sins. Come on, girls, we have cooking to do before mass.'

A shower crossed the field. For Isabella, information about family sins and shame could wait with the promise of cooking. Bianca was already on the move, hauling Isabella up.

'This place gives me the creeps, Izzy. Stop asking questions.'

Heavy steps passed Isabella as the tall boy caught up to Bianca. 'Can I call you?' he asked.

Bianca turned. 'Sure,' she replied huskily, staring into the boy's eyes. 'My family's number is in the phone book. Russo, G. and F., Silkwood.'

Isabella grimaced and shut her eyes. *Oh, Bianca, here? Really?*

2

FROM his desk in the school hall, twenty-one-year-old graduate teacher Darcy Grant farewelled departing parents and students. When Darcy had entered the hall earlier that evening, Douglas, a craggy-skinned Head of English, pulled him aside. 'You're new to the far north, so a little advice. You'll find cream rises to the top, but turds also float. You'll get both kinds tonight. Call it as it is.'

Darcy blinked, still adjusting to the northerner's straight talking after relocating from southern Queensland. As students and parents milled about, Darcy winced, recalling a recent event. *Was he a turd?* Most nights, he was woken by high heels on the stairs, clinking bottles, and his fellow teacher and flatmate Leo's slurred encouragement, 'Just a little further, love.'

After joining a drinking spree with Leo and his female guests, the next morning Darcy jolted awake from a nudge. A naked girl smiled. 'I'm Cindy, in case you don't remember. It's Darcy, isn't it? New to town? I like your fair skin and hair. Makes a change from the Mediterranean blokes.'

Startled, he'd pulled up the sheet, staring at the ceiling. His eyes streamed from the smell of metabolising alcohol and body odour. Darcy had wanted to sink and disappear into his mattress, only answering Cindy's questions with blunt responses. 'Yeah. No. Yeah.'

She'd rolled away. 'I can tell you're not really into this.'

He hadn't answered. A monochrome dawn glow reached in through his thin curtain. As she'd dressed in silence, he registered her weariness. It was a weariness far deeper than a late night. After Cindy had left, questions gnawed. *What did it mean?*

12

Leo, showing his own guest out the door, had provided counsel. 'Don't worry. Casual encounter. Cindy won't care, one way or another.'

'But I found an earring in my bed. Should I return it?'

'Nah, there's lost earrings all over town.' Leo smirked. 'I've quite a collection.'

In the hall, Douglas let him go after asking about the progress of a couple of Darcy's Aboriginal students, including the promising Clarissa.

'She's wary about standing out. It's their culture.' He gripped his arm tighter. 'She's cream, don't let her curdle.'

During the night, Darcy greeted students, mainly in the cream category. As parents departed, hugging their children, Darcy sighed, for he had never sat on the other side of a teacher's desk receiving credit for his effort. Clarissa arrived and was joined by her aunties, who clapped, hooted, and cuddled Clarissa with every compliment. Clarissa smiled but looked at her shoes.

Across the night, Darcy noticed most sun-wrinkled fathers looked around, while mothers listened and nodded. Men tugged at their collars as if trying to release the school uniforms that once held them back from their farming futures. *New to town*, they all asked him, or stated. At the bell, the men stood, extending mud-stained, calloused paws in farewell handshakes.

From his classroom, he'd seen workmen sheeting the hall, final repairs after a roaring, scything cyclone had torn the roof off the year before, pinging screws like bullets, scattering tin across the town. Metres above, large fans rotated and hummed, straining against the heavy humidity. Although sitting still, his shirt stuck to sweaty skin. When Darcy had arrived in town, he could barely read the blackened road signs. Mould and mildew embroidered most surfaces. One warning sign by the creek opposite his home was legible enough. Illustrated wide jaws – crocodile territory. At night, he often heard revving trucks in the distance, yells and gunshots. He felt *new to town*.

At the far end of the hall, Frances Russo, school office

administrator, greeted parents and students with a broad smile. Frances had showed him around on his first day. Her youngest of two daughters, Isabella, was at university, training to be a teacher. Isabella, he was told, was the first in their family to reach university. Farming had been their primary family occupation since their forebears immigrated to Australia, then going back illiterate generations working patches of dirt in Sicily. Her bright eyes had misted.

'One day, Isabella can be just like you, fresh-faced, ready to shape young lives. 'My education was…' She paused and frowned before continuing. 'Oh, never mind. Isabella is the future.'

Just yesterday, when he'd collected his parent-teacher meeting schedule, she'd returned to her favourite subject, saying she prayed to Saint Scholastica of Italy for her daughter's success. 'Isabella is divined to be an educator, returning to teach our Italian clans, including religion at Sunday School.'

Darcy noticed the cross on Frances' necklace and imagined Isabella as demure and plain, with a nun's veil.

Frances also explained Isabella was expected to marry well, *un buon matrimonio,* honouring her parents, with a local Catholic Italian suitor already matched. Thinking of Leo's cavalcade of guests – 'casual encounters' – Darcy realised other lives were more certain and organised.

In the hall, Frances circled around busy tables before arriving at his desk. He readied for more discussion of her daughter's destiny.

'I'm here to discuss something important.'

Darcy's heart raced. In this small farming town, everybody knew each other's business. He was only able to settle down his Monday classes after the weekend gossip round. *Might Frances know about Cindy, worried about his character?*

'Ah, something important?' he ventured.

Frances crossed her arms. '*Si.* Food.'

Darcy paused from responding, then laughed, pointing to a long table. 'Refreshments are at the back of the hall.'

She rolled her eyes. 'Refreshments? Ha! I'll show you. Please join us on Sunday for a traditional Italian lunch. You can meet Isabella, home on holidays, and pass along tips. You can also meet my older daughter, Bianca. She is very pretty, around your age.'

Darcy blushed and didn't reply.

'Don't worry Darcy, the parish priest blesses the meal.'

Still, Darcy didn't reply, and Frances touched his arm, seemingly used to bashful young men.

'Darcy, c'mon, you know what to say.'

'Of course,' he murmured, 'thanks for the invite.'

Frances scribbled their family address, drew a map, and left. *Ciao.*

Bruno, a Year 12 student, and his mother arrived. Boisterous Bruno, repeating Year 12 – *not cream* – was devoted to rugby league but not to his English studies. His red-eyed mother gripped Bruno's damning report card. Darcy imagined yelling and tears.

Douglas also had advice for these sorts of interviews: 'You don't need to be the bad guy. Don't make it look like you're part of the problem. Turn the tables around. Ask the student how they think they're going.'

Towering Bruno sat down with a deliberate scrape of his seat and a loud huff. The surface of Darcy's desk darkened in the twilight shadow of a man mountain. Bruno's seat appeared to be as small as a shoeshine's stool. He stared at Darcy with a sneer and a rearing, upturned jaw.

Nearby, Douglas nodded. Darcy commenced. 'I have notes here. But tell me, Bruno, how do you think you're going?'

Bruno's broad brow flexed as he concentrated – an unfamiliar expression to Darcy – his mouth opening and closing like a landed, gasping fish. Darcy relaxed, appreciative of Douglas' advice. As he tapped his fingers, waiting for Bruno's reply, he pictured Bianca at the Russo family lunch, with dark Italian eyes like her mother's, pools of warm chocolate, smiling in welcome. As Bruno took a deep breath, Darcy leant in to make sure he caught every word of Bruno's stammering excuses, partial compensation for his disruptive behaviour. Tables turned.

'Mr Grant,' Bruno bellowed, 'my cousin, Cindy, says she knows you *very well*.'

Darcy's eyes widened.

Bruno's mum arched an eyebrow.

Douglas paused from talking with a fellow teacher.

'Cindy says she had a night over at your place but hasn't heard from you since.' Bruno paused. 'So, tell me, Mr Grant, how do you think *you're* going?'

Darcy gripped the table to steady himself.

'Everything alright over here?' asked Leo, standing beside Darcy's desk, dressed in athletic sports teacher apparel. With his dark hair combed upwards and brown Mediterranean skin, Leo seemed to be a modern Roman centurion.

Darcy expected to hear earrings clinking in his pocket.

'Yes, Mr Scuderi,' Bruno replied. 'Never any problems with Mr Grant. He's not a bad bloke for a southerner.'

~

Next Saturday afternoon, Frances cooked with her daughters. Pasta sauces bubbled and plopped on the kitchen stove. The family dog scratched and whined at the door. Gino sniffed the rich tomato-scented air upon his return from the cane fields. As he approached the pots and reached for a crusty roll, Frances waved a wooden spoon.

'We don't need you to taste test. Out!'

Grumbling, Gino turned away, and Frances and her daughters kneaded pasta dough on their kitchen table. Light puffs of flour lifted as they thumped the elastic lumps. Bianca rolled a wooden pin up and down, flattening resistance, but she looked at their phone, wanting flattery.

'Bianca, concentrate, we're almost finished,' Frances said.

Frances thought of tomorrow's lunch, hoping Darcy would enjoy himself. Sunday lunches were rowdy traditions exported from their Sicilian homelands. She was sure her guests would be welcoming, although the men tended to be wary of southern strangers.

'Remember, girls, we have a special guest tomorrow – Mr Grant.'

'Is he good-looking?' Bianca asked, eyes twinkling.

'That's not for me to say,' replied Frances, with a coy smile. 'But, Bianca, I think you'll like him.'

Bianca sought her reflection in the window and smiled.

As Frances rolled the pasta sheets, she thought Darcy was sincere and polite – lovely qualities in a young man. At lunch, the elderly Silkwood nonnas would notice, for eligible young men were a useful match-making resource. They'd prefer him to be an Italian Catholic, even better, Sicilian Catholic. The nonnas schemed generations ahead about who would be matched to take over the family farm. If there hadn't been a wedding in a calendar year, suggestions would become urgent. *'Pronto!'* Frances knew the nosey nonnas were interfering, plotting matches for Bianca, worried about her virtue. She smiled. *Interfering? Hadn't she mentioned Bianca to Darcy?*

'Why are you smiling, Mamma?' Isabella asked.

Frances turned her head, admiring her angelic, youngest daughter, home on a short break from university. At 18, she was already within the nonna's range, promised to Carlo, from a good neighbouring Sicilian Catholic family. Frances re-rolled the pasts sheets, realising she was more traditional than she'd admit, tying her success as a Sicilian mother to Isabella's eventual Catholic marriage. At weddings, everyone congratulated parents for the proper marriage, as much as good wishes for newly married couples. Frances glanced at her eldest daughter, who still admired her reflection in the dark window. Vivacious, wilful Bianca wouldn't provide Frances with this honour. Every Sunday the parishioners arched their eyebrows when only Isabella knelt beside her and Gino in the pews.

When Gino overheard gossip about Bianca, he'd tell Frances she was failing as a mother. She'd curse, replying that he was failing as a father and defender of their family. Despite his famous arsenal, Frances was often woken at night by an idling truck on the near road, footsteps from their home, while her husband slept off his nightly grappa.

Before turning away, Gino would say, 'If you'd borne me a son, and he didn't turn out well, then you could lecture me.'

'Mamma, what is it?' Isabella asked. 'Why are you frowning?'

'Oh, nothing,' Frances replied. 'Let's cook Carlo's favourite pasta sauce. Good practice for when you're a housewife.'

'*Sì. Sì*, Mamma,' Isabella replied, eyes bright.

The phone rang. 'It will be for me,' cried Bianca, throwing down a kitchen towel. Soon, the curled, straining telephone extension lead trailed to her bedroom. From the bedroom came a loud hoarse reply. 'Maybe, if you ask nicely.'

Frances dropped her spoon and covered Isabella's ears, yelling, 'Shush, Bianca!'

Frowning at the closed bedroom door, Frances realised it was time for full nonna mode. Hopefully, steady Darcy could settle Bianca before there was trouble. The type of trouble when enraged Sicilian fathers tapped on a suitor's door with a shotgun.

~

Driving to the Russo family home, Darcy looked forward to meeting Frances' older daughter. Pretty. His age. Yet Bruno's question and allegation still hung. *How was he going?* Just yesterday, he'd seen Cindy at the town supermarket. Straggly hair fell over her face, eyes glazed. As she shuffled by, massaging her temples, Darcy had stood still by a display of out-of-date groceries. Up close, he noticed her supermarket uniform and 'manager' badge.

'It's okay, I'm used to being ignored afterwards,' she mumbled sideways.

Today, Darcy was glad to escape Leo's social scene. Last night, Leo shouldered his way through the front door in the early hours, *a little further love*, then bounced from wall to wall to his bedroom, accompanied by clicking high heels. Soon after, the sounds of ardour filled the eaves, only muffled by the pillow over his head.

Readying for lunch, he'd frowned in the mirror at his teachery tan shirt and fawn pants. He knew fashion expressed personality, like a bird's colourful, beckoning plumage. In the forest near the high school, he'd seen a rummaging cassowary. The huge bird sported bands of blue, purple, and orange. In comparison, his outfit was a long stripe of tobacco. He drove to Silkwood, hoping Bianca was a mild young lady, more impressed by education and manners, than fashion.

By the Silkwood Hotel, he pulled over to look at Frances' hand-drawn map. The tall timber pub reminded him of similar hotels in Toowoomba, his hometown. In a light trance, he was a boy again, hungry, alone, peering inside the hotel looking for his father.

Darcy edged back onto the road. *The Pearl* – his white 1970 Holden Kingswood – rumbled over tram lines which led away into dark, narrow alleys within the tall, thick cane. Darcy shivered. He wouldn't want to idle into the permanent gloom, where the stalks might scratchily push the venturer further into a maze.

He soon spotted a large, rusty barrel fashioned into a letterbox with RUSSO hand painted in large white letters. Shiny cars were parked beside a plastered Italianate stucco house. The home appeared as if it belonged on a farm under Mount Etna. Here, in Far North Queensland, he supposed the house was another Sicilian migrant stuck in a damp cane field. Chained to a shed, a big dog strained and barked at the strange car. Darcy tried to identify the breed. *Cane Farm Big?* Other dogs milled and yelped around a truck where the hairy hulk of a mud-caked pig was bound tight with thick ropes, blood dripping from its tusked snout. A young Mediterranean man, with a shotgun over his shoulder, wiped blood from a knife, and stared at Darcy's car.

Darcy's hands trembled on his steering wheel, selecting a place to park. After he parked, curtains parted, and he saw Frances' shining olive-skinned face and broad smile. Barely out of his car, he received a hug. 'Darcy, you found your way!'

Just inside the door, Frances introduced him to Bianca. '*Ciao!* Mamma didn't tell me the school has such handsome young teachers. I'm going back!'

In her Sunday best dress and makeup, Bianca looked like a model ready for a fashion photoshoot. The room seemed to glow around her. His face reddened as Frances led him outside, joining Gino and other men who placed tables together, cigarettes wagging in their mouths.

He met Giovanni, Giancarlo, and Giuseppe. Most seemed to answer to 'Joe'. Darcy heard the farmers were only paid once a year after the cane harvest. He touched his wallet for reassurance. The men cursed about the wild pigs that dug up their cane crops. *One fewer today*, Darcy thought.

'Hey, Mr Teacher, you'll have to join us at a pig hunt,' said one of the 'Joes'. He nudged Darcy. 'You want to see Gino's gun arsenal?'

Gino looked from the kitchen where Bianca stood, then back to Darcy. 'Don't worry, my guns are mainly aimed at pigs, not suitors.' Darcy stared at Gino's dark, squinting eyes. 'With the safety off,' he added. Darcy waited for a smile, indicating a joke, but Gino's face remained stern. In the background, the pig hunter stared at him, cleaning his hands with a fresh cloth.

Darcy swallowed and turned, hearing a loud voice. A 'Joe' explained the warm ocean temperature meant a cyclone was still possible. He waved his hat in a circular motion. 'Mr Teacher, over that horizon, a menace can come, just like last year.' He pointed to the sky towards the coastline. 'It zooms in and flattens our fields like a devil scorning God.' He slammed his hat down and the men blessed themselves.

A stooped, grey-haired man arrived, a glinting cross on his collar, nodding at the scenes of devotion. '*Pronto*,' the nonnas barked, carrying large bowls and baskets of bread. The men paced to their seats, rubbing their hands, cyclones and pigs forgotten. *Bene!*

Darcy turned at the sound of a soft voice. '*Ciao*, Mr Grant, here is your seat. My name is Isabella. Nice to meet you.'

He stared at the divined daughter, with warm olive skin and dark reflective eyes, a near replica of Frances and Bianca. 'Ah, ah, yeah, good to meet you too. Ah, ah, how's university?'

Gino brushed by with bottles of red wine encased in thickly woven baskets. '*Molto Bene!*' the men roared. Isabella's reply and the priest's blessing were drowned out.

In Darcy's hand, the warm bouquet of red wine merged with Italian food aromas. He heard clinking glasses, and Bianca, sitting opposite, raised her glass to him with a beautiful smile. His stomach grumbled. Yet, across the afternoon, her eyes darted around, and she jumped from her chair to top up glasses and clear plates. Frances frowned at her frenzy and looked to Darcy, shrugging her shoulders.

After the feast was devoured and the din of comradery lifted again, like the last lesson on a Friday afternoon, Darcy went to help clear the table. He held an empty bowl, jaw open, looking around the gregarious congregation. When their hands weren't waving and writhing in emphasis, men and women had arms around each other. *Bene. Bene.* It was a lifestyle and unity he didn't know existed. He stood heavy footed.

Frances called from the kitchen, 'If you're going to help, the kitchen is this way.'

'Oh, yes,' Darcy replied, re-focusing.

Mid-afternoon, Isabella sat beside him, sipping wine. She wore a large cross on a necklace, like Frances, and her voice was soft and polite as if in prayer. Looking from her mother to the nonnas, she explained her life was mapped out, with university, then a short engagement and marriage. Her eyes flicked to the pig hunter, who nodded and stared. Darcy heard an echo. Frances' expectations. Listening further, Darcy felt Isabella didn't seem to mind; her life coordinates, he supposed, were like constellations in the Silkwood sky: family, church, a profession, and marriage to an Italian farmer. With a full stomach and vino, ears ringing from the din, he understood the Sicilian traditions as care, not control. Darcy glanced back at the future husband, trying to recall introductions – *was his name Carlo?* Darcy shuffled on his seat, realising he was sitting where Carlo normally sat. Darcy studied his glass of dark red wine and thought of the pool of blood below the pig's snout. He held Carlo's eyes for a moment before accepting another top-up from Bianca.

Later, Isabella pointed to his stained scrunched napkin on the table. 'Many of the meals are ancient traditional family recipes traced back to our home village in Sicily. What was your favourite pasta?'

'Russo Pasta?' he ventured.

'Tick. Correct answer,' replied the trainee teacher, smiling.

At dusk, Frances called out to the congregation. 'Next, the Feast of The Three Saints. Then, Angelica can host.'

Bene! The men gathered their hats. Darcy felt thumping pats on his back. '*Ciao, Ciao.*'

In the kitchen, Darcy stood beside Isabella, readying to leave. Carlo bumped a shoulder as he passed by. Bouncing forward from another heavy pat, Darcy said, 'Isabella, I almost feel beaten up. I'm worried what they'd do if they didn't like someone.'

'You don't want to find out.'

Darcy laughed, but Isabella didn't smile. She flicked her long hair like a mane.

Oh, he realised. It wasn't a joke.

Carlo looked back from the door, sneered, then walked away heralded by baying dogs.

~

In the early evening, after prayers with Mamma, Isabella slid the forbidden *Dolly* magazine out from under her mattress. She opened the magazine cover, listening for footsteps approaching her room. She had little more than a Catholic mother's abridged explanation of intercourse, which sounded unpleasant. The sacrosanct, intimate act, her mamma instructed, was only to be undertaken within the sacrament of marriage for consecration and children, *Christian children.* Outside her bedroom, she heard Bianca's laughter, talking on the telephone. Bianca must have received the same instructions, but she wore a type of moral raincoat, sheeting away commandments like raindrops, *nothing sacrosanct.*

At her high school, a couple of library books, which somehow avoided censorship, had pages crumpled from re-reading. The school librarian would squint at the giggling and click her fingers. 'Hush!' Recently, in a university lecture room, a girl dropped her *Dolly* magazine as she stood up. Isabella had grabbed the magazine and shoved it deep in her bag. After her nightly prayers, a new devotion began. Gaps were filled as she flicked through the pages. *Ah. Really?*

She returned the magazine to the girl, who provided another. A teenage librarian. The girl had looked at her plain, country clothes, necklace and cross, and asked, 'Country Catholic?'

Isabella nodded and felt her cheeks burn.

'You'll need a few editions.'

Isabella flicked by the perfume advertisements to reader articles, where girls wrote about their experiences. Bianca might make a worthy *Dolly* correspondent, she thought, but Isabella also listened and learned. The month before, she went to a party at a university share house. The music was too loud to talk, and students drank to the point of not *being able to talk*. In the bathroom, with vomited pizza on the floor, drunk women messily reapplied lipstick, adjusting their dresses, talking about their experiences with men. At the time, she'd blushed at the women's vivid descriptions. She'd walked home, wondering whether her virginity at age eighteen was unusual. Carlo's hugs were uncomfortably long, and she sensed he wanted more than holding hands at family lunches. Isabella shuddered as she strode to her university lodgings.

Over the page, Isabella studied a magazine article. *You'll know when the time is right.* In candlelight, a partially dressed young couple looked across at a bed with a sheet folded back. Isabella looked up, reflecting. She wasn't in candlelight, more like a twilight, Carlo not really a boyfriend, but an assumed fiancé. Her future marriage was like a crease on her palm, a clairvoyant's guiding path to the altar. For her Catholic Debutante Ball, she had been paired with Carlo by Mamma, because he was a local Sicilian Catholic, and better still, an altar boy. Isabella accepted the pairing without question and smiled for photos, holding hands with Carlo.

On the next page, Isabella looked at a photo of the couple kissing, now sitting on the bed. The idea of Carlo kissing her, edging her across the bed, roused no emotion, no desire. She wondered why, and whether that was normal, or a sign. Isabella looked upward and imagined her wedding day. In the dark church, she would stand in virginal white, honouring her parents, her mamma sniffling with pride.

Later, as Carlo carried her into the hotel bridal suite, desire would surely arrive, her body tingling, *the time would be right.*

At a knock on the door, she shoved the magazine under a pillow. Bianca entered her room and grinned at the room's religious décor. Looking at the cross on the wall and the large portrait of Virgin Mary arranged by their mother, she asked whether Isabella was in training to be a nun. Her sister poked fun at the imprint of knees where Isabella and their mamma prayed.

'Izzy, the only religion I like is The Feast of the Three Saints. Plenty of cute guys. Speaking of which, I wonder if Mr Grant is coming along?'

3

THE following Sunday, Darcy joined a gathering crowd at the Feast of the Three Saints. Rows of red and green bunting flicked above, glinting the colours of Sicily and Italy.

Earlier in the week at school, Frances reminded him about the event, mentioning Bianca. Again, Darcy must have seemed anxious.

'C'mon, Darcy, come along, you know what to say.'

He nodded, saying, 'Thanks, for sure.' Yet Darcy heard Bianca's name as a message. *Had it come from Frances as a matchmaker or from Bianca?* Just her name made him wriggle damp fingers in his pockets.

The Silkwood church bell chimed, carrying a solemn tone from Sicily. A large, raised float appeared with shiny figurines: the martyred and beatified three brothers: Saints Alfio, Filadelfo, and Cirino, killed in Sicily for their Christian beliefs. There was another funereal chime like a forecast of doom. Stern-looking men held a large, mounted flag bearing the name of the church and an insignia. Darcy read their message in their faces – today was about remembering sacrifice and honour. A brass band struck up to support the march and Darcy sighed with relief, but the respite was short-lived as a stern looking man on a megaphone recited solemn prayers.

'Holy Lord, we remember the sacrifice of Sicily's three martyrs in your name.'

School-aged girls swept by wearing flowing red dresses with white pinafores, black tunics, and patterned headscarves. Ranks of young, upright Silkwood men marched behind them in white shirts adorned with diagonal red and green sashes, matching the flickering bunting. To Darcy, the men appeared to be junior Carabinieri gendarmerie conscripted to guard the saints. Darcy could now see the three saints aloft on a gilded altar protected by a heavy regal pelmet. They moved along on their motorised float, flanked by praying clergy. The saints' serene holy faces, encircled by golden halos, shone in the light sunshine. Heaped flowers rested at the martyrs' feet. As they moved by, the demure, sculpted saints stared sightless with delicate, painted eyes. The crowd clapped and threw money. After the saints rolled away, the faithful marched to a large marquee, noses upright, sniffing food carried by the breeze.

Darcy walked around market stalls, trying to appear casual, looking for the Russos, but hoping not to see Isabella's huntsman boyfriend. Inside the busy marquee, he felt landlocked around cheerful brown faces. Beyond, he heard a familiar bright voice. *Mi scusi.* Frances barged through and gave him a quick hug in welcome.

'*Ciao.* Where is Bianca I wonder?' Frances looked around, before an arm was hooked in hers and she was led away.

Later in the afternoon, Leo arrived, allowing Darcy to separate from a couple of farmers he'd met at the Russo lunch. Again, he received rough affection as he departed. *Ciao, Mr Teacher.*

'How's the form?' asked Leo, looking around.

'The saints were pretty.'

Leo groaned and rolled his eyes, then dragged Darcy into the marquee where the devout were loosening into revellers. By the busy bar, Darcy received an exaggerated hello and hug from Bianca.

'Hello! I hoped to see you. Welcome again to Silkwood.'

Their eyes held, and his heart began tripping. Leo appeared with drinks.

Bianca exclaimed, 'Behold, two more Silkwood saints.'

They toasted drinks. 'Can you see our halos?' Darcy asked.

'Yes, and your holy aura too!' Bianca replied.

They laughed, but Darcy struggled to converse as Bianca danced about. A young man in a shirt and sash arrived and reached for Bianca's hand. She slipped through near shoulders into the crowd, holding hands with the man. Darcy looked in the direction of departing Bianca for many moments.

'Isn't she a beauty,' commented Leo. 'Another drink?'

Leo found a drinks stall by the edge of the marquee. They clinked glasses of grappa. Darcy sniffed his glass. He felt like he was standing close to a petrol bowser. The marquee lights shone in the softening dusk and objects blurred and swam with every sip he took. At the edge of the bar, Bianca glowed, low sunlight shining on her face. Her Carabinieri costumed protector was not beside her, but other men milled around raising glasses seeking her attention. Between their shifting shoulders, her eyes found Darcy, and she raised her glass and smiled.

~

Isabella walked around the edge of the marquee. After the procession, she had changed from the peasant costume. She was embarrassed to resemble a young village girl, yet her mamma had insisted. Dressed in her best frock, Isabella stood tall, wanting to be grown up, like her sister. At home, hanging out their washing, she had noticed Bianca's large bra size, pleased she was catching up. She applied lipstick from a tube that Bianca had discarded in their bathroom bin. Nearby, a boy whistled. She turned, for sometimes she was mistaken for her beautiful sister. The whistling boy called out, 'Ciao, Isabella. Wow!' She blushed; Carlo would be nearby, but young Silkwood men were always daring.

The sun lowered, with only a light red trim remaining on top of the cane fields, like lipstick, as the marquee lights shone. Isabella heard a squawking announcement from the speakers. Chairs flung back and the marquee crowd bustled toward her. The press of bodies pushed her into the open field, where the revellers looked upward, wandering around. With a bump, then a trip over a farmer's boot, she stumbled, hair falling over her face. Crawling along grass, trying to stand, she felt a hand in hers. The palm was soft, and she thought of Bianca pulling her through the cemetery gates at Easter. But this grip enveloped her hand, stronger, maybe the whistling boy, but more likely Carlo, claiming her. Another farmer's boot stamped beside her, but the firm hand still guided her. She felt as if she was crawling in a rainforest among dancing tree trunks, free of their roots. When scrambling clear of another scrum of legs, she was lifted to her feet. Isabella looked up. Darcy held her hand.

Bumped again, she tried to free thick hair from her face. Isabella leaned into him as a shield, smelling grappa on his breath.

'Did you like the parade?' she asked, glancing at his silhouette. 'We Sicilians mix death and celebration.'

She heard him laugh but stiffen, examining her profile.

He rubbed his eyes. 'Bianca, is that you?'

Above, fireworks erupted, followed by thumping booms smashing the sky into violent, colourful sprays. Dogs howled in warning from nearby farms. The crowd jumped and shrieked. *Bravo!* Darcy steadied her from rollicking, boisterous shoulders. All other eyes were upward, but his face was close, looking at her, with explosive sprouts of light flashing in his eyes. His cheek brushed hers and their lips met, as if by a magnetic pull, with electrons vibrating in the sky. Her body felt as electrified as the ignited sky, and she pressed into him, surprised she felt no reluctance. Fireworks continued to flash and boom above; and they held tight, kissing for minutes, her chest pressed into his. When the skies quietened, he pulled away, blinking to focus, then his eyes widened.

'Isabella?' he asked. 'Oh, no, I'm so sorry,' he whispered.

The clapping crowd thinned. Cigarettes beaded and bobbed towards the marquee. Darcy dropped her hand and hurried away, not looking back. Recovering her breath, she walked towards Carlo, who weaved through the crowd calling her name.

~

Inside the marquee a short time later, Isabella swung, arm-in-arm with her mamma to the rhythm of a folk band and vigorous clapping and stomping. She rubbed her mouth with the back of a spare hand, worried her lipstick might be smeared. Isabella looked sideways. Carlo waited to dance. He had both sharp eyes and sharp knives. Carlo took her arm. After another song, she swung away, reflecting. Darcy's kiss was a shock, and she felt guilty for letting it continue.

The band leader began singing *That's Amore.* Her mamma

cheered, gripping Isabella's elbow and swinging her around. Minutes later, the band announced a break, *Ciao for now*. Carlo turned towards the bar, a mate's guiding arm over his shoulder. *Your round, Romeo!*

Her eyes flicked about to see if Darcy was nearby. The teacher was a slow learner Isabella thought; she told him not to rouse local anger. Darcy knew she was with Carlo. Darcy would have noticed Bianca was always surrounded by admirers. Isabella had been alone in the fields. Her mistaken identity as Bianca was unlikely. Southerners must be just as daring as young Silkwood men. Isabella walked to the edge of the marquee. He needed to be rebuked and warned. Perhaps Darcy was in the dark, keeping his distance. Maybe waiting for her. Glancing behind to be sure she wasn't being watched, she stepped into the gloom.

~

Leo slurred and rolled in the front seat as Darcy drove away from Silkwood close to midnight. Around a corner, Leo's head slumped, resting on Darcy's shoulder. Leo's face was sticky from the Italian liqueur and his clothes smelled of perfume. They rose through the dark forested pass, then to the plains where cane walls shone from his passing headlights. Darcy gripped the steering wheel, shaking his head. *No!* Isabella. Not Bianca.

He remembered the flashing lights of the fireworks. Now, there were other lights on the highway. Police waved drivers over, and Darcy pulled in behind a line of cars. A police officer dragged a sobbing man away from a parked car and shoved him in the back of a van. Although it had been hours since his last drink, Darcy's heart raced. The local Italian distillers brewed for impact as much as taste. He blew into his cupped hand but could only smell a feminine fragrance – Isabella's Impulse deodorant. Darcy wished instead he could smell alcohol. As the police officer waved the line forward, Darcy looked across to the cane fields beside the road.

Just a few hours earlier, he'd walked the fields around the marquee to avoid the Russo family and Isabella's boyfriend. At one point, Darcy had glanced back at the marquee. He squinted at bright light.

'Oh, Darcy, it's you,' Gino rasped as he lowered his torch. 'Sometimes the youngsters get up to mischief out here, eh.' Gino surveyed the fields. Darcy looked at the thick torch. Gino seemed happiest when holding a metallic instrument. 'What are you doing out here anyway? All the fun is inside.' His torch swept back to the marquee. An outline of a young woman with long, flowing hair appeared but then stopped and turned back.

'Just clearing my head. The grappa is strong.'

Gino tapped his heavy torch on Darcy's shoulder as he left.

The police officer tapped his window on the highway, shining a torch. Leo blinked like a startled owl. 'Ha!' roared the police officer. 'Tell Scuderi we expect him at footy training tomorrow. Get out of here!'

Trembling, Darcy pulled out of the police line, but he needed policing. Frances had trusted him, confiding plans for Isabella. Bianca had joked about his saintly halo. He was no more a saint than Silkwood's painted figurines. Low thunder grumbled overhead, then heavy rain streamed across his windscreen. Ahead, rear brake lights flashed, streaking red on his blurry windscreen like the dripping blood from the slaughtered pig.

4

MONDAY afternoon, Darcy walked to the school office, intending to bump into Frances. The percussion of the Silkwood fireworks and band still echoed, and he decided to face the music. He found Frances at the office door. With a dry mouth, he said, 'Thanks for the invite to the feast.'

'Thank you for coming.' Frances winked. 'Did you spend time with Bianca?'

'Ah, just a little.'

'I'm glad you enjoyed your return to our village.' She paused, touching his arm. 'I can tell you are coming under Silkwood's spell.'

Darcy relaxed, exhaling. Nothing indicated Frances knew.

'Darcy, will you keep trying with my daughter? I'd love you to be close to our family.'

Darcy blinked. *Keep trying with my daughter?*

'What's wrong, Darcy? Isn't my daughter your type?'

'No, gosh. She is lovely, it's—'

'You know where we live, and you are welcome any time.'

Frances turned to talk with a student with a bleeding finger.

'Oh no, my dear, come this way. I'll find you a band-aid.'

The school cleared quickly, as always, and a vehicle pulled into the car park. Darcy recognised the Russo family car. Darcy felt drilled by Isabella's black eyes. He saw more glare than stare.

Bianca smiled and waved. After a toot of the horn, Frances strode from the office. With a return quick wave, he glanced away and turned back towards his classroom.

~

As dawn's glow lit his bedroom curtains on Tuesday morning, Darcy heard high heels on the floor outside his room, accompanied by Leo's mumbling farewell. He closed his eyes, drifting into a light doze, for he had barely slept. His first daily thoughts were the same. *Where might his mother be? Did she think of him?* Dreaming, he visualised her happier than the only photo he'd seen of her, found in the back of a cupboard, missed by his father. His room brightened, and he remembered the bonfire in their backyard. *Bye,* said the girl at their door. *Bye,* his father had said, throwing his mother's clothes and photos into the fire. Darcy remembered a dress lifting from the inferno, like a scorched, crackling witch. His mother had disappeared before he started school – Darcy had worked out that much – for his report cards were only addressed to his father. His mother might have been surprised he'd become a teacher. *Teacher?* Darcy sat up and turned over his upended alarm clock. *No!*

Minutes later, he buttoned his tan shirt as he ran like a student trying to beat the school bell. The grey sky lowered and rain washed the town to start the day. He arrived soaked, panting. Water pooled on the classroom floor as his students filed in. Above, the fan blades hummed, struggling to part the heavy humidity. A musty teenage fug fogged the windows.

'Novels out, please,' he called, breath recovered. 'It's time for character analysis.'

'The main character is irresponsible,' a student called out.

The northerners were always straight talkers. Darcy gulped, feeling self-conscious about kissing Isabella.

'Cavalier,' murmured his best student, a bright-eyed girl, sitting in the front row.

Darcy went to commend the student's adjective selection, but he couldn't form the words. A boy traced his analysis into window condensation. *Reckless.*

Darcy thought of the report cards he would soon write. Mothers would be the first to read the results, extracting crushed envelopes from schoolbags. He thought again of his mother, who he couldn't remember, his school report cards unread. But he remembered the bonfire and his father's glassy-eyed stare into the flames. His mother's dress had drifted in the updraft like a kite flying to heaven, then fell, a surrendering flag. The dress clung to their barbed wire fence behind the vegetable patch, unnoticed by his often-absent father. Every term, he read out his report card to the remaining fibres, mother and son, both hanging on.

The bell rang and his mind returned to his classroom. Out shuffled the character analysts. The Year 12 students wandered in.

A girl held a tissue over her nose, gasping, 'Year Nines!'

A coughing student checked the fan settings, while another opened the windows wider and flapped a large notebook.

'It stinks like a cane farmer's armpit,' Bruno called out.

'They say the same about you,' replied Darcy.

'Give me the names of the Year Nines who said that,' Bruno challenged, eyes glinting.

The class laughed. The light-hearted start to the lesson settled Darcy's concern about Isabella. He would forget it happened, like she should. If they met again, she would receive the message like a naval semaphore. *Oh no. I kissed the wrong Russo.* Then it was time to get down to the real business of teaching – behaviour control, instructing Bruno to not kick chairs or flick the ears of students around him.

After the final bell, and students had cleared, he sneaked out a side gate only used during a fire drill to avoid Frances and more glares from Isabella. *Character analysis, eh*, he thought.

By Thursday night, lying in bed, Darcy calculated the week was winding down well enough. Frances hadn't arrived at his classroom with a raised hand. Leo's town gossip over dinner didn't include descriptions of southerner males carousing with 'spoken-for' Silkwood maidens. Isabella didn't reappear at school. Carlo hadn't parked by his home, tipped off by Isabella, window rolled down, weapon held low on his lap. Darcy snapped off his reading lamp, punching the air; he'd been lucky. Then he felt cross with himself, as he thought of Aunt Betty, his father's sister. She'd told him to never offend or mislead a woman with casual, thoughtless affection.

~

Aunt Betty visited when Darcy was in his first year of high school. She arrived with a Gold Coast tan as the fog was clearing. 'What's with this freezing Toowoomba climate? Are we still in Queensland?' Aunt Betty pulled on a cardigan, and his father disappeared, likely to the Returned Services Leagues Club, the RSL, to cash his veteran's pension cheque. She directed Darcy to a lounge chair.

'You're thirteen?' Betty enquired, sitting across from Darcy.

Darcy nodded, feeling like he agreed with an accusation.

'Well, then. Let's discuss a few facts about adult gender relations. Boys need to be taught. Girls communicate. There's a lot more going on for girls in a biological sense, as you can see.'

His aunt held an illustration of a nude woman. He rocked back to get away from the threatening breasts and other lines and swirls between the girl's legs.

'Open your eyes. Study the female erogenous zones.'

Darcy glanced at the various anatomical charts and wriggled about as his aunt described the act of sexual intercourse.

'Darcy, affection should only happen within a committed relationship. Understand?'

Young Darcy nodded to hurry the lesson along.

His aunt clicked her fingers. 'Be careful if you initiate affection. You wouldn't want to mislead a lovely girl, would you?

'Gosh. Of course not, Aunt Betty.'

Tonight, looking at his ceiling, Darcy wondered if he'd misled Isabella, like static interrupting a radio broadcast.

When Aunt Betty next returned during his later teenage years, Darcy waited for more discussion about adult gender relations. Those days, he'd studied the figures of girls around his age, becoming an expert at looking away *just in time.* He imagined their erogenous zones, summoning more detail than the illustrated curves and swirls. He imagined they'd have hair *there,* just as he'd grown. Other than Aunt Betty, Mrs Black – the elderly welfare worker who inspected their government home – was their only female visitor. He didn't *ever* try to imagine her erogenous zones.

Across the day, Darcy waited for his aunt to extend discussions on adult gender relations. He had a long list of numbered, written questions. *1. When might the described things take place? 2. How would he know? 3. Who took the lead?* The questions were numbered through to a neat dozen. However, his aunt didn't initiate any conversations on this subject. He grumbled, folding away his questions under a pillow on his bed. So much for girls communicating and boys needing to be taught.

Later that day, a car arrived at the house and his aunt greeted another arrival, also from the Gold Coast. He recognised Eliza, his cousin, although she was a curvy woman now compared to the last photo he'd seen. Later in the afternoon, Eliza joined Darcy on the lounge. She asked about school and books; subjects he could discuss freely. *Girls knew how to communicate.* She asked him whether he had a girlfriend.

'Me?' He covered a burst of acne with his hand. 'Of course not.'

'But you've become handsome. I'm surprised girls aren't breaking down the door.'

He shook his head, but he loved his cousin from then on.

'What about you? Do you have a boyfriend?' he'd asked.

With long legs, lovely female curves, and a beautiful face, he imagined many Gold Coast men would want to be in his very position.

'Not at the moment.' She leaned in and whispered, out of her mother's hearing, 'I've had a few flings with older guys to find out how things worked. That served a purpose.'

Darcy squinted in concentration, gathering the meaning, as Eliza uncrossed and crossed her tanned legs.

The next day, Darcy walked with Eliza around the cold, local streets. Eliza gripped his arm, and Darcy felt the stares of his neighbours, imagining their surprise at the welfare kid with a glamourous girlfriend. He walked tall, chin raised. A car drove by, and a young man in a check shirt tooted a musical horn.

Eliza sneered. 'What a creep. I don't think my kind of guy is in this town.'

'I don't think there's any girl in this town, or anywhere, for me,' Darcy replied.

Eliza faced him. 'No! One day, you will sweep a beautiful girl off her feet and be madly in love.' She squeezed his hand. 'You'll see.'

At the time, Darcy thought his cousin should write fantasy novels.

But now, in his bed in town, Darcy thought a sliver of this might be true. Isabella was beautiful, but the rest fantastical.

At the start of his Year 12, Eliza sent a postcard of herself with other tanned girls dressed as bikinied Gold Coast Meter Maids. The postcard had a short message: *I've plenty of golden girls for you to meet. Come any time. Love Eliza.* Across the year, Darcy studied the stunning, near blinding creatures in the gold bikinis so often that he risked good school results. To him, they appeared to be supremely evolved female specimens of a human super race.

5

SITTING in his air-conditioned office on Monday morning, Principal Rich Pierce pulled at his collar and rubbed his red neck. The previous Friday, he'd been over eager to start fishing from his boat *Salsa* in the warm, aquamarine waters off Dunk Island. With a baited rod and the giant shadows of fish passing below, he'd raggedly splashed sunscreen. By the end of the day, his neck resembled the florid red and orange livery of the coral trout flapping in his esky.

Rich reviewed first-year teacher progress reports. Most had settled in well enough; a few *too well*, with most of the department's fortnightly pay in the publican's bank account. Darcy Grant seemed dutiful, but in Rich's experience, the quiet ones were the ones to watch. Last year, the most outwardly sincere of his young staff turned out to be a marriage breaker. The teacher *learnt a hard lesson,* walking with a limp, aged 22. He asked around about young Mr Grant. Leo said Darcy was reserved, bookish, usually reading novels in his room on weekends, only visiting Silkwood a couple of times. Outside his office he heard Frances Russo shriek on the phone. Rich looked at Darcy's face in the staff photo, remembering newspaper articles about weapons and violence. Frances shrieked again. Darcy would want to be careful among the excitable Sicilian clans, Rich thought, especially if he were to mingle with their womenfolk.

Today, after one further meeting, he would unlock his safe and head to the bank with his margin of the tuckshop profits. Across the bank counter, he'd also slide stacked cash from his various schemes, including the rent from the dead teacher's flat, where he had installed Darcy and Leo without the knowledge of his former colleague's family.

'I'd appreciate a receipt and an update on the balance,' he'd say to his favourite female clerk, flashing his white teeth. He was in his late thirties but mistaken for younger. His wedding band would be tucked in his wallet. She might look up from his bank balance, glance at his luxury sedan parked out the front, considering his offer of a country drive.

In the afternoon, he would speak in fatherly tones at the first-year teachers principal's reception. He would roll out his usual 'commendation to the new generation' speech, just mouthing the script. The gullible, earnest young teachers, like Darcy Grant, would follow every word and think he meant it. Later, he would listen to a Rod Stewart record in his office, sipping vintage sherry, before heading home to ignore his wife.

He patted a cool towel to his neck, skimming a thick conduct file: *really*, an extensive misconduct file. The Year 12 boy sounded like a thug, with a likely future career as a nightclub bouncer. He read the letter from his deputy principal recommending expulsion. Rich closed the file, ready to deliver the bad news to Bruno DeLuca's mother. He should also personally provide the verdict to the condemned. However, his memory of Bruno destroying opposition school rugby league teams made him reconsider. This could be a job for the deputy who wanted Bruno dispatched. Rich smirked. Everyone had to do their bit.

Rich looked up at the knock on the door. He checked his blonde hair in the mirror, popped a mint, unlocked the door, and guided Mrs DeLuca to his leather lounges. Surprised at her slight figure, he wondered how she could have carried prenatal Bruno.

Rich sat the thick file on the small table before them. The over-stuffed file sprung open.

'Mr Pierce, I thought the worst when I heard you wanted to see me.' Mrs DeLuca stared, wide-eyed, at the file. 'What has he done now?'

'What do you want to know? Last week? Or a summary of this term? Even today, I expect he has been raising hell.'

At her sniffling, Rich slid a box of tissues across the table. He knew some principals felt this was one of the worst aspects of the job, but he didn't mind. An expulsion was just a thump to a fish's head to stop the flapping.

'Your son will need to complete his education elsewhere. My staff are exasperated.'

'Please, another chance? It's been a hard year for him. His father cleared out.'

Father cleared out? Rich took her hand. 'This is the most awful part of my job. I'm sorry. Unless—'

Rich felt the squeeze of her hand. 'Unless?'

'I need something to reward my team if he is to stay. Like a bonus.'

Mrs DeLuca paused from dabbing her eyes. 'Bonus? Like cash?'

'Cash? Mrs DeLuca, that's a good idea.'

Rich outlined his terms, including confidentiality.

Mrs DeLuca nodded at the instructions. 'A weekly cash contribution for the teachers? That should be fine. The sugar price has been reasonable. So, he can stay?'

'Yes, if we have a deal.'

She touched his neck. 'Poor thing, that sunburn looks painful.'

He placed his hand on her lean thigh. Trembling with excitement, he imagined a tugging line, hooking another prize coral trout.

~

At least Mamma had called, thought Isabella, to let her know about tomorrow's visitor. Mamma often phoned her university lodgings, passing along village gossip, talking about her favourite topics: new engagements within the Italian communities, births, and baptisms. Although Townsville was three hours' drive from Silkwood, it felt like she never left. *Si, Mamma, wonderful news.*

When the communal phone rang at 7pm, a party girl would call out, 'Isabella, it will be for you.' Her voice was flat, knowing it wasn't her latest man, following up after a party. Her friend was always right. In the early weeks, Isabella needed Mamma's news bulletins, for she missed home and family meals. She also missed Silkwood's rain, a light soothing drum beat on the roof, and watching the cane grow, week by week. During recent calls, she'd begun to listen for *his name*, not Carlo's. As her mamma spoke – Silkwood's radio news bulletin fading into the background – she frowned, wondering why she placed any significance in Darcy's improper affection. Yes, the kiss was better than the occasional wooden, closed mouth pecks with Carlo, but the mood was festive, overhead fireworks, with grappa on his breath. Bianca once told her about a New Years Eve party.

'Izzy, everyone kissed the stranger beside them under the fireworks after counting in the new year. So fun!'

Maybe it was much the same.

Dolly spoke of chance encounters. Perhaps, for her it was the thrill of the outsider, becoming more of herself, less the model daughter, *as modelled by Mamma*. She warned Darcy not to rouse Sicilian anger. Yet he risked the kiss, and she'd played a part, letting it continue. Or maybe he did mistake her for Bianca. She rubbed her temples. There would be no study tonight.

After tonight's call, she sat in her room. On her desk was a cross and family photo, arranged by Mamma, who'd inspected and approved of the room with a nun's single bed when they'd visited the former convent. She looked at the family photo she'd kissed with a sob every night in the early weeks. The family photo was taken at her 18th birthday, yet she felt guarded like an infant. She looked at her sister in the photo. Bianca was the intelligent daughter. Isabella was here because of tutoring, smart Carlo's help, hours of study after prayers, and her mamma's insistence. In the photo, Bianca's chin was raised, eyes gleaming, saying, *my life is mine*. Bright Bianca couldn't be tamed, *but she had*.

After birthday cake, a nonna croaked, 'Stability and a good family name are the best virtues for marriage. You must strive for *un buon matrimonio*. A good marriage.'

Carlo was by her side and reached for her hand.

'Loyalty can be expected,' explained the milky-eyed nonna.

'*Amore*, love, a bonus.'

'*Si. Si.*' She bowed, and felt Carlo squeeze her hand.

Isabella supposed her parents were matched, but Mamma was always vague about how they got together. The temperature dial of their relationship seemed to rest closer to loyalty than *amore*. While Mamma was a sun that glowed over Silkwood, warmth touching everyone with hugs and kisses, Papa seemed to be in a dark, cool eclipse. Perhaps this was the way it would be, or become, with Carlo. Yet, the affection between her and Darcy seemed natural, not guided. Her heart thumped. *Amore?*

Isabella reached for a novel. Her mamma disapproved of fantasies, but they were Isabella's favourite genre. After a couple of pages, she sighed and threw the book aside; Isabella and Darcy would only exist in a fantasy novel. Mamma said that most southerner teachers returned home as soon as they could; Darcy wouldn't want ties. Besides, she was matched, and loyalty was expected. Isabella blinked, concentrating. She had a visitor tomorrow, not fantastical Darcy, but Carlo. Her mamma would be pleased she would receive him. Isabella wondered which of her better dresses she should wear.

6

DARCY walked towards the staffroom after the last bell, mid-June, wondering why the young single teachers were herded together. At the staffroom door, principal Rich Pierce invited them to take refreshments. Frances stood by a table arranging biscuits and teacups. The welfare kid stiffened. Refreshments for teachers were rare.

At the front of the room, Rich addressed the group, explaining the mid-year staff transfer phase was nearing. 'It's time to even up teacher numbers in schools around the region, as student numbers change. We also need to transfer teachers in and out of the remote schools.' He paused and seemed to sneer. 'Single teachers, like you lot, are the easiest to relocate.'

Teachers murmured to those beside them.

'If you'd like to take a remote transfer,' continued Rich, 'you'll be rewarded with extra pay and holidays, and free air-conditioned housing.'

Darcy heard the beckoning pipes of a snake charmer's flute. He slid low, eyes peering over the seat in front. He noticed another young teacher, Liam Matthews, sliding even lower. Liam had told him earlier that he was dating the town hairdresser, Christie.

'I met her at the religious festival in Silkwood. But she's not that religious, if you know what I mean.' Liam had winked.

Darcy blushed, thinking of his dalliance in Silkwood.

Rich continued. 'I need volunteers, or else, you might be volunteered.' He clicked his fingers.

Darcy slumped lower. Liam was under the chair.

'At the end of your satisfying remote service, you'll have your pick of schools,' Rich went on. 'Say, on the Sunshine Coast or the Gold

Coast. You name it.'

The lights dimmed and a video began. The narrator introduced *Education in Remote Far North Queensland*. A smiling teacher walked off a plane holding a yellow departmental envelope. Laughing teachers relaxed in modern accommodation, tearing up their transfer envelopes, which rained down like golden confetti. Later, they drove along a rough rail in a thick, dark-green forest inside a new four-wheel drive vehicle. They sang '*A Land Down Under,*' as they swayed, then frolicked on a white sandy beach, clinking beers, admiring the sunset. There was a snippet of classrooms full of dark faces, interrupted by a plane buzzing overhead. The plane landed, delivering mail and supplies. A carton of beer was unloaded, and the ground attendant winked at the camera. Near Darcy, a few teachers laughed. The video concluded with a close-up of an air conditioner, followed by another beach scene with serene lapping water.

Darcy blinked, assessing this rendition of remote Queensland as propaganda. *If* the video was to be taken literally, teaching only briefly interrupted boundless outdoor leisure – an inverted version of schooling elsewhere. The lights came back on and Rich invited questions.

Leo, sitting beside him, whispered, 'He also moves on teachers who are causing him trouble.'

'Is that why you went away?'

'Ah, that's a long story.'

Rich squinted, trying to locate the talking. 'What's that? Are there any questions?'

'Surely, I can't be sent twice,' whispered Leo.

At the end of the meeting Rich handed out transfer application forms at the door. His eyes were cold like a cane toad. *Volunteer or be volunteered.* Darcy thanked Rich and placed the paperwork into his bag. He wanted to be regarded as a valuable team member not a sacrificial offering at the department's pagan altar. Darcy marched away from the threat. By the school gate, Liam dropped his form into a bin, touching his stylish, permed hair, and jogged away, bag bouncing on his back. Leo gathered a few transfer prospects who agreed to practice for the northern lifestyle with a few beers. Darcy watched the pied piper leading the band to the 'bottom pub.' He looked to where the Russo family car had parked weeks earlier. Isabella had held his eyes with a glare. Darcy blinked, imagining a hopeful stare, not an angry glare. Darcy heard the click of closing door. Frances called out. 'Hey Darcy, Bianca is still waiting for your call.'

~

Early evening, after lectures, Isabella walked in moonlight through the old convent gardens. The cross on the roof cast a shadow across the path. She thought of biblical calvary and their family mausoleum, hurrying towards the door.

In the foyer, the party girls mingled, waiting for cabs. The air held a thick mixture of hairspray, perfume, and cask wine.

A girl sneered. 'Look! Sister Isabella back at the convent.'

The girls laughed and blessed themselves.

A taxi arrived, tooted its horn, and the girls ran through the door, heels echoing in foyer, off to party houses and night clubs. A different calvary, thought Isabella.

Leaning through the taxi window, a girl yelled, 'When's your boyfriend visiting again? He looks like your type. Hairy religious wog.'

Shrieks of laughter only faded when the taxi taillights disappeared.

Isabella sat in the foyer lounge, head hung low. After a minute, she felt her cheeks cool, but the humiliation was settling much deeper. She sat opposite another cross, but also cross with herself, too ordained – her mother's perfect poised mannequin in a store window.

Isabella lifted her head. Carlo was undeserving of the insult. With his brains and marks, he should be at university, not her. Isabella rubbed her temples. During Carlo's last visit, he'd said his papa was buying a section of land beside their family farm, *for them*. If her life was organised in chapters, Isabella knew the contents page without reading. Listed midway: Isabella, Cane Farmer's Wife. Everyone would be happy, even gruff Papa would pat Carlo's back. She'd make an eligible Silkwood bride; Sister Isabella didn't puke cask wine and pizza onto a stranger's floor. Isabella looked in her mail pigeonhole. Sometimes her mamma sent articles from the *Town Times*, featuring photos of engagements, weddings, and babies. They'd arrive in a thick package. She'd only glance at these when replying to the 7pm call. *Si, Mamma, wonderful news.* She returned to the same thought. Everyone would be happy, but would their happiness make her happy? Isabella noticed an unusual shape. A thin envelope jutted in her pigeonhole.

~

Darcy looked about their drab house: no resemblance to the alluring video images. Damp mildewed curtains hung limp. He turned on the fans, then snapped the dial off to conserve power. Soon, there would be another electricity bill, followed by complaints from Leo, who found money for booze but not bills. Another shower passed overhead. His cousin Eliza occasionally wrote to him, confirming her gorgeous golden friends were still waiting for introductions. *Didn't returning teachers from remote postings have their pick of locations?* Darcy walked down the wet stairs to the letterbox. Thunder cracked overhead, reminding him of the Silkwood fireworks and Isabella. A fat cane toad hopped past his feet. As rain sprinkled, Darcy grabbed the mail and walked under the house for cover. The cane toad hopped away into the waterfall mist over the roof eaves. Darcy thumbed through the mail; *all the bills were in his name.*

He thought again of Isabella and the press of their bodies. During his childhood, he'd never minded being alone. Yet, these days, when rowdy Mediterranean chatter and laughter reached the eaves during neighbourhood parties, he'd remember the Russo lunch, now feeling both alone and lonely. Every Sunday lunchtime, he replayed Frances' bright greeting: 'Darcy, you found your way!' He wished he could find his way again, following cane tram lines to the Russo farm, feasting for hours. *But no, he'd kissed the wrong Russo.* Darcy doubted Bianca really awaited contact, remembering the Carabinieri costumed man. She was also circled by many other admirers, like she was the main act in a Roman Amphitheatre. The Carabinieri gendarmerie couldn't guard her as his, probably dismissed with Brigadier Bianca's salute and high laugh. *Besides, if he were to try with Bianca, how would he face Isabella?* She would think he was a carefree southerner rake, working his way through the Russo daughters, messing with their emotions and lives. Later, lying in bed, staring at the fan, imaging propellors, he wondered what it would be like to fly north on a small plane, jettisoning bills like unwanted cargo. Rain thumped the roof. Darcy hummed 'Riders on the Storm' by *The Doors*, his dad's favourite song. The transfer form was in his bag. He could ride out of this town as a rider on a storm, bills in Leo's name. His thoughts returned to the Russos and Silkwood. Isabella was at university. Carlo waited. He puffed a heavy breath. He'd leave them to their lives, imagining a small Cessna on the tarmac. Darcy groaned, he was over-thinking as usual, imagining inconsequential problems. Then he rolled onto his back.

Oh Shit. The letter.

~

Isabella retrieved the envelope, her quick clipping footsteps echoing along the corridor, paired with shadows, as if in pursuit. Sitting on her bed, she examined neat, unfamiliar handwriting on the envelope. She tried to steady her breathing before sliding a fingernail under the seal and unfolding the letter.

> *Dear Isabella, I wanted to write earlier, but I didn't have your address. I hope I overheard your mum correctly about where you are living. She was proudly telling a parent you'd settled in well in Townsville and university. That's great. I'm sorry about my affection, the magic of the Feast of the Three Saints overwhelmed me. I don't have a habit of randomly kissing girls, no matter how lovely. I must have been under Silkwood's spell. I apologise for any offence. I don't want to disrupt. Seems you have firm plans. It's great you have certainty. Some days I don't know how I ended up being a teacher in Far North Queensland; it just seemed to happen. It would be good to see you again when you're next on holidays. Good luck with your studies, Darcy.*

Isabella studied Darcy's elegant writing, remembering the handwriting of town boys, pens hacking shapes into paper. She had to guess Carlo's words scrawled within birthday and valentine cards. Across her school years, after essays were handed in, most teachers called the boys to the front desk, asking them to interpret.

'More hieroglyphics,' the teachers complained.

More than handwriting, she analysed the words. Darcy gave the impression he thought her lovely and the kiss was rare. She noticed what was missing, just as much as what was written. *Ah.* There was no mention that his affection was intended for Bianca. The ending was cool, yes, like her dropped hand in the fields, but she re-read her favourite line. *It would be good to see you again.* She blushed at the notion that an educated handsome older man thought her lovely, their kiss conjured by magic and spells. Perhaps fantasy had arrived in Silkwood.

Isabella checked the envelope for a return address, already framing a reply, arranging a place and time to meet, kept secret from Mamma and Carlo. She groaned – *Santa Maria* – there was no return home address. Her mamma managed all school correspondence. Isabella's handwriting, and the Townsville postmaster's stamp, would be noticed. She wasn't due home for weeks. She stood. Looking at the clear sky through the window, Isabella whispered a prayer, asking for a way to reach Darcy. After many minutes, Isabella swished the curtain closed. She was talking to winking, mocking stars, with no return address or possible reply.

~

Darcy looked out his bedroom window as clouds opened in stratospheric choreography. In the clear sky, stars seemed to blink with startled eyes at a rare audience in Queensland stormy tropics. He wondered whether Isabella looked at the same stars, whispering to a satellite in orbit to carry a return message. A comet shot by. Then grey muscular clouds closed shoulders overhead, and the only light was a misty halo around a streetlight. Again, he worried whether the letter was a further mistake. After he posted the letter with nervy fingers, Darcy had peered into the dark slot mounted into the post office wall.

His letter rested below, out of reach, likely askew, in a dark postmaster's purgatory, not sent, delivered, or read. An Australia Post truck had rumbled by and parked. Darcy swallowed. His letter would be retrieved, delivered, and read. He shuddered as the truck left, imagining Carlo sitting in Isabella's room, finding the note, scowling, interpreting salacious intent.

Darcy closed the bedroom curtain, wanting to also close his nightly musings about Isabella. In the Silkwood fields, he knew the Russo daughter was Isabella, taking her hand, remembering their easy conversation at lunch, admiring her curves and beauty, wanting to hold and kiss her. When he saw her stumble in the fields, fear of Gino and Carlo had been no match for his desire.

When he'd first kissed other girls, he broke for breath and asked whether they were single. They'd reply, *shhh enjoy the moment,* later explaining they were in patchy relationships. Perhaps, Isabella's car park stare was a question: *are you sincere?* Carlo didn't seem like a flowers type of guy, unless placing roses on an enemy's grave. Maybe Isabella was unhappy, her life a solemn hymn or funerial dirge written and sung by others. Perhaps she sang along, not wanting to be noticed, but in quiet lament.

Darcy blew out a long breath; yes, Isabella was the loveliest girl he'd kissed, but no more musings. Leo said Cindy circled the pub every weekend looking for him. Darcy closed his eyes, tonight he would try to dream of Cindy.

Yet later that night, Darcy dreamed of Isabella drafting a return letter. As words stretched across the page, he followed her written lines and curves, his pen joining hers on the page, tracing looping handwriting like the ribbons in her hair. All through the night, they held close together, his pen following the letters and shapes she formed for him. Her lines formed into limbs, and they curled together, entwining like forest vines. A flower budded and bloomed.

In the morning, he woke startled, vivid images clinging to him. He checked he was in bed alone, trembling fingers, fearing leaves and petals. He felt around, making sure there wasn't another lost earring, then looked to see if a shotgun barrel rested on his windowsill aimed at his head.

~

The classroom lights glowed in the early evening of the final week before the semester break. Teachers hunched over piles of examination papers with report cards to be written. Yellow departmental transfer envelopes arrived in the teachers' pigeonholes with air tickets, but one had yet to land for Darcy. Liam, his schoolteacher friend, said he was in love with Christie and hoped he was safe. *Love?* Darcy marvelled. *Or safe from love?* Earlier in the year, he might have thought Liam was weird, but he recollected his vivid dream and understood. Frances was right, Silkwood could cast spells.

In the classroom, Darcy ticked in time with the click of the departmental clock. A shadow reached from the door. He jumped; the shape looked like Isabella's outline.

Frances swept in, carrying a basket. 'It's me! With food of course!' Isabella's expressions played across her face. Darcy froze, wishing away memory of his dream.

'You're my last delivery and I have something special.' Frances unpacked her basket. 'No town pizza for you like the other teachers. Silkwood homemade fare.' She gestured across the dinner, a version of the Sicilian lunch, including red wine.

'Don't you know there's no escaping Sicilian hospitality?'

'Blessed by the priest, I hope,' Darcy joked to relieve his nerves.

Frances laughed. 'Not this time. I'm giving God a night off.'

Darcy thought of the letter he'd drafted to Isabella at *this* desk. He'd written many versions and still worried about the balance. No God in his classroom suited him, too.

'Darcy, marking students must be challenging when you work so closely with them. If it were me, I'd give them all A's.' Then she frowned. 'I hope Isabella concentrates on her studies. Her recent results were disappointing. I'm worried someone is distracting her.' Her eyes held him, still frowning. 'He'll be sorry when I find out.'

Darcy had a sudden hiccups, and Frances studied him.

'Anything wrong, Darcy? What do you know?'

'Nothing. Must be the wine,' he explained.

After Frances left, he went to reach for the Year 12 essays. Instead, Darcy opened a folder provided by Douglas. Within, were model essays from the previous year for the graduate teacher to reference. He stared for a minute at the cover page of the first essay.

Student name: *Isabella Russo.*

Mark: *A.*

He closed the folder. A few moments later, he took a deep breath and re-opened the folder. The lines of her handwriting were light and elegant. He closed his eyes, willing away the dream and their coiling limbs. Her prose was confident, clear, and carefully crafted, just like when she spoke. Darcy looked at the classroom window, imagining her reflected face, then cocked his ear, seeming to hear Isabella reading her essay. She explained the characterisation of the women in *Summer of the Seventeenth Doll.*

The women see their men as forever strong and heroic, working in demanding conditions in cane country. They remain loyal to their dreams. Isabella, reflected in the window, held his eyes. His breath caught. *They remain loyal to their dreams,* she repeated.

Darcy remembered to breathe, closed the folder and walked around the room, willing concentration. Isabella's voice still murmured in his ears. Alone in his childhood home, he was prone to daydreaming, visiting voices in his head, illusion overtaking reality. Isabella, in his classroom, felt like a religious visitation. He shook his head; he'd receive a different Russo visitation if he disrupted Frances' divine order.

Darcy thought of the letter. *It would be good to see you again.* This line had featured then omitted in various drafts; then retained. Darcy swallowed. The correspondence was too encouraging, too disruptive. Now he'd learned that Isabella was distracted, and Frances was on alert. Thinking of the cane trains that chugged around town, he'd changed the guidance points on the tracks, with Isabella a potential derailment. Darcy set the essays aside and teetered homeward, scraping his feet. By the sugar mill, he paused, admiring the strength of the monstrous steel beast venting steam. Industrial hum vibrated beneath his shoes. Darcy held the gates, wanting to harness the mill's might.

At home, Darcy opened his bag and removed the transfer application form. *He'll be sorry when I find out.* A few minutes later, Darcy rested his pen on his desk, then went to the fridge. Heels up on his desk, he held a beer. When his form was filed, a removalist truck would arrive, uproot his little life, *pronto,* and cart away a few boxes as if he had never existed. In days, he would alight from a tiny plane on a small dirt airstrip. Bills in Leo's name. By July, he could live in free, air-conditioned departmental accommodation with a pay rise – leaving Isabella and the Russos to their futures. Carlo's blade would be under other throats, not his. In a couple of years, he would arrive on the Gold Coast, another yellow transfer envelope in his pocket, mingling with the golden-brown female super race. Darcy reached high above the wardrobe and took down his suitcase.

7

AS dusk merged with darkening rain clouds, Matt Flint, owner and editor of the *Town Times,* locked the newspaper office from the inside, farewelling the last of his staff. Looking out the window, Matt could see other town businesses closing, reminding him that northerners always turned in early – only the two lively pubs signalled habitation as the sugar mill steamed below. The town cinema usually drew a crowd around now, but the owner, old Sid, was unwell. The cinema's soft foyer footlights no longer shone for the young town starlets, such as Bianca Russo, his new office trainee. A few sugar mill workers ambled by, gradually becoming silhouettes framed by the strengthening shop lights. Matt avoided his reflection in the dark window, not needing a news report on his unfortunate Flint facial genes. In his early forties, he still heard the taunts of his school bullies: *Flint sure has been hit with the ugly stick.* More mill workers passed by, then slowed, glancing through the window, probably seeking a glimpse of Bianca, who *hadn't* been hit with the ugly stick.

Matt planned to rise before dawn tomorrow to receive his newspaper's latest issue. After many years as a newsman, the thrill of holding the latest edition never dulled, though a few people named in tomorrow's paper for crimes would be less pleased. He checked to make sure the office door was locked. One of the lead stories involved a savage bashing, two men with designs on the same girl. The local got the upper hand, or fist, *as it were.* There were plenty of these stories and Matt left a page free in most editions. The assailant apparently waited for the police to arrive, a bloodied pulp lying in a gutter, vengeance worth a long stretch at Stuart Creek Prison. Matt rubbed his hands together, another dentist specialising in teeth replacement

52

might establish in town. A business in need of advertising. In full colour he'd persuade.

A familiar figure walked by: Dennis Deakin, the town detective. Matt had the jump on dozy Dennis, who would learn tomorrow about local gun smuggling, like the old days when the mafia half-ran the place. He checked the lock. Across the street, there were shouts from the 'top pub', confirming to Matt that it was time for a drink. Panting with effort, Matt mounted the worn stairs to his private rooms above the office. Moments later, he was gulping, lowering a tower of rum. Legs raised on the upstairs desk, Matt swirled his second rum, reflecting. A couple of years earlier, around his fortieth birthday, Matt had sat with his mother on a Saturday night at the Flint family home in Rockhampton, chewing on his steak and watching a pink ostrich on television. He'd stopped chewing, thinking. *When had he last spoken to Mandy, his girlfriend of sorts?* He wondered where she was and what she might be doing.

His mother had broken his reverie. 'Matthew, are you going to piss away all of your redundancy cheque?' She banged her cutlery on the table. 'How much is left?'

Matt had jumped, turning from the puppet ostrich to his mother. Her enquiry was timely; that afternoon, he'd stood in a car yard inspecting expensive imported vehicles. Matt hadn't taken his preferred car for a test drive, for he still felt drunk after his rum bender following his sacking from the local newspaper. He'd been zealous in his pursuit of politicians, developers, and a murky land deal. Influential people didn't like the headlines. There had been heat on the paper to cease reportage, and the owner rang him every hour.

'Flint, do you want the boot? Go back to reporting beef prices!'

The day after, he'd been sacked after the next damning headline. After being shoved out of the building with a, 'Fuck off, Flint,' by the burly sports reporter, he'd looked up; the owner stood at the window, waving with one hand and giving him 'the finger' with the other.

To his mother, Matt mumbled a figure well above the change in his pockets.

'Look after yourself, not the publicans. Now, look here.' His mother had pushed an advertisement across the table. Circled was a business for sale: a newspaper in a sugar town up the Queensland coast. 'We're going to check it out tomorrow.'

They'd driven north early the following day, Matt noticing neat, damp rows of sugar cane as they neared the town. At the newspaper office, his mother frowned, assessing the business assets and accounts. She shook her head, and the sales ledger, in mock annoyance at the sales vendor.

'This so-called business isn't worth shit.'

A couple of days later, she vigorously shook the vendor's hand as if she was swinging a skipping rope. 'We're doing you a favour.' As the crumpled man looked at the modest cheque, she winked at Matt and addressed the vendor. 'Your lucky day. I don't usually take on charity cases.' Her grey eyes twinkled. 'Cash the cheque. Give us the keys.'

Later, the newsman, with good news, called Mandy. He twirled the office keys between his fingers, knowing Mandy would be impressed and ready to relocate.

After many rings, she picked up. 'Yes?' Her voice sounded husky, tired. 'What? Nah.'

To the newsman, this was breaking news. 'Huh? Have I got the right number?'

In the background, he could hear a piano tinkling, a masculine voice, and a trumpet toot.

'Mandy, I thought you hated jazz.'

'I've moved on. I've wanted to say something for a long time.

'What's that?'

'Fuck off, Flint.'

Matt replaced the phone receiver – his second sacking in two weeks.

He now sat in the room's only chair, willing himself not to drink too much, the usual descent of the lonely bachelor. All over town, he heard despair among the womenfolk. In the town café, Matt eavesdropped behind a raised newspaper. Complaints reached over his print parapet. Lousy sex. No sex. Too much sex. Revenge sex. Weird sex. *Wow, women communicated.* Lowering the paper to his eyeline he sought out one of the unhappy women. Yet, at any eye contact, the women looked away. As the town women lifted the drawbridge, he raised his print in defeat.

Matt remembered his school bully, tall and handsome, with an arm around his latest girlfriend, taunting him by the classroom door.

'Hey, ugly stick.' He'd flicked his ears. 'Unbelievable. Even your ears are ugly. I never thought that was possible.'

Matt's face burned at the memory of the bully's deep chuckle and the girl's high-pitched giggle, sounding like a kookaburra testing its vocal range. Setting aside his rum, Matt rolled into bed. In his dream, charming Prince Matthew astride a chestnut mare clip-clopped up the town's main street, ready to claim a princess. The dream genre was Western, and he rode with a sidearm, square dimpled chin raised on his handsome face. As his steed clicked past the rowdy town saloon, women cheered. One burst from the crowd, lifting her long skirt. She called, 'Take me, Prince Matthew.' He helped the buxom maid into his saddle. A stumbling man burst from the saloon, calling, 'She's mine.' Half roused from his dream, Prince Matthew found himself holding a pistol before realising he was holding something else. He shuffled under his sheets.

~

The *Town Times* whacked the Pierce household door. Maria Pierce put down her tea. She could learn more about life in town. Her principal husband, Richard, never asked her to social events. A couple of fellow Sunday churchgoers were her only friends. After a brief chat, they'd wave from the church gate after mass, heading to parish lunches.

As she collected the paper, she thought she might busy herself with housework. A week earlier, her husband had fired their Filipino maid, Delores. Richard said she'd been stealing cash from his wallet.

'Really? Your wallet is never on display.'

'Shut up.'

Children skipped by. Their sweet voices rose and lilted on their way to school. She sniffled at their joy, instinctively holding her flat belly, which should have swelled over the years with babies, just as her husband had promised during their courting. Over a candlelit dinner with flowers and an engagement ring twinkling on the table, he told her his favourite names: Richard, Richie, Rich, Ricky, and Ricardo. She'd laughed at the time, thinking it was a joke, as she blushed and tried on the ring. This wasn't the first time he had misled her. After graduating as a veterinarian, she worked at a vet practice and started dating one of her colleagues. The day after their second date, when the two vets kissed like unpractised, pecking emus, Richard tearfully entered the clinic, carrying an injured dog. Later, she discovered that one loved her, while the other loved her family money. Her choice of the better-looking job candidate still haunted her as she was dragged along Queensland's endless coastline with Richard's promotions.

Maria unfolded the newspaper on the kitchen table and picked up her tea to savour her small window to the outside world. She turned pages, nibbling a biscuit in hope. A week earlier, she'd replied to an advertisement: *Ideas sought for new columns. Apply to Matt Flint, Editor in Chief.*

She'd explored ideas over coffee with Matt in the town cafe. 'I'm a qualified vet. What about a column about animal and pet wellbeing?'

'Okay, that's got legs.'

They laughed. Their eyes locked.

'Should I pen a feature as a trial?'

'Woof. Woof.'

Maria remembered his warm handshake as they left, her first physical touch in months. She felt his yearning bachelor eyes. With trembling fingers, Maria flicked through the newspaper, worrying her article might be too weak for publication or stuffed down the back. Yet, midway, she found Vet Maria's column interpreting a dog's wagging tail. She touched every line to be sure it was real, brushing away biscuit crumbs.

'Matt, thank you,' she murmured, thinking she would like to pat his hair, a messy dog coat. She laughed. Matt looked like a mournful pooch needing affection. Thinking of a dog's wagging tail, she visualised Matt's grin.

She placed her tea on the table, her joy cooling at Richard's response to her column. *He wouldn't be wagging a friendly tail.*

~

Matt roused into partial awareness before dawn. He rolled onto his back, concentrating. The day's early sounds provided the newsman with information. An intuitive observer, he tuned into daily routines. *There was always more to know.* He heard his delivery team at the office door, then footsteps down the street. *Thump.* A bale dropped at the newsagent's door. In the background, the sugar mill groaned, hissing steam. Cane trams scraped on steel tracks. He heard the dull pull and complaint of steel couplings between the cane bins, bustled along by the squat muscular trams. Barking dogs heralded thrown newspapers, for the town hounds were never sure whether the town rag was friendly fire. Matt was convinced barking was just occasional exercise for dogs. He'd ask the paper's new veterinary columnist.

There was another sound at the door, potentially another delivery. Then, light footsteps climbed his stairs. The insects finished their overnight broadcast. Tugging tiredness called for a near-dawn snooze. A shadow stretched into his room from the door. There was a slight buzz in his ears, and his radio survey across town tuned out. He may have heard the whispering of dropping fabric, coupled with falling underwear catching along the thighs, a little further at the knees, and almost free. He may have imagined a shuffle of light feet freeing 'smalls' caught around an ankle. Then, a ruffle of sheets. He'd found a town Mandy.

8

Isabella Russo, trainee teacher, walked tall across the school to a classroom. She approached senior students who crowded by the same door she'd stood by the year before, but this time in a dress, instead of a school uniform. Sandals, instead of school shoes and a pink ribbon in her hair.

At home, her mamma inspected her, beaming. 'A future teacher in our humble family. And so beautiful too, the boys will struggle to concentrate.'

Her mamma hugged her so often Isabella needed to re-iron her dress. She refused Carlo's offer of a lift, driving with her mamma.

When teacher training placements were being arranged, the university lecturer frowned at her completed form. Isabella needed to experience a different educational environment, he explained, rather than her former high school. In a drab, thin, crushed dress, with unbrushed hair and downcast misty eyes, Isabella said she was needed at home to help her frail, elderly parents. Darcy's letter was in her pocket.

'I'm sorry to hear,' replied the university lecturer.

At the Year 12 classroom door, students greeted her, mostly Year 11s from when she was in her senior year. A couple of the students were repeating Year 12 for better marks, including Bruno Deluca. As Bruno sneered down at her, she remembered the first two letters of his surname, his most common grades, *never the last*. Recalling his vile hectoring, Isabella was glad she would be an observer in the senior class, just helping the senior students with their work.

Inside the classroom, the young male teacher introduced her as Miss Russo.

58

'Miss Russo, ha!' Bruno snorted from the back row.

Isabella flinched but took a spare seat near Bruno to show her determination. As the teacher introduced the novel, Bruno murmured a decibel below the teacher's hearing, part of the bully's craft. She frowned at his heckling and looked from her adult dress to the student uniform she'd worn only months earlier, feeling like an imposter, considering the lecturer's logic. Towards the end of the lesson, Isabella felt a kick on her chair. Then, a further kick-kick-kick.

'Isabella, *sorry*, Miss Russo, do you know what this is?' Bruno rasped. Another kick.

Isabella stared ahead. The kicking increased.

'It's me banging your pussy, eh.'

Nearby girls yelled. One threw a ruler at Bruno, another a thick pencil case, which he swatted away with a laugh. The bell rang. Isabella marched out with heavy steps. Darcy surveyed the classroom, trying to locate the disturbance. He slumped into his chair. *What happened to Isabella?* He'd left his completed transfer request form in his bag. His father had fought worse battles at Darcy's age in the Vietnam jungles. To back out with a yellow envelope *would be yellow*, in his father's eyes.

The day before, Douglas, his head of department, explained a trainee teacher would be placed with him to observe a new graduate, compared to older teachers.

'We need to offer the trainee diverse experiences. Especially, as the trainee went to school here.'

Darcy felt a light headache pulse, asking, 'Ah, a former student?'

'Yes, Frances' daughter, Isabella Russo. Great student, fine young lady. You'll like her.'

Darcy looked away, wondering whether his letter had drawn Isabella back, and if her hunter boyfriend knew.

Below the classroom, Darcy heard a burst of male laughter. A usually demure girl yelled, 'Bruno, you talk about a girl's pussy, but you're the real cunt.'

Darcy jumped in shock, then stood and jogged down the stairs. Near the school gate, Isabella stood, head hung low. Darcy stopped, feeling weak. *This wasn't Douglas' intended diverse experience.* Nearby, another girl yelled at Bruno, who walked away with a sports bag swinging over his broad shoulders. Darcy's eyes narrowed and he followed Bruno.

From the athletics track, Darcy heard a shrill whistle and walked in the direction of the school fields. He looked over the vast, glossy green paddock: Leo's classroom. Athletic students stretched and warmed up with short sprints. In the centre of the oval running track, the school rugby league teams groaned with every push-up. Only Bruno completed the push-ups with ease, as if he was flattening the ground.

'Hey, Darce,' Leo welcomed Darcy. 'Looking for a job?' Without waiting for a reply, he added, 'Here, clock these guys,' throwing Darcy a stopwatch and pointing to sprinters lined up along a whitewashed stripe. 'They need a good time to head to the athletics championships in Cairns.' He pointed to another small group of four runners. 'This is their competition.'

Darcy stood beside three of his Year 12 students, who limbered up with springy jumps. He walked in front of them, standing in the lanes of the athletics track.

'Ready?' he asked.

'You're in the way, Mr Grant.'

Darcy clicked the stopwatch. They looked across at the rival group on the opposite side of the track, already stretching out in a fast sprint.

'Hey, Mr Grant, the others have started, and we need a chance.'

'We can get underway when you tell me what upset Miss Russo and the girls.'

He clicked the stopwatch to pause the time.

'Just some joking around,' one said, looking over at Bruno.

Darcy clicked the stopwatch. 'That's two seconds, soon three.'

'Hey, stop!' the athletes cried.

A wind brushed past them as the rival sprinters completed their circuit. Leo registered he had a role. He showed Darcy his stopped clock. 'A fast time, perhaps a school record.'

Behind, the finished sprinters gasped for air.

'Wow,' exclaimed Darcy, 'not sure there's any point you guys running.'

Darcy started the clock again.

'No! Please, Mr Grant!'

The rival group cheered as Leo called out the times. The stalled runners milled, frustrated. 'Can I have a private word?' asked one of the students.

They spoke away from the lanes. Darcy walked back. He clicked the stopwatch twice, returning to zero.

'Ready? On your marks!'

As the sprinters flew, Darcy asked Leo for a quiet chat.

~

'Yes, Mr Scuderi, I'd be happy to help,' confirmed Bruno.

Leo smiled with appreciation. Students were happy to help lug the training equipment back to the storage shed close to weekly team selection. Bruno broke his pile into two at the shed to carry through the door.

'Boots off, please, Bruno.'

Leo noticed Bruno looking at other students in their football boots as they left.

Leo asked Bruno to stand still inside the shed when the pads were stowed away. 'Close your eyes. I want to check your balance,' instructed Leo.

Bruno's eyes flicked about, especially at the close of the shed door.

'That's pretty good. Balance is essential. Okay, now feet together.'

Bruno pressed his feet together.

'Balance still good.'

Bruno looked through slitted eyes, then squeezed them shut as Leo stood before him.

'You can open your eyes now. But keep your feet together.'

Bruno's eyes bulged as Leo held a large lead shot put above his unprotected feet. 'W-w-what are you doing?'

'You know, Bruno, I once dropped a shot put on my foot as a trainee teacher. Broke a heap of small bones. Out for the season.'

'W-w-why?'

'You're in line to be selected for the Firsts. You're training so hard. It's a pity.'

'W-w-w-w-hat? W-why?'

'Anyone representing the school does so because of good skill and character. How would you describe your behaviour in class and around school?' Leo leaned in closely. 'How would you describe your respect towards girls and female teachers?'

Leo adjusted the heavy lead orb in his hands. It was like a cannonball. Bruno stared wide-eyed at the menace.

'It could be better, Mr Scuderi.'

'What about your respect towards the female trainee teacher in your English class?'

'Yeah, could be better, Mr Scuderi.'

'But will it be better? What will I hear tomorrow when I ask your teachers about your attitude and respect?'

'Good reports, sir.'

'Gosh, this is getting heavy now. Do I have your word, Bruno?'

They both looked at the pronounced veins weaving across Leo's arms.

'Yes, you do, sir.'

Bruno still stared at the shot put with sweat glistening on his brow. 'Can I leave?'

'Yes. Now we have an understanding.'

Bruno shuffled backward, and Leo dropped the heavy ball. A dull cannon boom filled the room. The ball rolled slightly, revealing a dent and a large crack in the concrete.

'Wow Brono! Look at that damage. Glad you weren't in the way of that, eh?'

~

On Friday afternoon, Darcy hoped the noise from his classroom didn't carry across the school. His Year 12 students were talkative and unproductive, as usual, during the last lesson of the week, waiting for the bell. At the start of the lesson, he'd written instructions in chalk on the blackboard. Only the academic girls in the front row seemed interested, as he too, counted down the minutes until the bell. Today, he was a poor role model for Miss Russo, like he'd been in the Silkwood fields. He still wondered whether she was here because of his letter, worrying too about Frances and Carlo.

During his first weeks, Darcy found that a teacher can try with just minutes to the weekend. He'd long given up. *Thirty of them. One of you.* Perhaps, this was a lesson for Miss Russo, after all. Yet, her determination was a lesson for him; after she was bullied, she arrived as if nothing had happened and looked Bruno in the eye. Then kicked him in the shins with pointy leather shoes, then stamped on his toes. Bruno hopped around, howling. The entire class was silent, in judgment. *Thirty of them. One of him.*

With the weekend just minutes away, Darcy daydreamed, looking out the window at the sugar mills stacks. Isabella would have discarded his pathetic words in the bin, seeking a training placement to be close to her boyfriend, then confirming her engagement with Carlo.

Later in the year, he imagined accepting Frances' lunch invite. Darcy would clink a glass of vino with Isabella, her engagement ring sparkling on a slender finger, smiling at the distant memory.

'I was under Silkwood's spell,' he'd say.

'I'd forgotten all about it,' she would say.

Carlo would shake his hand, asking whether Darcy would attend the nuptials. Of course, he'd reply, knowing what to say. Bianca would sit beside him in the church, mentioning she was single and lonely, brushing his hand with hers, not reaching for the church missal.

In the classroom, the din lifted, high, even by Friday standards, and Darcy blinked away his daydream, clearing his throat. 'Students, make some effort, you're leaving more work for next week.'

Darcy looked as stern as he could muster, then the chatter rose. Isabella smirked. He shrugged, *Friday afternoon, eh,* and she shrugged in response. Darcy blinked as if to clear away dust in his eyes. This wasn't a daydream. Isabella in his classroom wasn't a coincidence. He remembered her determination, also admiring her poise and care, helping students, mainly boys wanting her attention. He'd noticed her grace and beauty too.

The bell rang. Tables and chairs scraped on the lino floor, and bags banged and dragged from the outdoor lockers. *Bye, Miss Russo. Bye, Mr Grant.* Darcy went to the window and began drawing the curtains.

'Darcy? I have wanted to talk with you again all week.'

Darcy froze. Beside him, the Year Nine student's etching remained in the mossy grime. *Reckless.* He stood rigid, finding it difficult to turn around.

'It's been so hard being in the same room but unable to talk.'

He turned around.

'Ah, well, I—'

'You wrote, wanting to see me again.'

'I'm sorry. This isn't a good idea. You've too much at stake.'

Darcy could see her eyes moisten. He resisted an urge to hug her, especially after Bruno's bullying.

'Also, Isabella, it seems like your mum has some suspicions.'

'I can manage Mamma. She's always suspicious.'

Darcy noticed her wry grin.

'What about your boyfriend?' he asked, trying to relieve his guilt.

'He's not really—'

There was noise from a nearby classroom. Isabella walked to the door. Darcy recognised the effort. A close whispered discussion would be noticed, gossiped about. He watched her bobbing hair drop and disappear down the stairs. 'Oh, no,' he said, looking at her heading towards the school gate. Over the weekend, he would miss her.

~

A couple of days later, Frances knocked and entered Darcy's classroom. Frances didn't have the slightest spark of her usual joy. Darcy felt a chill, figuring slighted Isabella had finally confided in her mum about the kiss, his letter, and reasons for returning.

'Mr Grant, I would like to speak about Isabella.'

'Of course,' he replied, fussing about his desk to fake confidence.

'Isabella has been reluctant to attend your lessons, a bit nervous.'

'Frances, I'm sorry.'

'Yes, at the very start of her teacher training.'

Darcy stepped back, noticing Frances' glowing black eyes. 'I didn't mean—'

'I guess these things happen between young people.'

She pulled out a tissue from under her sleeve.

Darcy fought the urge to run. 'Frances, what are you going to do? I made a mistake.'

Huh? Frances appeared confused. 'Anyway, it's all stopped, and the brute apologised.'

Darcy laughed, recalling Bruno's surprise move to the front of the class, relocating from the bully's back row with its commanding view and furthest range. He then dedicated himself to the writing drills, saying goodbye and thanks to Miss Russo. Darcy owed Leo a six pack.

'What's so funny, Darcy?'

'Oh, just relief, sorry.'

'I'll tell you who should be relieved. The bully. We Sicilians have a protective streak.'

Darcy nodded, assuming Frances didn't know the might of the actual bully.

'Lucky Bruno,' she whispered, kissing Darcy's cheek. 'Isabella is thankful, too. She thinks you've got something to do with it. Thank you, too. My daughter's university education is so important to me.' Frances touched the cross on her necklace, then gripped his arm. 'Darcy, you must come for lunch again one day. I meant what I said. It would be wonderful to have you closer to my family. Bianca needs a steady influence, just like you are providing Isabella.'

When Frances left, he slumped into his chair, only stirring when the janitor wandered by, scraping a bin. 'Any rubbish in there, Darce?'

9

NEAR spring, a couple of weeks later, along the town's main street, Darcy heard the townsfolk buzzing like bees gathering and sharing pollen. *My harvest slot is next week. You? The week after.* Buzz. Buzz. In the fields, the mature cane waved with light straw-coloured flowers, wanting to be noticed by the mechanical harvesters. They, too, also waited for their slot. At a distance, the manicured, uniform fields resembled a bowling green surrounded by a dark grandstand of high shadowed mountains. To Darcy, the lumpy mountain tree spectators waited for the harvesters and play to begin. Inside the sugar mill, Darcy imagined a bloated queen bee demanding nectar. *More!* The cane trams bustled out to the farms with empty cane bins. Hours later, they rattled back, laden with jumbled thick stalks as dark soil stripes appeared in the fields. But still the queen bee was unsated. *More!*

The weather had changed in time for the harvest, as promised. In Douglas' office earlier in the year, Darcy had wiped his brow, drenched with sweat from standing still in his classroom. Douglas turned his fan up, saying the mild winter made the summer monsoon struggle worthwhile. For most of the year, the north had been a brooding misty grey green, with land and air barely distinct. Only the high mountain above the town and the soaring sugar mill stacks had stood out. These days, the sky was so bright that Rich Pierce was barely seen without his golden Onassis tycoon sunglasses. Most mornings, at the top of the town's prominent hill, Darcy squinted through plastic service-station sunglasses, his father's army cap pulled low. He counted three clear horizontal bands: bright blue sky, dark green mountains, and the light green of cane fields. It seemed to be the Mediterranean immigrant's flag of the north. He thought of

Clarissa, his Aboriginal student. He was sure the town Aboriginals didn't see it that way, living at the edges, within their land. Still, he remembered the contrasting red and green bunting flickering at the Silkwood festival and Isabella's warm olive skin. While he mostly held these thoughts outside of lessons, yawning Leo would continue to goad him, making his morning coffee.

'Another night in your room, Mr Grant. When will we be calling you Father Grant?'

Darcy always joked, 'I'll book you in for an extra-long session in the confessional.'

Today, walking to school, Darcy heard excited discussions in Italian and Greek along the main street. Fingers counted numbers, calculating the expected cane price per tonne following harvest.

Si. Si. Bene. Bene, the Italians chattered and hugged.

Kalos. Kalos, the serious Greek men nodded.

Today, mid-week and mid-term, Darcy noticed the Year 12 boys looking out the window more often than usual, hearing the increasing bustle at the sugar mill. Darcy figured they felt held back from their sugar futures and would be in the mill's recruitment room the day after graduation.

The mill exhaled sweet breath, and sugary essence filled the room with each rustle of the classroom's mouldy curtains. Raised noses inhaled candied air. Listening to his yawning students, Darcy smelled his irrelevance. He wouldn't blame his students if they threw down their novels, stormed out in protest, and hitched a ride on the cane trams out to their farms. In a daydream, he imagined joining them, whopping a crumpled leather hat on steel flanks, willing on the puffing iron horse.

Darcy blinked, rejoining his listless class. He supposed they sat equally bored in church every Sunday. *Was he just another priest to them? Father Grant?* In his classroom sat Isabella; she knew he wasn't priestly. At the sound of more loud yawning and Bruno's snoring, Darcy realised he wasn't much of a teacher on slow days like these. *Didn't Frances once say he was under a spell?* He wanted to vanish with a swish of a cape and tap of the magician's cane.

He stamped. 'Nah, fuck that.'

'Mr Grant, did you swear?' asked the demure girl in the front row who'd sworn at Bruno in defence of Isabella. 'That's against school rules.'

'Me? I'm sure you misheard.' He adopted a coy smile and leaned low. 'You can talk,' he whispered. 'Well said to Bruno the other day, but don't repeat those words in your next essay.'

The student blushed and covered her mouth, giggling.

Darcy addressed the class. 'Open your notebooks to a new page. Imagine it's two years from now, 1987. You'll be well out of school.'

'Yeah!' cheered the class.

'Some of you might be out of school. A few of you will probably be finishing assignments and detention.' He pointed to boys he knew could take the joke, including rousing domesticated Bruno. The class laughed again. 'Describe what you hope to be doing in two years. I know many of you will be at teacher training college, just as I was.'

'Noooooooooo!' they groaned. '*So, gammon, Mr Grant!*'

Darcy smirked. He was the teacher, but he was still learning. Gammon was a word used by Aboriginal students when something was improbable or bad. The term was adopted by all.

Soon, his students bent over notebooks. Some looked up and away, thinking, then scribbled. Minutes later, with minds in 1987, the students lifted their heads in surprise. 1985's clanging bell.

~

Two days later, the class continued to write. At the front of the classroom, Darcy drafted his two-year prediction as a model for his students. In 1987, he could be on the Gold Coast with the golden blonde hair postcard beauties, *not* in training to be a priest. Isabella was also drafting. He stared at her lustrous thick dark hair. In two years, she'd be engaged, close to attaining a teaching diploma. They'd be virtually at other ends of the state, and likely never see each other again. Darcy paused, wondering why this saddened him, a solitary welfare kid, who'd built emotional fortification around his little life.

Alone, hungry, in a cold house, he'd kept people at a distance, especially the nosy welfare worker, Mrs Black. Drafting the letter to Isabella was his first expression of emotion. He glanced up at Isabella; she looked at him. Students noticed he'd stopped drafting, pen frozen in the air, like a statue. Chatter rose among the scholars.

Darcy stood, cleared his throat, asking, 'Any Prime Ministers out there?'

The students hushed, recognising a teacher's standard tool: nabbing someone who was talking and putting them on the spot. They remained silent, eyes lowered, so he asked them to stand in a circle. They remained quiet, so he probed.

'Who expects to be living here? Working? What type of work?'

Hands went up and down, and students called out answers. Clarissa followed the other girls and raised her hand with the popular choices. After more questions, there were jeers as students called out their stories. Overconfident statements were called out with, *No way! Gammon, eh!* Darcy noticed Isabella laughing and smiling at the boys' responses. Most boys expected to work on their family farms or at the sugar mill. The girls expected to help at home and on the farm or work in administration at the sugar mill. They expected to marry and have children in just a few years. Darcy noticed the narrow list. They were in sugar country and little else seemed possible. This too was Isabella's intended future. He swallowed, wondering about her drafted plan.

Then Clarissa spoke – her first words in months. 'I just want to help my people, eh. Many of my mob can't read or write. I want to show the younger ones that trying at school is okay, eh.'

Darcy felt ignorant, trying to find fitting words. 'That's so good of you. I'm sure you can succeed,' he said, wondering whether his words sounded hollow.

'Gammon, eh,' Clarissa murmured, looking at her feet.

One of the girls hugged Clarissa, then another. *'No way*, not gammon,' they said. Isabella stood and touched Clarissa's shoulder, saying, 'If I can make university, you can.'

Darcy knew to not speak, wanting to hold the moment. After a minute of hushed murmuring among the class, Darcy drew the focus. 'Well done, everyone. Save your writing and look back in two years and then five. Perhaps update. And for the future Prime Ministers, remember this is where it all started: 12C! Not gammon, eh!'

The most boisterous boys cheered, the least likely to ever reside at the Prime Minister's Canberra Lodge. Isabella smiled. Darcy checked the clock.

One of the boys called, 'What's your two-year story, eh?'

Darcy's breath caught. He tried to step the question.

'Will you be here in two years?'

Darcy looked up at the clock, tilting an ear in hope for the bell.

'C'mon, Mr Grant, tell us your story.'

'I want to see you lot graduate and see what becomes of you.'

He felt Isabella's eyes on him. Darcy thought of the completed form in his bedroom and how close he'd come to departing.

'So, you'll go back south after we graduate?'

He rolled out verbal padding, not answering. Finally, the bell rang.

'Students, please say thanks and goodbye to Miss Russo. She's finished her time with us and is heading back to university.'

The boys sighed, many of whom had stolen glances at Isabella, calling for her help. The class clapped.

'Thanks, students,' Isabella said. 'Keep at your studies and good luck for the remainder of the year.' She paused, smiled, and held his eye. 'Thanks too, Mr Grant.'

Isabella left with the students. Darcy stood by the desk where she'd drafted. He touched the surface, wondering about her two-year plan, whether she'd just joined the dots plotted for her. He sensed a new plan, realising he hoped for it too.

So, gammon Mr Grant, eh, his students would have said.

~

Leo drove from town on Sunday morning, waving to Scuderi relatives resting in the town cemetery. Darcy was a wary passenger, focused on Leo's shaky hands and steering, knowing he must be weary from his overnight exertions. Somewhere near dawn, Darcy had heard chirping birds and Leo's stumbling return. *A little further, love.* He was surprised when Leo rose mid-morning, showed the girl out, grabbed his keys, and outlined his recovery plans to Darcy.

'A reviving swim up at the inland gorge. Then a nap.'

Leo explained he'd be ready for a few 'close out' weekend lagers at the 'top pub'.

Darcy's thoughts drifted in the direction of Silkwood, imagining Isabella in a light nightdress, rousing, rubbing her dark eyes, accepting a cup of tea from Frances, both whispering a joint prayer for the day. Carlo was not really her boyfriend, she'd said. Perhaps, though, Isabella was walking home, hair loose on her shoulders after a night with Carlo, following Darcy's stiff response in the classroom. He felt his forehead furrow.

By the car, Leo had flicked a towel at Darcy. 'Cindy looked lonely at the pub last night. As usual, you're missing when there's a good time on offer. Still in training to be a priest?'

As the car circled through the hills, Leo continued to joke and tease. Today, Darcy didn't mind Leo's playful goading. The trip also made his weekend seem busy as he fended off Frances' invitations.

High in a mountain range, Darcy held on to his seat as he was slung around on the ever-winding road. Leo sped as if the publican had called last drinks. Feeling a scrape on the passenger door, Darcy gripped the door handle and yelled, 'Hit the brakes! I'll take the wheel.'

Standing by the side of the road, Darcy could see smashed guardrails along the road's long curve behind them. The Ford Escort's scuffed paintwork had new dents and scratches. One remaining hubcap spun down the road. Leo tapped the bonnet with croaky praise. 'Runs like a dream.'

Without warning, a growling mechanical sound came from below. They both flinched. Ranks of black-leathered bikies were quickly upon them with howling engines and hyper-crackling exhausts: an orchestra of mayhem. The riders heckled and spat at Leo as they revved past. Darcy and Leo hunched low, covering their ears until the bikies disappeared around the corner ahead. Leo leaned on the car bonnet, *not running like a dream.* He threw Darcy the keys.

'Leo, do you know those blokes?' Darcy asked.

'Yeah. One time, I was in trouble with them.'

Darcy held the keys, chilled. He grimaced at the distant motorbike growls. 'Really?'

'Yeah, got involved with a biker's girl. That's when Pierce sent me away for a couple of years with the yellow envelope.'

Darcy studied Leo's glassy red eyes, which he slowly closed then painfully re-opened, like an unwilling roller door. They set off again with Darcy at the wheel. Leo clicked open a can of beer. Remembering the shotguns slung over the bikies' shoulders, Darcy slowed the car to a crawl. They climbed for a while, Leo chugging his beer, until the country opened and flattened onto a plateau. Leo pointed with his beer to the cars on the side of the road, and Darcy parked behind them. Towels over their shoulders, they walked through a clearing to the rapids. Above the roar of the rushing rapids, kids cheered as they bounced on huge, round black cylinders.

'Inflated tractor tyre tubes,' Leo explained. 'Farmers' kids, eh.'

Darcy sat on his towel as Leo waded in the shallows of a nearby pool, a quiet eddy beside the nearby riverbank. He watched Leo sink beneath the water as teenagers rolled the rubber tubes, teeth chattering, back to the top of the rapids.

Leo waved. 'Darce, come in for a dip.'

Darcy gasped as he entered the cold pool. He looked into the dark water. 'Are there crocs in here?' he stuttered. He'd heard a 'salty' could zoom in at any depth without warning.

'Too cold up here, but you never know.'

Leo grabbed his leg, and Darcy squealed. Leo then dropped low into the water to his eyeline, mimicking a crocodile. He drifted towards Darcy, unblinking and focused, a rapacious predator gliding on the surface. *A little further, love.* Darcy followed suit, and the two pretend alpha male crocodiles launched, teeth bared. They wrestled under the water, only rising when they were out of breath.

'I was going to get you into a death roll and drag your corpse to my den.' Leo puffed. 'But I need my driver to get me back for the afternoon session.'

At the mention of Leo's planned drinks, Darcy thought of their household finances. Bills in his name. Leo was always short on the rent and tapped Darcy for loans. His car was a near wreck and probably uninsured and unregistered – he had noticed the curled, lifting car registration sticker dated from many years earlier. His PE teacher clothes, once resembling a mighty legionnaire's uniform, were now dull and thin.

'Time for a snooze,' explained Leo, leaving the pool.

'Your finances are the death roll,' Darcy grumbled to Leo's back.

As Leo dozed in the dark forest's midnight cool, young women rose around Darcy from the water's edge, like marine nymphs testing the earth's fertile soil. They glistened, slippery and delicate as tadpoles. Darcy lowered his father's army cap, sneaking glances as the dripping sisterhood paraded by.

'Hey, Darcy,' said a soft voice.

Darcy glanced the tapering slide of Isabella's bare legs as she walked away. She looked back. He was too slow, no longer with quick teenage eyes. They locked eyes. Her magnificent shining hair lay long and wet over her shoulder. He looked away.

Darcy felt a dull thump as his cap flew off. Leo stretched and yawned. 'A free beauty parade, and you're staring into space. What's wrong with you?'

Darcy glanced back to Isabella, who was wringing her hair. He stared at the long drips. Tick. Tock.

~

That evening, Isabella retrieved *Dolly* from under her mattress. She rested the magazine on her upraised bare legs and re-read the articles on intimacy, shuffling her feet. She addressed the portrait of the Virgin Mary. 'Apparently, you don't know anything about this. *Apparently.*'

Isabella turned the page and read a new article away from the virgin's gaze. The story described a long, passionate kiss, a prelude. Her face reddened and she wondered whether her exhibition at the gorge might stir Darcy. *Dolly* explained a girl could give signals if a trustworthy guy was interested but not confident. In the classroom, their eyes caught and held, but she felt his restraint. She was due to return to university in a week but still waited for his next move, while Carlo circled. She recalled his teacher's assessment, it wasn't a good idea, too much at stake. Isabella looked at her long, lean brown legs, wondering if Darcy might like to stroke them, remembering his gaze at the gorge. She closed her eyes, daring to fantasise about the magazine's descriptions, also recalling overheard stories from the university party girls. Her body began to warm. She'd hadn't felt longing like this for Carlo, only Darcy.

At the sound of footsteps near her door, she stuffed the magazine under her pillow, hoping her face wasn't flushed. Her mamma knocked on the door and let herself in.

Isabella knelt beside her bed, devoted as a nun at a church pew, Mamma beside her. They crossed their foreheads, closed their eyes, and recited their nightly devotion.

'Now, once again, in Italian.'

'*Sì*, Mamma.'

Isabella squinted to be sure the magazine was covered. There was a particular article she wanted to re-read. She prayed onwards with memorised words, unthinking. Isabella imagined Darcy looking at her legs as she again felt strange warmth. Isabella wondered about Darcy's sexual experience. One day, could he guide her in more ways than teaching?

~

At university, Darcy studied literature combined with teaching for no better reason than he liked books and school. Schooling had scaffolded his childhood, bereft of parental presence. At school, his friends shared comics and lunch with the skinny welfare kid. In his first year, his cousin Eliza wrote, asking whether he'd been on any dates.

'I've heard about the wild university life,' she once wrote.

In the house across the street, students partied most nights.

Spying through curtains, amidst mist and fog, Darcy saw young men and women come and go. At night, he'd lowered his window to block the singing and shouts. Darcy would sigh, placing Eliza's letters on top of his comics, chess magazines, and stamp collection. Re-reading Eliza's letters, Darcy wondered whether the Gold Coast had universities, with single golden girls as abundant as grains of sand on their shimmering beaches.

One day in his second year, his welfare worker Mrs Black was joined by a female trainee during a routine welfare check. His father was out. Darcy lied. *Food shopping,* he mumbled to his feet, as Mrs Black looked through their empty pantry, making notes.

A few days later, he met the same girl at university, Kelly, where she was completing her qualification. After a couple of dates, they kissed outside a cinema. She whispered that her parents would be away for the weekend. In her bedroom, covers drawn back, many boyhood questions were struck from his list. Aunt Betty's vague, one-dimensional drawings were replaced with voluptuous, responsive, three-dimensional womankind. Looking from Kelly's body to her posters of Rod Stewart, Darcy felt like a rock star. University life had warmed up at long last. The mist had cleared.

Over those weeks of frantic intimacy, Darcy gradually felt he was a character in a novel, playing his part. Then he felt like a reader, hovering above, following the sexual adventures of Darcy Grant, each chapter, at a distance. At the three-month mark, the social worker trainee provided an assessment while they sat in a cafe. 'Initially, sex provides the illusion of love, but without love, the relationship and sex die. Do you know what I mean?'

The Darcy Grant character feigned surprise as Kelly continued, 'A lasting relationship must have love, without illusion.'

'Huh?'

Kelly continued, saying he was doing and saying the right things, but he seemed guarded, emotions hidden. 'I fear our relationship will only ever be lived on the surface.' She paused to study the café menu long after she had ordered, frowning, looking like she'd made a bad selection. 'I want to be with someone who truly wants to be with me and know me deeply.'

'Oh, but I thought we—'

'Of course, you would. You live in your head, but I live out here.'

Minutes later, Kelly asked for her spare house key.

When he next saw Kelly a few days later, her assessment continued. 'You didn't argue. You just let me go.' She'd grabbed his arm. 'Yes, I know your background, but you could have said you had feelings for me. There is something wrong with you.'

The next day, in the library, flicking through a chess magazine, Darcy considered the strange, remote idea of feelings. In the magazine, black and white pieces stood in opposition across the chequerboard. Men and women were opposites, sometimes opponents, he supposed.

Perhaps his heart was as cold as the ash the morning after his mother's belongings had been cremated. Most nights, he stared at the golden-brown postcard girls, tuning into his cousin's optimism. But he also heard Kelly's words. There was probably something wrong with him.

~

Sunday afternoon, the week after Isabella finished her placement, Darcy wandered the supermarket aisles with Leo. Pushing a wonky-wheeled trolley, he piled up groceries with only a vague idea of their household needs.

'More Vegemite?' Darcy ventured.

'Suppose,' Leo croakily agreed.

Months earlier, Darcy had suggested they prepare a meal plan and itemise an ingredients list. Leo had rolled his eyes, studying the label of his beer, explaining that he wasn't a domesticated pooch.

'I prefer to shop by instinct and impulse.'

'More likely, what's on special,' Darcy had quipped.

He expected a sharp retort, but Leo had laughed.

Long lines snaked towards the checkouts. Darcy played the game of guessing the fastest aisle. He craned his head about, counting the trolleys and volume of groceries within. There was no clear winner, so he shuffled forward in his chosen aisle.

Ahead, a skinny older man held a pack of sugar aloft, yelling, 'Wow, a buck. Don't we make the stuff here?'

'Whinging pensioner,' Leo muttered to Darcy.

The line stalled, but Darcy's arms jerked as Leo powered the trolley away into a newly opened checkout.

'We're in luck!' said Leo. 'The best checkout outfit in the entire supermarket.'

Isabella stood at the checkout, readying to tap prices into the register. Darcy was as frozen as the packet of peas in the trolley. Leo began joking with Carlo, who waited to pack groceries, while frowning at Darcy.

Isabella whispered to Darcy, 'I'm still a supermarket checkout chick when back home. No more "Miss Russo" for a while.' She smiled, then asked, 'Would you mind unpacking your trolley?'

'Oh. Yes. Sorry.' Darcy fetched and dropped articles.

'Mind the eggs,' Isabella suggested, smirking. 'Finally, some vegetables. I was beginning to worry.'

'I had... to insist,' Darcy stammered, then found a steady voice. 'Mr Scuderi thinks the supermarket finishes at the biscuit aisle.'

Isabella grinned and held his eyes. Darcy smiled with relief, relaxing, searching for another light remark. 'Isabella, how about the price of sugar? Don't we make it here?'

She laughed. 'You sound like a pensioner.'

'Hey, back to Townsville tomorrow?' he asked.

'Suppose.' Her voice was flat, eyes dull.

Darcy loaded a packet of pasta, thinking of her two-year plan.

Isabella squinted and shook her head. 'This isn't real pasta. Don't you remember your favourite pasta?' She held his eyes, then looked down, whispering, 'Russo pasta? Do you remember and feel anything?'

As Isabella tallied the last groceries, Darcy, red-faced, collected notes from his wallet.

'When do you finish work?' he whispered.

Her eyes lit up. She cupped a hand around her mouth. 'Four pm.'

~

A couple of hours later, rain slapped on Darcy's windscreen. He could only see blurry, washed shapes coming and going from the supermarket. Darcy had driven back to the supermarket in a trance as if he were returning to shop. Yet he jumped in surprise when his passenger door flung open, and Isabella slid into the car. To see her so close, with her shining, beautiful olive-skinned face, was startling. He sat stiff. Isabella glanced at him, shaking in her wet supermarket uniform. Water trailed across the seat. Darcy reached into the back seat for a towel. He patted the seat around her, soaking up the drips.

'Here.' He offered her the towel to finish drying.

'It's okay, you keep going.' She looked up. 'If you want to.'

Darcy shuffled closer. He patted around her dress. He looked away, noticing the heavy rain created a misty cocoon around the car. She edged a little closer as he did. He leaned towards her, and they kissed. Minutes later, she broke with erratic breathing.

'I've got to catch my bus back to Silkwood.' She opened the door and then slid back to hug him. 'See you next week?'

'You're not going back to university?'

Isabella shook her head, water drops flicking. 'No. You're here.'

Darcy watched Isabella disappear into an enveloping curtain of rain and mist. Again, he felt the sensation of warm affection carried from the Silkwood fields, then his heart raced. His digger father would have said Darcy was drawing battlelines he couldn't defend against a heavily armed opponent.

10

RETURNING from lunch at the town cafe, Matt paused in the *Times* office. *Why was his door closed?* The door was usually open, welcoming leads. Often, a head would peer in. 'Boss, I think I have something.' It was usually Peter, his star journalist cadet.

The closed door suggested a waiting visitor. Not the prospect of a promising story. He visualised the gun in the upstairs cupboard left by the previous owner. Matt had assumed the owner was just another regional Queensland 'gun nut' or paranoid. But perhaps retribution for his reportage was a real risk. Matt opened the door, taking a deep breath. School Principal, Rich Pierce, sat in Matt's seat, smiling and looking about.

'The door,' he instructed.

As Matt closed the door with a click, Rich gestured at the piles of past editions and framed front pages. 'Our Matt Flint, town's very own Kerry Packer, eh?'

Matt waited, thick carpet eyebrows twitching.

Rich flicked through the most recent paper and found his column, 'From the Principal's Desk'. He read his column, nodding and complimenting himself. He looked up at Matt and spoke. 'We've had a good arrangement so far?'

'We covered your school news. Placed your column early.'

Rich doodled on Matt's blotting paper. Without looking up, Rich said, 'I'm less interested in our news dealings. I'm more interested in our dealings as men.' Rich flicked through the newspaper until he got to his wife's column.

'My wife doesn't belong in your paper.'

Matt rallied, pointing to the article. 'This is a professional arrangement. It has nothing to do with the school.'

Rich scowled and stamped. 'My wife doesn't belong in your paper.' He paused. 'And she doesn't belong in your bed.' Rich pointed to the roof. 'You've been trying to keep your so-called professional arrangements with my wife a secret, but when the husband knows, it's time for men to talk.'

Rich arched his eyebrows, then winked.

'What do you want?' asked Matt, wondering why Rich seemed amused.

Rich slapped the table. 'Yes! I agree. I'm owed something.'

Pierce outlined his demands and Matt slumped against the wall. Matt would continue receiving hundreds of dollars in monthly advertising from the school. However, Matt was to return the exact amount and an additional hundred dollars in cash in an envelope, bound in an old newspaper edition, and delivered to his home.

'Hand-delivered on the first Sunday of the month, just after dark.'

Matt flinched at Rich's blithe pat as he passed by.

'I'm sure you know the way to my home.'

~

The following Sunday, Isabella shuffled in the car seat, kissing Darcy, lifting her skirt a little, should Darcy want to touch her thigh or higher. As they kissed, his hand brushed her breast. There was more they could do, she'd read and heard, but kissing was fabulous and enough for now. The previous Sunday helped overcome her confusion after their first kiss and the letter. He'd been the one who reached for her hand and initiated the kiss under the fireworks, pretending she was Bianca, then wrote a half apology, describing her as lovely and wanting to see her again. All the while, she was guided towards Carlo, wondering whether there was any point waiting.

Isabella felt Darcy's hand on her knee, then a little higher. She shuffled on the seat to help. She could feel his light shakes through his wrist and fingers.

The *Dolly* article outlined steps from kissing to touching. *You'll know when the time is right.* Isabella thought sex might be like a jigsaw.

For her and Darcy, pieces were still scattered and untouched. She hoped the pieces would one day complete their scene. Building romances also sounded like hopscotch too, skipping through stages. She thought of other games, too, like snakes and ladders. There would be opportunities and risks as they rose on the ladder, with the threat of landing on a snake – such as gun obsessed Carlo – and sliding towards an unfortunate fate.

The sky brightened and she hoped the car was still in shadow. She felt Darcy break away, looking about.

'Quick, duck your head.'

They huddled low. She heard voices, one of them Carlo's, as the remainder of the supermarket shift workers shuffled by, heading to the bus stop. When it was quiet, they raised their heads, looking over the dashboard at eye level.

'Isabella, this is too risky. We can't continue.'

'You don't want to see me?'

'Sorry, Isabella.'

'Sorry?' Isabella heard the sighs of *Dolly* readers across Australia.

'I can't do this.' He turned away.

'Darcy? What do you mean?'

He turned to face her. 'I want to see you, but not in this car park. Your mother and Carlo can never find out.'

Isabella hugged him, then she spoke. 'I have an idea, at least for next weekend.' She looked about. 'But, yes, we must be careful.'

~

Minutes later, in the car park, Darcy put his hand on the seat, feeling her warmth, drawing in her breath. He touched strands of her floating hair that curled down the car seat. A weird, new feeling was awakening in him. *Amore?* His desire was deeper than attraction, but risk prickled too. He looked in his rearview mirror. At the bus stop, Carlo seemed to scowl at Isabella's back. Darcy ducked his head again, thinking ahead to next weekend. The digger was leaving the safe foxhole, his father would have said, marching towards enemy lines.

<h1 style="text-align:center">11</h1>

DARCY drove with Leo the next Saturday afternoon to Mission Beach, just a few kilometres from town. During the week, Leo pointed to their calendar in the kitchen and said, 'The Mission Beach Music Festival is on Saturday. You're coming. We're camping the night.'

'For sure.'

'Well, well.' Leo rocked his head back in surprise. 'Really? It's high time you re-joined the local scene. If possible, you are getting even more morose listening to *The Doors* in your room.'

Darcy laughed, then turned away to hide his blushing face. In his pocket was a message from Isabella she'd slid across the counter when he paid for groceries the day before. *'My tent will be at the far end of the beach, at the back. Pink hair ribbon on the front rope.'*

Leo gave Darcy a vivid Hawaiian shirt. 'Beach festival mode,' he'd explained. 'Party mode,' he added with a wink. He danced around in his shirt. 'C'mon on, let's go. We want to get there before dark.'

Off the highway near Mission Beach, Leo pulled over. He reached into the esky and retrieved two beer bottles. 'It's at least a two-beer trip, perhaps three,' he said.

Darcy offered Leo a stubby cooler from the glove box.

'Bewdy, Darce, but this fella isn't going to have a chance to get warm.'

After several long gulps, Leo squeezed the beer between his thighs. Leo set off again with an extended belch, chatting about the festival, describing drinking and dancing.

'Plenty of girls, Darce.' Then it was time for another beer before he said, 'Even you could get lucky.' He hooted his car horn with self-amusement.

Darcy ran with the joke. 'Well, in that case, let's get going.'

Leo sped up and the lines of cane blurred into an indistinct green mass. Nearing the village, they turned around the corner towards a bright strip of beach with glittering, chalky blue water beneath a darkening sky. On the beach were bright light flashes from a DJ booth and flickering flames from campfires. Cars were parked around tents. Men in leather hats raised beer bottles as Leo tooted.

Leo wriggled his hips in a mock dance to the DJ's beat, winking at a waving girl. 'Oh man, the form is good.'

A man in a blue singlet jumped backward to slide over the car bonnet. Leo encouraged the car surfer. 'Yeah!' Another couple of blokes surfed over the bonnet, one spraying beer across their windscreen.

'This is going to be a crazy, crazy night, Darce.'

Leo slapped Darcy on his leg and asked for another beer. After a few minutes of weaving around drunk couples with empty beer bottles clinking in the car, Leo parked at the far end of the beach. He burped like a deflating accordion. Darcy thought the sound could have come from a large African mammal, a happy hippo on a mudbank.

Leo helped Darcy set up a tent in darkening dusk shadows. They agreed the car would be left unlocked, and the first back from the party could either claim the tent or the back seat.

'I'd say you'll have the first choice,' Leo said, already swaying towards the flashing lights and dancing girls. He threw an empty beer bottle into the bush, hitting others with a clink, before reaching the revellers. Darcy waited by the car, touching the instructions in his pocket. He stepped away with crinkling nostrils. Bonnet-baked beer.

~

A few metres away, Isabella waited alone in a dark tent. The beach soundtrack thumped like the pulse of a giant beast. She adjusted her singlet, feeling the outline of her new bikini. Earlier, in the festival campground, Bianca had left the tent with a skipping walk. 'I'll be back later,' she'd called over her shoulder.

'When? How late?'

'Late.' She blew Isabella a kiss. 'Join the party when you've finished setting up. This is a rare time Mamma has let you out of her sight. Time for you to finally have some fun.'

When Bianca left, Isabella tied a pink ribbon to the tent. Then she retreated into the tent to test her torch. As Isabella waited in the dark, she worried. *Would Darcy come; would he find her?* During the week, Bianca had taken numerous phone calls with the extension cord trailing into her bedroom. Isabella waited by the closed door, hearing Bianca laugh and shriek.

Her papa grumbled from the lounge. 'Does every bloke in town have our number?'

The night before, when there were many calls, Isabella placed an ear to the door.

'Well, maybe, if you ask nicely.'

Later, Isabella sat on her bed, wishing she was holding the telephone behind a closed bedroom door, confirming arrangements. She was sure Darcy would ask nicely. In the tent, adjusting her bikini again, she wondered what he would ask nicely for. She heard more heaving chaotic roars from the beach, then a light step nearby. A silhouette reared over the tent.

'Isabella?'

Isabella dropped the torch, fumbling for the zip. She squinted through a high slit. She pulled back at the sight of a shirt with large yellow flowers. It wasn't Darcy's style. Then his blue-grey eyes flashed in the torch light. She tore open the zip.

He held the ribbon. 'I found the doorbell.'

Isabella laughed and cuddled into Darcy on the mattress. They kissed against the backbeat of the beach party.

Darcy pulled away. 'Isabella, should we talk about what's going on? I'll be blamed for you dropping out of university. I doubt Carlo will give up on you. This could go so wrong.'

'I can manage Mamma, but yes, we need to keep this secret, at least for now. Forget Carlo. It was nothing.'

She took off her singlet and rolled it over the torch. They sat in a glowing cavern, staring at each other. He leaned in and kissed her.

After a few minutes, Isabella let him untie her bikini top, surprised she felt no embarrassment. He unbuttoned his shirt, and their bare skin touched. She gasped at the sensation.

'If we go further, will it be safe?' asked Darcy.

'I think so,' she said, trusting *Dolly Doctor.*

Blushing, she waited for Darcy's next move.

There was a sharp crack outside the tent. Isabella jumped. *Was Bianca returning?* They sat up rigid as shadows formed over the tent. Isabella slid inside her sleeping bag, retying her bikini top. Leaves and sticks crunched by the nearby tent.

'This could be the Russo's tent, eh,' a man slurred.

Isabella recognised Carlo's voice and began to shake.

The zip fastener lowered with a sharp rip. Darcy reached up and held the tab.

'Fuck, it's jammed, eh.'

The tent swayed, the fastener shifting a little. Darcy's shoulders arched, straining.

'Weak prick,' another man replied. He didn't sound as drunk. 'What's the idea anyway, Carlo? I thought we were just going to search through a few tents for booze.'

'Wanna see if she's here,' replied Carlo. 'Can't find her at the party.'

'Okay. Get outta the way. Let me try.'

The fastener jerked, and Darcy held the tab with two hands as the tent buckled. A rope snapped, and part of the tent slumped inwards.

'Fuck it, let's cut our way in,' Carlo mumbled.

With a sharp click, a point pricked the canvas. Isabella stifled a cry. Darcy drew a deep breath and picked up a shoe.

'C'mon, Carlo, you really going to slash the girls' tent? Calm down, mate. Let's head back. I saw Bianca, Isabella will be nearby. C'mon.'

After grumbling and footsteps, eventually Isabella could only hear the roaring surf of the beach party and Darcy's heaving breath. Darcy held the tent zipper tight for another couple of minutes, then unzipped a high section of the tent flap, looked out, then turned back to Isabella.

'Hey, find Bianca and hang out for a while. I'll move Leo's car and watch your tent.'

Darcy hugged Isabella before sliding through the opened tent flap. She peeked through the slit as he stole into the shadows, bright yellow flowers fading into the gloom. Placing hands over her ears, she tried to block out his last nervy-sounding words.

'I shouldn't have interfered with your life. I shouldn't have come.'

~

Around midnight, Isabella lay awake in her tent. Earlier at the beach party, she'd looked for Bianca. Strobe lights from the DJ booth crisscrossed the writhing crowd like helicopter blades. Within the whirling melee, she was bumped and groped. Carlo danced nearby, stubby in one hand, flaying arms spraying warm foamy lager. He tried to kiss her, but she pulled away. Among the sweaty, swaying bodies, she saw Bianca and waved. Bianca smiled, then turned back to kiss the man beside her. A few songs later, wriggling free from more clutching hands, Isabella left the beach and adjusted her clothes.

She strolled around couples who kissed in the shadows, trying to forget Darcy's final words. She sat on a log at a distance watching the mania, calculating what would have happened in the tent if they weren't interrupted. She stretched out her legs which shone in the moonlight, imagining Darcy stroking them after they'd made love. Closing her eyes, she swallowed, visualising the knife pressing into the canvas. As much as she wanted to be with Darcy, he'd been centimetres, seconds, from being stabbed. Isabella stood, bowed, retching.

Later, the moon lowered over the rainforest. The DJ played another thumping song, then a muffled *Ciao for now*. The strobe lights stilled, glowed, and faded. Silhouetted shapes staggered from the beach to their tents. Isabella looked for Bianca, needing to hold her sister. Bodies brushed by. Carlo stumbled out of the gloom, slumping in front of her, slurring, joining unformed words. She squinted to comprehend, eventually piecing together: *You've changed, turning away from me. Who is it?* Isabella tried to help him up, but he could only crawl, and rested against a palm tree, rocked his head against the trunk, and passed out. She found the flick-knife in his shorts, stood, and threw the weapon into the forest, then zig zagged through campers' canvas clumps to her tent. Car headlights flashed. Her silhouette shadow projected over her tent. She turned and whispered towards the dark outline in the car, '*Sto bene,*' I'm okay, placing a hand over heart.

Hours later, Isabella woke to a tearing zip, and she squinted at the early dawn light and the outline of her sister's face and messy hair. Bianca tumbled in, mumbling, 'What a night.'

In the closed confines of the tent, Isabella could smell Bianca's night. She coughed, turning away from her sister's body odour and sour breath. Bianca shook sand out of her hair. Then she slumped asleep, snoring, and Isabella could only rouse her hours later with vigorous shoving as the festival packed up with the clinking poles of collapsing tents and revving farm trucks.

'C'mon, Bianca. Wake up!'

On the way home, Bianca croaked, 'We got to bed at eleven. Mamma will ask.'

'One look at you and she will know better.'

'Disrupted sleep, looking after my rebellious little sister, the uni drop-out.' Bianca laughed, shaking more sand out of her hair, then glanced across. 'Carlo was in a state last night. Pissed, throwing punches at his mates, accusing them of stealing you.'

Isabella gripped her seat, snapping a fingernail, unable to reply.

Bianca continued, 'If you're breaking it off, tell him straight, that's what I do. Or if you're together, you need to calm him down.' She slapped Isabella's thigh. 'There's a way to calm him down. You act innocent, baby sister, but I bet you know what I mean.'

Isabella's face reddened, and she waited for Bianca's review of her night. Instead, as Bianca cornered from the highway to Silkwood, the conversation took a different turn.

'Izzy, do you know Mamma's birth year or actual age?'

Isabella thought for a moment before she replied. Their parents' birthdays were celebrated but not milestones. 'Whenever I ask, Mamma says she is close to becoming a nonna.'

'Gammon! Everyone says she barely looks older than us.'

'Mamma hinted last year she was close to forty, near Papa's age,' ventured Isabella.

'Gammon! Papa's older brother just turned forty. Papa is a few years younger than him, and Mamma looks way younger than Papa.'

'So, she's in her thirties? Maybe mid-thirties,' Isabella wagered. 'You're twenty. Mmmmm.'

The sisters' eyes locked and Bianca replied, 'Yep, Izzy, Mamma had me *very young*. That's the reason for the tears at the cemetery.'

Isabella thought of the years of her mamma's conditioning commandments, *un buon matrimonio*.

'That's why there aren't wedding photos?' Isabella asked.

Bianca nodded.

Turning by the Russo letterbox, they saw their mamma burst from the door, blessing herself. The sun lit up her youthful face like a Madonna. At a distance, Bianca honked the car horn. 'We figured it out, Mamma,' she whispered to the windscreen. She honked again.

Isabella realised she needed cover. 'Hey, Bianca, don't say anything about Carlo to mamma, we're just working things out.'

Hearing a tune, Bianca turned up the radio: '*My lips are sealed*' by the *Go Go's*. She winked and nodded.

Once home, Mamma skipped about as they exited the car, clapping her hands. 'I can see you had a long night! I have your favourite minestrone to revive you.'

Isabella smiled. Of course, Mamma would have cooked and prayed through her worry. She recalled Bianca's sandy hair and sour breath, face reddening at the memory of her untied bikini top. Her mamma's worries *were real*, her prayers weak defence.

Inside their home, Isabella dropped her bag with a thump beside her bedroom door. She paused and looked in: the bedroom of a young girl. A fabric doll lay on her bed. She thought of her soft doll's skin pressing into Darcy. Angel figurines were on her dresser, yet hours earlier, she wasn't angelic. The doll's glass eyes resembled Darcy's stunned, almost sightless orbs when he stared at her breasts. Above, Mary held vigil, admiring virginal order. Isabella squinted in annoyance. She felt a hand on her shoulder and flinched.

'Turn around *per favore.*'

Her mother inspected her lips, cheeks, and neck, as if she was a farm animal, then smelt her breath for cigarettes and alcohol.

Isabella felt a spike of spite. Her mamma, likely an unmarried, pregnant young teenager, was continuing to control her. She turned around, picked up her bag, entering the virgin's room, wriggling free of another touch on her shoulder. She wasn't her mother's display doll any longer. Nor in training to be a nun. Not Sister Isabella. Her Mamma was a talented artist, but Isabella wasn't another portrait of Mary.

<h1 style="text-align:center">12</h1>

EVERY day at school, Frances sketched during the many calls from fretful mothers. Illnesses close to exams. Forgotten tuckshop money. Missing books. Lost sports uniforms. As Frances drew, she soothed anxious mothers as the school's warm broadcast radio voice to the outside world.

'Don't worry. I'll keep an eye out. It will be okay.'

These days she tried to maintain a steady voice; Isabella, university paused, pulling at her tether. Instead of Isabella attending the music festival, Frances suggested she help arrange flowers at church for Sunday mass, as she had loved to do during her school years. Frances remembered schoolgirl Isabella standing with a flower in a hand, looking at the altar in a cocoon of heavenly light.

'Frances, are you there?' a mother asked.

'Sorry, you were saying?'

Despite her suggestion, Isabella shook her head and packed an overnight bag for the festival. Frances' slight relief was Isabella wearing a demure light frock, with her hair in a tight bun, as if ready for Sunday School. Bianca, however, wore a mini skirt and a tight-fitting top, hair loose, bright lipstick. From the shed, Gino scowled, pointing at Bianca then to her. Frances read his familiar look. *Shameless daughter, your shame.*

'Frances, are you listening?'

'*Si*, sorry, I'll register Mario as ill today.'

In the office, Rich Pierce passed by, touched her shoulder, and stared downwards at her cleavage, *again*. She said goodbye to the mother and turned her shoulder away. Frances knew some men had overactive hands like creeping vines. Rich seemed to be one of those men, connecting with touch to see if there was a chance. Then he might coil around if there was a positive signal. She'd heard stories about him but preferred to see his good side. He was a civic leader.

During the week, they organised his regular newspaper column. Reading his drafts, she sensed vanity. He was also showy with his wealth, which she was unused to. If a cane farmer was *going alright,* only their accountant knew while they grumbled about the sugar price. Meanwhile, Rich cruised the town in his luxury saloon and gold-framed sunglasses, tugging *Salsa,* his new boat.

When mothers arrived to collect their sick children, Rich wished them a speedy recovery, saying, 'You'll be missed until your return.'

Frances would sigh at his paternal care. *Lucky Mrs Pierce.* These were the pale children she'd helped into the sick bay, a cool cloth on a hot, beading forehead, an aspirin, and a call home to mum. Rich would often carry students' schoolbags, chatting with mothers, holding an umbrella over them if it was raining.

'Hurry back when you're well,' he'd say.

Sometimes, he would look up to catch her eye. Frances felt these gestures were for her benefit, that they were a team.

Today, Frances returned to her sketch, the phone finally quiet after the early morning spike in calls. Every sports carnival was the same, with the mothers of unfit students calling with fictitious maladies. She sketched Isabella, running with flowing hair and light beams from heaven.

'Frances, you are so talented.'

Rich had returned to her desk. Blond hair streamed over his shoulders. She saw the resemblance to Rod Stewart, the famous singer, just as the single mothers and female teachers gushed.

'Let's take a stroll. I have a new studio to show you.'

Studio? For Frances, this was a word from long ago. She turned on the office answering machine. As they walked, he said, 'I heard you were a talented artist when at this school.'

'A long time ago. These days, I just whitewash our stucco home.'

They looked up at the sound of a starter cap and cheering

students. Rich led the way to the art classrooms. Inside the art room, the background scent of varnished wooden easels mixed with paint and turpentine took Frances back many years earlier.

~

Fifteen-year-old Frances had shrunk at the sight of her frowning mamma at the art classroom door. Frances held a paint brush, red ochre dripping onto her smock. Students' heads peered around their easels as her mamma entered the room and whispered into her teacher's ear. Covering her mouth with one hand, her art teacher pointed to Frances, then the door. Frances walked to the door, face burning, and glanced back at her near-completed painting, destined for honours at the regional art awards. Her mamma drove to the doctor so Frances could hear the blood test result for herself.

Sitting under a cross, the doctor pointed at the red drips on Frances' blouse and seemed to mock her. 'No need for more blood, the laboratory analysis is clear enough. You're fifteen? The police should know about this.'

Her mamma muttered in agreement and Frances was dragged out by her collar. Her mother sped to the local police station where Gino worked and smacked her umbrella on the locked door, screeching, '*Figlio di puttana.* Come out!'

They heard scraping feet move to the back of the station, then silence. Only when her mamma pressed the car horn for a minute, did the duty sergeant peer through the partially opened shutters. As they left, the shutters snapped shut, just like the doctor's file. Frances stared at the parked police car until no longer in view.

'With child?' her teacher had gasped. 'She seems so pure.'

During her first week working back at the school as an office administrator, twenty-year-old Frances, a mum with two small daughters, took a lunch break and ventured to the art rooms, where she met Mrs Torre. Her art teacher took only a moment to recognise Frances, and they hugged.

'It must have been God's will for you to be a mother instead of an artist,' Mrs Torre said, 'but I kept samples of your art to remember you.'

Frances sighed, and her teacher invited her to sit. What seemed like moments later, Frances noticed students lining up for their afternoon class. Mrs Torre held her arm, inviting students into the classroom. 'Students, we have a special guest, Mrs Russo, one of the most talented artists ever to grace these rooms.'

She pointed to a large painting of men cutting cane in the rain, mounted high on the classroom wall. 'Look at the light and shade. Isn't it both miserable and beautiful?'

Students stood, craning necks, looking at the work anew. One student said, 'I thought the painting was from an art gallery.'

'That's kind, but no, Mrs Russo created this work of rare quality in this very room.'

Frances blushed. The student clapped and the entire class joined in. Frances bowed her head and covered her eyes. Mrs Torre led her shaking former prodigy away. She'd felt more miserable than beautiful as she crossed the school back to the office. *It must have been God's will for you to be a mother instead of an artist.* Back at the office, she recalled not God's will but Mrs Torre's prediction when she started Year 10.

'You have the talent to have an independent life as an artist. You will have a studio and a gallery that art collectors will flock to.'

But no, her mother smacked the police station door. Rough Gino, her teenage underwear yanked aside. No studio. A nursery instead. *God's will to be miserable, not beautiful.*

~

Frances felt Rich's arm brush hers as he turned about to look at the students' latest art. She didn't dare look upwards at the described miserable and beautiful painting; she would cry if she did. Frances felt nervous being this close to a man, admired for his good looks, alone in a room, where no one knew. She was conscious of her heartbeat.

Rich touched her shoulder. 'Are you okay, Frances?'

'I'm fine. This room brings back many memories.'

She struggled to say more. Rich guided her through to a small room, which she remembered as a storage room. Strong aftershave overpowered turpentine odour.

'This looks so different,' she said, looking about.

'Fitted out last week. I had a little left over after cyclone repairs. Funded from the principal's capital account.' He winked.

Frances glanced at Rich, uncertain of the meaning.

One easel stood in the room. The shelves she remembered as a student were gone. A small desk held a box with new paint tubes and a bottle containing clean paintbrushes. Lights illuminated the easel and the back of a framed canvas.

Rich spread his arms. 'Here we have your studio.'

'What? For me?'

Rich touched her arm. 'Your talent shouldn't go to waste.' He invited her to turn the canvas around. The canvas on the sides of the wooden frame looked aged.

Frances looked from Rich to the easel with a sense of ceremony and suspense. She turned the canvas around and shrieked, '*Santa Maria!*' The canvas was her near-completed painting from when she was a Year 10 student.

'H-H-How?' was all she could manage.

'Old Mrs Torre stored your unfinished painting. She told me when she retired.'

Frances felt a surge of joy and hugged him in thanks. Rich took her hug and lengthened it, then pulled out of the hug to kiss her. She was stunned and let it continue as he moved to kiss her neck.

Frances pushed him away. 'No, I can't. Stop! You know I'm married, and so are you!' Her sandals slipped on the floor as she ran from the room. To stop from falling, she gripped the desk she'd once sat at as a schoolgirl.

'Frances. Let's talk.' Rich grabbed her and tried to kiss her again.

'No! I'm not like that.'

She heard the starter gun and cheers from the school sports ground and launched free of his grip, feeling a rip on her sleeve. When through the door, she walked around the near-empty school in loops, holding her sleeve, avoiding the office. When she returned, a note sat on her desk.

I'm glad you liked the studio. Let's return sometime soon. RP.

She crushed the note and dropped it into the bin, no longer seeing the good in him. Frances felt miserable. Not talented. Not respected. *So, the things she heard were true. Poor Mrs Pierce.* Her sketchpad landed in the bin with a thump beside the crushed note. Finding a pin in her drawer, she held her sleeve in place while hissing at his smiling photo on the wall. She glared with her Sicilian evil eye, *malocchio.* She heard a gunshot before remembering it was a starter gun.

13

ON the Monday afternoon after the festival, Darcy walked through town, thinking of Isabella. If only he lived alone, as he'd done most of his life. Then he could invite Isabella over, talk, working out whether to continue. But he couldn't involve Leo or his cavalcade of guests. One day, Bianca might be at Leo's door as Isabella left his room. Bianca's shriek – *Santa Maria* – would surely be heard all over town.

Darcy paused in front of the closed cinema, thinking of the interruption at the festival; a warning he should heed. The knife pressed into the tent canvas was likely the same blade sliced under the pig's throat. Yet, in the headlights, by the tent, her eyes sought him, and she'd placed a hand to her heart.

By the cinema a truck revved. The bearded, olive-skinned driver and his girlfriend stared at him. In shops, men would state or accuse, *new to town*, although Darcy had lived among them for months. He sighed. Maybe he'd never belong. Southerners who'd lived in the north for decades weren't regarded as locals. Darcy looked in the direction of the highway, vehicles heading south. Perhaps Cousin Eliza's golden friends were waiting. With one of the tanned beauties, he might walk hand-in-hand through Surfers Paradise, without fear, in bright sunshine, not stalking in dusk to a tent. They'd turn into a surf store. Darcy would try on fashionable surf wear behind a curtain, the male salesman beckoning with a coat hanger, not a knife. Yet, beautiful, real-life Isabella held a hand over her heart searching for his eyes, reaching his heart. Darcy looked away from the southern edge of the highway, back towards Silkwood.

A young woman, who looked around his age, brushed by and began clearing envelopes from under the cinema door. Hearing her grumbling, Darcy stooped to help. She held up an envelope, shaking her head, addressing Darcy.

'My dad is too ill to reopen the place, but the bills keep coming.'

Darcy had looked at the cobwebs over the door hinges, sizing up the opportunity. He needed more private time with Isabella to work out where this was heading.

'Perhaps I can help reopen the cinema?' he offered.

The woman squinted, sizing him up, then replied with a grin, 'Well, that would be a godsend. My name's Simone. I would help, but I have a busy job at the newspaper office. Besides, my husband wants me home at night. We're trying for a baby.'

Darcy's eyes widened. He was still becoming accustomed to the locals' straight-talking.

'What do you know about the cinema business?' Simone asked.

'Nothing much, just watched a few movies when I was at uni.'

'Romances, I bet, eh.' Simone winked. 'Don't worry, a little training is all you will need. It's mostly about popcorn.'

~

Darcy knocked on the principal's office door the next morning. On the table in the lounge, Darcy folded out a document. 'My contract says that I need permission to take a second job.'

Rich frowned. 'Yes, it is a departmental requirement. We need energy focused on our students' education. It's also a consideration whether the job clashes with school values.'

Darcy tried to suppress thoughts about values. 'I'm just looking to help reopen the cinema, which would be after hours.'

From outside the room, Frances shrieked into the phone. '*Si. Si,* she's back home, *il disappunto.*'

Darcy looked away from the door, placing his trembling hands in his pocket.

Rich nodded after a few moments. 'Okay, that should be fine.'

Darcy stood, surprised at the ease of Rich's decision. The lines were blurred between them, as Rich was both his boss and landlord. Every fortnight, after the teacher's pay cycle, Rich called by their house in his luxury Holden Statesman to collect their rent in cash. The electric window would lower with a faint mechanical whirr and a gust of air-conditioning. Rich would extend his open palm, smiling. When Darcy had arrived in January, Rich handed him house keys. The rent seemed steep, but he knew nothing of the north. Mail kept arriving for the previous occupant. He asked his new housemate, Leo, where they should forward the mail.

'To heaven,' Leo had said, pointing at the clouds. 'The guy's dead. Teacher. Hit by a cane tram. I used to work with him.'

Darcy assumed Rich was kindly handling the rent on behalf of the bereaved family.

Last night, Rich arrived, towing a boat. The driver's window lowered, and Darcy passed the envelope. He spelled S-A-L-S-A as the boat paraded by, trying to calculate a principal's salary. Looking at the car and boat and feeling his near empty wallet, Darcy wondered what he and Leo might be funding. Then he became cross for unkind thoughts, the returning jealousy of the welfare kid. He shook his head. *Rich was a civic leader.*

In the principal's office, Darcy almost made it to the door before Rich spoke again.

'Before you go. We should treat this as an enterprise.'

'What do you mean?'

'One good turn deserves another. Doulgas says you're a bookworm with an excellent vocabulary. You know what the word enterprise means.'

Darcy frowned as he left the office. *Enterprise?* The office phone rang, and Darcy lingered in a corner, waiting for Frances to take the call. As he darted by her desk, he was grateful to see her sketchpad missing. Darcy didn't want to see another biblical-looking sketch of her angelic daughter. He especially didn't want another discussion with mournful Frances about her daughter's stalled education.

~

Darcy stood outside the cinema, keys jangling. Simone had given him the keys the night before, asking if he could tidy the cinema ahead of his training. Before entering, he paused to study the building's exterior. The Art Deco façade looked like the outside of a church. Although there wasn't a cross on the roof, Simone had explained the cinema was a place of homage. Inside, looking about the foyer, Darcy imagined Silkwood nonnas decades earlier: young, beautiful, nervous, powdered, and scented, holding hands with suitors watching black-and-white flicks. He thought of Isabella, she wasn't cinematic nostalgia – she was a modern-day starlet.

Darcy steadied his shaky hand on the confectionary counter, suspecting he was a seedy director preparing a salacious B-grade film script. Darcy crossed the foyer, shouldering through two heavy velvet curtains crossed like folded arms. The auditorium seats revealed themselves in sepia. The aisle narrowed towards a stage in the faint grey light. A curtain rippled in flutes on a stage in dark shadow. He felt back in the dusk at Mission Beach where he'd snuck towards Isabella's tent, easily the most daring act in his meek life. Darcy drew a deep breath, admiring his new realm. *Could he really do this?*

Darcy stole deeper into the building's interior. To the side of the auditorium, he found the manager's office. Famous actors peered out from dusty posters. Actress, Sophia Loren, resembling Frances, seemed to glare at him. Darcy took a backward step. He replayed Frances in his classroom. *We Sicilians have a protective streak.*

With a shove, he creaked open a side door. Outside, there was a narrow, damp alley to the street. He imagined a smiling Isabella running to hug him. Back in the foyer he prepared a confectionary display as colourful as a cassowary's plumage. The region's prolific sugar production would be sold back to the locals at jacked-up prices. *Sorry, pensioners.* Warming up the popcorn maker, he remembered the central part of the cinema's profitability: corn. Simone explained that the cinema charged a buck for just a few cents worth of kernels. He pulled out a bag of salt from a cupboard, following Simone's instructions: 'Always add plenty of salt. Dad makes a pretty penny on the drinks, too.'

He laughed. Salt, as much as sugar, kept the cinema doors open.

Simone dropped by after work and beamed. 'The place looks ready, well done. The teenagers will be pleased.' She paused and smirked. 'So many romances started here. I won't tell you what I used to get up to and get away with here as a teenage girl.'

Darcy's eyes widened.

Simone opened her bag and gave Darcy the new cinema advertisement: a screening on Saturday evening and a Sunday matinee.

Darcy walked outside to lift bulky cases with movie reels from Simone's car boot. The case was labelled *Witness*. Harrison Ford. Darcy hauled the cases into the cinema.

'This way,' Simone instructed.

They climbed a flight of stairs to a room just under the roofline. Simone turned on a light, which flickered before the projectionist's workplace became visible: two large metallic projection machines aimed through a slot in the wall. Simone took a reel from a case beside a sofa.

'Last year, the film distributor accidently provided duplicate reels of the movie *1984*. Dad has been meaning to return them, but these will be good for you to practice.'

Simone raised an arm at the projector's rear and mounted the reel. She showed him how to slot the film from the whirring reel through the machine. Then, with a click of a few other switches, she adjusted the film's motion through the machine. As the reels rolled through the clicking projector, Darcy peeked through a small window. Soft light coated the seats like dusted sugar. Numbers counted down, then a lion roared the auditorium into life. George Orwell's *1984* opening rally of yelling citizens chanted to empty seats.

'Let's leave this to roll on for a while,' said Simone.

They left the room and returned to the sales counter. Darcy piled popcorn from the machine into two cups. Inside the auditorium they watched the early scenes.

Simone hummed to the *Eurythmics*. 'I like the song *'Sexcrime'* on this soundtrack. What about you?'

Darcy mumbled a reply, glad to be in darkness, imagining what she used to get away with. Later, Simone showed him how to work the till, and they confirmed the ticket and confectionary prices. Simone then lifted a small section of the carpet. Cut into the boards below was a concealed safe. She rolled the carpet back and stamped it into place.

'Store the cash here,' Simone explained. 'Drop it to the bank during the week but leave money aside for bills and deliveries. Dad just wants to get the place reopened. We trust you.'

On their way out, Simone picked up a spare bucket of popcorn.

'That will be a dollar, Miss.'

'A dollar? You've got a nerve.' Simone laughed. 'But it looks like you've mastered the cinema trade. Remember. Plenty of salt. I must race home. I'm ovulating.'

14

DARCY stood at the school gate farewelling students on the final day of the third term. Earlier, he'd rested against the classroom doorframe. Another teacher stood alongside. Ready for the bell, his students were all at the door, ready to run.

As the final bell ushered in the holidays and the students barged past, they heard cheers and stamping feet across the school.

'Don't they hate being here?' The career teacher sighed. 'Why do we bother?'

Darcy sympathised with a pretend moan but recalled Isabella's joy. At her checkout, the day before, he'd whispered, 'I'm reopening the cinema. Knock on the side door any time after four p.m. Saturday.'

She beamed, fixing her already perfect hair. 'Wow! Can't wait.'

'Can you make sure you're not followed? You know?'

'I'll be alone. I saw Carlo yesterday,' she whispered, 'told him I need space.'

At the front of the school, Darcy watched the students cheer and jostle, stealing hats and throwing them skyward, and he walked to the school gates. Bruno stooped to Darcy's eyeline. 'Sir, do you reckon I will get a better report at the next parent-teacher meeting?'

'Of course, Bruno. I hope your mum is my first booking.'

He'd noticed Mrs DeLuca by the school office more regularly than usual and had meant to stop and praise her son's improvement.

'Mr Grant,' Bruno continued, 'I know it was a while ago, but I'm sorry for saying those things about Isabella, sorry, Miss Russo, in your classroom. I hear she's dropped out of university and doesn't want to be a teacher. I hope I'm not the reason.'

Darcy blinked at her name, before replying, 'I'm sure you're not the reason. She's a Silkwood girl, a tough northerner, eh!'

Bruno gave him an affectionate tap. Darcy stumbled, just managing to catch his footing. He bumped into a group of girls discussing the movie session times. 'Sorry, girls.'

'That's okay,' one of his students replied. 'But, Mr Grant, is it true you're reopening the cinema tomorrow?'

Darcy realised that news raced across town like a cyclonic rain squall. There was almost no need for the town newspaper. His nerves tingled. *Witness.*

'Yes, that's right,' he replied. 'I've learnt how to make popcorn.'

'Great.' The girl beamed. 'I'm going to raid my piggy bank.'

Frances came up alongside him. 'Hey, Mister Cinema Manager, I expect a family discount.'

'Okay, just for you,' he replied.

'No, that won't do. What about my daughters?'

Darcy smiled to hold his nerve, picturing Sophia Loren on the cinema poster. 'I'll see, but I must run a profitable business.'

'You'll get plenty of business from our household alone. Isabella wants to arrive early so she can be your first customer.' She stopped and looked into his eyes. 'Will you talk her into resuming her studies?'

Darcy nodded, mute.

'Also, Darcy, keep an eye out. I still suspect a man is holding back her education.'

~

On Saturday afternoon, after staring down the highway, barely blinking, Isabella finally relaxed with a sigh. The old local bus warbled towards her. Boarding the bus, she'd thought of her mamma as a sexually active, then pregnant teen; who must have also taken trips with secret intent. *It was her turn today.* She knew what would have progressed between her and Darcy in her tent if they weren't interrupted, for they'd been almost undressed within minutes. In the shopping centre carpark, he'd break from kissing and frown, likely from worry. But that time must have passed. His arrival at the tent confirmed that he liked her, wanted her, and the risk was worth it. She remembered his invitation. Four o'clock. Her body tingled. Nobody would be queuing until six.

Before leaving home she had paused by the religious calendar in the kitchen. Many dates in September had been struck off. Her mamma had lifted a pen to cross out another. Isabella had stared at the date. *It was her turn today.* Above the row of dates, St Nicholas glowed in holy light as the benefactor of souls in purgatory. Mamma had crossed off the date, then blessed herself after she'd placed the pen in the kitchen drawer beside her rosary beads.

'Another day in our mortal lives, Isabella,' her mamma had said. 'Who knows what the Lord has in store for us today?'

Isabella couldn't find words to reply and had blessed herself.

As the bus spluttered towards town, Isabella checked her reflection in the smudged window. In Bianca's bedroom, she asked her sister to inspect her after she had dressed. Isabella was covered in praise and her sister's perfume. In the car driving to the bus stop, her mamma had observed, 'It's so good of Mr Grant to give up his weekends. Isn't he a saint? The Silkwood saints have a new rival.'

Isabella had looked down at her best shoes. She reached for her mamma's hand, realising the more someone trusted you, the more likely you were to let them down. A truck passed them the other way. Carlo waved, but she lowered her eyes.

At the bus stop, her mamma turned to her. 'I will pick you up at the front of the cinema after the movie ends. Keep away from town boys. Don't wander away.'

Wriggling on the seat, she'd nodded, imagining Mamma with her town boys as a teenager. She withdrew her hand. *Hypocrite.*

On the bus, she checked the perfectly placed ribbons in her hair with nervy fingers. Doubts edged in as the bus neared town. *Dolly* included many articles about the unreliability of men driven by overpowering testosterone, then casting the girl away without further thought. *Could Darcy be one of those men?* She remembered her dropped hand by the marquee. *Would he ask nicely and remain nice afterward?* The *Dolly* checklist included clues to reveal whether a boy really liked you.

Frequent eye contact. Blushing when caught stealing glances. Initiating conversation. Compliments about looks and dress. Asking whether a girl was single. Requests for dates. Affection. Gifts. Giving a girl time, without pressure for sex. Interest after sex. In her bedroom, the night before, she'd wanted to tick through the checklist. She'd lowered the pen, after imagining ticks, biting her lip. She felt a little guilt, better knowing how Carlo felt. As the bus rumbled on, fresh anxiety shifted to the initial pain of sex, as she had read and heard. Perhaps she might melt in some way, softening like wax under heat, and it would be easy for her, and warm and pleasurable for him, but it probably wouldn't be like that.

'Miss! Can you hear?' The driver craned his head backward to catch her attention. 'Are you getting off?'

'Yes,' she called, hurrying to the front and down the steps.

On the main street, the closed cinema was dark, no wafting enticing popcorn scent. The reopening seemed unlikely, and she wondered whether she'd misunderstood. *Was it really her turn today?* A farmer's truck drove by, then stopped. A swarthy town boy leaned out the window.

'It's closed, eh. After some company?'

A shower brushed over, and she raised her umbrella and walked away.

'Frigid bitch.' A flicked cigarette hissed in a puddle at her feet.

Isabella shuffled around the block, trying to steady her umbrella. Back at the cinema, she found the narrow side path. The cinema still looked as lifeless as their family mausoleum. With a quick look both ways, she turned down the path. After knocking on the side door, she stood in the gloom. There was no sound, and she placed her ear to the door. Isabella listened for movement but could only hear farm trucks revving in the street. She wondered whether to knock again or walk away. As she went to knock again, the door creaked open. A wide eye peaked through the slender crack, then the door flung open, and she was pulled inside.

'Quick, no one must see you!'

She flinched. He seemed so formal that she almost called him Mr Grant.

'Is it okay that I came? I thought—'

Eventually he mumbled, 'You look lovely, Isabella.'

She grinned and examined his red and yellow polyester shirt with a popcorn logo. 'So do you,' she replied, smirking.

'I know. I look like an ice cream.' He smirked. 'The selfless things I do for this town.'

He guided her into twilight dusk of the foyer with a shaky hand. Isabella hoped for a daring kiss in the foyer, just a metre away from footsteps on the street. Instead, he looked to his feet.

He looked up, appearing to jolt upright. 'Are you sure about this?' His voice was the same husky, hushed lover's tone as when they were in the tent. She hoped it wasn't just a bolt of testosterone. Isabella took his hand and they ascended stairs opposite the counter. Isabella squeezed his hand, praying she was really connected to Darcy and could trust him. She tried to forget the unticked checklist.

They climbed into near darkness. Upstairs, in a small room in grey light, the mute projection equipment seemed to inspect her. *What are you doing here?* Darcy began kissing her again, and she felt a warming all over her body. Remembering the weekend before, she listened for approaching footsteps but could only hear her thumping heart. Darcy helped unfasten the buttons her mamma had helped fix into place.

'Are you sure?' Darcy asked many times.

'Yes, yes.'

With the rustle of clothing, Isabella knew Darcy was also undressing. Soon, they only wore underwear. He asked again whether she was sure, and she kissed him harder.

'Will it be safe?' he asked, as he removed his underwear.

'Yes, it should be.'

Darcy pulled away to grab the cushions from a sofa and lowered her to the floor. Then, after intimate caressing and a brush of his lips over her nipples, it was happening, after months of wondering, and article after article. She lay still, not knowing how to react, trying to imagine melting wax as a tide rose within her and waves began to crest. After a while, she could hear his breathing change, then a cry. Afterwards, they lay still, silent, and she waited for the last clue on the *Dolly* checklist – *interest after sex*. Darcy sat up, flinging on his clothes.

With his back to her, he barked, 'There's a cinema to open.'

He flicked several switches on the projectors, her stern witnesses. Isabella felt back at the marquee with her hand dropped. *Had she given herself too easily?* As he worked with his back to her, it was almost as if she wasn't there. She gathered her clothes and dressed in silence.

'Darcy?'

He either didn't hear or didn't care.

~

Later, Isabella sat motionless in the auditorium, awaiting the arrival of her friends and the film's start, absorbing what had happened. A secret part of her womanly identity had changed. She thought she would feel satisfied, like an achievement. *Her turn today.* Yet she felt used and discarded, as if she belonged in purgatory, where St Nicholas would pray for her. Isabella felt an open button at the back of her dress. It was the same button her mamma had fastened with a light touch and kiss on her shoulder. Isabella sighed. She had presented herself like a doll in her best dress and her sister's perfume. With a head full of *Dolly* bravado, she had laid on the floor of a small, probably dirty utility room, not remotely like the glowing lovers' cavern in her tent or the white linen of a bridal suite. Like a party girl, she had given herself like she was 'on special' in the supermarket discount aisle where the pensioners fingered the bruised produce, complaining. What she had traded couldn't be returned at the refund counter, where the manager, Cindy, crossed lines on shopping receipts and handed back cash.

'Sorry you aren't satisfied with your purchase,' Cindy would apologise.

With her head lowered, Isabella cried. She'd dishonoured her mamma too, who was controlling, but loved her, and had her best interests at heart. She'd let down Carlo too, in some way. She turned away from the sound of a rustling curtain.

'Hey, Isabella, are you okay?' whispered Darcy.

She couldn't answer and concentrated on the light pressure of his hand on her shoulders and his kiss on her cheek. He found the loose button and looped it into place.

'Sorry, I have to rush. Here, take this.'

She fumbled and then steadied a large box of popcorn. Drying her eyes, she re-felt Darcy's tenderly fixed button, as lovingly placed as her mamma's soft touch. Moments later, munching on Darcy's salty popcorn, alone and in the dark, she felt a kernel of hope. Then she sat up taller, feeling more fully a woman. If her mamma could have sex in her teens, so could she. At home, collecting the washing, she saw the tiny writing on the labels. She had grown into the same waist and bra size as Bianca. The date had been struck off the calendar. *Her turn today.* St Nicholas could pray for lost souls, *not hers.* Then Darcy returned with a bottle of water and a hug.

'Here, you'll need this.'

Her mouth was dry, but she needed the hug more. She didn't need any more of her mamma's moralising, rules, and control. She wriggled her legs. The first time, *done,* more to come.

15

FROM inside her home, alone, on Saturday evening, Maria Pierce looked up from re-reading the Saturday newspaper. Car traffic and chatter from town reached her through her open window.

'Ah, yes,' she murmured, 'the flicks are back.' She re-read Matt's article about the cinema reopening. The article reverentially reported her husband's inspiration as the town's 'father figure' to place a teacher as the acting cinema manager. Earlier, she had pushed the newspaper away with a snort of disgust. *Father figure?* 'Matt, my man of words, I can't believe you wrote, let alone, printed that rubbish.'

After walking around the kitchen, then retrieving the newspaper, she nodded, realising the purpose. Matt was keeping Rich happy. In a way, it was a love letter to her. She sighed, tracing her forefinger over her lover's printed name.

Thinking of Matt and Rich, the lines of her marriage and affair ran too close together like the narrow cane-tram tracks lacing across town. She prayed that her tracks wouldn't ever intersect like the large cross she wore on a necklace. Trembling at the prospect of discovery, she touched each of the four points on her crucifix, whispering, 'He. Must. Never. Know.'

Maria walked outside onto a small balcony to settle her nerves and to feel closer to Matt. The air was rich with the town's humid, sugared air. Maria sniffed the air, also smelling popcorn. She wished she could sit with Matt, holding hands among the happy townsfolk, sharing a box of salty kernels. But she was bound by her Catholic faith on the tram track of marriage. For now, Matt was patient. Yet, as he came, he would grunt, 'Soon, Maria.'

'Yes. Soon,' she'd reply, then listen for God's condemnation, a grumble of celestial thunder.

Whenever Maria heard police sirens in town, she hoped for intervention. Becoming a widow could be an easier way out if God decreed. She thought of the town's cold stone church and God's judgment of her adulterous sinning. Yet, without love, she could remain deserted by her husband and abandon herself to her faith. Or she could allow herself a ray of happiness in this sodden town.

She touched the four points on her crucifix. 'Let. Me. Be. Loved.' Maria whispered in the direction of Matt's musky upstairs' bedroom across town, 'Soon, Matt. Soon.'

~

Darcy's customers gathered outside the cinema, sharing movie reviews. *The baddie got what he deserved.* Students and parents thanked him. Someone patted his shoulder. His colleague, Liam, shook his hand, Christie kissed his cheek, all the while, he nodded, looking for Isabella, worrying. He felt as if he'd marched Isabella upstairs to his wolf's lair and deflowered the trembling lamb. Had he, the wolf, *really* stopped to check? During the movie, he studied Isabella through the projection window. Her black Sicilian eyes gave nothing away. He half expected actor Harrison Ford to enter the projection booth holding up his police badge, loosening his handcuffs.

Showers unfolded over the town in sheets, like the curtain closing across the screen. With a quick, practiced snap of umbrellas, patrons huddled together then dispersed with goodbyes. Just at the edge of the cinema awning, teenage girls surrounded Frances. Isabella stood among them.

Frances spotted him and called out, 'Hello there. Seems like the first night was a wonderful success.' She gathered the girls and said, 'Thank Mr Grant before I take you home.'

The girls mumbled shy thanks.

Frances looked around. 'Isabella. Where are you?'

Isabella moved from behind Frances.

'Thanks very much. It was a great first night.'

Isabella held his eye and smiled. He took a step forward, then remembered to stop.

Frances called back to Darcy as the girls settled into the car. 'Please come to our home on Sunday week for lunch. It's Isabella's nineteenth birthday. Gosh, my daughters are so grown up. Before long, they'll be married off by the old nonnas.'

Darcy felt a pressure in his chest, and he turned back to the cinema door. Ahead, a tight group still gathered in front of the cinema sign. Darcy walked by. A photographer asked the group to pose. The newsman, Matt Flint, walked to the side of the group and reorganised the shot, positioning Rich in the centre.

'Okay, Matt,' said Rich, 'another, with me and the mayor.'

Matt looked at Darcy. 'Hey, Rich, shall we get a photo with the new manager too?'

Darcy walked closer to the cinema door, needing to clean the cinema for the Sunday matinee. He was sure popcorn was cast around the auditorium like a spray of stars. Over his shoulder, he heard Rich's loud principal voice. 'No need to photograph Darcy. This is an enterprise facilitated by the school.'

Darcy slowed his steps, and Rich seemed to speak louder.

'It was Darcy's shift tonight, then a different teacher each week as caretaker manager.'

Darcy groaned, shuffled through the door, and looked up at the projection room. The agreement didn't include the involvement of other staff. Darcy stood where the safe was hidden with the night's takings. Yesterday, when he returned to confirm with Rich that he was taking over the management of the cinema, his principal revealed the meaning of enterprise.

'You manage the place. I will manage the money.'

'But, you already have so much responsibility,' Darcy rebutted. 'Besides, this wasn't agreed with Simone.'

A snarl cut into Rich's bright smile. 'Remember, a good turn deserves another. Do you want the yellow transfer envelope?'

There was a knock on the cinema door and Rich appeared in the foyer. 'Tonight seemed like a success. There must be quite some takings to manage?'

After a few minutes, Rich left, slapping Darcy on the back.

'Now we have reached a better agreement about our enterprise. Good luck for the weeks ahead. Doesn't seem like the old owner will ever be well enough to return.'

Rich's blue eyes twinkled as if they shared an understanding. Darcy stamped the section of the carpet where the safe was concealed, takings safe for now; however, Rich would be cruising by in his mafia mobster saloon after the Sunday matinee to collect the revenue.

~

The following Saturday morning, Darcy spied through his bedroom window to be sure Leo had left, then picked up the phone to call his cousin, Eliza. Immediately recognising his voice, she fired questions about his life in the far north. 'Do the students call you Mr Grant? How do you keep a straight face?'

After a few minutes, Darcy asked a question of his own; one that would reveal too much. 'I want to buy a birthday present for a young woman. What do you suggest?'

'Well, well, well, tell me more. So, you've got a girlfriend? I told you so.' She clucked. 'Who is the lucky lady? Where did you meet?' Darcy was evasive, and she continued to probe before providing advice. 'Okay, lover boy, most girls like any present. It's the thought that counts.'

Rain drummed on his roof.

'A new raincoat might be the best present around here.'

'Huh?' Eliza grunted. 'Are you trying to impress or depress this girl? Maybe in your case, it really is the actual present that counts.'

Darcy's face reddened at the memory of birthday presents. Over the years, his father jotted dates into a calendar whenever he heard neighbours singing 'Happy Birthday'. After consulting the calendar in the years that followed, he'd trot behind the postie's red motorcycle, later picking through the neighbours' mail, pocketing cards. His father would grin at his harvest of bank notes, admiring the generosity of relatives. Darcy burned the neighbourhood kids' birthday cards in their backyard incinerator, eyes misting in shame. The cards were reduced to cinders, like his mother's belongings. Every birthday, Darcy received ten dollars, intended for someone else. One Christmas, his father's prolific harvest led to police patrols and a knock on the door. On Christmas Day, his father pinned five, ten, and twenty-dollar notes to his shirt, like military citations, saluting the decorated Private Darcy Grant.

Darcy wrote to his father every month, and sent a card for his birthday. He didn't reply, but Darcy's letters would be read. That was enough for Darcy. Enough for his father too.

Eliza asked, 'How old is your girlfriend? Is she your age? Younger? Older?'

'Ah. She's—'

Eliza filled the silence. 'You know, a great experience is just as good, like a romantic weekend away. Or surprise her with lingerie before a night over. That's what I like.'

Darcy coughed, needing a few seconds to recover.

As he went to finish the call, she asked, 'Hey, Darcy, before you go, what's your girlfriend's name?'

Darcy hesitated. He hadn't said her name to anyone in this context.

'C'mon, Darcy, you're not letting on whether she is younger or older or where you met. Surely you must know her name?'

'Her name… her name…' It felt like a confession. 'Isabella. Her name is Isabella.'

'Isabella. What a beautiful name. I can tell in your voice that you really like her. That's so sweet.'

After the call, he felt a mix of satisfaction and guilt, like devious salt in popcorn. Mostly he felt relief. He had told someone. It was real. He smiled. Eliza hadn't mentioned her golden super race female friends. *Of course.* The mention of her friends had just been Eliza's encouragement to boost his confidence. Remembering Isabella in the projection room, he stood tall, feeling as mighty as a chessboard king, for he had his very own member of the supreme female super race.

~

Turning by the Russo letterbox for Isabella's birthday, Darcy remembered his first arrival, pensive about his unattractive plumage. The idea of Bianca had made him tingle; now, his heart raced like the Russo hound, *Cane Farm Big*, running alongside, barking at the rolling tyres. Today, his conscience howled, like the hound at his tyres, recalling Isabella's return to the projection room the afternoon before.

Unclicking his seat belt, Darcy realised he hadn't needed to come. From the supermarket carpark to the festival camping ground to the cinema, one thoughtless action had followed another. A sequence, but not a sensible one.

Muddy farm trucks parked by the shed, likely with dried pig's blood caked into mud. Young men smoked by the trucks, not returning his wave. Beside him, Isabella's birthday gift rested on the seat like an exhibit for a jury of nonnas. Evidence for Carlo too.

Isabella had assured him, dressing in the cinema. There was no affection from her side. 'He was always just a friend. But I have to pretend.'

Darcy understood. A type of blinding Toowoomba fog.

The Russo curtain flickered, and Frances was soon beside his car. 'Welcome back, my dear!'

Darcy wondered whether he could hold his nerve. 'Ah, yeah, it's great to be back.'

'Well, it has taken some effort. I assumed you had a girlfriend and didn't have time for my family.'

Darcy tripped, almost losing his footing.

'Please spend some time with the birthday girl. Talk to her about returning to university. That would be like a birthday present for me.'

Darcy fumbled, then carried the present behind his back to conceal it from the nosy nonnas. Inside the Russo home, the nonnas were busy in the kitchen, arms waving like orchestra conductors, and he nestled his gift on the table, obscuring it with the others. Bianca waved with a coy smile and led guests to their seats. A couple of the young men stared at him. Carlo gave him a severe look, *what are you doing here?*

Isabella walked from the kitchen with an aunt who admired her gifts. Darcy stood back. At the table, a nonna held her hand. 'Isabella, today, you will receive many additions to your glory box to take into marriage in the near future.'

'How wonderful,' Isabella replied.

Frances called from the kitchen, and the nonna shuffled back to help. Isabella and Darcy locked eyes. To Darcy, the bright wrapping of the gifts appeared to fade. Looking into her eyes, he felt like he was staring into car headlights at night. He could only see her smiling, beautiful face in a silent cocoon aura, like a glimpse of the divine. A nonna's clapping shook him back, and women hurried outside with food bowls.

Isabella held Darcy's gift and whispered. 'I will open your present later in my room.'

Darcy looked across to Isabella's bedroom. The décor revealed the room as a place of prayer, and he felt the wolfish guilt of the violator. Isabella brushed by and hooked a finger in his, low under the table. They turned, hearing Frances' instruction. 'Come on now. Lunch is ready, and the parish priest is about to bless the food. *Pronto!*'

Darcy waved by the door, and Frances walked over. 'What? You can't spare a few minutes for lunch?'

'I have a cinema to open. Your lunches take hours, and there is never enough to eat.'

She playfully flicked him with a dishcloth.

Outside, the loud congregation was hushed into prayer. He drove away, reflecting on his own divine experience. Religion was described as a mystery. To Darcy, it didn't seem possible to know either way. But remembering Isabella's voice channelled into his classroom, weeks earlier, he wondered. There might be more to it. Yet he didn't want to think any more about the Russo's religion. Passing the silent Silkwood church, the shared knowledge of the hooked finger felt like the real knowing. Yet, their knowing needed to be unknown. Pages of newsprint lifted in the breeze from the side of the road, town gossip made real. Chances were, they would be found out. He grimaced, wondering about the safety switch on Gino's favourite rifle. Carlo, too, would have a gun in his truck. In the rearview mirror, he looked back at the Silkwood church in hope that Isabella's religion might protect them. Surely Silkwood had enough martyrs.

~

Isabella cried during her birthday song. Her mamma had placed a small ballerina figurine in the middle of the cake, with a one and nine arranged in candles. She smiled for the many photos with the birthday cake lit with candles. All the while, she thought of Darcy's gift on her bed. She clutched her dress, wanting Darcy's hand. During more photos, she imagined Darcy waiting in her bedroom. Behind the unnoticed closed door, while the guests drank and sang, she would lift her dress in shadow, and they would make love in a corner where the Virgin Mary couldn't see. At the thought, her skin glowed.

Her mamma called out, 'Isabella, you look like a radiant Sicilian princess. Bianca, you've got competition as the village beauty.'

Bianca shrieked. 'Papa, get a rifle. Guard the door!'

The crowd laughed. Isabella noticed Carlo, stony faced. She took a deep breath to blow out the candles. One remained defiant, flickering. The nonnas studied the tiny flame. It meant Isabella had one true love. The nonna who mentioned her glory box, croaked, 'Who is it?'

A nonna looked at Carlo who winced, then found a slight grin.

~

In the early evening, Isabella lay on her bed in a light nightdress, gripping Darcy's gift. It almost felt enough to hold it. At the gift table, she'd opened Carlo's gift, exclaiming joy for show, and gave him a quick peck on the cheek.

Isabella had waited until after her prayers with Mamma before tearing at the wrapping of Darcy's gift. Inside was a small card. It was pleasant but not romantic, signed 'Darcy Grant'. Isabella sighed; there was no expression of any emotion, the feeling of a dropped hand returned. *Ah*, then she understood. Her mamma loved to read her birthday cards. Darcy would have guessed. Inside the card was a movie flyer for *Witness*. She frowned, grumbling, 'An old movie flyer? So much for gifts for my glory box.' She then looked again. There were little annotations. Like a crossword puzzle, he'd overlain words across W-I-T-N-E-S-S only she would know.

'Silkwood' stretched over the 'W'.

'Cinema' projected an 'I'.

'Three Saints' offered the 'T'.

'Mission Beach' rocked with an 'N'.

'Side Door' snuck an 'E'.

'S' sat on the sofa cushions.'

Saturdays gifted another 'S'.

Isabella laughed and rolled over on the bed. This was a love letter beyond anything she could have imagined. She held it to her breast, vowing to keep the movie flyer forever, and look at it every birthday. She listened for her mamma's footsteps. The inscriptions were also a confession. Then, she opened the small box; inside was a pair of glittering earrings. She jumped up and tried them on and addressed the portrait of Mary. 'Yeah, I know what you're thinking.'

The final part of her present was a book. She turned the cover over. *Under Milk Wood* by Dylan Thomas. Darcy had overwritten the 'M' with an 'S,' so it read 'Under Silk Wood.'

Written inside the cover was a message. 'Remember Reverend Eli Jenkins. I will always see your best side. Hope you'll always see mine.'

She scanned the book, which read like a play, looking for mentions of Eli Jenkins. The sections she found were confusing as the Reverend seemed to pray in poetry. One page opened. The 'M' in Milk Wood was corrected, like a teacher's pen would, to an 'S'.

We are not wholly bad or good
Who live our lives under <u>Silk</u> Wood
And thou, I know wilt be the first
To see our best side, not our worst.'

Isabella re-read the lines. She looked at Mary. 'I know in your eyes I am sinning, Divine Mother, but can you see my best side?'

She held the book all night, dreaming in ways neither Mary in Silkwood nor the Reverend in Milk Wood would approve.

16

THE following weekend, Frances waved to her daughters from the front steps. Their family sedan turned by the letterbox and edged away towards town. Frances whispered a prayer, for she could not always protect them as they left the shelter of her wing. Male deceit was often veiled by charm. She shivered, imagining Pierce's smug photo in the office. Frances stamped. She'd only stayed at the school and tolerated Pierce to avoid gossip. But she hadn't forgotten nor forgiven, although this was meant to be the Christian way. Her eyes narrowed. She'd also need many re-readings of the bible to find forgiveness for whoever was distracting Isabella from her study. Carlo confided she hadn't returned to spend more time with him.

Her thoughts shifted to the town boys. They would have their versions of an art studio to seduce. Isolated farm shacks, *vino* in the fridge, with a worn-in spring mattress. She cringed with dread. Bianca could stand up for herself, although she encouraged men's attention. Perhaps the same boys had turned their attention to her pretty younger sister. The chaste, chased. Although Gino liked his gunslinger reputation, an impassioned young man might take his chances. Gino's famous arsenal hadn't deterred Pierce. Frances sighed, wringing a tea towel in her hands. At least Bianca was protected, for she'd taken her daughter to the doctor for *a secret prescription* when she heard another truck idling at their farm boundary and found Bianca's bed was empty and cold. Frances' teenage pregnancy had dishonoured their family name. Frances stamped. There would be no further family dishonour.

Yesterday, arranging flowers in the church, her friend confided that she'd been dutiful, allowing sex close to and just after her cycle. 'Even on nights when I didn't want it,' she'd added, glancing up at the

119

statue of Mary. She'd whispered that her many pregnancies were the result of her husband's crocodile-eyed promises to withdraw during the other times of her cycle.

'Most years, another baby. Another mouth to feed while he is in the fields,' she'd said, placing a hand on her belly. 'And now another.' Looking through the church door, she'd added, 'non-Catholic women have it easier.'

Every morning, away from Isabella's hearing, Frances whispered to Bianca, 'Have you taken your pill today?'

After the flower arranging, Frances looked up to a figurine of Jesus. She felt a blush of shame and lowered her eyes. She believed because she wanted to believe. Yet, when Frances prayed, she felt like she was speaking to outer space without an ear or care.

When holding Bianca at her baptism, the dark church walls felt like men's shoulders closing in around her. The priest had stood over her as if the baby were his. A crucifix was held over Bianca's face as if the church had delivered Bianca, not her. As she held her baby, who was painfully delivered *by her* and suckled on *her body*, Frances lifted tall, arching her back to meet the threat. As Bianca was blessed, Frances decided that God would only be allowed into her home to the extent that was good for her family. Yes, the priest could bless their food if this kept the parish happy. She'd raised her daughters as Catholics, so they had the choice to believe. Her doubts shouldn't block their opportunity to enter heaven, forever stuck in purgatory, as St Nicholas hovered over Silkwood, praying for their ascension.

Bianca hadn't cried when anointed, only opening her holy eyes to stare at her mother with the look she'd have for evermore: *Let's get this show on the road*. Every morning, Bianca confirmed, '*Si*, Mamma. I have taken my pill.'

At the church, during flower arranging, her friend asked, 'How do you manage, Frances? You had only two babies, now long ago.'

'I suppose God only intended for me to have two.'

'I'd say your husband is more disciplined than mine.'

Every morning, after reminding Bianca, Frances whispered a

short prayer of contrition to the holy papa in Rome, behind a closed bathroom door.

'After what happened to me, papa, I want a say.'

She placed the pill on her tongue. After staring in the mirror for minutes, Frances swallowed and blessed herself.

~

On the way to town, Isabella half listened as Bianca listed the boys who liked her. Isabella's decision to *pause* university was vexing her ever frowning Mamma, but she thumbed through dull textbooks, yawning, at the dinner table as a pretence. She'd selectively described university life to alarm her Mamma, saying, 'I'll be able to better cope when I'm a little older. Perhaps next year.'

As Bianca murmured beside her, Isabella dreamily looked at the passing cane, thinking of Darcy and shuffling her legs. Isabella felt a little punch on her arm.

'Izzy, are you listening? I'm also keen on a cute, muscly journalist at work, Peter, my partner for my Deb Ball. We kissed by the side door a couple of times last week.'

Isabella barely listened. She had heard many versions of this story. Bianca parked the car and said, 'C'mon, join me at the café before the movies. Plenty of cute guys.'

'Not today,' Isabella replied. 'I want to look at the new dresses in the shop window.'

'You're the world's most boring sister,' Bianca said, pulling a pretend sad face. 'So much for giving me competition.'

She soon walked towards the café, where boys turned from playing a pinball machine and whistled. Beside the car, Isabella opened her umbrella, stooping to ward off heavy rain. Strong wind caught and fanned her long hair. Hunched undercover, she ambled towards the shops, doubling back to the cinema when heavier rain forced people inside the café, and the street was empty.

~

Matt spent most Saturdays in his office. Maria crept upstairs early most Saturday mornings – a divine start to his weekend. Mid-morning, the delivery boys returned with empty satchels. Strong sales – more divinity. Today, Matt sat at his desk to review his accounts. He winced. There was less divinity in his ledger these days. He thought of Maria. She had a wonderful figure. But it wasn't a figure he could list in the accounts for his mother. Looking at a framed photo of his mother, he rehearsed his response to her inevitable enquiry about the hole in their revenue.

'Mother, listen.' Matt cleared his throat with a deep rumble, imagining a prominent Adam's apple. 'It's been a tough cane season. I've offered temporary discounts to retain customers.'

After rehearsals, he felt managerial. He almost wished for his mother to call. Matt stood, for his weekends included gathering news for the mid-week edition. Sometimes he called Dennis, the town detective, for a chat. *Always a newsroom!* Dennis often let something slip after a few minutes of cursing about Matt's crime reportage. But their last conversation hadn't gone that well. 'Fuck off, Flint,' was the extent of their exchange. He decided to leave a call to Dennis for another day. Instead, he sought his raincoat from a hook by the front door. As he opened the door, horizontal wind sprayed rain inside the foyer. 'NO! Not the new editions.' He patted the paper stand dry with his hanky.

Matt looked around at the street. Road gutters overtopped and the roads were slickly wet like a dam spillway, with twin rivers bouncing down either side of the street. Around him, shop awnings sheeted heavy water, an early taste of the summer monsoon.

'Nah,' he mumbled and hung up his raincoat.

Down the wet street, a few people looked out from the café. Although the rain blurred his aspect, he saw Bianca Russo's dark eyes looking out, long flowing hair in the breeze. Matt returned to where she sat in the office and studied her family photo. He looked at Bianca's beautiful mum. She would be famous in another place, a model or actress. Perhaps a television weather girl. Yet here, she was bogged on a soggy cane farm with the same daily weather report. The journalist in him began to frame a story about the lost Sophia Loren of Far North Queensland.

He glanced outside to see if the weather might have improved for a snoop, but rain still lashed the town. He guessed the young cinema manager would have a quiet night. Yet, despite the weather, a girl with long, thin legs huddled low under a black umbrella in front of the cinema. He rubbed his eyes. After Maria's departure, the early tot of rum had been more than a tot. A gust caught her umbrella and fanned out her black wavy hair: Bianca, again, he surmised. The cinema doors were closed, and Matt thought he saw his office trainee dart down the side of the cinema. She didn't reappear.

'Ah, I see,' mumbled Matt.

17

DURING the week, Simone stopped by Darcy's home to drop off more movie reels. Darcy liked this aspect of Far North Queensland town life. If you wanted to talk to somebody, you called by, *eh*. But he needed to move; Pierce kept jacking up the rent, and Leo was in severe arrears. Darcy had trawled the camping store looking for a makeshift bed. He planned to reside in the cinema office for the remainder of the year, subsisting on a diet of ice cream, popcorn, and twisties. He'd wash from a hand basin, hoping teenage acne wouldn't return.

Darcy smiled at Simone in welcome. In his dreams, he endured a less-welcome drop around: traffic noise would conjure an image of Carlo ramming their gate with his heavy farm truck, honking his horn with a shotgun across his lap. Darcy would sit up in bed, panting in fear. During the day, he suppressed thinking about the risks he was taking, but his subconscious wouldn't let him off so easily.

In the fading light, near dusk, he and Simone sat on the small deck, waving away mosquitos. 'How's Sid getting on?' he enquired.

'Oh, it's so sad – he's in hospital now. But he's proud that the cinema is back in action. Can I ask another favour, Darcy?'

'Of course.'

Later, Darcy drove Simone home in Sid's truck. A house key rattled in the console.

~

The following Saturday morning, Darcy drove to Sid's home. Large trees shrouded the house, a few streets from the town centre. Simone waited out the front. Upstairs, she showed Darcy through her childhood home. Mounted photos from weddings, parties, and holidays covered most walls. Darcy could see this was a home more than a house; where people loved as much as they lived, with framed happy memories, just like at the Russo's. One wall held photos of Simone in school uniforms, from primary to high school. Simone sighed at a picture of an older woman, touched the photo, and blessed herself. Darcy's eyes misted, thinking of his missing mother, and a lonely boyhood in a quiet, cold house without photos and connections.

'Are you having second thoughts?' Simone asked.

'No, it's fine. I'm just admiring Sid's setup.'

Darcy was led to the spare room, which contained a wardrobe and mirror. He stared at the large double bed. Simone caught him and playfully elbowed him, asking whether he was planning to ask anyone over.

'No. Ah, no, no,' he stammered.

When the tour was completed, Simone said, 'Darcy, thanks for looking after the place while Dad is in hospital. At the newspaper, we hear everything. Unoccupied places are usually broken into. I know I can trust you.'

Hear everything? He swallowed. *Trust?* He coughed to shield a moan, worrying again about the cinema revenue.

'Anyway, Darcy, it's good you're clearing out from that house. An out-of-town lawyer popped in to see our boss during the week.'

'Yeah?'

'The lawyer said he was surprised your address was occupied. Said the property was part of what he called a "contested deceased estate" and the dead teacher's house was meant to be empty.'

'Really?'

'Yeah. He's representing the family of the old teacher who owned the place. The spare keys were left in the principal's office in case of an emergency. The lawyer is surprised there are tenants.'

'Interesting, but why was the lawyer seeing your boss?'

'He carried the paper into our office, then opened it to the principal's feature article. He asked Matt if he was close to the principal, as he wasn't getting anywhere with Mr Pierce. How about that?'

'Yeah, that's strange,' said Darcy.

Heading outside with Simone, Darcy calculated the rent he'd passed through Pierce's car window. He recalled the mechanical click as the window pressed into the Statesman's door frame, around half of his salary sealed within. The timing wasn't ideal to ask for a refund. At school, the staff whispered in close huddles about the end-of-year transfer phase. Pierce carried around a staff list and red pen. Between lessons, his teacher friend Liam hid under a desk in his classroom, patting his streaked perm. Darcy hoped the cinema enterprise would shield him from a northern posting, but he couldn't be sure. Pierce would miss the rent; a scowl would replace his cheesy smile.

'Sure you're okay?' Simone asked again.

Darcy reassured Simone and she walked to her car. Simone's car backfired like a gunshot as she revved, and Darcy jumped. He ran up the steep driveway to the fence – wanting to explain that Pierce was handling the cinema money – but he pulled back. He should have discussed this much earlier. Puffing, he walked back to the house. He'd turned from a private person into a sneak. Perhaps, too, Pierce's accomplice.

Later, in his new room, Darcy looked out between the curtains at the thick shrubbery by the fence line. Light peaked through gaps in the leaves. He felt secluded, but not secure, wishing he was hidden behind a thick wall of impenetrable sugar cane. Looking at the double bed, he sighed, resolving that he couldn't, wouldn't, shouldn't, invite Isabella over. The cinema was a credible ruse, but Isabella's movements would be more public if they were to meet here. Simone had pointed to pot plants at the back steps, where spare keys lay rusting but ready. Although he thought of giving Isabella one of the spare keys, that's where they would stay. He'd see Isabella at the cinema. No invite. No key. Although a sneak, he was better than that.

Later that day, lying on the double bed, he tried to see the relationship from Isabella's perspective. She probably liked the furtive, daring spree with an older man. *But was it enough? Would it remain enough?* Without signals he could read, Kelly, his previous girlfriend, had called it off. In Silkwood, Isabella and Carlo would be still presumed to be matched. The presumption would turn into pressure, with the eventuality of joint Italian surnames written within a marriage registry after confetti was cast over the couple. *Darcy who?*

Picturing the spare key under the pot plant, he imagined Isabella lying beside him. He turned to his side, touching the cool mattress, wishing for her warmth. But no, he was better than that.

Yesterday, as he packed up his belongings in the dead teacher's house, Leo confirmed he was also making other living arrangements. Darcy was relieved Leo hadn't asked to move in, although he asked for the address. Darcy had joked, saying he'd be placing a lock on Sid's beer fridge.

Darcy sat up and travelled to the cinema to prepare for the Sunday matinee. Later that afternoon, at the top of the projection room, Isabella adjusted her dress and walked down the stairs. From the foyer, Darcy pointed at famous actresses. Posters of Hollywood stars hung high on a foyer wall, out of hibernation from the cinema office. He called out, 'I could do with some good-looking female company now that I'm living out on my own.'

Isabella squinted, trying to understand. 'Huh?'

She walked to him and looked up at the posters. Darcy asked Isabella to close her eyes. He placed a key into her open palm and whispered in her ear. Isabella absorbed the news, her eyes wide and shining. He looked away. His resolution had barely lasted hours. He was a meek, weak sneak. During the week, he wondered whether he'd have the nerve to act superior, disciplining the talkative year nines. He drew a deep breath and repeated his want for company, alone in a house. Beneath the portrait of Sophia Loren, Isabella pranced like a starlet, swinging her hips and pretending to smoke. She addressed him in a deep, hoarse Italian accent, holding the key and considering his request. 'You know, Mr Grant, a Silkwood beauty like me has many offers. I'll see what I can do.'

Darcy reached over to the service counter to find a temptation. 'Stale popcorn?'

'How enchanting, Signor Grant. I'm yours.'

~

Darcy drove Sid's truck to the town centre the following afternoon. The truck was big: farmer-style, like most unwashed town rigs. The use of Sid's truck was a deception as Pierce maintained a register of teacher vehicles, in addition to their home addresses. If his principal was to find out about Isabella, Frances would be next, then hostile Carlo. It would be a combustible chain reaction, a trail of fizzing gunpowder, not a movie script with a happy ending, sighing patrons squeezing hands, hoping for a sequel.

On the dashboard, old movie posters rolled around as he rumbled along. A magazine with a semi-clad woman on the front cover slid sideways as he took a corner. Darcy stopped, grabbed the *Playboy* magazine, and shoved it under the seat. There was a long object underneath that felt like a broom handle. Darcy sat upright and gasped when he felt the rifle stock. He drove on, heart beating fast, assuming Sid handled any personal or business issues firmly, without police assistance. Darcy hoped the cinema takings were making it to the bank. Parked under a tree near the supermarket, Darcy thought that meeting a young teacher in an old truck may not have suited Sophia Loren, yet just after three p.m., an Italian beauty ran to the vehicle. She hid low, holding onto the edge of the seat as he drove away.

'What's this under the seat? Feels like a *Dolly* magazine.'

'Not quite. More for a male audience.'

'A porno? How boring. Heaps of those around the shed.'

'What's this?' asked Isabella, reaching further back. 'A gun, I suppose. Typical.'

Darcy smiled; country teens had a well-rounded life education.

Inside the house, he led her to his room.

Isabella smiled. 'Wow, a real bedroom.'

'How long have we got?' he asked.

'Don't you get any ideas, Signor Grant,' Isabella said, addressing him again as husky Sophia Loren. 'How's a movie star meant to get in the mood without projection equipment?'

'I'll be your director.'

'Okay, I know the plot,' she said, undressing.

~

Afterward, Isabella lay recovering under a sheet. The fan clicked above them. Their limbs were loose and askew, like clock hands. Isabella followed the slow rotations of the fan blades in sync with the ticking clock on the bedside table. Although happy, she felt restrained. They could find places but couldn't stretch time. They could find pleasure but little peace.

A little after four p.m., Isabella squirmed out of Darcy's embrace and dressed into her supermarket uniform. 'Sorry.' She sighed. 'It's time again.'

The street was Sunday-afternoon quiet as she left, and Isabella crept along the fence line, one soft foot at a time, marching, this time, to the beat of the bus timetable. Time organised her life during the day, with her monthly cycle, another internal clock. Her period was due, and, for once, she hoped it would come soon.

She couldn't make more time; it went faster when you needed more. The hour today, from three to four, seemed like minutes. The hours of Mass, with Carlo looking over at her, *dragged*. Isabella stopped with an idea. Though she couldn't create more time, she could better arrange the time she had. She would ask her manager, Cindy, for a two-p.m. finish. *Yes!* She could make time, after all, arriving at the bus stop with a broad smile.

'What are you so happy about?' asked Carlo, waiting at the bus stop in his supermarket uniform. 'Will this bus ever leave on time? Will you ever have time for me?'

18

RICH Pierce stared at the two envelopes on his desk. He smiled at the familiar elegant female handwriting on one scented envelope, filled with bank notes. There was a note among the cash: an invitation for a further rendezvous. Into his diary, he jotted: *Important school business,* for the following afternoon. Rich opened his safe, whistling, and added the cash to the growing stack. He was still surprised that town parents paid him to keep their misbehaving spawn at school. He'd been a schemer for a few years, but the far north was the best scene. Perhaps it was parents' misguided belief that education would give their children better life prospects. Yet all they needed around here was the ability to farm, fight, swear, drink, shoot, smoke, and screw. That all came naturally enough. Schooling only got in the way. Back at his desk, Rich examined the other envelope. It was lumpy, not with cash but with the returned keys to the dead teacher's house.

'Grant. Scuderi. Worthless pricks,' he cursed at the 1985 staff photo. Flicking the keys around his desk, he considered where he might find new tenants.

Another letter from a southern legal firm about the house tenure sat in thin strips in his shredder. Ignore the first three legal letters, he'd once read. Last week, he'd assured the visiting southerner lawyer with a bright smile that the house had only been occupied for emergency accommodation after a nasty relationship breakup.

'I'm seen as a father figure around here,' he'd explained. 'It's a weakness of mine, but I have to help when I see a person in need.'

The mute stony-faced lawyer studied the framed photo of the media article with Rich shaking the mayor's hand in front of the cinema. The man looked unconvinced in a lawyerly way and left, still issuing letters, probably to crank up his fees. This confirmed to Rich everyone thieved in their own way.

Rich reached into a lower desk drawer. It was time to transfer a couple of teachers to remote postings. In return, he would receive a couple of war-weary teachers: new tenants.

Rich pulled the staff list out of his drawer and picked up his pen. *Who would the regional office accept in return for teachers from remote posts?* He nodded. Young, male, with no runs on the board. He rested his pen on *Grant, D.* and looked up again at the staff photo, smiling at the thought of Darcy struggling in Far North Queensland's rebellious wilds. He'd seen Darcy on morning walks wearing an army cap, as if he was a big deal. Rich chuckled, for Darcy would need military quartermaster skills in the frontier. Rich clicked his pen, then paused. The cinema had become his private mint, a virtual money press. *Yes,* Darcy was handing over the cinema loot, but he could sense reluctance. Rich's usual method was to involve someone in his schemes and blackmail them into silence as a collaborator. But Darcy wouldn't take any payment. Since Darcy arrived in town, he'd been his special project. Darcy was his father's name. His father had beaten him every day of his childhood until Rich was old enough to fight back — and then fight the world. Rich looked back at the staff photo. Darcy looked like his father as a young man.

Rich addressed the staff photo. 'Darcy Grant. I will break you.'

Yes, Darcy had stepped into line at the suggestion of a replacement cinema manager, but something wasn't quite right. A young bloke giving up his weekends didn't make sense. Rich reached into his drawer for a yellow envelope. It was time to test Darcy's motive to continue their enterprise. He would use his reliable transfer threat to shake him up. In the meantime, he needed to transfer out a teacher or two. He spotted a prospective transfer victim: Liam Matthews, the recently engaged teacher.

He addressed the staff photograph again. 'So sorry, Liam, we all must take our turn. The town boys will be happy to keep Christie company.'

Rich chuckled. Just yesterday, he'd signed the engagement congratulations card. He laughed, anticipating the farewell card. He shuffled the two transfer papers on his desk. Liam was about to be dispatched. *But what about Darcy?*

19

IN bed with Isabella on a Sunday afternoon, Darcy stared at the ceiling. His mattress seemed to sink, and he was back in his chilly Toowoomba lounge room, listening to Eliza.

'I've just had a few short flings with older boys to find out how things worked. That served a purpose.'

Darcy looked from the ceiling to the window. *Was Isabella a roused new arrival into womanhood, eyes broadening at a bright dawn?* He sighed. Isabella rolled away. *As Isabella's eyes adjusted to the light, would she look further afield?*

As Sophia Loren, Isabella joked in the cinema, saying she had many offers. It was possible. Probable. The town boys would soon paw at her, knowing what she knew and could offer. He remembered her laughing in the Year 12 lesson when the boys made outrageous claims about their futures. If Isabella could be amused, she could be seduced and taken away. When their fun died down, Isabella may well conform. Darcy had heard of pre-marital flings. At the Russo home, he'd noticed the framed photo of Carlo and Isabella at the Debutante Ball, looking like shy newlyweds with anxious thoughts of their honeymoon. One day soon, Carlo might sit again beside Isabella at a family lunch, holding hands. *Let's set a date*, Frances would say, placing hands on their shoulders.

Darcy sighed again, for an average guy like him couldn't hold a beauty like Isabella. He wasn't the one – just the lucky first. Like Leo's stopwatch, he wondered when his good run would end.

Shivering despite their body heat, he stroked her thick hair. Darcy wondered whether his fear and jealousy was a form of love. He didn't feel sad after his split with Kelly, his university girlfriend. When he saw her with boyfriends, sometimes she'd catch his eye. No emotion registered. He was more worried about being late to the next lecture.

He gave Isabella a light shake, waking her. 'Isabella, what about we plan a car trip together like a normal couple?'

She stretched and yawned. '*Si, Signor*,' she replied as husky Sophia Loren. 'But what's wrong? You're shaking.'

~

Darcy drove along a narrow, muddy Silkwood cane trail the following Saturday. He parked at a fork. Isabella's green dress shimmered from the tall clumps of cane as she ran to the car. Darcy concentrated on her broad smile and shining eyes, trying to forget his cousin's short flings with older guys. He held and kissed Isabella for minutes, only roused into action when he heard a tractor. Isabella lay low on his lap as they left Silkwood, eyes upright and warm.

From the Bruce Highway at Mourilyan they curved towards a dark green mountain range resembling a long, high castle guarding the coastline. Darcy's car engine roared, lifting around the corkscrew turns up the steep range. Below, they caught a glimpse of Etty Bay's blue-green water. They pulled over to peer at the sea through the palms and tropical foliage.

'Wow. Is this a glimpse of Eden?' asked Darcy.

'Look,' exclaimed Isabella. 'There's a mountain silkwood,' she said, pointing at a large tree in the jungle. To Darcy, the hardy-looking specimen with smooth bark seemed well named. He stroked Isabella's skin, admiring her Silkwood silky exterior. As they drove down the range, more shards of ocean blue sliced through trees and vines.

'Let's see if it is Eden. Hurry down, Adam,' she whispered. 'I can be your Eve.'

At the base of the range, a caravan park and surf club snuggled into the forest. Towering cliffs overshadowed the sandy cove. Separately, they walked and met at the end of the cove. In the foliage, twigs snapped – a tall cassowary stood. Darcy squeezed Isabella's hand into a closed ball. The bulky cassowary passed by.

They ventured onto the beach near the waves, stepping around low rocks pitted by salt. Shells and broken coral scrunched under their feet. Isabella skipped through deeper water, splashing out of Darcy's sight behind a large boulder. Darcy followed her lead, finding her bikini cast over a large rock.

Within moments, they were swimming, naked as porpoises, touching beneath the water. Wading back to the shore, Isabella leaned back on a large, smooth boulder. Darcy's shadow moved over her. Isabella's heart rate soon matched the lapping ocean. She lay against the warm boulder for many moments afterward, looking stupefied at the horizon. When dressed, they walked around the bay again and then separated. Darcy collected Isabella by the beach's edge and drove up and over the steep rainforest incline away from Etty Bay. Isabella's head lay on his lap, sleeping, and he stroked her hair. He thought of their hooked finger under the table at her nineteenth birthday. *The real knowing.* Then he placed two hands on the steering wheel, reminded of his premonition as he drove by the Silkwood Church. They'd likely be found out. There'd be a line up to shoot him.

~

'Darcy, thanks for dropping by.' Rich shook Darcy's hand and led him to the principal's lounge. 'Something unexpected. Please take a seat.'

Darcy stared at the yellow envelope on the small table. Rich noticed Darcy blinking, registering the implication.

'Is that…?'

'Yes, Darcy, it is.'

Rich figured Darcy would have heard the news about Liam Matthews. When he'd delivered the yellow envelope to Liam that morning, he'd retreated to his office. Rich had rubbed his hands, ready to witness the entertainment. The morning bell rang. Right on cue, Liam had shuffled to the school gate. Christie ran from her car. Rich smirked as Liam held up the yellow envelope, shaking his head. The couple hugged, with Christie's engagement ring glinting in the sun. Rich imagined Christie saying she would wait.

'Don't count on it, Liam.' Rich chuckled at his reflection. 'Two years is a long stretch. The town boys will circle. I might take a turn too.'

Next year, Rich would also poison the well. Over his regular cut, wash, tint, and blow-dry at Christie's salon, he would say he'd heard Liam had taken up with a local. At the window, Rich murmured, 'It's for the best. The incoming teachers are taking the rental.'

In the office, Darcy stared at the envelope. 'I'm only in my first year. Why so soon?'

'Everyone must do their bit. I'm sure you want to do what is best for the department.' Rich patted Darcy on the shoulder. 'Probably only three years.'

Darcy slumped in the chair. 'Can anything be done?'

Rich enjoyed his pleading. 'Are you asking me to challenge the department's wishes?'

'Do you have a say? Why… why, now?'

'Why not now?'

Darcy still stared at the envelope. To Rich, this confirmed his suspicions that there was more to Darcy than his loner persona.

'Don't worry about the cinema. I can make other arrangements. Why not now?'

'Can I confide in you?'

'Of course, I'm your principal. You shouldn't hesitate.'

Darcy stammered. 'I can't go… because… of a girl.'

'*A girl?* Rich leaned in. 'Well, well, tell me more.'

A few minutes later, Rich watched Darcy as he walked out of his office. Rich smiled, for he was happy with the deal. Oh, *how easily* Darcy had agreed. From next week, Darcy would provide a portion of his pay as a presumed sweetener for the department's transfer officer. Rich would handle the transaction. Darcy would also edge up the price of the cinema confectionery without involving Simone. Rich reflected at his desk, tapping the envelope. *A girl in the mix? Darcy's childhood sweetheart coming to town?* He'd suspected bullshit, so he'd pressed Darcy.

He'd asked, 'If you two are so committed, surely you have a photo?'

Darcy opened his diary without hesitation and provided a postcard featuring pretty girls in gold bikinis. He pointed out his girlfriend. Rich had turned over the card. The writing was faded, but the card was addressed to him in Toowoomba. Darcy was too dull for a quick, clever lie.

'Okay, hotshot, what's her name?' he'd asked.

'Eliza.'

'I'll see what I can do.'

Rich placed his favourite, empty yellow envelope back in his drawer a few minutes later. It would be ready to unsettle on another day. At the ringing school bell, he brushed his hair and picked up his car keys. It was time to meet Bruno's mum and take her for a country drive in the Statesman. She could again appreciate the sedan's broad and deep rear seats. Passing Frances' desk, he noticed she no longer sketched. 'Studio. Soon,' he whispered in her ear. Frances jumped, and he chuckled, clinking his car keys.

20

'NEXT! *Ciao*. Mrs Caltabiano. Nice to see you,' welcomed Isabella in her supermarket uniform. Carlo watched her nimble fingers as she tapped prices into the cash register and slid groceries down the ramp. Hairs on his neck bristled from the air conditioning, and he imagined impressions of her nipples pressing through her bra into thin supermarket uniform cotton. He shifted on his feet. Cindy, his manager, walked by, eyeing him.

Carlo sped up his packing, then paused. He stared at her hips, remembering his hand on her waist, at the Deb Ball the year before, in their senior year.

Cindy whirled back and clicked her fingers. 'Move it.'

Carlo glanced at Isabella again. She was a little taller, and they were nearly eye to eye. He wouldn't need to lean down to kiss her if she let him again. Her lips looked both silky soft and as firm as tractor tyre rubber. He fumbled a couple of groceries, and Isabella frowned.

'Careful of the eggs, Carlo!'

Carlo resumed packing, feeling Isabella both present and distant. She was present at the ball the year before, especially during the dancing. During parish lunches they'd often sat together, as they had at Sunday School and on the school bus. Sometimes at family lunches she had let him take her hand. His parents had been childhood friends, then sweethearts, with marriage a natural path. Mrs Russo built his confidence, *they were matched,* but Isabella kept her distance, as if he was a mismatch. Carlo's stirring nightly dreams made Isabella feel close, then distant afterward.

When he'd visited Isabella at her university lodgings, she gave him a hug and kiss on the cheek. Alone in the dining room, he wanted to reach for her hand, but she sat beyond arms reach. With her hair pulled back, and a cross on the wall, she could have been a trainee nun completing her novitiate, memorising her vows. *Sister Isabella.* She had frowned when he described the power of his new gun, a fulfilled birthday wish. Her brief hug goodbye felt sisterly. He felt confused and angry as he drove home. Carlo remembered Isabella walking away to her convent room, not looking back, as if she had done her duty. Less nun-like girls, with thick mascara and spiky hair, smirked and pointed at his truck. Near Silkwood, he'd pulled over, blasted a road sign with his shotgun. For once, this didn't make him feel happy. Looking at the shredded sign, Carlo tried to recall memory fragments at the end of the music festival when he crawled to her. He could only remember her eyes, as if she was truly seeing him for the first time, not liking what she saw. These days he wondered what it would take for her to like what she saw.

At the checkout, a customer grunted. 'Are you paid not to pack?'

Isabella glared at the stack of unpacked groceries and half-filled bags. Cindy poked him in the ribs. Carlo concentrated, catching up, but still, he stole glimpses. He noticed that Isabella studied her watch, yet it was only early afternoon. A few customers later, she halted progress and called Cindy. A new cashier replaced Isabella, and soon, more groceries slid towards him. He checked his watch. It was only two p.m. A minute later, she flashed by in her raincoat, her hips and breasts hidden away. Distant again.

~

On Sunday, the Catholic faithful milled outside the door of the Silkwood Church, their pent-up chatter released after the last hymn and solemn exodus from the pews. Last from the church, Frances swept among the flock, kissing passers-by. She stood to admire the new dress of one of Isabella's friends.

'Wow! Almost as beautiful as you,' she exclaimed.

The sky darkened, and rain swept across with a gust of wind. Frances and the parishioners opened their black umbrellas. Carlo rushed to the nearest umbrella, which Frances raised to receive him.

'Well, hello, Carlo, this is my lucky day.'

The rain intensified, and pods of parishioners made their way to shiny sedans.

Frances escorted Carlo towards his parents' car, holding the umbrella high. 'Gosh, you're getting more handsome by the day, Carlo.'

'If only Isabella noticed.'

Frances turned and kissed him on the cheek. 'I'm sure she will. Remember, you've been matched. Sometimes, a girl needs time. Now, speaking of Isabella, are you working the afternoon shift, too?'

'Yes, Mrs Russo.'

'You're such a good worker. They'll make you manager one day.'

'No way. I'm the first to leave at four.'

Frances laughed. 'I thought Isabella would be first out the door at four.'

'She beats me out of there, alright. She finishes at two.'

Frances frowned. 'But don't you both catch the last bus at four-thirty? I thought her shift was 12 to four, like you?'

Carlo ran to his parents' car.

Frances turned around. Isabella pulled up her sleeve to look at her watch. Frances' throat caught. Carlo closed his car door with a thud, head hung low. Frances looked up at the cross mounted on the church roof. She'd followed the priest's sermon, but in the car park, she'd received a real message. The background stopwatch of Isabella's life, from birth to womanhood, was ticking on. Frances thought she was holding the stopwatch. Stop. Go. But no, there were two missing hours, and Isabella was running free.

~

In the early afternoon, Frances surveyed the supermarket exit through her car windscreen. Shoppers puffed, wheeling heavy trolleys. She trusted Carlo but hoped he was wrong. Frances touched the magnetic image of the Madonna fixed to a metal strip. She drummed her fingers on the steering wheel, praying for a simple, innocent explanation, trying to control her dire, spiralling imagination. Isabella was saving for cassettes and new dresses, sure signs of a girl growing up. But now she was giving up two hours of income. *What was her secret?*

Frances knew mothers had many roles, and she unwillingly fulfilled the task of a spy. It seemed not so long ago that Frances would play 'I Spy' driving around with her young daughters. Today, she was spying for something starting with 'I'.

Showers thumped her car roof, and the rain soon streaked the windscreen, morphing the colours and shapes of the shopping townsfolk. It was finally two p.m., but she couldn't properly see. Frances turned on the car engine to start the wipers. The water sheeted away, and the blurry shapes became people. The familiar figure of Isabella strode away from the store.

'Oh, Isabella!' She looked to her passenger seat, recalling her skinny, large-eyed daughter in an oversized uniform, kicking her legs, ready for her first day of school. Now, a self-assured, upright young woman marched away without Frances's knowledge, formerly her permission.

Frances opened her car door as more heavy rain squalls swept over town. Under a lowered umbrella, she climbed a hill away from the supermarket, glancing up to keep on Isabella's trail. Ahead, Isabella took a corner into a quiet suburban street, well away from the shops. They were above the highway, and even the mighty sugar mill stacks seemed small. Frances shuddered, as she didn't know anyone in this corner of town. Noticing Isabella's confidence, Frances realised this was a walk completed many times. She wondered whether it was time to schedule a secret consultation with the doctor, as she'd done for Bianca. *Or was it too late?*

~

In Darcy's bed, Isabella marvelled at their private space, much better than the makeshift lovemaking locations around the cinema.

Darcy dozed beside her, and she tip-toed around, noticing it was becoming their place. Her pink ribbon was still placed as a bookmark in a book on his bedside table. A little photo of her, cut from the 1984 Year 12 class photo was stuck to the wall. A shy, obedient girl stared back. The photo already seemed like an archive of her, like those at the family mausoleum. She looked in the mirror to see if she appeared more womanly compared to her photo. She wasn't surprised that her dark Sicilian eyes gave little away. She jumped at Darcy's touch. He stood behind her, also looking into the mirror. To Isabella, the reflection was a shock. The mirror framed them as a couple after secret months. They pulled faces, laughing and posing as if for a camera.

'C'mon, Darcy, let's rehearse one more time for Mamma. You know what to say.'

He heard an echo. *You know what to say.* Frances at the parent-teacher night, when he'd been first asked to lunch. 'Okay, Isabella, but you go first.'

Isabella cleared her throat. 'Mamma, Darcy and I talk regularly at the cinema, almost like good friends and he's asked me on a date. I'm 19, so maybe it's time for a boyfriend. I want to make my own match and then head back to university next year. Darcy can help me with my studies. What do you think?'

Darcy replied in a high voice, as Frances. 'Really? What a surprise! Oh, yes, he is a fine young man. Let's keep the nosy nonnas out of our lives. Back to university too! How wonderful!'

They jumped up and down on the bed, hugging and laughing, with the mirror shaking as if there were earth tremors.

21

THE street was Sunday afternoon quiet. Frances heard the click of a closing door and footsteps. From behind bushy vegetation, Isabella crept along the fence line. Frances stood back, noticing her daughter's coy smile before she hid her face under her raincoat hood. The spy thought about returning to her car and confronting Isabella at home. Instead, she walked to the driveway, where Isabella had appeared. At the house, she went to climb the front steps, then stopped. Footmark scuffs on a side path led to the back of the house.

Frances' sharp knock on the back door sounded like a thunderclap. There was a muffled voice at the door.

'Isabella, is it you?'

The door opened. Frances registered Darcy's wide-eyed horror as he stepped back. Frances, mouth open in shock, gripped the stair railing.

After a few moments, she scowled and asked, 'Mr Grant, are you still accepting visitors from my family?' She shoved past him. 'You creep.'

Inside, Frances studied the disarray of the bedsheets, barely listening to Darcy's pitiful, broken voice. Her anger rose, with a burst of heat across her neck. She arched her shoulder, then launched, slapping Darcy. She felt the muscles around his cheek splay as his head rocked back. Frances dropped her tingling, stinging hand to her side.

'You! Her mentor!' she screamed. 'The person meant to guide her back to university, not threaten her future! I curse you with *malocchio*.'

Darcy held his face, trying to keep his jaw, teeth, skin, and eyes in place.

'We opened our home to you. Our thanks? Your contempt and disrespect.'

Darcy mumbled, holding his jaw. 'I know I betrayed your trust. I'm so sorry. We, we, we fell in love.'

'Love? I bet you just took advantage of your position and a teenager's curiosity!'

Frances sat down with her back to Darcy. Over her shoulder, she heard Darcy's explanation and sobbing pleas. She went to ask how long it had been going on, then remembered Darcy and Isabella standing close by the table at her birthday.

'Will you tell Isabella you know?' Darcy asked.

'I haven't decided.'

'Will you tell Gino?'

'That's for me to decide,' she paused, 'and for you to fear. Do the right thing and call it off. Leave Isabella to her life.'

She glanced at the bedsheets and kicked Darcy's shin as she stomped to the door.

~

Later, Frances sat in her car, waiting for reality and reason to merge. *Isabella and Darcy!* Darcy, the boy-teacher. Now, the teacher-boyfriend. It was like finding a cockroach at the bottom of a bowl of minestrone. Frances gagged. Although the image of the rumpled lovers' room stayed with her, Frances couldn't assign angelic Isabella as the temptress or boyish Darcy as the seducer. She started the car. With Bianca, it was obvious she wanted a love life as she fought to open her world. Frances realised Isabella had been gliding in Bianca's wake, reading university textbooks at the dining table as a deception, while secretly meeting Darcy. Frances grumbled. Carlo was sidelined, *buon matrimonio* to honour her parents was imperilled. Besides, Isabella was too young for a serious relationship when she should be focused on returning to university. Frances strangled an ironic laugh. Too young? *Who was she to talk?*

Driving home, a reel of memories lit up her windscreen. Her uncle's slide nights when she was a girl came to life. She would dance in front of the screen, pointing at the images. 'Papa,' she'd exclaim at the picture of her father installing their large letterbox with a pipe jutting from the corner of his mouth. 'Mamma and Papa!' at an image of her parents standing outside their partially built house in the early 1950s, cradling her as a baby. Then Papa in front of their bare fields, holding their first cheque from the sugar company.

'Oh, Papa, you've dark hair,' she cried. Relatives would laugh.

Her papa laughed. 'Oh, my bella, sit down, *per favore*. Come, sit on my knee.'

Today, other snapshot memories crossed before her. In the warmth of her car, Frances shivered. An image rose of the tall farmer's son, Gino Russo, leaving Silkwood to train as a policeman. In early high school, she'd heard his loud boasts.

'I won't be another grubby wog farmer in these muddy fields.'

Then, posted to a nearby town, Gino returned in uniform patrolling around the sugar towns in a spotless, late-model police sedan. He stood out, transformed in a crisp, superhero uniform, contrasting with gum-booted, sweat-streaked local farmers' sons astride muddy tractors. Concentrating, Frances gripped the wheel, resisting what came next. Still, recollections rose. One year, Gino worked at the local show, where she received first prize in the open-age art competition at just fifteen. He asked her to drive with him. The young policeman's eyes made her heart skip, then race. She somehow knew this wasn't an invitation she should check with her mamma. Down a quiet farm trail, she'd been guided into the backseat. He pushed her backward and yanked up her dress. Her underwear tore and her insides too. Afterward, Gino grinned outside the car, pulling up his uniform trousers and zipper, lighting a cigarette. Back at the edge of the showgrounds, he pushed open the passenger door with a nod.

Frances' steering became unsteady, and she remembered weak trotting steps through the showgrounds. She stood amid the mechanical rides, with chaotic lights, laughter and shrieks, holding her first-prize ribbon. Her friends ran to her to play and dance, but she was in a desolate trance.

'Frances. Let's ride the zipper.'

She felt ruined and didn't feel the ribbon fall from her fingers into the mud.

'Oh, Frances, your ribbon!'

Over the next few weeks, she felt trapped in an unspoken arrangement. 'Next weekend, eh', ordered the policeman, as he opened the door. He found excuses to patrol Silkwood every Sunday. They took the only time possible, the hour after Sunday Mass when the adults congregated while the children played unsupervised around the church. She would drift away with heavy feet to the end of the road, where he would be waiting with the passenger door already open.

'Jump in the back. Save us a bit of time, eh.'

She had supposed Gino must like her because of what he did, but he never said. To make her sin worthwhile, she wanted Gino to be the hero he'd first seemed and less the rough villain he'd become. She later prayed for Gino to be sent away to patrol elsewhere when she knew. In the back seat, her long skirt lifted to her shoulders, she was easy pleasure without love. After the realisation, every night, young Frances sobbed in her bed after prayers. Gino stopped calling by in his car after church. Her prayers were answered, but only in part, for she waited, but there was no monthly bleeding. Three months went by. Miserable, she painted in a frenzy. Then, a tearful confession to her shocked mamma. Around that time, there was a blood test, with knowledge passed to her father. Her enraged papa stood before his gun cupboard most nights, cursing the Russo family and their defiling son. *Figlio di puttana.* He took down Frances' paintings, turning his back in her presence.

Frances remembered the family meeting that followed. No cake, just terms. Papa's shotgun on the table. Gino, arms crossed, didn't look at her, yet his baby was growing inside her. The parents organised a quiet wedding away from Silkwood at the Ingham Catholic Church, many miles down the Bruce Highway: a parish with Russo family ties and many old bones in the cemetery.

On the day of the wedding, both families travelled separately. Gino and Frances' dates of birth were entered in the church marriage registry. Frances added four years to her age as instructed, and Gino was listed as slightly younger than his true age. A stooped, thin priest with skin as dry as Old Testament parchment blinked in surprise, for their dates meant they were both nearly twenty. He looked at Frances' baby bump and nodded. The pale, green-eyed priest glanced at Gino scowling in the shadows, and he took Frances' hand. His skin was as soft as Silkwood bark, for his work only involved turning scripture pages, baptising babies, and holding Eucharist.

'No lucky shamrock for you, dear *Cailín*?' he asked.

Frances shook her head.

'Ah, then, let's get ye married, hen.'

If possible, the father's Irish accent sounded as warm as his kind words. In front of the priest, Frances stood in her mamma's plain white dress, arms across her belly. Her grim groom stood to one side in his father's suit. Soon the priest held biblical arms aloft, pronouncing them man and wife. The men marched out, passing around beer bottles. Down the steps of the church Frances walked, head down, trailing her parents. Her school shoes, painted white for the occasion, scrunched through rice, still brittle from a previous wedding. Confetti from weeks earlier faded under the baking sun. Frances imagined the confetti falling like a colourful waterfall from the bride's veil as cameras clicked and the crowd cheered.

On the road home, the couple sat in silence in the backseat of the Russo family car. Gino stared out the window the entire return journey. Frances squirmed, for it was the backseat where she was *undone*, dishonouring her parents. Later, she sat, eyes lowered, through a quiet supper at the Russo farm, where there was a brief toast. She tried to smile but felt crushed, remembering the joyous reception at her cousin's wedding a couple of years earlier. The florists across Far North Queensland had been emptied, and her cousin was covered in flowers. At the altar, Frances just held a hanky. For her cousin, there were incessant toasts and dancing and then, properly, a baby a year later. Around the quiet Russo family table, the grumble of overhead thunder and the accompanying patter of rain was a relief. Her father stared at Gino. His father stared at her. *Rain. Blame. Shame.*

Gino and Frances were provided with the granny flat at the rear of her family home. A small, musty room was nominated for a nursery. If the nursery door was open, Gino shouldered it closed with a slam whenever he stomped by in his police uniform. Inside, Frances winced, pausing from re-painting the walls and dusting her childhood crib.

Frances now sobbed in memory of her parents, wiping away tears to see ahead. After many lost pregnancies, they'd become surprised, proud parents in their forties, with Frances their only child. She was adored like a Madonna, seated between her parents at Sunday lunch, from an infant in a highchair to a teenager in a high-backed chair. Yet after news that Silkwood's most eligible bachelor was to marry, and why, their Sunday family lunches, once rowdy, quietened, invitations unanswered. Across the fields, they heard toasting and feasting. Her father thought of cancelling their *telefono* account because the phone hardly rang. As Frances grew, her parents withered. During Frances' childhood, her parents described the sea breeze blowing into their young faces from the deck of the migration ship when they'd left Palermo, then again at their first sighting of the Australian coastline. Now, because of her, the breeze which blew them from Sicily to Silkwood was out of puff.

Frances wanted the slide carousel to stop, but she visualised Gino speeding from their home, gravel flying, a couple of months after their wedding. On the car seat slid his police uniform, folded inside a large paper bag. He'd been fired when Frances' true age was revealed. Gino cursed and stamped around the house for weeks afterward; the police were meant to look after their own. Every night, when Gino's shouting overpowered her parents' loud television, her thin, sickly father would stare from the kitchen window looking for Frances. *Sto bene*, she would mouth. *I'm okay.* One night he didn't appear, and her mother was at the window, crying. They carried her papa to bed.

When her papa died, Gino sat in her father's favourite chair, feet dangling, drinking all day, cursing at the rising cane. 'Fuck, everything gets plump in fertile Silkwood.'

Later, he grudgingly helped with farm work when Frances was too heavily pregnant to climb into the tractor. Her heartbroken mamma who only wanted to lie by her husband again since his funeral, died in the final month of Frances' pregnancy.

Turning from the highway into Silkwood, Frances recalled their first wedding anniversary. Gino had painted over her family name on the letterbox. In large white letters, he'd painted R-U-S-S-O. She'd stood crying with baby Bianca in her arms as her family name was covered, letter by letter. Frances' parents rested in the family mausoleum, now painted away.

Frances parked by the same letterbox, staring at Gino's painted lettering. She hadn't forgotten nor forgiven.

'Mamma and Papa, I'm not much of a Christian,' she whispered.

Forgiveness of Darcy also seemed a long way off, if ever. She'd joked that Darcy was under Silkwood's spell. But really, he wasn't spellbound. He'd visited the Garden of Eden, devouring unblemished Isabella as forbidden fruit, the serpent devil flickering a forked tongue over the virgin's soft skin in lust. In nonna mode, she'd invited him to take an interest in her daughter. He had, but not the right one. Frances hung her head. *Stupido.*

Frances recalled her hesitancy to talk with Isabella more directly about sexual relationships before the debutante ball. She approached her daughter after family photos when Carlo had stepped away. 'Isabella, you look so beautiful. You will dance tonight. Carlo may expect… he may ask you to—'

'Yes, Mamma?'

Dressed in virginal white, Isabella radiated cherubic purity.

'Oh, never mind, Angel.'

At the time, she felt it wasn't right to put obscene notions into her daughter's mind. The talk could wait. For Frances, this was a further lesson in motherhood. When you think it might be time to talk, the time was long ago. After this afternoon, she knew her daughter better. But that didn't make it better.

'Mamma, I've let you down again,' Frances cried. 'I'm a hopeless mother. So much for a proper wedding to honour you, when I didn't.' She hung her head.

Frances looked up. Gino sat deep in his shed, grinning as he read a men's magazine in the shadows. Her eyes narrowed. She bore their daughters and all household and parenting responsibility, also providing an income during the year. Most mornings, just after dawn, she toured the farm in their truck, inspecting the health of the rising cane stalks, while Gino polished rifle barrels after eating his prepared breakfast. Her husband tilted the magazine sideways, two pages unfolding. Frances' body shook. Today was their wedding anniversary. No card. No flowers. Just like their wedding. Gino threw a bone, a gift, to the farm hound. This morning, her wedding anniversary began with the crunch of Gino butchering a feral pig with an axe outside their bedroom window. Beside her, the baked paint on their letterbox was flaking and lifting. As paint curled, letter by letter, she began to see more of her family name and less of his. She drove in. Gino didn't look up. The dog licked inside the shank. Frances shuddered, braked, and felt something deep inside her shift, quite possibly her marrow.

22

IN the *Times* office, Matt rolled around on his office chair. Thinking about his suspicions of Bianca's secret romance with the cinema manager, Matt wondered why discretion was needed. Bianca's furtive romance wouldn't be as scandalous as his. Perhaps, it was because the cinema manager wasn't local or Italian. He started to frame another headline; another southern interloper dealt with.

Not for the first time, he glanced sideways at Bianca, remembering lustrous black hair fanned under the umbrella. Rain had shrouded the cinema, and he wondered whether his observation was mistaken. Matt tapped a pen on his desk. Something was amiss.

Cheers distracted him. It was mid-week, and his team had again performed their miracle. From across town and beyond, they'd filed articles to meet the immovable print deadline and his mother's strict revenue targets. His staff chatted and laughed. The tension of the deadline, *history*. The next deadline too far away to worry about. The team began to pack up, and as one left, it was a signal for a stampede to the pub. Matt smiled, for it was the same in every newsroom. The first drop became a trickle, then a torrent. He smiled at his analogy in this forever rainy town.

From his office, he heard the scrape of chairs and hurried footsteps.

Matt called out, 'Don't forget the staff meeting tomorrow at nine o'clock. It's time to start planning the Christmas bumper edition.'

'Yeah, whatever, boss,' they all mocked in unison.

Matt laughed. They may have well said, 'Fuck off, Flint.'

He went to the side door and the small alcove, which was usually empty apart from deliveries. It was also a space Maria passed through around dawn on her personal newspaper round. But the alcove wasn't empty, for Bianca was kissing his star journalist, Peter.

Matt retreated. His mental dossier imagined Bianca as receptive to attention but not the town bike. *Should he warn Peter about the cinema manager?* As a journalist, he knew there was power in what you wrote and didn't write. He could warn Peter about Bianca's other boyfriend, or not. Matt could let life take its course, just like Mandy's retreat into jazz. He heard a trumpet toot.

~

The following Saturday afternoon, Darcy jumped at the light knock on the side door of the cinema. *Knock. Knock.* He waited, for this could be another knock from Frances.

He felt his face. Students had stared at him all week and he wanted to wear sunglasses. Bruno asked him if he needed protection. The welt across his cheek was now less swollen, and he could almost chew without pain. Only one tooth felt loose. His black eye and the burst capillaries had faded to a mild malarial yellow.

'Darcy? Darcy, are you there?'

Darcy felt relief at her soft voice but then nervy trepidation as he opened the door. Isabella touched his face. 'Are you okay?'

'Oh yes, just a bit clumsy at home.'

'Were you hit? Has Carlo found out?'

He turned away and called over his shoulder. 'Don't worry. How are things at home?'

'Fine, but Mamma seems tense. She keeps ironing my best dress for my delayed school graduation. Did I tell you about last year when the cyclone blew most of the town away? There was nowhere to hold the graduation, and everyone was cleaning up, so our ceremony is going to be after this year's seniors.'

Darcy strode ahead, hearing that Frances was tense.

Tense? Yep, he knew tense. He felt dread with every heavy step to school. He skulked away from school when he spied the Russo sedan with his good eye, edging away. At night, he cried, thinking of his playful rehearsal as Frances with Isabella. He'd imagined himself as a fine character as Isabella introduced the idea of them dating. Instead of a mother's hug, he could expect vitriol and violence if he didn't call it off.

Isabella met him at the projection room steps. He wanted to guide her back to the side door and wave from a safe distance. But he took her hand and ascended the stairs, listening for screeching brakes. Afterward, on the projection room floor, they lay shoulder to shoulder. Darcy lay still, fear overtaking brief pleasure. Beside him, Isabella rolled towards him. Frances' discovery needed to be heeded as a warning shot over his shoulder. It was time for a break, like a film intermission, at least until after Isabella's re-admission into university. Then contrition, kneeling before Frances, as if in a confessional.

'Darcy let's take another trip,' Isabella suggested.

Darcy lay frozen. With Isabella beside him, he hoped Frances might accept their relationship as the shock wore off. Neither Gino nor Carlo had pulled up beside him, window lowered, in a dark street on his walk home from school.

'C'mon, Darcy. Let's have a little trial as a normal couple, like our trip to Etty Bay.'

Darcy ground his teeth. They needed to cool it.

'Darcy, why are you so quiet? What about a day trip to Dunk Island?' Darcy felt the nudge of her naked hip on his. 'An adventure!'

Isabella's breast pressed into his chest. 'Darcy? I thought you'd be keen. C'mon you know what to say.'

'Sure. What about tomorrow?'

~

'Darcy, Aunt Betty here. Sorry to ring with bad news.'

Standing in Sid's kitchen early Sunday morning, Darcy dropped his packed bag. 'What bad news? Dad?'

'Sorry, yes. He died a few days ago. A major stroke at the RSL Club. Died within seconds.'

Darcy gripped the kitchen bench, fumbling the phone. 'No, no, not Dad.'

'Sorry, I've have been trying to reach you all week, but the number kept ringing out. Have you moved? I contacted the school and spoke to your principal. He said you were away, touring remote schools as you were hoping for a transfer north. He said you were out of reach, but he'd pass along the sad news.

'That's not—'

'Huh? Anyway, Darcy, then he called me back, saying there was bad weather up north, you were stranded and couldn't make the funeral, but that we should go ahead with the service. I rang every school up that way. I'm so sorry I couldn't reach you. We buried your father yesterday.'

They fell silent.

'It comforts me, Darcy, that you have good people to lean on, like your principal.'

'No—'

'Eliza passes on her sympathy. She says you've got a girlfriend. Isabella? I hope she and her family can comfort you, because, sadly, we are so far away.'

Darcy held the phone away from his ear, trembling.

'Darcy, are you okay?'

'I'll never be okay. Will you tell me about my mother now?'

Darcy hung up after a few more minutes.

'PIERCE!' he yelled, frightening the birds outside the window into flight. Darcy thought of Sid's rifle and stomped to the truck. He reached under the seat. Bulky slugs lay in twin chambers. Back upstairs, with the gun on his lap, he stared misty-eyed at Simone's family photos. He lent in to study a photo of Simone in school uniform holding her graduation certificate, flanked by her beaming parents. In a week, Isabella and her parents would form the same tableau, after a year's delay. Frances wouldn't want him in the photo, or any photo, ever. Darcy looked back at a second graduation photo. Principal Pierce smiled, shaking hands with Simone. Breathing heavily, Darcy put the barrel of the gun over Pierce's forehead. Tugging on his father's army cap, he looked away from the photos, realising he had no one, other than Isabella, at least for another day. Bag over his shoulder, gun in hand, he marched to his car. Isabella would be waiting, so he returned the gun to Sid's truck.

Darcy sped through Silkwood, fearing Frances patrolling about in the Russo family sedan as if it were an army tank. He wished Frances might take him in her motherly arms, cradle him, as he sobbed about his loss and Pierce's wickedness. Now, he was scorned. Today's trip would entrench his damnation if she found out. Darcy bumped along the cane trail to their meeting place. Isabella, smiling, ran to his car. Light shone on her face. He leaned into her hug. On the straight of Silkwood's main street, he raced, head low, past the church, feeling like a raiding pirate extracting treasure.

With her head on his lap, Darcy's eyes darted about.

'You're very quiet, Darcy. Are you okay?'

'Just thinking about a phone call I took this morning from my aunt. Bad—'

Isabella interrupted. 'You're going to love Dunk Island.'

Darcy frowned, staring ahead as he drove through thick roadside jungle in silence towards the coastline. Beside him, Isabella sung along to *Madonna* songs from her cassette collection.

At Mission Beach, Dunk Island sat off the coast like a huge, rounded turtle surrounded by a curtain of glistening water. Ferry staff walked along the foreshore, selling tickets and counting passengers. Isabella merged with other queuing travellers on the pier beside the gently rocking ferry. Darcy waited alone on the shore until it was departure time and passengers hurried onboard at the honk of the ferry's horn. Darcy took his ticket, spotting an empty row of seats at the stern. He pulled his father's army cap down low, his eyes misting. Across the rolling journey from the bay, he gazed into the water, thinking of his father. His dad was deeply flawed but had stuck with him. Military loyalty, maybe a form of love.

Faster, smaller boats crossed their bow, creating a foamy trail, and Darcy hung onto his seat as their craft rocked through their wake. Ahead, he could see Isabella's hair whipping and flying with the wind. A couple of boys stared at her, nudging each other.

After they crossed the bay, individual palm trees emerged from the green mass like stick figures in greeting. Coconuts and palm fronds sat lumpen on the sandy beach. The roofline of the island resort peaked above the trees. At the island pier, they docked with a bump.

'Last ferry at four p.m. sharp,' instructed the skipper.

'Welcome, folks, to Dunk Island,' cried a resort attendant from the beach. 'Air-conditioned café and gift store right this way.'

Darcy stole away along the beach. Back from the main group, Isabella waited and looked about. Darcy waved from under a large palm tree at the far end of the beach. After a few minutes, they walked hand-in-hand on a trail in the forest, and into a small clearing where a large tree had fallen. Misty rays of light reached from above. Tall trees surrounded them, decorated with cascading, coiling vines like ropes from heaven. Isabella gasped and twirled with her arms lifted like a ballerina. Darcy came to her, and they kissed. He rolled out his towel and lowered her onto the leafy floor. Two electric blue Ulysses butterflies circled and curled above in a love parade.

'Isabella and Darcy's butterfly lovers' cavern,' she whispered a few minutes later. 'This is the real gift store.' She laughed.

Small leaves fell slowly, silently. Tiny web tresses fell on their faces from invisible weavers high in the trees. Darcy blinked to clear his eyes, the forest filling a void in its timeless routine to replenish. Both naked, he felt like Adam with Eve in Eden at the dawn of time. Isabella clung to him, yet he felt alone, unsure whether he and Isabella were meant to fill a void or were a void themselves. She hadn't asked what was troubling him, and he hadn't confided. He found his father's army cap and pulled it over his eyes.

Later, from a lookout, they viewed other small islands resembling dark brooding jewels in a crown. Below, boats buzzed over the water. Darcy thought he recognised one of the boats but dropped the notion.

Isabella leaned in and said, 'You know these are called the Family Islands?'

'Really?' Darcy replied, recalling his last conversation with one of his few family members.

Isabella pointed to two islands. 'There's Darcy and Isabella. You're in town, and there is lonely Isabella in Silkwood. Look! There's Mamma and Papa.' She pointed to a smaller island further away. 'There's Bianca. How unusual, she is on her own!'

Darcy stared ahead in silence as Isabella laughed.

Isabella nudged Darcy. 'C'mon, I thought that was funny.'

They followed a creek down the hill, stepping over smooth rocks that formed a pool above the beach. The creek line provided the only corridor of light as large trees crowded in, shoulder to shoulder. Later, they held hands and splashed around rocky coves and along narrow beaches, following the island's curve back to the resort and the return ferry. After meeting the trail close to the beach, Darcy stopped. 'Wait. I can hear a voice.'

Ahead, a boat hull swayed in the lapping shallows. The letter 'S' on the hull became visible, then an 'A'. He heard a man swear. Darcy pulled at a branch. A man leaned over an outboard motor. The boat shuffled, revealing her name: *Salsa*. The man turned. Reflective gold sunglasses flickered. Darcy felt twin spikes of hatred and fear.

Pierce slammed his fist on the top of the motor. 'Fuck! This engine is new.'

Darcy lowered the branch and edged back to Isabella, explaining the quandary.

'Oh no. *So, gammon*,' she whispered.

'Let's just wait and see. Hopefully, he starts the engine and heads away.'

They peered through parted branches. Rich worked the engine with a rope, then tried the switch in the skipper's console. *Salsa* rolled, subdued in the swell. A horn from the ferry sounded. Rich looked up. Cursing, he anchored the boat and waded to the beach.

Darcy whispered, 'We can't return together. You go. I will get the first boat back tomorrow morning.'

Isabella sat down. 'No. I will stay with you.'

The ferry horn honked again.

Darcy's welt burned. Before he took a bullet, he could expect a matching pair of bruised eyes if Isabella was missing overnight. He lifted Isabella, saying, 'Please. It's our best option. Otherwise, there will be police greeting the boat tomorrow, along with your parents.'

'Okay, okay.'

'Please avoid Mr Pierce,' he instructed. Darcy wanted to add: *if you do talk with him, slap him as hard as your mother can.*

Isabella grabbed belongings, including their clothes and towels which had been shoved in each other's bags throughout the day.

Isabella held Darcy with moist eyes. 'I'll find a way to get home. Don't worry.' She kissed Darcy on the cheek and ran under the tree line to the ferry.

Darcy watched Isabella, his Eve, run from their Eden. The ferry honked an urgent, insistent horn. Young men lifted from dozing under the trees and ran to the pier. Boarding the ferry, one of the men seemed to appraise her, and Isabella didn't look back in Darcy's direction.

<h1 style="text-align:center">23</h1>

WHEN the ferry moored at Mission Beach with a thump, Isabella waited behind two tall men, ready to disembark. Mr Pierce let ladies leave in front of and around him, then seemed to admire them. The crowd of passengers thinned out, heading to parked cars. Isabella edged behind her former principal. A couple of female tourists she'd befriended on the boat were many metres ahead, almost off the pier. On board, they'd confirmed their help.

'You need a lift to the highway? No worries. Where?'

'Silkwood.'

'*Huh?* Never heard of it.'

As Mr Pierce sauntered, she fell a long way behind. The tourists, many metres away, turned around, perhaps looking for her, then walked on. With a smile she spied the taxi rank. A taxi waited, as if for her, with its light on. *Phew.* Then a couple opened the back door, and the taxi joined many other departing cars.

The tourists she befriended paused at their car. Looking back again, the driver shrugged, and Isabella soon heard crunching gravel under the tyres. A headache pulsed.

A young man she'd briefly spoken with on the ferry stood at her side. 'You said your boyfriend was picking you up. Lucky guy, eh. Where is he?' He looked at the near empty car park and clinked car keys.

The ferry skipper walked past and then stopped near her. Holding up a clipboard, he called, 'Hey, does anyone know about a missing male passenger? A bloke bought a same day return ticket but didn't board. Does anyone know who this might be?'

A few remaining people stopped and talked among themselves.

She froze when Mr Pierce turned around, and drew her hat down lower, heart racing. The skipper crouched to look under her hat.

'Miss, are you on your own? Did you travel with a male companion?'

'No,' she whispered, returning to shuffle behind Mr Pierce.

Isabella glanced at the young man nearby who stared at her, his car keys glinting in the sun. *Perhaps she could trust him?* Entering a stranger's car would be breaking another of her mamma's rules. But she had dishonoured many of her mamma's commandments, and she had to get home before dark.

'Hey, aren't you from Silkwood?' The man asked. 'Wow, haven't you grown up.'

She paused from answering, figuring what he might want in exchange for a ride.

'Yeah, I'm sure, you're the younger of the Russo daughters.'

At the sound of her surname, Mr Pierce turned around. She felt her hat being lifted.

'Isabella?'

'Oh, hello, Mr Pierce,' she mumbled.

The man walked away, looking from Isabella to the principal.

Rich asked, 'How about that missing passenger?' He looked back towards the island. 'Are you on your own?'

She felt heat around her neck. 'I was with friends. They must have left.'

She was guided to his car. After unhitching his boat trailer, Mr Pierce took a long loop of the carpark. There was one remaining car, which Mr Pierce slowed to study.

On the return drive, she murmured short responses to his questions, glancing at his speedometer. *Come on. Come on.* As he asked questions, and she mumbled replies, Isabella wondered what might have happened if she accepted the man's offer. He probably would have pulled over into a cane track, saying that one good turn deserves another. Now, her whistling former principal was looking sideways at her with a grin, and she felt as imperilled as if the man drove further into the cane fields and turned off the engine. Her heart thumped in fear, understanding her mother's commandments: guidance and care. The adult world was full of snakes and venom. The principal's whistling seemed to become shrill, adding to her headache.

As they passed the Silkwood Hotel, Mr Pierce asked, 'Do you know anything about the missing male passenger?'

She couldn't find words to reply and blushed, clutching her bag for comfort. The zip shifted. After a minute, she stammered, 'Just right here, Mr Pierce. My house is straight ahead, so there is no need to drop me off at the door. Thanks.'

Her principal looked at her opened bag. Darcy's army cap peaked out and Isabella felt more heat on her face and neck.

'Ouch, Isabella. That's a nasty case of sunburn.'

~

On Dunk Island, the late afternoon glow faded. Soon after, stars illuminated the sand. The sea lifted and rolled under a silver starlight coat. Offshore, *Salsa*'s hips swayed in the swell.

Darcy stared towards the mainland, a blank backdrop, like a dark cinema screen. At the town cinema, there would be no roaring lion tonight. There would be no movie, applause, or credits, just the static of Dunk Island's buzzing insects reaching the mainland. *He's here.* Darcy imagined a replacement projectionist in the booth. As a cassowary, Frances sniffed his offensive odour, looking for her chick, kicking the sofa, ripping the cushions, and tipping over the projector. With a peck, she hit the button, curtains closing across the screen with a slap. From the cinema microphone, 'That's all folks, just a final word from our sponsors.' *'Sexcrime'* by *The Eurythmics* boomed from the speakers. He felt a headache pulse. Simone would hear the cinema hadn't opened, no beckoning popcorn scent, frustrated patrons banging on the door. She'd take more interest, reflecting on her teenage years, wondering what Darcy was getting up to at the cinema and trying to get away with. The headache gripped him like a migraine, for Simone worked at the newspaper where the reportage was ruthless.

Through the night, he sifted sand between his toes, trying to sort out his faults from Pierce's actions. They were locked in a cat-and-mouse tussle. Rough tabby Pierce toyed with timid, mousy Darcy. With a paw swipe, Darcy scurried, evading his claws. He sighed in frustration. Over on the mainland, he hoped Isabella lay safe within her bedroom chapel, not as cheese mounted on Pierce's mousetrap. Darcy grumbled. *Was he even a mouse?* He was more like a ball of wool, for even a mouse didn't play along, thinking life was a game like a child's cartoon.

A distant light glowed from the resort bar. He heard laughter and clinking glasses and remembered walking across a park to the Toowoomba RSL Club as a boy, frost scrunching under his feet. The manager had called their home. Police were at the club door, breaking up a fight, and he'd helped his father home. Blood poured from his father's lip, who slurred about a run-in with the navy guys.

'The sailors said the army let everyone down in Vietnam,' he explained. 'While we were in the jungle getting our arses shot off, they were safely firing their cannons offshore sipping the captain's sherry.' His father had gripped his arm. 'I tell you, son, the best boat is a sunk boat. Remember that.'

Darcy wiped a tear, imagining his father's name on the club service honours board at the RSL. There would be a freshly painted gold cross besides his name. *Deceased.* A light wind brushed the shore. *Salsa* nodded her dolphin nose. Darcy took off his shirt, entered the water and waded to *Salsa*, dancing in the swell. He mounted the stern from a rear step by the failed motor and stepped on.

'C'mon, *Salsa*, another jig.'

Darcy tried the ignition, just in case. The switch only clicked, and the engine remained mute, so he tugged at the anchor rope. Soon, a rising chain sawed along Salsa's nose, then a shiny crucifix-looking anchor glinted. The breeze shifted, and they floated away from the shore. The resort bar light eventually became a tiny winking star.

Darcy looked over the side of the boat into the inky water, wondering what might be below. Pierce wasn't the only creature with teeth. Darcy heard a noise. Flap. Flap. He kicked the esky – another strong flap. Yep, the fish were large around here. Like everything else. Cassowaries. Crocodiles. The sugar mills. Leo's thirst. The cruelty of his principal.

Darcy knelt, feeling along the bottom of the boat. After he unscrewed the plug in the base of the hull – *Sorry, girl* – water began to fill the vessel and the esky soon lifted and floated. Above the lapping water in the console, Pierce's mobster sunglasses glinted in the starlight. Darcy buttoned them inside his shirt pocket. The spare fuel tank floated and bumped by. Gripping a life vest, Darcy tapped *Salsa*'s stern, *Bye, girl*, and rolled over the side, swimming back to the shore. A few minutes later, Darcy gripped coarse coral and sand under his feet. On the beach, he heard a loud gurgle and swivelled around. *Salsa*'s raised bow, like a salute, gave a final wave and slid below. Darcy stood and returned the salute.

'I remember, Dad. Rest in peace, digger.'

24

EARLY Sunday evening, Matt sat in his office, swivelling in his office chair. Nursing a large, neat rum, he admired his framed front pages. One of his favourites was the stooped, corrupt bookie, Rob Dodds, in a loose, borrowed suit being led into court. Matt had taken the photo, and the article led with his headline: 'Short Odds for Robber Dodds'. The newspaper edition had sold out and there were skirmishes in the Rockhampton cafes whenever an idle paper was left on a table. When the librarian had asked for replacements for stolen copies, the editor patted Matt's back and mentioned a raise. Matt had shrugged off the gesture. To Matt, being a journalist had never been about money. Journalism was a high calling, in his view, and tonight he raised his rum with a shaky hand. Rum sloshed onto his already stained beige slacks. *High calling? Oh yeah*, he slurred, lowering his rum, glancing at his safe. He was due again at the Pierce household, but not for the secret knock on the door, opened with a gust of perfumed air.

In journalism terms, he'd declined, to his way of thinking, from the venerated front-page crusader to the office administrator accepting copy for classified ads. In the Rockhampton newspaper office, the female teenage trainee blushed and stammered on the phone, receiving advertisement copy for sexual services. Matt would help, taking calls, confirming copy. Weary, husky female voices would repeat the phone number, along with described services and prowess. *Everything, any time*. Matt's bushy eyebrows arched with intrigue, but he was a guy that would never pay for it. Matt agreed with his mates at the pub, chugging beers. *Nah, it would never get to that*. But he'd taken up the editor's offer of a raise.

'From the Principal's Desk' article lay on his desk. Matt stared at the photo of Pierce and took another gulp. Pierce seemed to wink. Setting aside his empty glass, Matt knelt low, opening his safe. As he retrieved the notes, Matt reasoned he was just in a temporary snare from a hustler. *Not paying for it.* Just a custom tariff for handled goods. Export tax from the marital bed. Ticket for entry. Matt sighed. *He knew.* The eyes in his mounted newspaper pictures seemed to look away in dismay as he rolled the notes inside a spare newspaper. By his ear, a mosquito sang. *Pimped.* Matt stopped rolling the newspaper, wondering whether he should tell Maria, restoring her dignity. She said, *soon, Matt soon,* and if he ceased the payments and told her, the soon might become now. Or it might become never again.

During the week, he'd stared into Maria's light-brown eyes, lit with dawn's soft glow. With rain on the roof, he wanted to stay in bed all day. After she'd left, tip toeing down the stairs, he hummed a 70's tune that had played yesterday on the staff radio in the kitchen: '*Sugar Baby Love*'. It was a hit around ten years earlier when he'd cruised around Rockhampton in his Chrysler Valiant. Then, *valiant* had been a motto for his patchy love life. In his glovebox, a section of the classified ads was folded into a map. He and Maria had been together for a few months, but he often wondered why she risked herself for him; even the most unhappy of the town women had passed him over like rotten fruit at the supermarket. She was valiant too, he supposed.

In bed, he'd nibbled on her ear and whispered, 'Maria, my sweet bella, I know you're not in this for my good looks. I'm not the best deal going in this town.'

With another nibble she squealed and kissed his cheek. 'Oh, Matt, my man of words. You're a package,' she'd said.

'My bella, is that a charitable way of saying I'm ugly, but I have other virtues?'

'You're a very caring package. Looks aren't everything. I've been fooled before.'

'Well, don't let my good looks fool you.'

Matt smiled now, hearing Maria's laugh — *his bella* — as if she was in his office tonight while he finished folding the dollar bills inside the newspaper. He sighed, realising he'd *always paid for it.*

The loud ring of his telephone shifted his focus. Sunday night calls were infrequent, but this was always a newsroom. He grabbed the receiver. '*Town Times*'.

'Matthew, it's your mother speaking.'

Matt grinned. His mother was from a generation who spoke formally on the telephone. He settled back in his chair, readying for his mother's meandering news round of Rockhampton gossip, hopefully without updates about Mandy and the local jazz scene.

'I have looked over our accounts. Revenue is slipping.'

Matt rocked forward in his seat. He provided his rehearsed managerial explanation.

'Temporary discounts in a tight market? What a load of shit!'

Matt recoiled. 'Mother, please. I'm on the ground here. That's how things are.'

'Well, I will be on the ground soon enough too. I will be seeing these so-called businesses who are holding out.'

'Mother!'

'I'll be wearing boots. There will be sore arses when I'm through!'

So much for her formal telephone style, thought Matt.

'You're getting worked over. Can't you see? See you tomorrow.'

'Stay where you are, Mother. Give me a little time to tackle this.'

Matt looked at his framed newspaper articles, a vanity when he believed he'd answered the *high calling* of professional journalism. Matt looked at the rolled newspaper, shaken.

His mother yelled, 'Don't be a softie. Pull on your boots. *Kick arse!*'

~

Rich Pierce sat in his study as the window curtain ruffled from the fan. Instead, he wanted to fan Matt's cash across his table. He always enjoyed hearing Matt's steps by his study window, then the light plop of a newspaper delivery, with a gruff, 'Here, prick,' or even 'fucker' when the delivery man was more spirited. Rich would rub his hands together, striding by his unfaithful wife, who serviced Matt like a client.

'For services rendered,' he would mouth to Maria's back.

Rich looked at his watch. He was due at the cinema. Tonight, it seemed necessary to receive Matt's payment instead of waiting for delivery. Rich grumbled. This extended the day's inconvenience as he thought of *Salsa* pulling at her anchor in the shallows. Walking to town, he pondered. *What's your game, Flint?* He doubted Flint had called it off with his wife. In the early evening, Maria hummed as she drafted her latest newspaper column. It was also improbable that an unfortunate-looking mutt like Matt had found another woman. Dogs barked as he passed by, one after another, like a pianist's finger running along a keyboard. Closer to the main street, another dog snapped at a gate. He stopped, bent down, and threw a rock at the dog.

'Pretend it's a kitten.'

A berserk series of snarls erupted, and other town dogs joined the hysteria. Rich laughed, hoping Matt would hear the herald of barking dogs and fearfully retrieve his kitty from the office safe.

At the office, Rich knocked on the door. The outline of lifeless desks and chairs filled the interior like a Pompeii exhibition. He heard the click of a side door. Matt stood in the narrow alley beside an opened doorway.

'Hi, Matt.'

'Hi, Rich.'

Both men stared at each other for a few moments.

'Matt, this is rather nice catching up in person on a Sunday night. But it's also a little inconvenient.' He paused. 'I should be at home with my wife. Sunday night in bed with Maria has always been a divine way to end the weekend.'

Matt frowned. Rich grinned.

'Matt, I don't know whether my wife is tiring of you, but you've fired up her sexual appetite. She might be a vet, but in bed, she's the real animal.'

Rich felt Matt's glare.

'Matt, you're sullen. Have you anything to say?'

'Yeah. One day, you'll be on the front page. It won't be good news.'

'Nice one, mummy's boy. With my next payment, which I will receive in a minute, I will buy you a new sign for your office door. "Matt Flint. Pussy Hustler in Chief. Married Pussy Preferred." Now, go to your safe. Otherwise.'

'Otherwise?' asked Matt.

'Otherwise, no more pussy for the town's ugliest man.'

Rich noticed Matt reach inside. He held something that looked like a thick broom handle.

~

The police patrol car ambled in another loop around town. For the two policemen, there was just the 'top pub' and the 'bottom pub' to monitor. But the regulars were winding down, zapped by Friday-night fervour and Saturday-night fever. The younger policeman drove, as the older policeman took his privilege of being driven around. On this humid night, he was happy to complete their shift in the air-conditioned car. Pulling at his collar, he asked, 'Can you crank up the air?'

A couple of bare-footed Aboriginal men sat under a dark shop awning, and the police car stopped. The policemen looked at their passive faces. They were *regulars* in their own way but weren't trouble.

'Should we haul them in to show we're working?' asked the younger policeman.

'Nah, leave them. For now.'

The two policemen agreed to head back to the station. It was a night for television and crosswords. Parked outside the cinema, they heard an argument up the street. The noise seemed to be coming from the newspaper office. The policemen discussed whether they should attend the scene or ignore the noise. If the police didn't see anything, there was nothing to police.

'Let the locals sort out their problems,' the older policeman instructed. 'Too many guns in these country towns.'

A call came in over their radio. The younger policeman picked up the microphone on the car dashboard and untangled the thickly curled connecting cable.

'Yep, receiving, go ahead.'

The men listened to the brief. The station had received a complaint about the cinema: financial irregularities.

'We are outside the cinema now,' the younger policeman replied. 'The place looks closed, but we can see if the young bloke you're after is here.'

~

Rich walked from the side of the *Times* office to the main street, shaking his head at Matt's impertinence. Matt had embarrassed himself, yelling and shaking a rifle about as if he knew one end from the other. Rich turned down the street towards the cinema, his mood lifting, for Darcy was a soft touch. His eyes bulged. A police car was parked in front of the cinema, and a police officer was shining a torch into the inky interior. *What?* Rich withdrew under a dark awning, reflecting on a weird day. Perhaps the cinema hadn't opened at all. The probabilities were adding up. Rich jogged home with more barking dogs as an escort.

A few minutes later, Rich stood between the television and the sofa. Maria moved her head to look around him. Rich shuffled to block her view, and Maria shifted along the sofa to gain a fresh vantage of the telly. Rich followed, then swivelled, snapping off the television switch. He stood over his wife. 'Now, do I have your attention?' He glared, the principal waiting for obedience.

Rich wasn't bothered that Maria probably hated him; he had her family's money. Their joint bank account was near empty, but his private account was full. Maria was just another landed fish, scaled, filleted, and consumed. Years earlier, he'd stopped in the main street of a small Queensland town where he worked, listening to local chatter. Feigning interest in country bumpkin menswear in a store window display, he tuned in. *Family wealth. Filipino maids. Single daughter. Inheritance. Vet. New Holden Statesman.*

A sales assistant had walked outside. 'Can I help you?'

'I'm going to help myself,' he'd mocked and walked away.

At the sight of the shiny Holden Statesman in the vet's car park he'd winked at his reflection in the side window as he drove by. On the outskirts of town, Rich approached the dog pound, holding his nose. He selected a dog with mournful, pleading eyes, hauling the yelping hound to the car by its collar.

'Hope he settles in well,' called the despatcher.

He'd tied up the abandoned pet to his rear bumper bar, then reversed in a figure of eight pattern on a quiet road. On hearing a crunch and howl, Rich had dragged the injured hound into the front seat and raced to the vet.

The dog whimpered at every bump in the road.

'Fuck teachers' pay,' he'd replied.

Bounding into the vet's clinic, he'd called for help. Maria had appeared. Rich saw beautiful wealth, not beauty. On the surgery bench, they'd patted fur, hands glancing, as the dog panted.

'You're so caring, picking up an injured dog,' she'd murmured, patting the crumpled mutt. 'Most people wouldn't bother.'

Rich had thought she might cry.

'I look after enough animals at school, why not another?' he'd joked. 'Can I come by tomorrow?'

Maria had blushed and nodded. From a nearby room, Rich had heard a male yell and a door slam.

In their lounge room, Rich still stood over his wife. At the Catholic altar with Maria, he'd been poor. Now, he was rich. Today, he felt like a priest standing before his Catholic wife, readying with damnation. To date, Matt had paid hundreds for the husband's pimping consent. *Wouldn't it be wonderful to tell her that?*

~

Maria studied her husband's glare. She knew her husband was ruthless. Somehow, he hadn't discovered her affair, but he easily could. She looked at him, and his brow looked tight with tension. *He probably did know.* Of course. He'd waited for a time that best suited him to punish. She clenched her hands into fists, thinking of his hypocrisy. The bible warned about false idols. Most Sundays at church, she felt the stares of the town women. She just caught their glances as they looked away. It was the same as other towns. *They knew about his other women.* She thought of the fired maid, Delores. *Of course.* Maria buried her humiliation deeper. She felt like the broken dog in her clinic, touching her cross with trembling fingers.

'Sorry, Richard,' she replied. 'You have my full attention.'

Looking at Maria, Rich weighed up his options. He still wanted Matt's payment and a hold over his publicity machine. If he accepted Matt's defiance, the deal would be over. Matt wanted the payments to be over, not the relationship. Rich smiled; a plan was firming.

'Maria, my dear, I'm so sorry to interrupt your program. Can I sit beside you?' Rich took his wife's hand for the first time that year. 'From tomorrow, the end-of-year hell is going to start. Reports to be signed. An additional Year 12 graduation after the cyclone last year. Awards nights. Timetabling for next year. Pack a couple of cases, and I'll put you on the overnight train to your family home.'

'What? No.' Maria withdrew her hand.

'Maria, you've always said you'd like to spend time with your mother for her birthday. Isn't that Tuesday? Well, now is the year.'

'No, it's too soon.'

'Why? You're just waiting out the year.'

Rich pulled his wife up from the sofa.

'But my column—'

'Finish it on the train and post it. I'll pop by to see Matt and explain.' He saw his wife stiffen. Rich went to her bedroom, reached high into the wardrobe, and pulled down two suitcases. He called out, 'I'll be back in ten minutes to take you to the station.'

Rich walked through his garage to a storage room, waiting for Maria to pack. The door was open for ventilation. Rich kicked away hopping cane toads, then shoved a man lying on a mattress on the floor. A small fan whirred on a crate beside the bed, creating a strained melody with the man's snores.

Rich kicked the man. 'Get up. Get up.'

The man rolled over, unwilling to rouse, but with another kick, he sat up, blinking, croakily asking, 'Hell. What's going on?'

Rich knelt by the bed, giving instructions and a roll of paper bound with an elastic band. 'No more payments after tonight. Our deal is done, if you make this delivery.'

Leo rose from the floor.

25

MISTY rain created foggy saintly halos around the streetlights. Leo's head was foggy, too, from the afternoon drinking. Asleep just minutes ago, he meandered like a dazed sleepwalker up the town's main hill. His blurry vision suited him, as he didn't want to focus on his mission. Pierce's small package pressed uncomfortably against his hip. Rousing a little, Leo replayed Pierce's promise: *no more payments*. With full pay restored, he could leave town for the long summer break with a repaired, insured, and registered car, loans repaid too. With money in his wallet, he could drift around as he pleased. Better still, he could find Penny, Cindy's lost sister, his former girlfriend.

Leo wandered into darker streets, close to his destination. He willed focus, needing to deliver Pierce's 'gift' to the right place so he could change the course of his life. He rubbed his temples, remembering.

'I'm trying to change the course of my life,' pretty Penny once said to him. They'd met at the school gates late one afternoon when he was a graduate teacher. Leo noticed her long legs and closely cropped, blonde punk hairstyle.

'Are you lost?' he'd asked.

'No.' She'd laughed. 'Not lost. This is the same school I left in a hurry, as a teenager.'

Leo had walked with Penny towards a classroom where other adults gathered for night classes to complete their broken education.

She whispered, 'I'm not lost here. I'm more lost in my life.'

At the classroom door, Penny hesitated at Leo's suggestion of a date. 'You seem nice, but I have some dark history I'm trying to get away from,' she said.

'Ah, okay, but are you single?'

'Technically single.'

Leo stood, swaying at a dark corner. 'Technically single, eh,' he slurred.

He would frequently stay late at school to see her and ask again for a date.

'Okay, okay, you are persistent,' she eventually replied. 'We can meet at my house, but no one must know.'

She shared a small house with Cindy.

Leo and Penny met every afternoon before night school. Over a month, he fell in love at her place on a quiet town street. But it wasn't so quiet one afternoon as a spluttering motorbike pulled into the driveway. The rider was masked, wearing leather from head to toe, with a painted skull on his helmet. Glancing through a part in the curtain, Penny rocked back, then ducked. In tears, she whispered that the rider was the brother of her jailed boyfriend, a fellow bikie. Leo ducked, too.

The brother revved his engine loudly three times.

'Shit, Leo, this is a warning from the gang I used to ride with.'

The bikie climbed back on his motorbike after repeating the warning: *snarl, snarl, snarl.* The biker took an interest in Leo's car and looked inside. Leo sweated. Athletic gear and envelopes were on his front seat. The biker looked at the house again, yelling, 'Leo, you dog! Penny, you slut!'

In the dark, Leo searched letterboxes for the correct number, stumbling, almost missing the driveway. Surprisingly, for early Sunday night, no lights were on. Following the path by the side of the house, he found the back door. He patted under the pot plants in the dark, feeling for a spare key. *Please.* The pot plant spare key was the Far North Queensland way. He found success, a dull bronze key, under the third pot.

He stood to listen for approaching cars or footsteps, but all was still. He unlocked the back door. 'Technically, not a break-in, eh.'

A streetlight shone into the smaller of two bedrooms. Books were stacked beside a bedside table. Leo inspected Pierce's delivery in the dim light. His vision gradually made out a folded movie advertising flyer covering a roll of bank notes.

'Technically trouble, eh,' he muttered.

He closed his eyes, returning to sleepwalker mode.

Leo placed the roll under the bed mattress. The bikie's accusation echoed. *Leo you dog.* Before heading up the driveway, he checked the downstairs' fridge for beer.

'Technically paid for, eh. Technically asleep, eh.'

~

From the cinema, the police radioed back with their report. 'No one here, boss.'

The station gave them another address. 'The bloke should know his location.'

They knocked on the door at the front of this address, just a few streets away, but again, no one was home.

'Feels like we are in a ghost town,' the older policeman ventured.

'Yeah, no one is out, and no one's at home.'

'Okay, let's leave this to the morning shift. We've worked hard enough tonight.' The policemen smiled to each other.

As they turned back to their car, they heard a car engine. The glow of headlights peaked over a slight rise. A luxurious car pulled into the garage.

'Hello,' the driver called from his car, with a wide, beaming smile. 'Can I help you?'

The older officer walked to the car. 'Mr Pierce, we are looking for one of your staff. Do you know where Darcy Grant resides? The electoral roll address details aren't up to date.'

'I think he moved recently. Perhaps I can confirm tomorrow? Why do you ask?'

'We haven't established anything yet, but the cinema owner is concerned about aspects of his management.'

'Oh, really?' Rich frowned, unbuckling his seatbelt. 'Anything I should know about?'

'Do you know whether Grant has sticky fingers?' the older policeman asked.

'I've never had cause to consider this question before.' Rich glanced about, as if looking for someone. 'Now that I think about it, he asked permission to take a second job. Perhaps he does have money troubles.' Rich paused. 'It disappoints me to say, officers, that yes, he likely has sticky fingers. Have a good night.'

Inside the car, the police radio crackled, and the younger officer remembered to radio in with an update.

'Well, that was interesting,' observed the older policeman. 'I gave the fish a taste of the bait and he grabbed it.'

'Huh, what do you mean?'

'Instead of defending his team member, the principal sold him out. He's one to watch if you ask me. But I guess that will be up to the detective.' He punched his partner's arm. 'If a policeman sold out one of his own like that, they'd have a limp and desk duty for life.'

Both officers turned their heads and focused on a swaying figure haloed in the streetlight, walking towards them through the hazy rain.

26

TO Darcy, the morning boat journey back across the bay from Dunk Island seemed far longer than the way over. He drummed his fingers. The mainland didn't appear to be getting any closer. Scowling at the wheelhouse, Darcy imagined the skipper drawing out the experience to charge high prices.

The swell lowered. *Mind skipper, submerged hazard.* Darcy grabbed the rail, smiling. His satisfaction ebbed a second later, thinking of his dad, also knowing he'd been miserable company for Isabella. He'd not given Isabella a chance to understand. *But how could he explain emotions he couldn't put into words?* A large bird with white, salty-looking feathers flew over the bow. Emotionally, he was an uninhabited rocky outcrop a tired bird would fly over, not part of a verdant island chain nestling as a family. Through his island childhood, he'd found a way to cope, building fortifications, lying to the welfare workers to cover for his absent father. He could remain isolated and survive, but that wasn't living *la dolce vita*, the beautiful life. The Russo family and the gregarious Silkwood Sicilians taught him that.

Adrift, he wished the skipper would continue to take his time.

Onshore, Darcy squeezed past people queuing for the ferry journey to the island. He weighed up whether to call in sick or request bereavement leave. But if he called the school, he would reach Frances. He decided to drive and consider his options, perhaps driving past the Russo home a couple of times. Isabella might hear his engine and wave. Then he'd drive the back road to the school, parking at the sports ground fence, call out to Leo that he was sick and to pass a message to the deputy principal. Darcy strode to the car, happy with his plan, looking forward to a day at home.

As Darcy opened his car door, a figure stepped out from the shadows, standing in speckled light.

'Did you have a nice day with Isabella yesterday?' asked Rich.

Darcy's legs twitched. 'Huh. What? What are you talking about?'

'STOP!' yelled Rich as if Darcy was a petulant student. 'I gave Isabella a lift home yesterday afternoon. She admitted what's been going on. Childhood sweetheart coming to town? A child in town more like it.'

Darcy rocked back at Pierce's word blows.

'You need to shoot through for your own sake,' barked Rich.

Darcy slumped against the car, almost unable to stand. 'No. What about my students? NO!'

'No? You made your choice, screwing a girl barely out of school. A trainee teacher too, under your supervision.'

'This has nothing to do with university.'

'It will. I know the university people. I sign the certificates of training completion. I'll be ringing the university this morning to explain Isabella exchanged sex for a good report.'

'That's not true.'

'It will be when I tell them. While I'm at it, I'll say I'm so disgusted at her conduct I won't accept another trainee teacher unless they kick her out.'

Darcy clenched his fist, wanting to lunge.

'I'll also tell Frances you seduced Isabella to ensure a good report.'

'That's not true either.'

'It will be when I tell her that you confessed this to me. She'll be furious at your conduct. For your sake, that should be reason enough to hightail it.' Rich studied his face. 'Looks like someone has made a start. Her other guy? Smart kid, but a terrible brawler when at school.'

'C'mon Rich. You once said that one good turn deserves another. Give me a break. Look the other way.'

'Nah, that doesn't work for me.'

Darcy stared into the twinkling pupils of a tormentor. Rage erupted. 'YOU DIDN'T TELL ME MY DAD DIED. YOU

DESERVE TO DIE!'

Rich chuckled. 'Nice fighting words. I bet you're a lover, not a fighter.'

Darcy grabbed a large branch from the ground. Rich looked at him, unmoved.

'Okay, lover boy. Give it your best shot.'

Darcy swung low, aiming at Pierce's groin. Rich blocked and kicked the branch away with his shoe, laughing.

'Yep, a lover not a fighter. You're to leave.'

'No way. I'm staying.' Darcy opened his car door.

Rich held out Isabella's senior certificate. 'I'm due to present Isabella's certificate on Friday, but I will tear it up here, on the spot, unless you leave. Kicked out of university. No senior certificate. Her parents won't be pleased. Leave. Face your failings like a man.'

'WHAT SORT OF MAN ARE YOU?' Darcy yelled. 'Taking our rent for a place that isn't yours! Taking the money from the cinema! I bet my supposed transfer north and nibble on my pay was another scam.'

'SHUT UP! I'll tear up Isabella's certificate now. Clear out, or else.'

He held up Isabella's certificate again. A fat tear plopped onto Darcy's shirt. *Salsa* was on the bottom, and so was he.

Rich called from his car. 'You lead, Romeo. I'll follow.'

Darcy revved his engine and ground his wheels, lifting gravel towards the Statesman, like a shower of asteroids. Rich braked, but then sped up, stalking behind. Across the cane plains, Darcy sped, swerving around corners, screeching at the road's edge, not caring if he crashed. The forest and cane fields formed into bruises as he rushed by. Ahead, a farm tractor putted and bounced. The tree branch swing and shower of gravel was pathetic, but Darcy spied a truck coming the other way. He would avenge his father with more than a sunk boat. Darcy aimed to pass around the tractor at the last second, leaving Pierce with no time or room to avoid a collision. Behind, Pierce's engine rev growled, and the grill of the Statesman filled most of his rear mirror. With a yank of his steering wheel, Darcy swerved, tyres screeching. Then, Pierce's reflected grill was all he could see, insects visible in the radiator mesh. Pierce curled around the tractor as the truck turned away down a side road. Darcy retched as he weaved to correct his steering. Pierce honked his horn and flashed his lights.

At the stop sign on the highway, Rich set his car indicator to head back to town. Darcy's car engine ticked with the animal heat of unusual exertion, almost like the panting sprinters on the athletics track he'd clocked months ago.

Darcy, too, indicated and turned towards town, thinking of students he would never see again. Every day, wide-eyed juniors, elbows reaching up to high desks, stared at him with sweet little faces. His older students treated him with respect. Simone confided when she was ovulating. He didn't just have roots and branches growing around Isabella; he'd become part of the town in a way he'd never achieved in twenty years in Toowoomba. A wry, reluctant smile formed; he was no longer asked whether he was new to town. The north was a safer place, too, following Bruno's domestication. But he'd let people down too. Frances and Gino. Isabella too, for he'd placed her at great risk. *Will it be safe?* She'd never refused him, breaking from university to be with him. He'd let down Simone and Sid too, earnings, takings. His students too. His senior students, especially, *gammon*, for he'd not even seen out their year, much less than a two-year forecast. Douglas, his head of department would curse in Latin.

Darcy recalled passing the Silkwood Church after Isabella's birthday when he had the premonition they'd eventually be found out; yet he persisted. The teacher had avoided the lesson – observe the warning signs. He turned into town and drove to Sid's home. Darcy thought of his father. He'd told him to play along during the welfare checks to gain more time. *Yes, Mrs Black, Dad's at the shops now; spending the pension cheque on food.* The cooperation with authorities worked then and could work now. He went to frame a plan, but paused, worrying about Rich's final threat when they walked to their cars.

'If you reappear, I'll call Gino Russo and tell him that you defiled his young daughter. He's an ex-copper with plenty of guns. He will finish you, of course, but I'm concerned about Isabella. I'll tell him that his daughter was far from an innocent party. Who knows what an enraged father is capable of?'

Darcy remembered the Sicilian's rough affection as he'd left the Russo lunch. He'd joked with Isabella that he was worried what might happen if the Sicilians didn't like someone. He remembered her reply. *You don't want to find out.*

~

'Boss, wake up. I want to pitch you a story.' Matt glimpsed Peter through low slits as he slumped, crumpled in his office chair. Matt wasn't equipped for the young journalist's zeal after his showdown with Pierce. He'd rocked and rolled in his armchair with his rum bottle until dawn, suspecting his favourite columnist wouldn't call by for another early morning edition. She hadn't.

Peter fanned the air with a notebook. 'Boss, did you have a few last night?'

'Leave me be, Pete,' Matt croaked. 'Can't it wait? Can you lower the curtain?'

'C'mon boss, this is a hot prospect.'

Matt, editorial debate in his blood and ample rum, pushed himself upright. They walked towards the whiteboard. Peter paused at Bianca's desk, studying the family photo. Matt registered Peter's sad look.

'C'mon, Pete,' Matt rasped, 'would you have preferred to know or not know?'

'I guess it's best to know. She never mentioned the cinema manager guy.'

Matt leaned on the wall beside the whiteboard, eyelids lowering. Usually, the journalist would hook the editor with the story and reinforce it with sources, with excitement building between them. But this morning, Peter explained his sources first.

'On Friday, Simone mentioned her father had been feeling a bit better and has been going through his books. Apparently, there has been plenty of cinema revenue but little in his bank. I went to the Sunday matinee last night to sniff around and have a chat with the manager, but the cinema didn't open. I waited in the car, and the police turned up.'

Matt opened his eyes. 'What's the angle?' Matt massaged his temples. 'Fraud?'

'Yep, the cinema bloke is pocketing the takings, counting on Sid croaking it and Simone's grief.'

With a shaky hand, Matt listed the story on the whiteboard. Simone would be a reliable source. Too many stories pitched at his whiteboard came from town gossip and loose hearsay. Matt noticed Peter's beaming smile, sensing adrenaline coursing in the young journalist's veins with the prospect of breaking a big story. It was a fever he hadn't experienced in years.

Outside, townsfolk shuffled by, heads lowered, realising Monday wasn't a hoax. Matt and Peter admired Bianca as she walked towards the office. Both men exhaled. Matt dropped the whiteboard pen.

'Pete, I need to know this isn't personal. Are you trying to neck the cinema guy for his relationship with Bianca?'

27

DETECTIVE Dennis Deakin sat in a small, plain room at the rear of the police station. A giant typewriter dominated his desk. He flicked through the notes from the officers on the night shift. The notes included the promise of an early call from the principal to provide Darcy's home address.

'Define early, principal,' said Dennis as he checked his watch: nine o'clock. Even the night shift would be stirring by now. With a sigh, he brushed away hair falling from his balding scalp.

Dennis drummed his fingers with a detective's impatience. Events could unfold quickly, and he liked to get on with a case and close it fast before the actors dispersed. He prided himself on sharp, conclusive briefs for the prosecutor to send the perpetrator to Stuart Creek for a stretch. To Dennis, most policing television shows like the *Rockford Files* were a combination of fiction and fantasy. To fill the hour, the detectives imagined various scenarios and chased obscure leads to create intrigue. Yet most detective work was straightforward. The bloke who looked guilty almost always was, and there was no need to invent other angles.

'Nabbed,' he'd often say to the first suspect.

'Nah, gammon, eh,' they'd defend.

'Nabbed, not gammon.'

Violence and property crime kept him busy enough, and the annoying blokes from the newspaper sometimes brought him leads through their sources. Alleged fraud like this was familiar, too. People often drifted through the far north to escape their past, make fast bucks, and scurry away like roaches. Most locals clung to the cane industry and led honest lives with prayer. It was mainly the recent arrivals 'on the make' who filled his briefs for the prosecutor and later the grimy, claustrophobic van to Stuart Creek. Looking at the notes again, Darcy Grant might also be a drifter, for he'd only been in town since the start of the year. But a teacher-criminal was a change.

'C'mon, ring,' he willed his telephone.

However, one of the challenges in the north was a culture of silence. It was pointless to investigate crime in the small sugar villages. Thumbing through his notes again, he doubted he'd have the usual silence in this case, for the principal wasn't looking after his own. He read again: *PIERCE states that the potential perpetrator, GRANT, probably has thieving tendencies.*

Studying the mountains through his window, Dennis thought of police television shows. What *was* true among the drawn-out television fiction was that women hated calls in the middle of the night, straining already strained relationships. He sighed. He was here after one too many of those calls, taking the transfer when he came home one morning to an empty house and a handwritten note on the table. He looked back to his telephone. A word with Darcy Grant would clear up this matter. *Nabbed, not gammon.* Then, he would tap his brief into the waiting typewriter, then relax, a devious drifter interned within a correctional mausoleum.

'C'mon, c'mon ring,' he willed his telephone.

~

On the back seat of his car, Darcy's suitcase slid with every corner. Everything was shifting in his life. Darcy braked at the highway intersection. Close behind, the haunting Statesman revved and honked. He intended to drive down the highway and double back. Then hide. He could call Isabella after a couple of days. He sighed. Considering Isabella's graduation certificate, Rich's threats, Frances' demands he call it off, and Carlo and Gino's guns, he couldn't stay, call, or return. He indicated right to head south where Toowoomba lay on a cool plateau hundreds of kilometres away. The Gold Coast was in the same direction.

'C'mon, Pearl, we can do it again.'

An old farm truck, generic red from rust and tinted soil, trundled past on the highway. He watched the old red truck drive north, possibly to Silkwood. Darcy recalled the light pressure of Isabella's head on his lap, her beautiful face looking up at him.

'Hey, Darcy, remember your favourite pasta?' she'd asked.

'Of course. Homemade Russo.'

Isabella Russo was his secret, special, and beautiful slice of the local silkwood tree. He hoped she was a real silkwood with a rugged interior. She would need to be tough for what lay ahead, for he supposed a disappearance would be far more difficult than a breakup.

He looked at his reflection in the side window and visualised their poses in his bedroom mirror, her eyes shining and beckoning like pools of dark chocolate. They practised their introduction as a couple. *Darcy, you know what to say.* He blinked and glanced again, but she was no longer there.

He pulled away and took a final glance back. Through the rearview mirror, he could see the broad shoulders of the nearby mountain and the steaming stacks of the sugar mill. He drove past the school with his window down. At least he was leaving alive, he mused, not in a hearse. In the sweetened air, the clanging school bell urged everyone into class. Reflected in the mirror, the Statesman's flashing headlights winked, wishing him away. Darcy heard a toot from the mill, farewelling another southerner.

28

FRANCES heard a knock on the office door. 'Mrs Russo, our teacher hasn't arrived.'

'Oh, which teacher?'

'Mr Grant.'

Hearing his name called out across the office wasn't a surprise, as she expected Darcy would be late this morning. After Sunday evening prayers, Isabella confided. It was late when Frances left her bedroom, and she blessed herself, fearing a Sicilian tragic twist. Bianca was protected with contraception, but not Isabella. Between sobs, Isabella had replied to her question.

'He withdraws most of the time.'

'*Merdi!* Most of the time? I thought you were more intelligent. It only takes once. When are you due?'

'I'm waiting.'

Frances had felt a chill on the warm night.

This morning, they'd travelled in rare silence, except for a brief exchange.

'Still no period?'

'No.'

'*Stupido!*' she had hissed.

In the office, Frances clenched a fist. Darcy would be best to keep his distance. Thinking of Gino's heavy arsenal, she felt capable of more than a slap. The deputy principal grumbled and left the office to flush out a teacher from the staffroom to take Darcy's first lesson.

Across the day, Frances looked to the school gate to see whether Darcy had arrived. Like a scratched opera record on repeat, she kept hearing the final part of Isabella's confession. *Mr Pierce dropped me home.*

Mr Pierce dropped me home. She spilled her jangling cup of tea. If Rich found out about Isabella and Darcy, he would use it to his advantage. She feared another invitation to the studio. Frances kept hearing Isabella's admission on repeat, almost not hearing the telephone. She lifted the phone receiver. The man asked for Rich. Frances could hear his irritation. Like Darcy, Rich hadn't yet arrived.

'I've been expecting a call from early morning.'

Frances wrote the detective's name on the message notepad. She guessed what the police matter might be. Year 12 boys were always a handful in their final week.

'Hey, since you're in the school office, can you tell me whether Darcy Grant is at school or where he lives?'

She fumbled and then regathered the phone. 'No. I don't know.' She hung up and found Darcy in the staff photo – smiling, sweet-faced. She hissed, 'Darcy, you are the devil's spawn. Your mother would be ashamed. I'll try to find her, and give her a call. To think, I feel like a lousy mother!'

~

'Thanks,' rasped Leo, grabbing the Coca-Cola from his student. Sunday night with the police had been a late, late night. He stood in the shade under the only tree on the huge school sports field. Today's 'lesson' would be laps of the school oval. The students could run, walk, or stand still; he didn't care. Leo leaned back against the tree and lowered his sunglasses. Shutting his eyes, half dozing, Leo recalled his night.

When he'd seen the police car in front of Pierce's house, he figured that Pierce was framing him. The police car door had opened.

'Leo Scuderi. Come with us.'

He hung his head in the backseat as they drove to the station. Escorted to the back of the station from the parked police car, he imagined he was re-tracing the steps of Penny's arrested bikie boyfriend. The iron bars of the watch house loomed, and he thought that at least he would have a more comfortable night than lying on Pierce's garage floor. An insect crackled, incinerated in the ultraviolet bug zapper. He was next.

The younger policeman addressed him. 'I have a couple of questions. Are you ready?'

Leo murmured his acceptance, wondering whether he should have a lawyer.

'Beer? Or rum?'

Leo squinted to comprehend. The officers roared with laughter. Leo joined in, laughing away his nerves.

'Beer, I have work tomorrow and should take it easy.'

But he didn't think of work as he sat with the younger officer, his mate from the cricket club. They drank for hours, with rain on the roof and frequent zaps of departing bugs.

At one point, his friend confided, 'Cindy and I are an item. I'm feeling lucky.'

This coupling confirmed what Leo had assumed, recalling a recent pub scene. At the time, it looked like Queensland pub physics where the lonely and the willing edged closer, drink by drink.

'Oh yeah? Good for you,' Leo replied.

'Thanks. Also, here's something interesting for you,' the policeman leaned forward. 'Cindy mentioned when the bikie was hassling her sister, Penny.'

Leo lowered his drink. Concentrating, he coaxed his friend along. 'Oh yeah?'

'We had that bikie guy in here a few times.' He pointed to the watchhouse. 'Acted tough on a motorbike. Cried all night in the cell.'

'Oh yeah?'

'Those brothers were disowned by their gang for drawing police interest. Cindy's sister and you were never in any danger. Our boss told your boss not to worry.'

'WHAT! Your boss told my boss?'

Leo declined another drink, not wanting booze to scramble his memory. With heavy scraping steps, Leo trudged back to his room, wondering if he could kill Pierce and get away with it.

'Sir. Sir.' A student shook him. 'Mr Pierce is coming.'

Leo shook his head, remembering the older policeman's words when he stood to leave the station. 'Pierce is a snake. I can tell his type.'

Leo squinted. The snake stared at him.

'You were in late. Just making sure your delivery went well.'

Leo felt as if his skin was tightening into scales. His overnight delivery could only harm Darcy. The deal with Pierce released his boa constrictor grip, but the antidote would inflict a venomous snakebite on Darcy. He owed Darcy hundreds of dollars yet repaid him with a tainted deposit. He nodded. As Pierce left, whistling, Leo figured he couldn't risk a return to Darcy's house, but he could warn him to tidy his room. The bell rang, and Leo walked to the tuckshop for another Coke on the way to Darcy's classroom.

~

After the long bell sounded at the end of the lunch break, Rich looked across the school from the vantage of his chilled office. The students sat in the shade, unwilling to raise a sweat. It took a second bell and insistent teachers, like cattle dogs, to guide the docile herds to their pens.

'Zombies on a conveyor belt,' he muttered into the mirror. 'The students aren't much better.'

As the school settled under late November's thick, humid blanket, he fanned messages across his desk, then stacked and re-ordered them like a poker dealer: first, last, alphabetical order, reverse, and random. But whatever the method, the detective's message remained at the bottom. The message from Mrs DeLuca had rested midway but now was on top. Rich looked away from the stack of messages. It was time to organise his week and the months ahead, especially with police interest in the cinema. Ignoring his messages, he dialled Maria's family home seeking his mother-in-law.

'Hello?'

'Mary, it's so good to reach you before your birthday.'

'Richard, my dear. Thank you for suggesting Maria visit for my birthday. I may not have many more. You never know when the Lord calls time.'

'No chance, you're a tough old boot. You will outlive us all.' Rich suggested she throw away her cane. Hearing her laugh, he lowered his voice into confidential mode. 'Mary, do you still have a minute? It's a sensitive matter.'

'Of course, Richard.'

'It's just struck me, Mary. I have dedicated my care to many within the school community, but not sufficiently at home. I'm worried Maria has sought the company of men outside of our marriage.' Rich registered Mary's gasp with a smile and continued. 'The preservation of our marriage is my highest priority. It would help to live closer to you, where we can raise our future children.'

'Oh, Richard, this is a wonderful, early birthday present. I have been so worried. Maria seemed unhappy when she arrived.'

'You know, just one night without Maria makes me realise that marriages can drift away like a sun crossing the sky, with a quiet sunset. But I would like a new dawn.'

'Oh, Richard, so poetic. And children on the horizon, too.'

'Mary, can you please pass on a message to my dear wife? I need to get on with business here at the school.'

'Of course, Richard.'

'Please tell Maria I have called the regional office to seek a transfer close to your home. She should stay until I arrive in a couple of weeks. Could she look for a house? It's her choice, as long as it's close to you.'

'Of course, Richard. This is very exciting.'

Rich hung up, snickered, then returned calls from across town. Still, the detective's message lay at the bottom of the pile. He looked out the window as rain streaked the glazing. With his schemes at risk, he felt sick of the dreary, sodden place. He didn't know how he might feign pride as he handed out the 1984 and 1985 Year 12 graduation certificates on Friday night. Thinking of the graduation, Isabella Russo's certificate was among the pile, at least for now. At this thought, he calculated Darcy's distance from town. He should be a few hours down the road where he needed to be, while the incriminating roll of bank notes was right here in town, where it needed to be. Looking at the office clock, he decided it was time to call the detective.

'I'm so sorry for the delay,' Rich apologised, 'but we've had a hectic day.'

'Is Darcy Grant at school? I'd like a word.'

'He's likely to be in the staffroom marking exams. It might take a few minutes. Please hold.'

Rich drummed his fingers as he waited in pretence, wondering whether it was prudent to interfere further with the police investigation. However, he needed Darcy to evade the police until the end of the week.

'Detective, I can't reach the staffroom at present. I will ring you back later.'

'Hang on!'

Rich hung up with a chuckle.

~

In the detective's office, Dennis felt his eyes blur. The dull room became too bright. Pressure pulsed and raced from one side of his forehead to the other.

'Oh, no, not today,' he panted.

The migraine crackled, and with delicate, slow movements, Dennis closed his door and lowered the blinds. Lying still on the office floor, he clenched his fists at his forehead to withstand the banging drum. Dennis groaned, not only from pain. There would be no closed case today, and he blamed his migraine and the principal, which seemed to be one and the same.

29

IN the newspaper office, Matt listened to Peter's update. Simone suggested the cinema finances were awry, but their accountant was yet to confirm. The police weren't commenting.

'Money has been pinched. It all points to Darcy Grant,' implored Peter, flexing his muscles after a gym session.

'Okay, but the story must be tighter. You have a personal agenda.'

Peter went to complain, but Matt turned to answer the ringing phone. On his news floor, he was happiest with a long list of stories on the whiteboard. This may be another lead, and he was planning a bumper Christmas edition. He picked up the phone. Maria's voice made his heart jump, and he turned his back to Peter, waving him away. With closed eyes, he listened to her cries as though she was in the room, not hundreds of kilometres away along Queensland's vast coastline. The newsman absorbed the news. Maria wouldn't be returning. He remembered Pierce's taunt. *No more pussy for the town's ugliest man.*

'Matt, there is now talk of children. My mother keeps reminding me of my Catholic faith and marriage vows.'

Matt ground his teeth. Maria sounded captive within high prison walls of morality. Infidel Pierce guarded her from heaven's high sentry box. 'Kids? You're kidding me!' Matt roared. 'You told me he's barely touched you in years. Don't fall for that bullshit!'

A few moments later, he realised he had been shouting. The receiver was back in its cradle, but he couldn't remember saying goodbye. Matt studied his headline posters, remembering he'd once had a feared, steely edge. He sat down to concentrate, drumming his fingers. There must be a way of skewering Pierce.

Matt rifled through past editions, tearing at and throwing useless copy aside. After half an hour, Matt peered around his office. He looked as if he was domiciled inside a shredder. Then he found what he was looking for: the photo of town celebrities in front of the cinema at the re-opening. Just inside the frame of the photo – Darcy's frown. Squinting, he remembered. One Sunday night, snooping out his window, he'd seen the Statesman down by the cinema. He'd assumed this was Pierce in 'father figure' mode, assisting the fledging manager.

Maria's news confirmed that Pierce's conniving had no limits. Before he mentioned his suspicions to anyone, he would further sniff about. He hated Pierce, but a good journalist couldn't take a story personally. Thinking of Maria, he needed to take his own advice.

He glanced to the office beauty. Bianca was greeting visitors at the office door. She had taken over responsibility for some of the paper's operations from Simone, including distribution. Matt still took an interest in all facets of his newspaper and stepped out of the thick snowy paper around his ankles, joining Bianca in the reception area. He was introduced to new delivery boys.

Holding one of the boys by the hand, Bianca gushed, 'Mr Flint, here's a fine young man from Silkwood who will be a great addition to our team. He's looking for a second job.'

Matt smiled at the brawny-looking fellow who looked like a cane farmer's son.

'What's your name?'

'Carlo, sir.'

~

At a small, squalid roadside garage Darcy consulted a mechanic. He was somewhere south of Townsville, only three hours from town, but north of Mackay, his intended overnight destination. The bang he'd heard under his engine bonnet when he raced with Pierce like a rally driver had become a clanging rattle. Over the past hour it felt as if Frances was punching his bonnet.

The mechanic in stained blue overalls looked under the bonnet with smeared spectacles. His face cut into deep crow's feet around his eyes as he squinted.

'Oh, that's bad. Oh, no, that looks bent too. Gee, don't see that often.'

The mechanic closed the bonnet and rubbed his whiskers with calloused hands, blackened from engine oil. Darcy was sure no woman would ever consent to being handled by those mitts. He thought the cane farmer's paws were bad, *but wow*.

'Lad, we've got some problems here.'

Darcy tried to follow the mechanic's jargon. Although confusing, it was clear the repairs would be costly and time-consuming. The mechanic grinned. 'It's a good thing you pulled in here.'

Darcy surveyed the junkyard beyond the garage, where dozens of rusty cars were arranged for scrap. *Uh-huh*. This was where the unlucky pulled in, and the priest in filthy oil-stained robes officiated last rites. From the junkyard, a couple of shiny black crows cawed in confirmation.

'Given the parts needed, it's touch and go whether your car is worth repairing, especially when my labour is factored in.'

'Huh? What are my options?'

'Well, you could get your rig towed back to Townsville for repairs. But that's going to be expensive.' He grimaced before adding, 'You see, son, you're kinda in the middle of nowhere here.'

Darcy felt in a vice for the second time that day. He thought, *let's get this over with*.

'Your best choice is to scrap your rig,' the mechanic continued. 'It's a shock, I know, but this car has done some miles. Don't worry, I'll give you a fair price.'

Darcy saw another swindler. He would have been sized up as soon as he drove in: Southerner-looking car. Young guy. Delicate hands. Clueless. He went to complain, as he'd kissed Isabella in this car, but it was also the same car he'd meekly driven from town. The mechanic unfolded a pocket in his overalls and handed him a few twenty-dollar notes from a fat billfold. Counting the notes, Darcy felt like his car was being stolen. Darcy trudged back to *The Pearl,* retrieving his suitcase.

'Is there anywhere around here I could stay?'

'Around here?' The mechanic laughed, shaking his head.

'Okay, I'll sleep in my car. I'll hitch a lift tomorrow.'

The mechanic rubbed his jaw, adding new grease to his stubble. 'Wait, we've done a good deal. You can stay here for the night.'

He pointed with a blackened, crooked finger to a level above the garage.

'C'mon, lad.' He slapped Darcy on the back with his greasy paw. Darcy worried about his favourite tan shirt. In the last few hours, he'd lost his girl, his job, and now his car. *Why not a shirt as well?* His father was dead. His aunt had told him about his mother too.

In response to his pleading after news of his father's death, Aunt Betty sighed and explained. The day after his birth, the hospital matron looked through a window. His mother ran down the street, wearing only a thin maternity gown and arms aloft like a biblical prophet. They returned her to the hospital, but this time to a different ward. She left again with a male warden on a motorbike, arms wide like she had wings. Mostly she rode with a bikie gang. Sometimes, she visited baby Darcy, but there were arguments. One day, she rode alone into a deep fog along the Toowoomba escarpment. There was a rockfall, and she wasn't seen again.

'I often wondered about you, Darcy, whether you had her madness, lost in your thoughts, mixing dreams for reality.'

'Doesn't everybody?' he'd replied.

The mechanic led him to the stairs by the side of the building. Darcy hung his head. Everything was gone in just his early twenties. If his name was on a clubhouse honours board, like his father, the manager would be gathering the cross stencil and gold paint.

'I'll get my wife to set up the spare room.'

'Wife? *Really?*' The questions were out of his mouth before he could hold them back. Upstairs, an attractive woman greeted them, rising from watching television. Darcy blinked, thinking the woman must be a fellow stranded traveller.

'The spare, Daphne.'

'Yes, love.'

She nodded with a wink. The room was made up, and he sat on the bed. Darcy knew he was working with a team. He wasn't the first trapped traveller, just another fly caught in their web. Downstairs, he heard his car start. The mechanic rolled the vehicle deeper into the garage, not towards the scrapyard. Darcy grunted and lay on the bed, staring at the ceiling. He heard the crows cackle and craw, heckling. *Fool.* Later in the afternoon, Daphne knocked on the door.

'Hey, looks like the next bus or train isn't until a few days. If you're not in a rush, I can run you down to Bowen later in the week. Then you can take it from there. It's a pity about your car.' She paused. 'You'll be okay here.'

Darcy turned away to hide his eyes. He didn't think he could cope with being pitied.

'What's her name?'

Darcy looked at his watch, pretending not to hear. It was nearly the end of the school day. Frances would know he was missing. Isabella might be curious about his whereabouts.

'Hey, what's her name?'

Darcy turned back to Daphne. His mouth felt dry.

'Isabella,' he croaked. 'Her name is Isabella.'

~

In the school car park after her supermarket shift, Isabella lent on the Russo family sedan to support her weak legs. She'd walked from the supermarket to the school to seek a glimpse. An unfamiliar teacher in Darcy's classroom waved his arms to settle down disruptive students. Her breath caught. He wasn't at school and maybe hadn't made it off the island. Mr Pierce passed through the carpark with a cheerful greeting. 'Hello again, Isabella.'

'Good afternoon, Mr Pierce,' she replied.

Based on his excellent mood, Isabella surmised he hadn't made the association with Darcy and was just joking about sunburn. Yesterday, they'd been unlucky, but overall, they had been careful.

There was barely anything that could connect them. They'd covered their tracks like the waves washing away their footprints at Etty Bay. She blocked her ears to cover her principal's loud whistling as he doubled back.

'Strange about that missing passenger yesterday, hey?' He chuckled. 'I hope he's okay,' he added as he passed by. 'See you at the graduation. It's been a long wait.'

A long wait? Isabella thought of her period, long overdue. She muffled a cry, she might be pregnant. They hadn't been that careful after all. The university party girls would jeer. *Sister Isabella! Ha!*

Sitting low by the car, kicking her feet in the gravel, she wondered why Darcy had been withdrawn yesterday. Whenever he became quiet, she sensed his worry and guilt. He'd always said that the risk was worth it. *Had it become too much?* He'd been vague about his facial injury. Perhaps they'd been found out. But even if he needed to leave to save his skin, he would have surely explained, and they would have made plans for a reunion. She reflected further. Yesterday he had been *too willing* to remain on the island, like the dropped hand by the marquee. Her throat caught. *Was he getting ready to dump her? Dolly* featured articles about men moving on to their next conquest when the novelty wore off. Darcy loved novels, but perhaps she wasn't novel anymore. Whenever they expressed feelings, he'd blush and stammer like a bashful boy. She'd sensed he didn't have much experience, which she'd liked. Isabella had felt special. Now she wondered, re-checking a mental version of the *Dolly* checklist, helping to know whether a boy really liked you. Maybe he wasn't bashful, just struggling to find the right sounding words to end it without hurting her feelings. Ticks became question marks. *What if she was pregnant?* Perhaps Darcy had an inkling of Isabella's situation, he could count weeks also, knowing he'd face the wrath of her parents. *Was this the way it was with Mamma? Fear, then sorrow? Weeping, slumped on knees in front of graves?* Carlo would be humiliated. Darcy could guess the consequences, remembering the knife prick in the canvas tent. Isabella looked towards the coast. The journey from the island to the school didn't take all day. Her eyes began to well with tears.

~

In the car, Frances passed Isabella tissues from their glovebox. Her daughters cried in happiness and sadness, their Sicilian temperament always at the surface, but Isabella had never sobbed like this. 'Can we look for him, Mamma? *Per favore?*'

Frances didn't want to look for, find, or see Darcy, but she let Isabella guide her to his home. From the driveway, Isabella looked about. There was no car. The windows were closed, and the curtains were drawn. 'Mamma, he's not here! I must know whether he's left the island!'

They drove to Mission Beach, Isabella sniffling all the way. Seeking distraction, Frances looked out the window as they passed newly planted, orderly cane fields, contrasting with the gloomy chaos of rainforest limbs and vines. Frances didn't see order, only chaos. At Mission Beach, Isabella guided her to the far end of the car park. Isabella stood where Darcy's car had been parked, then walked his tyre trail. She frowned. Broken branches were scattered, which hadn't been there yesterday. The hitched ferry bobbed by the pier. Isabella ran to the ticket booth by the dock. It was closed. Isabella stared over at Dunk Island. The dark island wasn't giving up family secrets.

'Oh, Mamma. Where could he be?'

Frances thought of the police. They could find him, but she wondered whether that would be good news. It was time to act.

'C'mon, let's have a better look around his place.'

Half an hour later, they were back at the house. Isabella pulled her hair back and wiped her eyes. Walking down the driveway, she took her mamma's hand. Isabella let herself in, calling, 'Darcy? Darcy?'

She returned to his bedroom. It took just a few moments to notice the changes. In a corner, his discarded, twisted cinema shirt looked like a *Twistie* from the confectionary stand. His version of *Under Milkwood* was torn up, pages cast about. Isabella noticed gaps in his small wardrobe. His suitcase was missing. She sobbed. This meant he'd left without explaining or saying goodbye. Only a few of his books remained, but none contained her pink ribbon. The movie tickets with her lipstick kisses weren't in his drawer. Yet his *The Doors* cassettes were left. Some of his things remained, but not them. He'd left, taking a version of her. Perhaps souvenirs, like tourists fossicking in the Dunk Island gift shop.

Isabella glanced back to the mirror where they'd first seen themselves as a couple, then rehearsed for Frances. *You know what to say.* Only her bleak, puffy eyes stared back. Isabella lifted a torn page resting on his pillow. Reverend Eli's prayer. 'It's bullshit,' was written across the verse about seeing the best in people. She lay on the cold bed looking up, imagining Darcy above her. Through her tears, she saw her mamma, who helped her up.

Isabella looked back at the bed.

'Come back, Darcy. Why is it bullshit? Come back to me.'

She shuffled away with her head in her hands. 'Oh, Mamma, where could he be?'

Frances remained in Darcy's bedroom and brushed away strands of her daughter's long black hair from the pillows. She picked up Isabella's dropped tissue. Although the reasons for Darcy's sudden departure weren't clear, she didn't want Isabella in this room. She shivered at the memory of the detective's call. They left the house as the streetlights flickered on.

'Where could he be?' Isabella asked, sobbing.

Frances heard this question in the car, at home, and in Isabella's bedroom all night.

30

AT his police desk just before dawn, Dennis waited for his buffet breakfast of aspirin, black coffee, and numerous cigarettes to kick in, determined to overcome a lost day. If the teacher was on the run, he'd need to widen the net, but the evidence dragnet started here in town. Dennis reached for his car keys.

Headlights off, he drove an unmarked car with a plain clothed police officer. Dennis wanted the advantage of a low-profile investigation, as Far North Queensland was notorious for tip-offs. Then, the trail went colder than a freshly poured beer at the Silkwood Hotel. They cruised in low gears to Darcy's confirmed home address. Dennis now knew Darcy lived in Sid's house while nicking his money. The guy was a turd. By the driveway, Dennis rifled through the letterbox, then tossed envelopes into the grass. Under streetlight, Dennis and the policeman strolled down the driveway. Dennis knocked on the front door. After no response, they walked to a mossy side path, and Dennis halted their progress.

'Wait. There's more traffic here than on the Bruce Highway.'

They stepped around the footmarks along a narrow strip of overgrown grass.

'Remind me to take photos when the light is better,' said Dennis.

He knocked on the back door. There was no reply. As he went to invite the policeman to force the door, Dennis noticed pot plants tilted, askew from their damp saucers. A key poked out.

'Well, what do we have here?'

Inside, they searched throughout the house and established Darcy's sparse room. The two men took the room apart. They looked in and above the cupboard. They lifted the wardrobe – a sleepy cockroach crawled away. After upending the drawers of the bedside bureau, Dennis scratched through a few letters. He kicked at the carpet, seeking loose sections that might have been lifted.

The men shook the bedsheets, noticing semen stains.

'Looks like he hasn't just been screwing old Sid,' observed Dennis. 'Let's run some checks. See if we can find his girl. Might help us locate him.'

The men took the mattress off the base. Dennis' eyes gleamed. 'Well, what do we have here?' Dennis held the roll, smiling at the exhibit for the prosecutor.

Standing by the door, he admired the dishevelled room, which appeared to have been scythed by a cyclone. The cockroach wandered across his path. He pressed his boot down, flattening the roach with a crunch.

'It's always good to do a little housekeeping when we make a call,' Dennis hooted in amusement. 'We've got our man. The next roach under my boot will be that thieving teacher. Let's find his girl and see what she knows.'

~

Carlo strode around town in dawn's grey mist, a newspaper satchel bobbing on his back, a reminder of the rocking rub of a heavy ammo belt. He trod through thick, wet grass along a fence line, tossing newspapers, thinking about his future. A dropped newspaper sprung open. The headline was about the sugar price. *Again.* Carlo grumbled. Although his father had bought him a property, he didn't want to become another grubby farmer stuck in a muddy cane field. His strong school marks from the year before meant he could still go to university, but that meant leaving Silkwood for years, maybe forever. Carlo threw another newspaper, wondering what he would be throwing away if he left Silkwood. *Isabella.* She'd left, then returned; and seemed she was staying. He sighed. Their hugs at the debutante ball had just been for the cameras. The match by the nonnas *was pure gammon.* Isabella said she needed space. The entire Silkwood postcode area didn't seem enough. These days she was just fake friendly, talking with him for show in front of the church congregation and nodding nonnas. A police car patrolled by. He studied the new model car and the well-dressed authority figures. *Maybe he could become a policeman?* The town girls gushed at the cops in their superhero outfits. Mr Russo had been a policeman before sacrificing his career to help Mrs Russo's parents, so he was told. Although he suspected Isabella had a secret boyfriend, she would be impressed by his clean, crisp uniform; crimefighter firearm on his hip. Gino would think of him as a son, perhaps bringing Isabella closer again. Carlo took another stride, throwing another newspaper over a fence, but slid and fell back. He sat up, panting in pain, lifting a twisted leg out of a hole covered by sprouting grass. He grimaced, feeling his crumpled ankle. Hobbling on, he threw newspapers. Another paper hit a door. A dog yelped, and so did he. Over the next hour, he completed his round, bouncing along on one leg. Limping back to the office, a dented, old car tooted and pulled beside him.

'Hey. I noticed the *Times* satchel. Need a ride to the office?'

Carlo stared wide-eyed at the driver. It was journalist Peter, his childhood hero. One day, Peter had broken up a fight outside of Carlo's classroom, and the two brawlers turned on Peter. He knocked them both out. To young Carlo, he became a god.

Peter asked, 'You're new to the paper?'

'Yes, first day.'

'That's bad luck.' He looked at Carlo's fat ankle. 'Wow, you would struggle to get a gumboot over that.'

'I'll be right.'

'That sounds like the stoicism of a young man from the land. Where are you from?'

'Silkwood.'

Carlo noticed Peter's face harden into a frown. 'Silkwood, eh? I suppose you know the Russo family?'

'Yeah. They are just two farms across from ours. I went to school with Isabella.' He paused, with a sigh. 'Bianca from the office is the eldest daughter.'

Peter closed his eyes, clenching his jaw. 'Ah, yes, Bianca.'

Carlo thought he understood Peter's pained response. Males were enthralled with Bianca. When Bianca held his hand at the office, he'd felt touched by an angel.

Carlo frowned, thinking of Isabella, who had turned away from him like a flag, picking up a stronger, preferred breeze. He closed his eyes in anguish, for her flag no longer flew over Silkwood. After delivering his final newspaper, he was sure which direction it flew. He saw the teacher's name on an envelope beside the letterbox. One Sunday afternoon, he'd taken a break when Isabella left and followed her to this address. So, she had a secret boyfriend, but *not so secret now*.

Peter pulled into the *Times* car park and turned to his passenger. 'I thought I had something going with Bianca. Turns out the teacher, the cinema guy, is her main man.'

Carlo replied, with a light sob. 'Oh, no. Wrong Russo.'

'Oh really? Her sister?' Peter asked, eyes blazing.

Peter hummed, drumming his fingers on the steering wheel.

Carlo groaned, oblivious to his throbbing ankle. He'd been cocky, trying to impress his hero. He heard an imaginary cock crow, like Judas in the bible. Judas had betrayed Jesus three times. Carlo had already betrayed his friend twice. Isabella might have turned away, but he felt miserable, turning her in.

'Hey, Carlo, you look in pain. Let's get some ice on that ankle.'

~

Later that morning, when Bianca was busy on a phone call, Peter whispered an update to Matt. 'Boss, it wasn't Bianca you saw by the cinema. It was her younger sister, just out of school last year.'

'Oh.' Matt pursed his lips, absorbing the possibility. It was the time all veteran journalists feared. Yep, he'd lost his edge. Matt turned away so that Peter couldn't read his expression.

'An honest mistake, Boss.'

Matt stood tall, rallying, 'Ah, I can see the story more clearly.' He addressed his reflection in the window. 'A devious man has been using the cinema to siphon money while debauching and corrupting a young woman into being his accomplice. This will be a bumper edition. The most delicious combination.' He clicked his fingers. 'Crime and sex.'

'Hang on, Boss.' Peter grabbed Matt's arm. 'Let's concentrate on the crime. Best keep the Russo family out of this.'

Matt turned around and glared at Peter. His junior journalist was already thinking about rekindling his romance. Again, this story was filtered by personal interests. He shook his head.

'Nah, full profile. The Russo girl is in. She's a probable collaborator.'

'Hey, hold it there,' Peter whispered, 'do you really want to stir up the Silkwood locals? It might be a bumper edition in a way you might regret.'

Walking back to his desk, Matt waved away the suggestion.

When Bianca left for lunch, Matt strolled by her desk, looking at her family photo. He leaned lower to study the image. The sisters were nearly identical. His mistake was understandable, perhaps, but the decay of his journalism standards wasn't. He stood; chin raised. Back in his Rockhampton heyday, when his reportage was ferocious, his editor nicknamed him *Matt Man*. One year, on his birthday, he received an embroidered cape. Riding a maniacal whirring mechanical bull at the pub in his cape, Matt held the bridle of the chiropractor's dream in one hand and a bottle of rum in the other. When he regained his footing after vomiting, a girl glanced from his face to his rum-soaked cape. 'You look interesting. My name's Mandy.'

Later, Matt slid twenty cents into the jukebox in the Ladies Lounge.

'Mandy, can I select a song for you?' he'd asked.

'Sure, Matt Man, anything but jazz.'

Her voice was husky. Matt tried to place the familiar voice. Adjusting his cape, Matt selected *'Tonight's the Night'* by Rod Stewart.

And so, it was.

In the *Times* office, the imaginary *Matt Man* swept in, cape swishing, stepping off the weary mechanical bull. On the office whiteboard, the returning *Matt Man* added 'Unsavoury Behaviour' to

'Missing Money' and his initials: 'MF'. Peter was personally involved and no longer on the story.

The high calling. Editorial standards, eh.

31

MID-WEEK, early morning, Frances stood at the office window, looking for Darcy among the arriving teachers. He'd never had a sick day and still hadn't phoned in to explain his absence. Wringing her hands, she supposed he would be wary. The night before in Isabella's bedroom, there were tears instead of prayers, but still no period. Cradling her shaking daughter, Frances looked at the expressionless Virgin Mother. Human tears in the room, but just a useless, sightless divine stare.

~

In the bright, slanting light of the early morning, Darcy squinted at a bus and train timetable posted on a wall in Bowen's main street. Daphne stood nearby, talking to a couple she'd recognised. Darcy couldn't locate his father's army cap, so he pulled on Pierce's sunglasses. The glasses relieved his raw eyes after two sleepless nights. Every creak in the house or blast of a truck horn on the highway fed his imagination that the mechanic had a shallow travellers' graveyard beyond the stacks of rusting car skeletons. Headlights cast shadows in the room, and he waited for the outline of the mechanic holding a heavy wrench. During fretful hours, he replayed his last discussion with Pierce.

'Nah, that doesn't work for me,' Pierce had said.

What did work? The realisation last night made him sit upright in bed, gasping for breath. What worked for Pierce was Darcy's criminal cinema enterprise. After learning about the rent scheme, he realised Pierce was capable of theft. This meant that the cinema takings were also in the funnel. He couldn't agitate about the rent scam, as he hung on to a future with Isabella.

Darcy imagined inquisitive sea creatures brushing past sunk *Salsa*. Vengeance felt good at the time, but today, it didn't feel enough. He wanted to sink more than Pierce's boat. Adrenaline surged. He thought again of Sid's loaded gun back in town.

Around dawn, he and Daphne had left the mechanic's yard for the hour's drive south to Bowen. He'd closed his eyes as they pulled out onto the highway, unable to look back at his car, ignoring the mechanic's smug smile and wave.

Tracing a finger down the timetable, Darcy considered his choices. From here, he could travel by train or bus. He chewed his lip. North or South? By bus or train?

Under the bright sun, he already felt far away from cloudy, rainy Far North Queensland and further away from Isabella. A young couple walked by, holding hands. Darcy stared at the girl's thick, swaying black hair. *How long would Isabella wait before assuming it was over?* She'd assume he'd left her, not worthy of a goodbye. Beyond murmurings when he held her, Darcy couldn't remember expressing deep feelings. The Italians expressed *amore*. He sighed. After a few days she'd assume he was an uninhabited island without *amore*, not one of the family islands like Dunk Island.

The couple kissed in shadow under a tree in the park. Her olive face was raised, and dark hair hung across her shoulder. At this distance, she could have been Isabella. He could be Carlo. *Was he seeing into the future?* Unable to watch anymore, Darcy turned back to look at the timetable, then hauled his suitcase to a telephone box.

After the long-distance beeps ended, his cousin Eliza answered. 'Darcy is that you? I'm sorry to hear about your dad. Do you want to come to stay during your holidays?'

Her invite was warm, but the Gold Coast wasn't his home. He looked north, which had become his place. He kicked a glass panel. There must be a way to atone, particularly if Isabella resumed her studies. North it was.

'Darcy are you there?' pleaded Eliza.

He replayed Pierce's threats. He visualised Gino's guns and

Frances' raised hand. No, south it was.

'Darcy? Are you okay? Will you come to stay?'

Daphne tapped on the phone booth. 'So, love, where are you heading?'

~

At the police station, Dennis repeated the details into the phone to the intelligence officer in Brisbane, trying to contain his irritation. Feeling typewriter tapping around his temples, he whispered the description of 'the person of interest' along with a make of the car and registration, expected to be travelling south.

The crime was confirmed. Sid's accountant had called. The cinema takings had really become takings. Simone confirmed Darcy handled the money. As Dennis knew, Darcy stashed the cash in his room, and the evidence was in a secure room at the courthouse, ready for Darcy's hearing before the magistrate. The roll contained a hundred dollars, but the accountant figured thousands had been pocketed. Although Dennis tried to remain detached from his cases, he shook his head. Ripping off a dying man was despicable. Yet, it was decent of Darcy to leave evidence to help ensure a straightforward conviction.

The intelligence officer reported back. 'Nothing. No motel records. No car sightings. No bank withdrawals for days.'

Dennis grimaced and nodded. The culprit had taken off just as the complaint was raised, hiding his trail, thereby confirming his guilt.

He'd followed up the girlfriend angle. On one case, he'd nabbed the missing crim's girlfriend and falsely charged her as an accomplice. This smoked out the real culprit. At the sight of the stained sheets, Dennis planned the same scheme. He'd called the school. When he asked the lady in the office for the name of Darcy Grant's girlfriend, it sounded like she had dropped the phone. With a shaky voice, she'd said he didn't have a girlfriend.

'He's not that way inclined,' the lady confided.

The lady offered her name. Frances Russo. Unusually, Italians were talking to him. 'Darcy is *sensitive*, you know, *private*, the way his type can be,' Frances had added.

Dennis remembered the many scuffed footprints by the side path and the stained sheets. A private Bruce Highway for the sensitive. Wanting to erase mental images, Dennis had sought an alternative point of view. He'd popped by the school carpark, cornering Leo Scuderi after the final bell rang. Leo had said he didn't know Darcy's whereabouts and was surprised at the idea of Darcy having a girlfriend. 'Always thought he was in training to be a priest. Disinterested in females. He's a bit delicate, eh.'

Dennis' eyes had widened. More information from an Italian. This case was irregular.

In his office, Dennis banged his table. He was much more interested in Darcy's whereabouts than his inclinations. He hadn't been too sensitive or delicate towards Sid. By now, he should be tapping his typewriter rather than wasting time learning about the thief's predilections. Dennis found a grin. Delicate Darcy would have a tough time at Stuart Creek.

The policeman who'd helped him upend Darcy's bedroom stepped into the office. 'What's the latest?' he asked.

'We have our man, but we just need to nab our man. Forget the girlfriend angle.'

'Okay. Matt Flint is out the front. Says he wants to confirm something before his deadline.'

Dennis gripped the table as if speared in the head. This migraine had given little warning and didn't like being ignored. Reaching for his sunglasses, he waved the officer away. Lowering the blind, he triaged his office hospice and locked the door.

~

Turning away from the police counter, Matt snorted at the prominent sign: 'Crime Watch. Report a Crime.' He stomped to the carpark.

'Pathetic,' he snorted. 'Does Matt Man need to tidy this up?'

In other places where he'd worked, the police and media had a grudging working relationship. Here, the detective acted as if there was no public interest in criminal activity. Simone had become wary, preferring good news about the cinema and wanting the police to lead the commentary. He visualised 'MF' on the whiteboard and felt the pressure.

Grumbling, Matt circled the car park, driving from one watchhouse to another, the town bank. The squat concrete building with reinforced windows said it was here to stay. He smiled, for the bank's generous advertising revenue meant his business was also here to stay.

He bounded up the stairs, wondering whether the manager might give him some clues about the cinema's finances or, even better, Pierce's accounts. He was only hopeful, as he knew bank staff were hired for their discretion as much as their ability to count.

The bank manager, a smiley round man, offered Matt a seat in his office. Matt soon held a whisky tumbler and settled into comfortable lounge cushions. He answered questions about his business, crossing his legs and moving into flattering, coaxing snoop mode. 'You know, our relationship with the bank is central to our business success.'

The manager beamed. Matt could tell the manager enjoyed but rarely received flattery. After topping up their drinks, the manager leaned forward. 'While I could talk business all day, can I help you with anything in particular?'

Matt pretended to admire his tumbler's warm, brown contents. 'Say, this is fine whisky. I usually take rum, but you're making me reconsider.'

'Wonderful. Very few people appreciate Irish malt.'

'I have an uncle in Ireland. I'll make sure he ships you out a few bottles.'

'How marvellous. A top-up?' As Matt accepted more murky liquor, the manager spoke. 'Let me guess why you're here. Rich Pierce?'

Matt blinked in surprise, returning to studying his glass.

The manager sat back. 'So that you know, Rich Pierce sat in that very seat yesterday and tearfully said you are having intimate relations with his wife. He said you would likely be here. He said you were coming after his wife, his marriage, and his hard-earned.'

Matt flinched, admiring Rich's guile.

'I won't ask whether it's true. But if you take his money, will you bank with us?' The bank manager looked at Matt with a blank expression, then slapped his thigh and hooted with self-amusement. 'You should have seen your face Matt. Priceless.'

'Yeah, you got me there, alright.'

The manager leaned in and lowered his voice. 'If you are after his money, you won't get it through his wife. He's the only signatory. Private account. We settled the final paperwork yesterday, but you didn't hear that from me.'

Matt reassessed banking diplomacy. He worried that everyone on the street knew his bank balance and rum bill.

'Anyway, he's a good saver. Good deposits every week. Lots of small notes and change. Every Monday. It drives the tellers crazy. But you didn't hear that from me.'

Matt nodded, figuring out the source of the small denominations handed over by the cinema manager for a cut.

The manager continued, 'They were good ol' days, though.'

'How so?'

'It's offshore. International wire this morning, but you didn't hear that from me.'

'Where to?'

'Asia. But you didn't—'

'No, of course, I didn't get this from you.'

'Another top-up?'

About thirty minutes later, Matt stood and swayed. On the lower steps of the bank, he felt light-headed. He'd gulped a fourth, massive whisky to close the discussion. *Or was it a fifth?* Leaning on the *Matt Mobile* for support, he smiled. He'd winkled details out of the manager he wasn't entitled to know. Matt's smile faded at the gradual realisation. *Ah.* The manager recognised one of his own, a fellow booze hound, not a news hound. From the window on the second floor, the manager raised a full tumbler, then appeared to fall.

Chewing a mint in his car, Matt assessed his options, including finding a long-lost uncle in Ireland. He couldn't ring Maria. Rich would have poisoned that well.

Swerving across the road, Matt sped back to the police station. At the enquiries counter, he again asked for Dennis.

'Sorry, Detective Deakin is actively investigating a crime and can't be disturbed.'

'Listen to me, sport,' Matt slurred. 'He's not actively trying to solve it.'

'Sir, have you been drinking?' The police officer sniffed the air.

'Sure have, *actively* you might say, drink driving and speeding too, but it doesn't look like you guys are interested in crime.' Matt belched. 'Tell the so-called detective that!'

'If you have information about a crime, you must report it.'

'Nah, finders, keepers. I need a quote for my article in exchange.' He blew victualler's breath in the man's face.

The policeman retreated, coughing.

Matt ran around to the side of the office. Most station windows were open, but the corner office window was closed, with the curtain drawn. Yet the sun was on the other side of the building, with this corner in the shade. He belted on the window.

'Dennis! I've got a hot lead on the cinema money.'

Inside, lying on the floor, Dennis massaged his temples.

32

THE fans in the town café rotated all day, slicing thick, humid air. The blades ticked above, reminding glistening patrons below *they were trying*. Ancient, dusty cobwebs swayed on a crucifix above the door, ruffling like Jesus' robes. Below, Simone and Bianca fanned themselves with laminated menus.

Simone frowned and confirmed the office chatter. 'Cinema revenue is missing. My father is distraught. The cinema manager is also missing. I trusted the guy, eh.'

Bianca gasped and reached for Simone's hand. 'That's terrible, your poor family. Are we covering the story? I saw it listed on the board.'

'I think so. Matt has written a few versions of the story. He wants to name everyone suspected to be involved.'

Bianca leaned in. Still learning, she loved every detail of the newspaper craft. Names in print made a person sound more real and important, unlike names etched into cemetery granite. Bianca asked if Matt was waiting for more information.

'I think so. If Matt receives a comment from the police, he wants to fully profile the character of the real Darcy Grant and his suspected female accomplice.'

'Really?' Bianca replied, wide eyed.

'Yes, he wants to report that he is romantically involved with a young university student, who was once training at the school.'

'Really?' Bianca repeated, a vague memory rising.

'Yep, Matt reckons its more than a romance, more likely they're partners in crime.'

Bianca blinked, reconsidering her opinion of Darcy. She had liked him for a while, yet he hadn't called. She now knew why. He preferred young, forbidden fruit.

'Do you know the girl?' Bianca asked.

'Yes, and so do you.' Simone paused, squeezing Bianca's hands. 'Your sister.'

Bianca stood and shrieked, 'NO! My baby sister with a crim? He's as good as dead!'

~

Toward the close of the day, Matt sat in his office, weighing up the story. He glanced at a framed front page on his office wall featuring a corrupt mayor, his former school bully, being led to a cell. It was one of his finest articles. He swivelled in his chair. *Could Matt Man mount a stirring comeback?* In his planned article, the Russo girl collaborator would add intrigue to the trio's criminal capers. His reveal would also be a salve for his mistaken observation. He looked towards Bianca's desk. He would be sorry for Bianca, but the austere *Matt Man* of old reported without fear or favour.

He stood. 'Nah.'

Peter had warned him. Matt imagined a pyre in Silkwood stacked high with his Saturday edition if he named the Russo girl. Like the Feast of the Three Saints fireworks, the region would see the glow in the sky. All over town, shop owners would sweep away the ash of his newspaper on Monday morning.

Matt walked into the newsroom to wipe the story off the whiteboard. If he could conclusively tie in Pierce, he would have a true scandal. Yet the signs were that Pierce was on the move, or at least his money was. *But Asia?* It didn't sound as tight at the Swiss, but it might be tighter than the town bank as he thought of the whisky bottle he'd helped drain.

Matt paused, looking at the bottom stair to his lair. The flapping of the office curtains reminded him of rustling sheets as Maria slid into his bed. *He hadn't been too tight either.* If he reported about Pierce, the real story would become the ruination of the devout Catholic wife and the bribes from the newspaperman.

'Nah.'

At the whiteboard, he paused to make sure he was alone. He never liked wiping away an 'MF' assigned story. Newsrooms were ultra-competitive, and he felt Peter at his heels. He held his hanky, then stuck it in his pocket, for there was a noise at the door. Two pairs of black Sicilian eyes drilled him: Bianca and her mother, Frances. Bianca unlocked the door and they marched inside. Bianca pointed to the whiteboard and explained their system.

'Mamma, here it is listed.'

Frances swivelled, facing Matt. 'Mr Flint. No, please, no. Her whole life is in front of her. *Per favore.*'

Matt went to push his hanky deeper but paused. The *Times* wouldn't exist if he agreed with every argument not to report. He needed to maintain his edge despite the beauty's entreaties. Frances worked in Pierce's office. *Leverage.* Matt stared into Frances' red-rimmed, black eyes, then pointed to the whiteboard.

'Mrs Russo, I need a better story then. Help me out.' He turned to Bianca. 'Can I have a private word with your mum?'

'Of course, Boss.' Bianca rested her hand on her mother's shoulder, kissed her cheek, and left.

'Mrs Russo, I've got a hunch about the real crim. Tell me the full story about Pierce.'

Frances clenched her jaw, and Matt heard a click. Her eyes glowed. Guiding her to his office, Matt tried to hold his nerve.

After ten minutes, Matt reviewed his notes.

'Let me read this back to you to ensure I have it right. A lawyer writes and calls most weeks. Pierce rented out a house that wasn't his. It was his decision whether Darcy ran the cinema and Pierce set the terms. You saw Pierce waiting late on Sunday at the cinema when you collected your daughter. You heard rumours that he threatened teachers with transfers unless he received a payment. The deputy said his letters of recommended expulsions were never approved, yet the mothers of these students regularly dropped off envelopes.'

Frances nodded, then seemed to study him before asking, 'Why the questions about Rich? The police are asking about Darcy Grant.'

'I initially thought the lad took the job to take advantage of the ailing manager. My contact with Pierce tells me that he is conniving. I'm almost certain Pierce took the cinema money. He likely brought Darcy into his scheme to keep him quiet and top up his pay. It doesn't look good for your daughter, close to the scene.'

Frances frowned, then reached for a tissue.

Matt continued. 'So, Grant fled, which focused the cops' attention. That works for Pierce but not Grant. I wonder—'

'I now wonder, too. He loves teaching, his students, and—' She sighed. 'And my daughter. During the week, I went to his home with Isabella—'

'And?' The snoop leaned forward.

'I could tell he left unhappy, like it wasn't his choice. Perhaps Pierce ordered him away to set him up?'

'I think you're on the right track. Did Pierce know about Isabella and Darcy?'

'Yes, I think so.'

'When?'

'Sunday afternoon. He was on Dunk Island at the same time as Isabella and Darcy.'

Matt stood. 'Sunday night or Monday is when the police started investigating. Then Darcy never reaches school, disappears, and becomes the main suspect. You're in his office. I need you to push Pierce about this.'

Frances nodded. '*Si*, I will do my best.'

'*Grazie*. Come with me.' At the whiteboard, he gave Frances his hanky. 'We're not done. Keep Isabella off this board. Find out what she knows and whether my suspicions of her are incorrect.'

'*Comprendere*, Mr Flint.'

'And grill anyone else close to Darcy.'

'*Si. Si.*'

'Also, Mrs Russo, aside from the Pierce matter, I assume, your family isn't happy with this murky romance and criminality? Will there be consequences?'

Frances' eyes brightened. 'Mr Flint. Forget the stereotypes.' Frances smiled. 'Sicilians are peaceful people.'

~

Bianca ran through the door. She burst through Isabella's closed door where Isabella lay on her bed, holding a book to her chest as she cried.

They hugged. 'Izzy, I didn't know. I'm sorry.'

Isabella cried. 'He's gone. I don't know why or where.'

'You poor thing. How terrible.'

Bianca held her sister, willing away the suggestion of Darcy as a thief and her sister as a collaborator. As Isabella sobbed, Bianca realised her sister didn't know about the allegations. Soon, the sisters were held by Frances, and the small bed sagged as the three women pressed together.

'What's wrong, eh?'

The women separated, staring at Gino by the door.

'Oh, nothing, Papa,' Bianca said as she rose. 'C'mon, let me pour you a grappa.'

'I asked, what's going on?'

'C'mon, Papa, the news will be on the telly,' Bianca said, guiding Gino's arm. 'I'll get you a grappa after a long day.'

'Nah, I'm sick of being parked in front of the telly all week with my grappa topped up, kept away from family business, eh.'

~

Together, Frances and Gino walked the fields around their home for the first time in years. Tonight, they weren't walking to settle a crying baby to sleep. Their babies, now women, were crying in their home. Frances provided a bulletin. She told him there was trouble at school because Darcy had disappeared with concerns about his cinema management, which had upset Isabella.

'What's that got to do with us?'

'There is more, but I need you to be calm.'

Gino said he would try, but soon, his yell carried across the cane fields.

'Isabella's dumped Carlo? We took that southerner into our home! He best keep his distance, or perhaps I should go after him.'

'Please be calm. We must think of Isabella.'

'Is she... in the family way?' Gino asked.

'I don't know. Maybe.'

'Maybe? Shit, we don't want to be back at the Ingham Church.'

Frances glared at Gino's back. *Do you remember why we were in that church?*

'Two shameless daughters! What a mamma you are!'

Frances stopped from yelling a rebuke, and considered a new focus for his anger.

'Also, husband, I don't feel comfortable working in the school office.'

'Huh, why?'

She explained. Foraging birds flew at the loud bellow that could have been heard all over Silkwood.

'I want to shoot that guy in the nuts.'

Mosquitos chased them home. Later, Frances watched Gino through the kitchen window. He paced around outside, puffing on back-to-back cigarettes. After dinner, she heard Gino in the shed loading and unloading rifles as if he were preparing for a pig hunt. Gino was a husband, father, and provider. It was a nice feeling to have a protector, too.

~

Later, when Gino was settled into his lounge chair and downing Bianca's generous grappa service, Frances sat with sobbing Isabella in her bedroom.

'Cut the tears.'

'What? Mamma, I'm so sad. I need a hug.'

'Sit up.' She hauled Isabella up by the arm. 'The time for being miserable is over. Forget the slutty *Dolly* articles too.'

Isabella gasped and covered her mouth.

'Isabella, it's time to grow up. Listen.' Frances described Isabella and Darcy's troubles.

Isabella sat tall, pushing the box of tissues away. 'So, he really did leave? He's on the run from the police? We might be named in the paper?'

Frances nodded, gripping her daughter's hand. 'We could both see he didn't leave happy, but I need you to be truthful.' She held her daughter's eyes. 'Isabella, did Darcy ever give you money?'

'No.'

'Did he ever ask you to hide money?'

'Oh, Mamma, never. He only took the job so we could have a place to meet.'

Frances took her daughter's hand. 'Tell me, has Darcy ever mentioned taking or hiding cinema money?'

'No, just—'

'*Just?* Just what, Isabella?'

'Just that he hated Mr Pierce coming to the cinema on Sunday nights.'

<h1 align="center">33</h1>

EVERY day, the school telephone answering machine blinked a morning 'hello' and summonsed a winking 'over here' when Frances arrived. Her first job was to listen, record, and clear the messages. Today, after rewinding the tape, she pressed 'play'. She scribbled messages, then erased the messages from the detective.

'Sorry, detective. I'm now in charge of this investigation.'

Later that morning, Frances strode across the school under her black umbrella, and entered the hall, where multiple PE classes collided in crazed mania around numerous ball games. Frances noticed the PE teachers scatter when they saw her. She was usually armed with paper slips for classroom cover for absent teachers. Friday cover lessons were always the worst, as they didn't resemble education, just riot control without the aid of tear gas and batons. Although the PE faculty were athletic, she always ran them down. She'd corner her victims like a black widow spider. Today, she squinted in concentration. Her beady eyes scanned for prey. At the sight of Leo, her spider legs bounced from her web.

~

Leo took a few steps back when Frances lowered her umbrella, eyes glowing in his direction. Frances, the compassionate school first aider, stepped over an injured student. *Oh, this is bad.* Leo hid behind mountainous Bruno, fearing another cover lesson.

'Stand still damn you,' he grumbled.

Leo had covered Darcy's Year 12 class earlier in the week. He'd described an exaggerated account of the drive to the gorge and escaping the bikies. In the front row, Bruno, arms crossed, had followed every word, holding Leo's eye. Leo hoped for cheers, but

220

Darcy's students looked sad.

An Aboriginal girl asked if Mr Grant was coming back. She looked down at her scuffed shoes. 'This is gammon, eh. Mr Grant said he wanted to see us graduate. Pure gammon, eh.'

'Yeah, gammon!' the class roared.

The bell was a relief. Leo fled, trying not to vomit.

In the hall, Leo still hid, protected in Bruno's twilight.

Frances peered around the human peninsula, and she and Leo were eye to eye.

'Mr Scuderi, can I have a quiet word?'

'Around here?' He laughed amidst the manic yells and jeering.

Frances didn't smile and shouldered him against the wall. 'Has Rich Pierce ever handled your money? Or other money?'

Leo blinked. 'Ah, well, once there was a girl, and—'

'Tell me, Leo.'

Leo thought back to the revving motorbike. 'Yep, first my money, then—'

'Keep talking.' Her notebook snapped open.

'When Pierce found out about the bikie girl, he demanded money, saying he would pay the bikie's ransom. He told me to take the yellow envelope and pay down his generosity with half of my pay.'

'Was the bikie ransom real?' Frances asked.

'No. I was just told the bikies didn't care. Apparently, the police boss told our boss.'

Frances scratched in her notebook. 'So, you were scammed?'

A student walked by, cradling an arm, twisted and bent in an unusual direction. 'Mrs Russo,' panted the student, 'can you please help?'

'Move on,' she snapped. 'Wait in the sick bay.'

'Anything else, Leo?'

Leo stared into Frances' dark, reflective eyes. Surely, she could see a snake.

'Leo, you look unsure. Anything else?'

'Yeah, something else, eh.'

Leo shed his snakeskin and described the Sunday night delivery. Frances' hand shook as she wrote.

~

In his office, Matt listened to Frances over the telephone, beaming. 'This is gold. Planted evidence.' He asked Frances to stay on the line, wanting her to confirm details with the police. Reaching the policeman on the counter, he was invited to leave a message. Matt rolled his eyes and formed the words stuck in his head all week.

'You know, Frances, he may get away with this.'

'I don't think so. I've informed my husband.'

Matt wanted the court's justice with Pierce off for a long stretch at Stuart Creek – all with extensive newspaper coverage. But a separate line of justice had been instigated. The Sicilians. In his warm office, he suddenly felt chilled. *I don't think so.* Matt wondered how much time the police and Pierce had left. Matt gleamed, looking down the street towards the highway, muttering, 'Pierce, you might want to give the Statesman a rev.'

~

Rich looked up and smiled at Frances at his office door. He welcomed her in, for it felt like an overdue visit. As the week dragged on and Darcy hadn't been located, he knew there must be great intrigue in the Russo household. He guided her to his lounge chairs.

Running the cops around might have consequences, but he wasn't hanging around to find out. His luggage was packed and tomorrow afternoon the Statesman would be on a car lot in Cairns for cash, twinkling her bright paintwork to draw the next owner. *Salsa* had slipped her leash – just a hiccup. When located, she would also be gone as quick as a jig for cash. His cash booty would ensure his moves were untraceable across Asia while he surfaced at an obscure, unregulated airstrip north of Manila.

Strangely, he longed for his reunion with Delores, his former maid, now heavy with their child. When she explained her pregnancy with a burst of tears, Rich fired her and kicked her out. Yet, when Delores wrote from Manila to say they would soon have a son, he'd looked out at the constant rain, sick of dragging Maria, unloved luggage, from town to town. Besides, it was getting a *bit tight*. Over the years, he'd extracted money as a sport. He'd started schemes at teacher training college when he lived in a dishevelled boarding house and mowed the yard to reduce rent. The mower was mechanically sound, but he extracted cash from the owner for fake repairs, also overcharging fuel. Then, he was hooked.

He'd been promoted via deft blackmails of senior departmental staff, honeypot traps performed by women he'd also compromised. He climbed the ladder, rung by rung, year by year, and one scam after another. Here, he'd racked up plenty of candy in this frontier sugar town. His remaining responsibilities were officiating at the rescheduled graduation for the 1984 seniors and 1985's Year 12s, then seeing off the sports teams early on Saturday morning. By the time there was an alert about his disappearance, like a stuck, clanging school bell, he would have become just another Far North Queensland bloke who had 'shot through'. By the end of next week, he would have selected a pretty maid, installing her beside Delores' room and the nursery.

Rich blinked, concentrating and staring at Frances. Her blouse looked more open than usual. He admired the smooth, curved incline of her breasts. They formed into a warm ravine, scaling to intimate twilight just below and behind the next closed button. He tried to control his breathing.

'Rich, do you know any more about Darcy's whereabouts?'

'Just as much as you,' he replied. 'Why do you ask?'

'Our family has become close to him.'

'Close? How close?' he asked, raising an eyebrow.

'We were all close, especially Isabella.'

As Frances crossed her legs, Rich was offered a glimpse of intimate dusk.

'Isabella, really? How close?'

'They were very close. Intimate.'

Rich conjured a mix of surprise and rage. 'INTIMATE?' Rich

enjoyed her wide-eyed alarm, and he took her hand, soothing. 'A member of my team. I'm very sorry.'

'It's quite unexpected.' Frances felt the cross on her necklace. 'Darcy loved teaching here.' She sighed. 'He loves my daughter too. Why wouldn't he complete the school year?'

Rich crossed his arms. 'Only Darcy could tell us why he left.'

'I can tell you what he told Isabella. You managed the cinema money. Now the police are asking questions.'

Rich smiled to calm his nerves. 'Frances, do you want to know what I think?'

'Please, it's all so confusing.'

'I think your daughter seduced a lonely teacher for a good report while she was on placement here. In clear conscience, I must contact the university. She will be kicked out.'

'NO! How dare you suggest that.' Frances glared and her hand twitched.

Rich gestured to a pile a graduation certificates. 'Isabella's graduation is in doubt, unless we come to some suitable arrangement.'

One day in the future, he hoped to reflect on this as his 'studio move' with Frances' sensual submission, revering his masculinity. Instead, Frances was calm and called to the door. Leo walked in.

'Leo and I had the most interesting conversation today.' She stared at him. 'Mr Scuderi was *very* forthcoming about your dealings.'

Rich leaned back on his chair, scowling. 'You two. How pathetic. Get out of my office. I have a busy school to run and don't have time for your tall tales.'

Rich jumped at the slammed door, and then the door frame shook from Leo's kick. His car keys shone on the desk. The V8 could move, and so should he, but leaving would be an admission of guilt. Rich opened his cupboard to admire his recent haircut and bleached tint in the mirror. 'Rocking Rod' would never be forced off his stage until after the encore. Also, Mrs DeLuca would be upset if he didn't honour their planned liaison before Bruno's graduation. He stamped; he would stay until he was ready. Frances and Leo were just making a point. Italians would *never* talk to the police. The Silkwood men, including Gino Russo, would be virtually embalmed in grappa after the cane harvest. They'd still be snoring tomorrow when his muscular Statesman stormed north past Silkwood to Cairns, their rifles mute and cold. He sang and danced in the mirror as Rod Stewart, tending his hair. Admiring his reflection, he hummed and sang, *Do you think I'm sexy?'*

~

Early Friday night, Frances covered her ears in pain. The re-opened school auditorium buzzed with the energetic frisson of the departing class of 1984, after a year's delay. The roar was their test of the repaired auditorium's acoustics, almost as fearsome as the cyclone that raged overhead the year before, tearing off the roof. Seesawing violins played on stage, but Frances couldn't register a note. The humid air was thick with jubilation, deodorant, perfume, and booze. Most students dressed in odd elements of their former uniforms, as encouraged by the deputy. Among the students, she spotted a few uniform articles she'd helped locate and return, always the warm, reassuring radio voice for thrifty mums. School mums called out as she passed.

'*Prego,*' she replied, nodding. Mums were finally graduating, too.

Mothers tidied their son's hair for photographs. Frances laughed as their fingers were swiped away. They'd outgrown their mother's preening. At home, it was okay for photos, but not in front of their mates.

'Mum, no!'

Sprays of loose fringe hair sagged forward. Mothers groaned.

Frances could see this wasn't a problem for Isabella, hair cemented with Bianca's hairspray, although her pink ribbon colour and birthday earrings weren't school uniform. Her eyes narrowed remembering Darcy's birthday gift. At the time, jewellery felt *too personal,* but she'd focused on the generosity, not the clue. Frances sighed, she would far prefer Isabella wear his earrings, set aside later, rather than carry his baby. She blinked at flickering light. Across the room, photographic flashes lit up a tableau of family generations.

Frances looked for Gino with their family camera. After a day of scribbling as a newspaper's hack, she wanted photo memories.

Bruno, a volunteer usher, guided and pushed his former classmates to their seats. The crowd hushed as the deputy stood at the lectern on the stage. The musical strains of the violin could finally be heard. Rich stood a few steps behind, smiling into the crowd. From her seat, Frances frowned. Rich had nerves of steel. He hadn't looked bothered by the accusations. Perhaps he was a cat that would always land paws first. She lowered her eyes, for she didn't deserve Matt's confidence, an office administrator out of her depth. Hopefully, Leo's confession was enough to keep Isabella out of the newspaper.

Gino sat in his all-occasion suit between Frances and Bianca. Each woman held a farmer's calloused hand. Frances noticed Gino scowling at Rich Pierce on the stage.

'Not now,' she whispered. 'Tonight is for Isabella.'

He turned. 'Tonight, okay, but not much longer.'

Frances and Bianca's hands were squeezed.

From the stage, the deputy welcomed the former students, confirming their instructions. They were to file in alphabetical order to collect their belated certificates. As he barked names, the alphabet-ordered teenagers trotted like sheep across the stage. Loud clapping broke out in patches for family favourites. Below, the school photographer clicked away, with Peter also taking shots for the newspaper. On the sheep trotted. The *Ns* were a large group, with a few Irish families responsible for the *Os*. As the students filed around, there were just a few remaining students from the tail end of the alphabet. There was a cheer for the Paronella lad. Then, it was time for the *Rs,* and the Russo family saw Isabella's bobbing pink ribbon by the edge of the stage. Gino focused his camera as Bianca and Frances leaned forward. Cheers broke out around them for the Santo cousins, then the Termini twins.

'Huh? What's this?' grumbled Gino.

Isabella cowered into the shadows at the furthest edge of the stage. Frances noticed her pink ribbon warbling on her dark head, then darting upstairs to the rear of the auditorium.

Frances bumped past jutting knees in their row. She raced up the stairs and held her crying daughter. At the end of the ceremony, there were cheers, clapping, and laughter.

The deputy called for order. 'Now, the academic awards.'

Below them, more students gathered. The stage glowed like a warm cocoon, and little insect figures crossed to fresh applause.

The academic award winners stood together for a group photo with Principal Pierce. As the deputy announced it was time to recognise the 1984 school dux, Frances held Isabella back from leaving. The deputy announced the 1984 dux. To applause, Carlo hobbled away from the academic group with a gumboot on one foot.

Pierce beamed, holding a certificate and medal, but Carlo stood away and called out. 'What about Isabella Russo?'

Rich smiled and gestured him forward.

'What about Isabella Russo?' he yelled.

At the rear, Isabella turned her head from her mother's side, eyes brimming but shining. There was a murmur among the student group. Isabella heard her name called out by her former classmates. Then Bruno yelled, 'Yeah! What about Isabella, Miss Russo?' Bruno bellowed again, 'And where is Mr Grant, eh?'

On the stage, Rich looked at his deputy and clicked his fingers. The deputy shuffled through a smaller file. Frances knew the remaining certificates were for the students who'd left town, were at university, or were working a shift at the sugar mill. Rich stepped back from the glow of the stage lights.

The deputy spoke. 'We seem to have overlooked one of the 1984 graduates.' His eyes flicked to Rich in annoyance. 'Our apologies. Isabella Russo, please come forward.'

Frances helped Isabella take her first few steps, and below, Gino refocused his camera. Isabella strode down the stairs to applause, which became louder when she was sighted. On stage, she hugged Carlo and crossed the stage. Principal Pierce crossed his arms. When Rich refused to take and present Isabella's certificate, the deputy stepped forward and congratulated Isabella. The deputy realised it was also his role to award gum-booted Carlo with his school dux medal. The photographer looked for the principal to include in the photograph, but he was gone.

34

FRIDAY night, Gino inspected his arsenal in a small room in his farm shed under bright electric light. His polished rifles stood in salute as if on a parade ground. The shed dog whimpered at the door anticipating a pig hunt. Gino clicked his fingers, and the dog dropped, silent but watching. He addressed the mutt, 'I have a different hunt planned.'

Gino reached for a small can of gun oil and a rag. He still missed the police firing range and carrying a weapon on his hip, always first to the farmers' pig hunts, rifles slung over both shoulders, as if ready for battle. The dog lifted its head, saliva drooling, as if reading Gino's mind.

Silkwood men approached him after the graduation, firing questions. His uncle was impassioned. 'Hey, Gino, was your family deliberately insulted?' He shoved him. 'Doesn't your wife work with him? How could he miss your daughter?' He'd punched Gino's arm. 'What are you going to do about it?'

The men gathered around him. Gino felt the press of dark suit jackets usually worn to funerals. Jabbing fingers felt like revolvers. '*Si*, Russo, what are you going to do about it?'

Gino grumbled along with them as he drew on cigarettes. Through the haze and light rain, he'd seen Isabella surrounded by the Silkwood womenfolk like a flock of birds tending to a wounded chick. Frances had cried, and his throat tightened. The man had handled his wife too.

'Hey, what's the talk about your daughter with the southerner teacher?' Another relation nudged him in the ribs. 'Remember, family honour!'

Gino walked away from the men to the carpark, but the

principal's parking bay was empty. Fresh tyre tracks stretched away. He'd ground the cigarette butt, hissing Sicilian curses at the retreating Statesman's taillights.

In the shed, Gino paused from polishing, thinking of his cornered wife in the art studio. He lit a ciggie. Tonight, he should be reflecting on what he had already done about it. Pierce shouldn't have lived long enough to stand on the stage with an audience to insult his daughter and family. As for Darcy Grant, *well,* that was another job. Gino picked up his heaviest rifle. The stock was hardwood, and the barrels were pure steel perfection, manufactured with American know-how. Puffing on the cigarette, he varnished the wooden stock. On the police firing range, he'd been told by the armourer, 'The chest, larger mass, better prospects for a hit. Only the head if you want to make a statement.'

He'd killed plenty of pigs, usually with a hit to the mid-forequarters. Now it was time, he supposed, to kill a man. He heard a cry from the house, sounding like young, wronged Isabella. *Time to kill a man or men?* He turned on the shed radio, trying to shut out his memory of young, whimpering Frances in his back seat, looking from his police badge on his partially unbuttoned shirt to the car roof.

The heavy rifle now felt as light as a stick. Pierce's smug face appeared in the crosshairs as he checked the sights. *A hit to the head to make a statement?* Yep, this weapon was the one. 'The Favourite'. He reached for his shotgun ammo and sniffed the gunpowder. Dry. Drier than the damp town street. His eyes squinted in concentration. Along the main street on Saturday mornings, men huddled in conversation in a shroud of cigarette smoke. The men's chatter hushed when he'd walk by with his wife and daughters. The men's wide eyes and gaping mouths did the talking. He'd hear one word on repeat over his shoulder: *Bellissimo. Bellissimo. Bellissimo.* Gino had assumed their eyes were trained on sultry Bianca. The word wasn't on repeat. *Bellissimo. Bellissimo. Bellissimo.* The men were counting the Russo women – one, two, three – hoping their number might come up, like a lucky ticket in the Silkwood Hotel pub raffle. Gino swallowed, reaching for a flask of grappa. Yes, his daughters were beautiful. His wife too. One. Two. Three.

The newspaper featured the principal's self-promotional columns. Earlier in the year, the column included a photo of the principal, arm embracing Frances, the office receptionist, with the caption: *The lady who really runs the show, making me look good.* Pierce, looking like a gameshow celebrity, smiled as if he had won the TV sponsor's loot. Gino clicked off the safety, wanting to fire a shot. The dog stood. It was impossible Frances found herself innocently alone with the principal with hundreds of students and teachers around. Gino's throat tightened. *Why did she stay if she felt uncomfortable?*

'Nah,' Gino grumbled.

Along the main street, the men had counted: one, two, three. Frances the only one with a wedding ring, but that hadn't seemed to bother the admirers. It hadn't mattered to Pierce either. Among the admirers, *was it hope or knowledge?*

'*Stupido,*' Gino moaned with realisation.

Frances. Probable adulteress. Acting saintly, sitting in the front pew every Sunday, but really, St Frances the Fake. He looked in the direction of their home. *Ah.* Frances was lining him up to gun down Pierce to avenge the insult to Isabella, while tidying up evidence of her infidelity. But of all men to cuckold him, *Pierce.* Gino stamped and chugged on the flask, warm grappa burning his throat. Pierce, with his feline luxury rig, the blond-haired glamour puss with soft hands, who made the local women purr. Gino looked at his hands, a replica of his father's crenulated mitts, with deep dirt crevasses. The very hands he'd despised as a boy, barely able to shake his father's hand as he readied to board the bus to the Brisbane police training academy.

Whenever he went to touch his wife, she'd inspect his rough hands. 'Yuk. No way. Get back to the shed sink and properly scrub.'

'I have,' he'd insist.

'*Mamma Mia.* It doesn't look like it.'

Pierce's soft hands on his receptive wife, *the receptionist.*

Gino studied a faded photo pinned beside his gun cupboard.

Uniformed police recruit Gino Russo stood erect, alongside the gun armourer, who held a tattered target with a peppered bullseye. Gino counted: *uno, due, tre, quattro, cinque*, calculating his likely promotions and rank if Frances hadn't deliberately become pregnant to trap him. By now, he would have been a gun instructor at the police cadet shooting range. Tonight was a rare occasion in fine, leather dress shoes, a reminder of marching on the parade ground. Young St Frances the Fake, sensing frailty in her ageing parents, willingly lay on the back seat, selecting him as a successor for the farm. Gino tore down the photo of him with the armourer. 'I was the real bullseye.'

Gino still visited his father-in-law at the family mausoleum. Every month, he emptied his bladder over Old Joe's ceramic photo, staring into his father-in-law's eyes like he'd looked into Joe's barrel in the mid-1960s. He'd stood with Old Joe beside lofty, rustling cane on family farm boundaries.

'Your family honour that side, Gino Russo,' Joe had ordered. 'This side. My honour. Gino, when a man looks into the barrel, he fully sees his sins. My daughter, fifteen. Look into the barrel. Face what you have done.'

Gino brushed the gun away. 'Honour? You need to know this. She undressed and jumped on me. I'll spare you the rest. It's not the sort of the thing a father needs to hear, eh.'

Joe shook, gun still lowered. 'You liar. Not my daughter.'

'Well, it's true. It could be any bloke from around here.'

Old Joe hissed, raising his rifle. 'You want it in the guts or the nuts?'

'Okay, okay. I'll marry the hussy. Help you out.'

Joe cried, fat tears running down his face, plopping onto his boots. 'Gino Russo,' he sobbed, 'I hope you have daughters, so you know the true meaning of love.'

He'd scoffed. 'No way, I want a son.'

'You're right. You don't deserve a daughter. You don't deserve my daughter or my farm when I pass on.'

Gino had laughed and pushed the old man. 'Your farm! Fuck that!

There's no way I'm standing in your muddy farm all day like a stupid wog migrant.'

When Joe trudged away from the family line of honour, Gino returned to his police car, trying to shut out Joe's last words.

'You've no soul.'

In the shed, Gino looked across to a family photo from Isabella's christening. He'd only sired two, when every year most Catholic families beamed for photos at the baptismal font. Gino noticed the parishioners look from his glowing young wife who radiated fertility like a blossom, their narrow-slitted eyes resting on him. *Only two?* During a pig hunt, a farmer with a brood of kids, said he'd be happy to pay Frances a visit to help out. Gino's shot over the farmer's shoulder silenced any further humour about his virility.

Back when he wanted to add to his family, he'd calculate the days since Frances' period. After dinner, young Bianca would laugh, tug at his trouser leg and shriek, 'Wow. Look Mamma, look, Papa is washing up. Is it your birthday?'

Bianca, cheeky from the moment she could talk.

Frances, with a Mona Lisa coy expression, nursed baby Isabella.

'It must be time for your prayers,' he'd instruct Bianca, taking baby Isabella, laying her in the cot. In bed, Frances' lay motionless, dull eyes stared unblinking at the ceiling, as if she was looking into outer space. But no more babies, no son, with just the mother hen and the two chicks on the nest. He'd stopped counting and was confined to the shed, allowed into the house to eat, watch telly and sleep, as if he was a tolerated unloved pet. Most nights he sat on the couch, ignored, as if he was a piece of farm machinery. Gino reached again for his ciggies, muffling a dry cough. He took a long drag.

Around the dinner table, he'd always act like he was listening to the TV news, but he tuned into family business. He could have made detective too. Bianca's latest guy was Peter, the journalist. Over the dinner table, before her deb ball, Bianca had whispered to Isabella, 'Peter's so cool. He could be a professional boxer, but he's going to be a writer. Brawn and brains. All the girls are jealous he picked me.'

After the ball, Gino had pretended to be dozing on the couch when Bianca returned with Frances. They'd marched to the laundry. Through slitted eyes, he'd noticed bloodstains on Bianca's dress. As he stole past the laundry on the way to bed, he'd tilted a detective's keen ear. Peter had punched a rival who asked Bianca for a dance, then threatened to shoot him.

Outside the shed, he heard light footsteps and turned up the radio, humming, as if he couldn't hear. Frances' perfume mixed with his cigarette smoke. The dog wagged its tail, then stilled at Gino's cold stare.

'Pierce, you *figlio di puttana*,' he cursed for his audience, pretending not to notice the shadow at the door.

Clutching 'The Favourite', Gino released the safety. There was a growl at his side. Gino followed the line of the dog's long snout into the inky darkness. Two pink eyes flashed, upraised tusks glinting. *The chest, Russo.* Gino walked to the edge of the shed as the shadow retreated. He aimed a few inches below the eyes at the squat, strong forequarters. *The head if you want to make a statement.* He lifted his aim, training the rifle between the two shiny eyes, visualising Pierce. He fired. The shape slumped with a squeal, and the dog raced into the field.

'That's what I'm going to do about it,' he yelled, retreating to his armoury.

After a minute, there was a scraping shuffle at his door, as if the listener had just arrived. Frances entered the room and lowered his raised rifle with a firm hand.

'Enough shooting, it's time for family photos,' she instructed.

'I don't think my hands are steady enough to hold the camera after tonight.'

She looked at him, still holding 'The Favourite'. 'You look steady enough. You dropped that pig easily enough.'

Gino wanted a confession from Frances, or at least more information to help further inform his plan. 'There is more I'd like to know about this Pierce business, eh'. He covered his weak, croaky warble with a cough.

'Is there?' Frances replied, hands on hips, voice icy. 'Go right ahead. Ask me.' Frances scowled at him, as if reading his thoughts. 'Ask me,' she repeated. 'What more does an honourable husband need to know? I hope that pig was target practice.'

Moments later, head lowered, Gino trudged to the house, following his wife's long strides. Within the warm light of their home, almost a holy glow, he readied to photograph the magnificent Russo women, *one, two, three,* with Isabella holding her certificate.

'Focus,' ordered Frances. He took a photo. 'Another,' she snapped.

Gino wound the film forward. *What would unsettle St Frances the Fake?* He smiled. Frances' romantic dream of Isabella's honourable wedding was turning wonderfully tawdry. *Would Isabella's baby look like her? Or more like the pale non-Catholic?* He half laughed and coughed, imagining Isabella pushing a pram with a fair-skinned infant, baby blue eyes drawn to the passing shapes of frowning parishioners.

'C'mon, Gino, we're waiting,' called Frances.

Gino focused the camera.

'Isabella, this one's for Darcy.'

He heard Frances' hiss and stamp.

Isabella beamed at his words and for the photo. Afterward, she rushed to him, hugging him longer than she had in years. Gino knew what he was saying to Isabella, and she knew what he meant. Darcy would be welcomed into their home. He hoped her belly would soon swell. Frances would sit in the rear pews, relegated from the front where the most holy knelt. She'd no longer pray for Isabella's perfect wedding, no *un buon matrimonio.* Instead, she should seek forgiveness for being a lousy mother. Gino grinned. After a quiet Ingham wedding, the young couple would live in the musty, mouldy flat behind the house, which at the time had felt like a cell, with Frances the swollen-bellied jailer. Darcy could serve his time in the same confinement. In time, Darcy could paint GRANT over their letterbox, with neat teacher strokes.

'See you lot in a while. I'm takin' a smoke outside. Bianca, a grappa, *per favore.*'

'*Sì*, Papa.'

~

Frances wrinkled her nose at Gino's cigarette smoke, frowning at the flyscreen door. *How many times had she asked him to only smoke in the shed?* The red cigarette bead swung by the door as he marched back and forth, smoke wafting into the house.

Her arm was around Isabella as she considered Gino's gesture towards Darcy. His kindness toward Isabella hinted at easy forgiveness towards Darcy. *Man, forgiving man.* Isabella burrowed into her, just as she had since she was a toddler, but her childhood innocence was long lost. Most likely pregnant. She looked in her husband's direction. *What was Gino made of?* A decent husband and father should be enraged enough to have already whacked Rich Pierce, with Darcy next when he was found. A more honourable husband would stakeout back roads and local motels in search of the southerner and organise a search party like a pig hunt. Her Papa had only spared Gino, so his daughter and her baby had a provider: an unwilling concession after weeks of cursing, with nightly visits to his gun cupboard. Perhaps though, Gino's grumbling in the shed was a rare glimpse of honour. Equally likely was that he'd seen her in the shadows, and this was another fake demonstration of masculinity, hoping she would later lift her nightdress.

As Isabella held her, Frances allowed herself a slight smirk. The day before her papa had died, he rose from his bed, yellow, not his native olive hue, looking more dead than alive. 'My bella,' he'd croaked, 'do you know where I'm going and why?'

These were the first words spoken to her for months.

'Yes, Papa. Do it. You know what to say.'

For weeks, she'd passed her papa on the couch as he stuffed his pipe with homegrown tobacco. Leaning down she'd whispered, 'Get him out of uniform, Papa. Unworthy of *poliziotto uniforme, sì?*'

He never replied, but sometimes he'd pause from his routine. But one night, he nodded and put down his pipe. In the mid-1960s, the local police sergeant must have been shocked at a Sicilian's voluntary presentation at the police counter.

'Daughter. Fifteen. *Bambino.* Russo *il poliziotto. Arrivederci to his uniforme? Sì?*

Although the officer was unlikely to have been Italian, he would have pieced it together; understanding the *lingo* was part of local policing. *Comprendere signor,* the officer might have replied.

'I hope I can show Darcy the photo soon.' Isabella sighed.

'For sure,' heckled Gino from the door.

Isabella faced her. 'Mamma, do you have a photo from your graduation? Do we look alike?'

From outside, Gino laughed. 'Graduation? Ha!'

'What's wrong with Papa?' Isabella asked.

Frances scowled, closing the front door, waving away cigarette smoke. 'Graduation? Oh, well, that was so long ago… You know, I'm almost a nonna.'

'Gammon, Mamma, you are young and beautiful,' assured Bianca.

Frances hugged them both. 'Oh, I don't deserve such wonderful daughters. Forget photos. Let's toast Isabella. Bianca, set out our best vino glasses, *per favore.*'

~

'The bastard is going to get away with it,' Matt Flint mumbled in his bedroom. He was a few rums 'deep'. Below, he could hear the men on the street shuffling away from the 'top pub' at closing time. 'Pissheads,' Matt toasted in admiration.

Frances had called in the afternoon. Pierce was defiant. After the call, Matt had sighed with disappointment. Matt thought he'd released weaponry, *the Sicilians,* but Frances just rang through with information, not action. Peter had also called with his account. Pathetic Gino Russo just smoked, glared, and grumbled. So much for Sicilian family honour. At the end of Peter's call though, he felt optimistic about the town's future. The schoolboys had stood up for their friend. Male brain and brawn had rallied to the damsel in distress. Matt raised a refreshed glass at the prospect of a mid-week feature about dux Carlo. He shuffled towards the steps to his downstairs office. The 'MF' article must be listed on the whiteboard. *Always a newsroom!* He stumbled and gripped a chair to steady himself. His elation sank. Maria still hadn't called. Although their severance had been less than a week, he felt back where he'd started in town. Single. Scorned. The better-looking blokes in Rockhampton would often critique the form of their lady friends. Over beers, they'd compare notes, while ogling the barmaids. *Wouldn't mind a decent night's sleep. You know how it is, Matt.* He'd stare into his beer, nodding. Hours later, he'd shuffle out, wallet empty, bladder full. On the street, one prolific mate would regularly hold up a beer coaster with blurry scribbles on the back. Name and phone number, with a red lipstick kiss. One night, his mate was joined by two ladies. Holding one, he'd asked the other, what about my mate? The girl had turned to inspect the wobbly two a.m. post-pub prospect. *What? Him?*

In his office bedroom, Matt stamped his feet. His mates had choice, but his cupboard was bare. He rubbed his eyes at the mirror, then focused on the reflected wardrobe. It wasn't bare; the office gun was propped in view. Matt whirled around, wondering about the former newspaper owner. Maybe he'd been a principled crimefighter, like *Batman*. Perhaps he'd donned a Far North Queensland cameo bat suit and cleaned up deeds that couldn't be reported. Perhaps he'd felled the baddies when the police were distracted by *The Joker*. A joker like Pierce.

Matt stared in the mirror to see if his looks had improved. Rum, the 'deaf and dumb', had the power to enhance. He squinted, seeking a dashing Romeo, Matt Flint. The rum was strong, but not that strong. Yep, he'd been struck hard with the ugly stick.

He reached into the cupboard. The gun felt good in his hands. This time, he felt capable, not like the earlier showdown with Pierce. Then, he'd felt like an amateur extra in a western, the gun a mere prop. He took a long hit of rum, feeling mighty, ready to spring from his cave to save Gotham. He stood in front of his mirror. *Matt Man* appeared, draped in a polyester cape.

'Robin,' he murmured to the mirror, 'Gotham needs us. Into the Matt Mobile.' He lay down on his bed with the gun and his rum bottle. 'Full revs, Robin, we may not have much time.'

Above him, Robin saluted. *Okay, Matt Man. Who are the likely vigilantes?*

'First, Gino Russo, heavily armed. Sicilian blood. A disappointment tonight but will rally. Second, Darcy Grant, a dark knight. On the loose. Highly motivated. Third, Leo Scuderi. Ripped off and an unwilling accessory. A sportsman too. Will want to hit the target and even the score. Fourth, Maria Pierce. Hates her husband. Wants to become a widow. She's in love with her handsome lover, a master in the sack. Maria has put down many animals as a vet. She'll be happy to put down another.'

Matt Man recalled Pierce's cruel taunt. *No more pussy for the town's ugliest man.*

'Robin, add me to the list.'

As Matt rolled his head around, the *Matt Mobile* roamed around town. He felt ill. The crimefighter saloon pulled up with a screech, and Matt returned to the room. Brown, viscous liquid dribbled from his chin. Sweating, with vomit on his pillow, he held the gun upwards, aiming at an imaginary Statesman that sliced in his whirring fan blades. He pulled the bolt back and opened the chamber. A copper cartridge rested in sinister repose.

Wiping his chin, Matt recalled reports of JFK's assassination, described as a 'turkey shoot' with countless brigands on the grassy knoll in Dallas as the presidential limousine murmured by. Pierce had made plenty of enemies. It could well be a turkey shoot, or here in Far North Queensland, more aptly, a mob feral pig shoot. The downstairs door opened with a creak. Matt's eyes gleamed from rum and hope. *Maria?*

'Just me, boss,' called Peter. 'Just in from the graduation. I want to get on with the feature. You okay up there?'

'Oh yeah, never better,' Matt slurred.

'Boss, I know you're close with the principal, working with his column, eh, but he was in bad form tonight. Someone should do something about it. The Russo guy seems like a weakling to me.'

Matt heard typing below, the tap, tap, tap in time with the throb within his temples. Among the typing and tapping came a ringing sound. After a few moments, he realised it was the phone. *Always a newsroom! Maria?* He clutched below his bed for his upstairs phone extension before Peter reached the editor's office. He heard Peter swear, reminding Matt of a journalist's pet hate: being interrupted when on a roll. The phone still rang, and Matt's hand patted around, like a swaying elephant trunk looking for peanuts. Peter's chair rolled back. More cursing. Peter's heavy steps paused at the ping of the answering machine.

'Message for Peter. About your girlfriend.' The voice sounded Mediterranean, but muffled, as if speaking at a distance through a handkerchief. 'I saw her jump in the principal's car in town tonight. He's probably feeling her up in the back of his Statesman right now.' The caller coughed. 'It's a nice car. What girl wouldn't be tempted by a slice of luxury? We've all seen your cheap heap.' The caller coughed again. 'The guy is a real sleaze, eh. The question is, what are you going to do about it? Weren't you a champion boxer?'

A typewriter crashed to the office floor. Matt murmured, 'Robin, add Peter up the list. Yep, this is going to be a turkey shoot.'

35

'WHERE are you going, love?' Daphne asked Darcy again in Bowen, early Friday morning, squinting in the bright morning sun.

'South by train,' replied Darcy from the phone booth.

With a departing toot, she'd turned her car around, returning to her oil-caked husband. Darcy watched the car depart down the long main street to be sure he'd seen off another Mrs Black, a type of welfare lady. Darcy suspected the sly mechanic – Mr Black, judging by his mitts – had been working on *The Pearl* from the minute they'd left for Bowen that morning. Mr Black was probably considering which Townsville car lot would give him the best price. Darcy felt the spare car key in his pocket.

Near midnight, Darcy approached a wizened, wrinkled truck driver at a roadside service station. 'I'm looking for a ride north.'

The driver looked him up and down, then stared at his bruised face. Darcy understood. He'd also made a rough assessment. There were plenty of stories about serial killer truckers in Australia. Darcy smiled sweetly.

'Okay, but one good turn deserves another,' growled the driver. 'A pack of Chesterfield Kings. Unfiltered. Full tar, too.' The driver pointed a nicotine-stained finger at the shop beyond the petrol bowsers. 'My name's Desmond.'

In the smoke-filled cab a few minutes later, Darcy asked, 'How far are you going?'

'All the way through.' The driver drew on the cigarette. About half of the ciggie crackled until he took a breath.

'Cairns?' Darcy asked, coughing.

'Yep, how far are you going?'

Darcy squinted through nightclub haze in the truck cab, listening to the smack of bugs on the windscreen.

'That depends.'

Looking up from his lap on the drive homewards from Etty Bay, Isabella had asked, 'What's *Under Milkwood* about? I get the bit about always seeing the good in people, but the rest is confusing.'

'I don't want to sound like a teacher, but I will give it a go.'

'That's okay, Darcy. You can be Mr Grant again for a few minutes. I can be Miss Russo, still learning.'

'Well, that's the point. The characters play many roles in their minds and dreams, carrying around versions of themselves, often different people inside the one person.'

'Like you are Darcy, my boyfriend, on weekends? Then Mr Grant at school?'

'Yes, Miss Russo, a jumbled mix of personalities. Then acting within expected roles during the day to suit the audience.'

Isabella counted on her fingers. 'I'm a daughter, sister, supermarket checkout chick, uni dropout, and girlfriend.' She'd paused, then adopted her husky Sophia Loren persona. 'So many roles to play, *signor*, but my favourite role is being your girlfriend.'

As the truck bumped along the highway, Darcy wiped his eyes.

'You okay?' asked Desmond. 'Ciggie smoke a bit too much?'

The CB radio crackled. Darcy asked the driver whether he enjoyed driving, for Darcy felt tall and mighty, bouncing high in the cab as the truck cleared away hopping kangaroos. It was a similar feeling to when he drove Sid's big truck.

'Yeah, it's good to be your own boss.'

Darcy nodded as a rain burst smacked the windscreen.

Over the squawk of the CB radio, Darcy tilted his head towards the radio speaker, recognising a familiar tune. As he hummed along to 'Riders on the Storm' by *The Doors*, in time with the swiping windscreen wipers, a smile formed, the first for days. He visualised Sid's truck; he could be a rider on the storm. An hour later, the truck lifted over a slight rise, headlights illuminating a long, treeless plain. In the distance, a tiny light glowed by the road.

'Do you know that place?' asked Darcy, pointing at the light.

Desmond laughed. 'I know every damn metre on this endless highway. You mean the mechanic's scrapyard?'

'Yep, do you mind if we pull over?'

'Sure, I could use a piss and another ciggie.'

From the truck, Darcy crept low by the highway. There were no lights upstairs. Outside the garage, he gasped in joy. 'Oh, Pearl.' Starlit moisture streaked her bonnet like tears. Darcy rolled down the window, releasing an acrid mechanic odour. The silent highway made the squeak of the handle sound loud. 'C'mon,' he whispered, glancing upstairs, hoping for truck lights on the highway. He inserted his spare key in the ignition, waiting. As a convoy of trucks neared and roared past, he turned the ignition, easing *The Pearl* away from her roadside clam shell.

On the highway a few minutes later, fast-approaching blinding lights shocked Darcy's eyes. The truck roared past with a 'toot' and a thumb out the window with a blazing cigarette firefly.

Darcy tried to remember the back roads to town. When he arrived around dawn, the police station should be his first stop, but ratting on Pierce didn't seem enough. Sinking *Salsa* didn't feel like he was square with Pierce. He thought of his conversation with Isabella: Mr Grant during the day and Darcy after hours. *What was his role to play in 'Under Silkwood'?* From his roaming around, he knew of farmer rigs he could borrow, always keys on the floor and a gun under the seat. Sid had the equivalent of a hand cannon, almost the size of a sugar mill chimney. The rig came with the standard Far North Queensland sweat-stained cap that could be pulled low in disguise. Darcy thought of his father.

'That's my boy,' his father had said with a laugh as Darcy blasted a beer bottle at long range with his first shot. They stood in a patch of dry bush down the Toowoomba Range. 'A man just needs to be able to shoot, loot, root, and scoot.'

His dad threw a bottle high, and Darcy blasted again, his father cheering at his fireworks of blooming shiny glass slivers. His father guzzled another beer and threw it higher than the first. Darcy spotted the shadow near the sun and lifted the rifle. But he was reminded of his mother's smouldering frock heading to heaven. The bottle thumped into soft gum leaves. His father grabbed the gun and butted him in the sternum.

'You only get one sight. Never pull out. Take the shot.'

Awaiting dawn's glow, Darcy calculated that the school sport send-off was just a couple of hours away. Pierce always farewelled the teams, parading his flowing blond locks as if on a catwalk for the town mums.

He heard his father from the grave. *Take the shot.*

'Yes, Dad,' he growled towards the brightening horizon.

~

'Well, Leo, like I said, it's great to see you,' his uncle slurred. 'Must nearly be dawn, eh.'

Leo and his uncle sat on large wooden chairs in a high-ceiling farmer's shed overlooking cane fields on Murdering Point Road, close to the turn-off to Silkwood. Between them, empty beer bottles stood shoulder to shoulder, covering a low table. Leo's uncle tried to place an empty beer bottle on the table, but it smashed on the shed floor. Neither of the men noticed.

'Yeah, you too, Uncle Joe,' Leo replied, 'it's been too long.'

Joe belched, lighting a cigarette. 'Leo, I admit, I would have liked to have seen more of you since you came back, but I understand a handsome young buck like you must have a busy social life.'

'Sorry, Joe, I have let many important things in my life go, eh.'

Joe looked at Leo's car parked inside the shed.

'Yeah, I can see.'

'I intend to make amends,' Leo replied.

'I didn't expect you to call out here late on a Friday night, that's for sure. Isn't Friday a big night at the town pubs? Plenty of skirt around, eh?'

'Yeah. But tonight was different. Delayed Year 12 graduation from last year. Amazing scenes at the end. A couple of young blokes stood up for their friend.'

Leo stood, stretched, and sighed. At the start of the school year, he'd never imagined Bruno would have volunteered as an usher at the graduation of his former classmates, also offering to help Leo with Saturday morning school sport. After the graduation, he'd put an arm around Leo's shoulders, saying, 'Mr Scuderi, I want to be like you, a PE teacher and a good sport, eh.'

Leo had stared up at Bruno, blinking. 'I dunno about that, Bruno, eh,' he'd managed to reply.

'Leo, I'm sure you have set a good example,' his uncle said. 'I read the principal's column every week. It sounds like there are many great people at the school, starting with the exceptional principal.'

Leo looked away, shaking his head, thinking about Darcy's disappearance. Perhaps he'd helped Bruno correct his course, but he'd spun Darcy's life out of control. Leo sighed, stifling a belch. *The teenagers stood up for their friends.*

Uncle Joe stood, gripping the armchair for support. 'I need to get to bed. It's nearly light.' He paused, cocking an ear towards the fields. 'Hang on—'

Leo watched his uncle stumbling towards the edge of the shed, kicking cane toads. 'Leo, did you hear that?'

'What is it, Joe?'

Leo tilted an ear but could only hear the murmur of distant vehicles on the highway.

'There it is again, Leo. Pigs!'

Leo heard distant squeaks and squeals, reminding him of naked Penny's giggling shrieks as he tickled her on the spring mattress.

Pulling back the tarp and reaching into his old, rusty truck, Joe pulled out two rifles. 'Here you go, Leo. It's time to drive vermin off our patch. What do you say?'

Moments later, Leo held a giant shotgun, still familiar after years of shooting on Joe's farm when he was a gun-crazy boy.

'You drive,' his uncle encouraged. 'Need to hit them before dawn.'

Leo caught the thrown truck keys. 'Vermin, eh?' Leo asked, thinking of Rich Pierce. 'Pigs will be a good place to start.'

36

THE old farm truck spluttered and puttered along the Bruce Highway toward town early Saturday morning. The driver felt vibration and looseness in the steering as the tyres rolled inwards and outwards. The truck eventually found a vibrating rhythm in the higher gears. Loose mud flew off, while the hardened soil remained forged with the paint and rust, clinging on for another cane season. Later, when the truck was back under its tarp, it would be like it didn't exist, hidden in just one of hundreds of identical sheds in the far north. Although the vehicle was difficult to handle, it would be more difficult to find.

The driver steered the vehicle around a corner in town, correcting direction with seesawing hand movements, lowering a sweat-stained farmer's cap. Ahead was the school. Right on time, the school bus was departing for Saturday morning district sport. Parents' cars filed away, with their sporty kids dropped off.

With a newspaper photo smile, the principal waved to the departing bus, standing beside his Statesman with the driver's door open as if he were looking for an express departure. The driver edged the truck alongside the school gate, parking with screeching brakes.

~

Matt Man approached the principal's home near the school, trembling and sweating. His headache was *special.* It was the same pain after his first night in town, when he'd finally reached Mandy by phone. Back in Rockhampton, she'd let him share a bed with her, but only mid-week in motel rooms. In bed, she was managerial. Practical, instead of passionate, but Matt didn't mind. He would wake alone, as the thin grey curtains brightened to pink, his wallet lighter, driving home in twilight as the newspaper delivery team threw his copy over fences.

When she took his call after the *Times* deal, he'd heard more than her gravelly voice; classified advert calls had echoed. The night they'd first met, he adorned in a vomit-strewn *Matt Man* cape, she'd said he looked interesting. It had felt like a compliment. As they'd swayed outside the pub, night bugs whirling above in the streetlamp, Mandy had explained she was between places. 'But I know a location,' she'd said, or offered.

In town, *Matt Man* turned the corner towards the school, feet sliding, trying not to trip, thoughts of Maria, Mandy too.

Later, he and Mandy travelled by taxi to a motel, with the stench of cow manure in the air. Empty cattle trucks parked on the edge of the road. Truckers smoked, pacing by their rigs, as if waiting. The night motel manager nodded when Mandy stepped out of the car and walked into the unlocked room with the key in the door. Matt stumbled into a sterile motel room. Mandy unbuckled his belt, suggesting he desist reportage about personal services crime.

'Matt, everyone is entitled to a good time and a good living.'

Matt's cape had fallen to the floor.

The next week, when he filed insipid stories, the editor scowled, asking what had happened to *Matt Man*. He'd turned away, chasing stories but not vice, for he had a 5-6 p.m. slot with Mandy.

Outside the Pierce premises, Matt stamped and took a breather. Matt glanced at the kitchen window where Maria once flashed her breasts. He closed and opened his eyes, wanting her again, but the curtains were drawn. His bella in Queensland's sugar Italy. With a hoarse rattle of his throat, he hummed *'Sugar Baby Love'*. Matt looked at the garage door where he'd placed the rolled newspaper, thinking of Mandy. He hung his head. He'd always paid for it, one way or another, compromising himself along the way.

Matt wobbled towards the school, steaming inside his long raincoat superhero costume. He caught a whiff of his armpits. *Ouch.* Worse than the smell of cow shit in a Rockhampton motel. He stomped sideways and forwards, gradually making progress towards the school, adjusting the bouncing gun inside his coat. By the school gates, he'd met Pierce many times to gather stories. Today, the final chapter. After a long pull on his rum bottle, he threw it aside, not hearing the smash.

~

After the truck's deep honk by the school gate, the principal looked over and then walked toward the farmer's rig. 'C'mon, a little closer,' the driver whispered, wondering whether Pierce would recognise the generic muddy DeLuca farm rig.

Everyone knew.

Pierce's porn star limo streaked like a shooting star for everyone to see, long blonde hair blowing out the window. Twice a week, the newspaper landed over town fences, dated stories tightly edited. Town gossip was the real town crier, with salacious, delicious news carried on the breeze 24-7.

Everyone knew.

Word reaching the husband. Bruno had roared and destroyed a school toilet door after reading his mother's name scratched into the woodwork, along with other etched particulars.

Watching Pierce's saunter, hearing his whistle, the driver wondered whether the pursuer ever worried about being pursued – the predator becoming prey. After pulling up his pants and thinking of his next appointment, *did Pierce ever worry about the husband? Or the monstrous son?* At a distance, Pierce slowed a little, stooping, trying to identify the driver.

'C'mon, a little closer,' the driver whispered again.

Earlier, a derailed cane tram delayed road traffic. The Italians stood around blessing themselves, for it was an omen, adding to stories of a worldwide sugar-supply glut and a collapse of the cane price. The early morning radio bulletin reported boat debris washed up on Dunk Island – an esky and fuel tank – and the feared loss of life. News was also circulating about a crocodile attack, a chilling cry heard by a riverbank, possibly linked to town chatter about a missing teacher. The cinema owner had died, and the flicks were closed again. There were more death notices than births in the newspaper. A dread had settled over town like ash; tomorrow, there would be a stampede to the church confessionals. Locals felt a sense of pending doom, like another cyclone building on the horizon.

The driver honked the DeLuca truck horn again and flashed the headlights. Pierce was closer, stooping lower to peer inside the open window, probably hoping to spy Mrs DeLuca presenting for another sneaky liaison, blouse already unbuttoned.

'Can I help—' Pierce asked, his mouth open.

'You?' the driver completed Pierce's sentence.

Varnished, shiny wood and metal reflected the principal's wide-eyed fear. With a nod, the driver raised the rifle. The chest offered body mass. The head a statement. After a booming rifle blast, thick, caustic smoke filled the driver's cab. Pierce disappeared in the choking fog. The driver coughed, eyes streaming, ears ringing.

As the smoke cleared, a hazy outline appeared. With trembling fingers, the driver reached for ammo. Another shot was needed.

Pierce wobbled, then toppled over with his head blown clean off. Strands of fine blonde hair hung in the air like puffs of dandelion filaments. The driver lowered the rifle, but there was no time to admire the principal's expulsion, for a truck had turned the corner. With a rev, the rig lurched forward, blood streaked along the door mixing with the mud and the rust.

~

Nearing the school, Matt *Man* heard a blast or bang. Then, a revving engine. Noises, no doubt, from the mill, disturbing residents' peaceful enjoyment of the weekend. *Shame on the mill manager.* He'd write and publish an anonymous 'letter to the editor' in complaint, then demand a full-page apology advertisement, in colour. *Kicking arse*, Mother.

After a few more steps, *Matt Man* stood trembling across from the school gates. The Statesman's paintwork flashed just metres away. Bianca Russo apparently another notch on the leather seat upholstery. *Poor Peter.* Matt adjusted his sunglasses. Sweat stung his raw eyes. He shuffled the rifle inside his raincoat sleeve, clicking the safety off. As he rubbed his eyes, a second vehicle swam in his eyesight. *Peter?* The rig looked like a farm truck that sometimes parked in front of the cinema.

'Robin, yep, it's starting to look like a turkey shoot.'

From his pocket, he lifted a spare flask. A blurry fair-haired man appeared with pale southerner skin, Pierce, but skinnier than he remembered. Pierce must be keeping clear of the tuckshop sausage rolls, Matt surmised. Matt coughed; his breath stung his eyes. The Pierce outline shimmered in the mirage, kicking a large lump on the ground. *Matt Man* shuffled, trying to aim and focus the crime fighter gun despite stinging sweat and blinding flashes. Then, a golden spark. Ah, Pierce's egomaniac sunnies. *Target confirmed, Robin.* He heard voices. *Fuck off, Flint. No more pussy for the town's ugliest man. Nah, I'd never pay for it. Don't be a softie.*

'This is for my bella!' he yelled.

His superhero gun blasted, and the skinny, fair-haired figure flipped backward, joining the other lump on the ground.

Retreating, Matt framed a story on the whiteboard. 'Honour killing. Sicilians suspected. Closed case.' He'd assign 'MF' to keep the copy under close control.

The greasy, stinking rum soak trudged up the hill, the gun barrel hot within his raincoat sleeve. Rambling back to his office, he remembered the skinny, fresh-faced, fair-haired young man in the corner of the photo from the night the cinema reopened. *Pierce: skinnier than he remembered.* His head pounded, already promising to be a killer. *Killer?* Matt stopped and looked back. *Oh, what have I done? Was that Pierce?* He stumbled along, needing to be at his office as an alibi when the sirens howled and the phone began to ring.

~

Once on the Bruce Highway, the driver rolled down the stiff window to clear away the gunpowder odour. Closer to the farm, heavy rain lashed the windshield. The truck wipers scraped and scratched, trying to clear the rain. The driver smiled; the rain would wash away Pierce's cold crocodile blood. Heavy rain was a welcome disguise too, for no one could identify the truck or driver, as the road was barely visible.

The constant scraping of the wipers began to sound like a screeching accusation.

Don't-Take-The-Law-Into-Your-Own-Hands.

The driver reached towards the ancient radio, seeking to shut out this judgment. Radio station frequencies were etched on opaque plastic, with a vertical red wire to tune. With a tweak, the radio dial turned, but not the red line. After pressing buttons like tiny piano keys, a strained static crackled from the speakers. Muffled by dust, a hint of a musical tune tinkled. The driver thumped the radio console. The music became clearer. High keyboard notes emulated rainfall, and the driver turned up the volume, recognising 'Riders on the Storm' by *The Doors*. The driver smiled, feeling like a rider on the storm, high in the cab with rain on the roof and water sloshing under the discordant wheels.

~

Darcy lay in his childhood bath on the road at the front of the school. The plug popped, blood emptying away. Isabella appeared above in his imagining, hooking a finger.

'I'm a strong Silkwood. I'll be okay.'

As the bathwater lowered, he reached for the fluffy towel offered by his mum, with twinkling green-blue eyes, just as he imagined as a boy. 'You're so grown-up, Darcy. I've missed you over the years.'

Darcy closed his eyes, and his mum disappeared with a motorcycle rev into a Toowoomba fog.

A large vehicle idled close by – maybe the school bus. Kids screaming. A shadow was over his eyes. Then a familiar male voice, with alcoholic breath like ether.

'Darce, hang in there. An ambulance is on the way. I need to settle my debts, eh.' He felt a shove. 'DARCY GRANT. Eyes open. HOLD IN THERE. EYES OPEN, EH.'

The Pearl was on the highway, idling, ready to return. Tears streaked her bonnet. 'Ready, Darcy?' she asked.

'Yep. Ready.'

He turned on the ignition. His dad saluted.

Isabella unhooked his finger. 'Bye. I'll never forget you.'

Within heavenly clouds, his father and mother waved and beckoned. Darcy felt shaken as there was turbulence on his skyward travel to the afterlife.

'Steady there, Bruno. He's injured.'

'Never mind the ambo, Mr Scuderi. I'll carry him. Some southerners are worth saving.'

37

FRANCES pulled the tarp over the DeLuca farm truck, kicked the cleaned, warm rifle with her heel deep under the seat, and walked the cane track home. The DeLucas were rarely at home; Bruno was usually at football training or studying at the school library, and Mrs DeLuca had a busy social life after her husband had left. Anyway, farm equipment and vehicles were borrowed without asking – always keys on the floor. Farm sheds were a type of church. The favour repaid with an unspoken fuel top-up, like a few coins thrown into the offertory plate during mass.

Still asleep at their home, Gino wouldn't know she'd left, following Bianca's heavy Friday night grappa service. Like a barmaid at the Silkwood Hotel during happy hour, Gino was regularly topped up when he'd returned from the shed after making a phone call. To Frances, the clicks on the home phone had suggested a brief chat. When Gino sat down, he was jovial as he toasted Isabella. Happy hours. Frances had crushed a few sleeping pills in his last large glass. When she'd left at dawn, he was still on the lounge, rolling his head from side to side, mumbling about family honour. Gino didn't know about family honour, but he soon would. He'd mumbled too about fixing someone to do the job, as if he had a plan.

When she was a young teen in disgrace, her father had taken down her paintings, hissing and pointing at her belly. In their lounge room, she learnt what Gino had said by the farm boundary.

'*Bambino potrebbe essere di chiunque.*'

Her baby could have been anyone's.

'Oh, Papa, that's not true.'

She'd sobbed as he slapped away her outstretched arms.

Last week, during Bianca's rare return to church, she complained. 'Mamma, c'mon, give God a break. He'll still be here next week.'

Still, she'd knelt, long after the priest was out of his vestments, with keys jangling, ready to lock up, keen for his long Sunday lunch hosted by a parish family.

Bianca had stroked her hair. 'C'mon, Mamma.'

Frances had hissed upwards at the religious figurines, 'I want redemption and resolution. Isn't that what you're about?'

'Mamma, c'mon, you're not making sense. C'mon. *Per favore.*'

The priest had rattled his keys, hurrying them out. As they'd stood, Frances stared at the baptismal font, holding Bianca's hand. She'd remembered baby Bianca, looking upwards at her for protection – not Gino, not the priest, not Jesus. Bianca had smelled her milk, whimpering. As they'd walked towards the door, Frances paused at the confessional.

Bianca had pulled her mamma's arm. 'Oh no, Mamma, let's leave.'

'It's okay, Bianca, dear, I'm done.'

With angelic baby Bianca suckling on a dummy in a bassinet outside the confessional, she'd knelt in the dark. Allowed back, for she'd worn a wedding band, Frances had whispered through the metal gauze, 'Sorry, Father, for I have sinned.'

She'd sought the Lord's forgiveness from the male priest for the male things done to her. She'd sought repentance for the immoral swelling that had shamed her parents, particularly the accusation: *The baby could be anyone's,* the angelic daughter with a parish award for perfect attendance at Sunday School. Frances had bowed her head at the priest's instruction, listening to the path for absolution of sin.

'You must be truly sorry to be forgiven.'

Inside the tiny box, she'd gagged at the priest's stale breath and vestments with baked-in body odour. Outside, Bianca slurped and suckled on her rubber dummy, *the comforter.* Frances had left, ignoring the terms of atonement. *Comforter? Not here.* Her school friends had stayed to talk with her, hoping to admire and hold her baby, but they were hurried away by long-skirted mothers.

During primary school, she'd held hands under the school desk with cute, polite Joseph. They'd read fables about princes and princesses as she'd stared into his warm brown eyes. He'd asked for her middle name while reading Bible stories together at Sunday School.

'Mary,' she'd replied with a smile, taking his hand.

Over the years, she'd seen handsome Joseph at church. He would look from his plain wife to thuggish Gino and shrug. Frances knew what he was saying: *Look where we ended up.* No princess for him. No prince for her. No Joseph and Mary.

As Frances walked the trail away from the shed and the truck, the roof of her home jutted above the ever-rising cane stalks. Her father had modelled the house on his memory of his boyhood home in Sicily before it was bombed during the war. Her father, *not Gino's.* Her family, *not his.* Gino's filthy boots at the back door. Her papa cleaned his boots in the shed every afternoon, only approaching the house in his 'outdoors slippers', the only present he ever wanted on his birthday, besides an extra-long hug from his daughter.

'Call that extra-long? Don't stop, *per favore.* I want to feel your hug forever.' Then he would place both hands on her slight shoulders, looking deeply into her eyes. '*Bella,* you must marry well, *un buon matrimonio* to honour your parents, and carry on the *fare l'agricoltore,* the farm. It wasn't possible for my parents in Sicily, with no farm left, but you can do it here. *Comprehende?*'

'*Si, papa, un buon matrimonio.*'

Gino's gnarled feet with scaly yellow toenails. Bulbous purple legs draped over her papa's chair with an outstretched hand. 'Grappa, woman,' he'd call. 'After a long day.'

Frances stood where uniformed Gino had parked in his police car, pulling up her dress, drawing her into dishonour.

'C'mon,' he'd say above her, 'make some noise. I'd love your God to hear.'

'You pig.'

'Yeah, I like that. Tell me again.'

He squinted, concentrating.

'Open your eyes, pig.'

Her legs were open, but her eyes were wider.

'Can you see, Gino?'

He'd stared into her open, widening eyes as he grunted.

'*Malocchio*,' she'd whispered.

Today, the police would be coming. Before the graduation, she'd placed Isabella's certificate in the wrong folder. She laughed, remembering Pierce frozen on the stage. Everyone would have seen Gino swearing at the principal's empty parking bay. She'd smiled at the sight of the unpleasant, pasty-skinned town detective skirting the crowd, ready to pounce on Darcy.

She'd called during the day. 'Detective, people at school have a feeling Mr Grant will be returning at graduation time.'

She'd held her hand over her mouth in delight as the detective studied Gino, who'd roared at the departing Statesman.

This morning, one of his guns was also missing from the rack, his favourite, which he'd discharged the night before. *Sorry, husband.* 'The Favourite' with fresh residue and his fingerprints was under the seat of his truck, which she'd idled for fifteen minutes, after dragging the slain pig into the dog kennel. The cops would pat the warm truck bonnet. Nodding. *Sorry, husband, the truck keys are deep in your pocket.* She undressed and tore her discarded clothes, sections ripping along seams, and threw them into the rag bin. Engine oil added dark stains, like blood.

As a girl, her papa had walked with her, hand-in-hand from church, crossing the farms, guiding her best shoes away from the muddy tractor ruts. Her mamma would stay behind, gathering village news, helping assemble food parcels for widows and the poor. Week by week, the cane would rise, starting from her knees. She loved to run a hand over the soft leaves as if patting a pet. Before long though, the stalks would soar over her head, creating a permanent gloom, and she held her papa's hand tight. Sometimes, if there was a breeze, the stalks would shake, and she imagined they were dancing, and skipped in rhythm. At a slight rise they would pause, and her papa would share a home-baked biscuit. Looking over their farm, his lined brown face with its own ruts would further crease into a broad smile. We left with nothing; he would often tell her, *il nulla*.

'As we boarded the ship in Palermo, it was hard to believe we could make a new home in such a beautiful green place as Silkwood.'

He told her his parents died with regret, because they had nothing to leave their *bambini*. This was before the regular talk of marrying well, honouring her parents, but she remembered her papa looking away to neighbouring farms, his smile fading. He grumbled about a farming family who took over smaller farms when the opportunity arose, through forced marriage, financial strain, illness, or death. At every opportunity, their chequebook was out. The initial offer was always insultingly well below market value. When the farm was secured, the family painted their name in thick white letters on letterbox barrels, the previous owners erased and to be forgotten.

'Not our *casa, my bella*,' he would say, kissing her cheek.

From the rise, they would walk down a slope, and his cheer would return. He'd puff on his pipe, his hand stroking their family name on the barrel post-box. As a girl, Frances thought nothing of the other family name because it was so common. Looking around her papa's shed, she thought of it today.

'Oh, Papa,' she whispered, 'it's taken me years, because of my *bambini*, but I'm going to make it right.'

She took a deep breath, thinking of the police knocking on the door of the Pierce household. A knock Mrs Pierce may have been hoping for. Maybe she'd already left her husband, finishing her life sentence. Bianca mentioned office gossip. Also, 'Vet Maria' hadn't been published this week.

Frances touched her paintings stacked under hessian cloth. Later in the week, with Gino in the watchhouse, she would rehang her 'miserable and beautiful' paintings. Whenever she'd dusted off her paintings, selecting a wall to rehang them, Gino would complain, saying he once went to an art show, then his dreams turned into a nightmare.

'What nightmare, Papa?' asked inquisitive Bianca.

It had taken Frances many distractions, driving to the 'big shops' in Cairns, for Bianca to forget. They'd returned with clothes they couldn't afford.

Frances caught her reflection in the greasy truck window. Soon she would hold the stares of the town men, competing with glorious Bianca. After feeling miserable her entire marriage, she didn't want another man or men, just yet. First, Gino's trial and sentence. She looked back to appraise her face. For a rare time, Frances enjoyed her reflection. She'd always been told she was beautiful, the village's Sophia Loren, but with Gino, she wondered whether it was a waste. The best use of her supposed beauty, she'd thought, was to pass her parent's olive complexion and luminous dark brown eyes to her daughters. Realising she was near naked, she gasped, thinking, *yes*. In her mid-thirties, she could enjoy sex for the first time, making love on the beach at beautiful Etty Bay, cassowaries as lifeguards. Her eyes flickered. She could try the things described in Isabella's magazines and Bianca's diaries. After her lover's visits, she would paint, with the gun room converted into a studio. Paint brushes instead of rifles. Paint pots replacing ammo.

Frances halted; before she could establish herself as a painter with a lover, she needed to remain the diligent housewife. There was tidying up to do, a few sweeps of a broom. In town, in the rearview mirror, she'd seen the other truck as the school bus doubled back. There, too, Matt Flint staggered around, then scurried away like a loony scarecrow on the loose; so much for the pen being mightier than the sword. There couldn't be a suggestion of two firearms. On Monday, Bianca would need to locate Matt's office peashooter and toss it into a deep farm drain. The sinking firearm would join many others, rusting in red mud. With Darcy at the scene, Leo would need to explain his role in planting false evidence. Leo could make the case he was manipulated by the late, dearly departed Richard Pierce, helping to clear Darcy's name. Later today she would probably see the detective. She knew what to say.

'I suppose delicate Darcy tried to prevent injury to his father figure. He's drawn to strong male characters, the way *his type* can be. I never thought my husband could be so wicked.'

The single detective would be receptive as she hugged him for comfort, letting him get ideas. Bianca's strong perfume on his shirt would cast a long reminder. The detective seemed drawn to easy, simple conclusions. If he returned to Darcy's home, with grass as high as sugar cane, he would only see scrubbed side paths. Darcy's bedroom and bathroom were also forensically clean, with no trace of Russo female visitors. Darcy's semen-streaked sheets were washed and folded in the cupboard. Although a practical woman from the land, *that* was a difficult job, and she'd mumbled Sicilian curses. Only the dead cockroach, who she'd named 'Darcy', remained pressed into the carpet.

Frances touched the cross on her necklace. *What if Darcy was dead or seriously injured?* She'd heard the shot, like a firecracker at Feast of the Three Saints. For the time being, she hoped, his greatest risk was hospital food. But she couldn't fool herself; Darcy had laid as still as Pierce. At least Isabella wasn't one of the students on the school bus, looking down in horror at her splayed, maybe slayed, boyfriend. Isabella had barely coped with Darcy's brief disappearance. *What if she was pregnant and the baby without a father?* If he survived, she'd have to try to forgive him, at least for Isabella's sake.

Inside the Russo home, Gino snored, laying prone across the lounge. Rain swept over with a grumble of thunder. Gino often said he missed the police uniform, looking at the rain saturating the fields. *Plenty of uniforms where you're going, pig.*

She listened for sirens.

A black and white photo of her parents caught her eye. They smiled back at her, not like the stern portraits embedded in mausoleum granite. Frances kissed the photo. There would be no more tears at Easter, with her parents finally at rest. *Maloccio at peace.*

Still, she waited for sirens.

In the months ahead, she might pop down to Stuart Creek to visit Gino, maintaining appearances. Under a long modest dress, she would wear new, sheer lingerie to be discarded immodestly on a motel floor. Between 'prayers of the faithful' last Sunday, church gossip had reached Frances; Joseph had separated from his wife.

Over the months and years ahead, Gino, with mounting layers of scar tissue over his eye sockets, might notice that Frances looked more relaxed, *fulfilled,* asking why she no long wore a wedding band. He'd complain about her court testimony. Frances would reply that she'd been raised to always to be truthful. Listening to his theories – *I've been stitched up, Fran* – she'd sniffle at the injustice, agreeing to pass along his appraisal to Dennis. Driving out of the prison car park she'd smirk. Gino would never receive a visit from the detective, pen out, notebook open, receptive ear cocked.

Frances showered and dried her hair, rinsed, wrung and hung her underwear to dry. In a thin white nightdress she'd hung overnight, Frances walked to Isabella's room. The night before, she'd given her daughter a glass of tainted water when entering the bedroom chapel for prayers. Isabella would still be passed out from dissolved sleeping pills layering the celebration vinos. She opened Isabella's bedroom door and slid in beside her sleeping daughter, *where she'd been all night, officers*, comforting her distraught daughter, embarrassed about the graduation debacle. Isabella snuffled, then groaned, her face wincing from cramps, holding her belly. Frances lay a soft palm over her daughter's stomach, glanced at the virgin's holy glow in the portrait, blessed herself, mouthing, *Grazie, Madonna mia.* Frances closed her eyes, drifting to sleep, praying for Darcy, hearing sirens in her dreams, ignoring the ringing telephone.

<h1 style="text-align:center">38</h1>

DARCY drifted high above the earth, rolling through soft cloud pillows. Below, were Silkwood's patchwork quilt of farms. Then he lifted higher, touching the sun, ecstatic, with a tube in his arm. A satellite whistled by, emptying popcorn, which turned into stars. Darcy hovered over Etty Bay. Isabella's cast-off bikini lay on a recumbent boulder. Aunt Betty held an illustration of a woman's erogenous zones. Naked Isabella walked towards him.

'Hello, I'm Eve.'

Annie Lennox from the *Eurythmics*, wearing Cindy's missing earring, hummed '*Sexcrime*'.

Darcy returned to his hospital pillow at the squeak of shoes on institutional lino. After a groan, a slight chilling pressure pulsed in his veins. A meteor shower filled the entire galaxy. In the Silkwood fields, he was kissing Isabella under fireworks – a shooting star whizzed by.

For at least two days, by his rough calculations, Darcy rested like a crocodile on a riverbank, with pretend sleepy lids, lying in muddy camo. Listening. Recalling. He remembered pulling into the school carpark. Pierce was on the ground. Sid's cap pulled low, Pierce's sunglasses covering his face, Darcy kicked Sid's gun back under the seat, for there was no need. Blood pooled around the Statesman's front tyres. By the truck, he heard a man call out. Then *smash*. Later, he rode like Silkwood's fourth martyr, not on a motorised float, but bouncing along on the back of what felt like a cassowary.

He groaned – wanting to forget the pulverised remnants of Rich's head with its flaxen bloodied hair – receiving more welcome pressure and chill in his veins, drifting again into dreamy bliss. Through the mist, Isabella walked by in swimwear at the inland gorge. They jumped on his bed, readying to rehearse for Frances, announcing themselves as a couple. Then he was back in teachery brown at the parent-teacher night. He'd been speechless at Frances' lunch invite, in awe of her beauty. She'd helped bashful Darcy.

'C'mon Darcy, you know what to say.'

Rousing in the hospital bed hours later, Darcy's hip ached under a bulky bandage. His head felt grazed, combined with a bruised shoulder. When he wasn't touring Darcy Dreamland, he wondered whether Isabella knew he'd returned and was in hospital. His pulse quickened, not because someone had killed Pierce and he was at the scene, but Frances might find him, adding to his injuries. Perhaps he was the real target, not Pierce.

The hospital ward was quiet, so he peeked about with low croc-like eyes. A bag of blood drained into his arm. Darcy wondered whose blood it was, and whether it could make him a better person, for he couldn't trust his blood or his bloodline. The bedside table was bare. No cards, no flowers. Darcy sighed. So, no one knew or cared. Isabella, lost to him, probably guarded. A tear trickled, itched and he winked it away. *The Pearl* was parked at Sid's house. Keys on the floor. He'd roll out of town, like Desmond, the truckie, a rider on the storm. Hearing shoes squeaking towards him, he snapped his eyes shut.

Fingers touched the bandage on his head. 'Detective, he's likely to be concussed. I can feel swelling, but I hope he can remember what happened. His blood pressure is nearly normal, so he is improving.'

'Good. I need answers,' a gruff man replied.

Later, Darcy woke, remembering Isabella's green dress emerging from the backdrop of shimmering cane when he collected her for a road trip. Swaying cane stalks formed into long lean legs as she ran to him, beaming, as if he was the only thing that mattered in the whole world. Isabella was a glimpse of the divine, like at her birthday, rays of heavenly light beatifying her angelic face. Nothing else existed. *Just Isabella.*

Darcy remembered too, seeing his parents in a cloudy, heavenly shroud as he bled on the ground. They'd stopped beckoning. His mother whispered, 'Your girlfriend is so beautiful and in love with you, what are you doing here?'

Darcy felt the bumps as he returned through the stratosphere, lowered from a great height. 'There you go, sir,' said a familiar voice, 'so gammon, Mr Grant.'

'Detective, he's rousing.'

He felt a shove.

'Darcy! Darcy Grant!'

He closed his eyes, returning to his quiet internal reptilian realm, slumping into a warm mud mattress in the mangroves.

'He's out again,' a woman observed.

Later, he heard light steps nearing his bed, curtains closing with a swoosh. Someone placed flowers beside him. Floral notes filled his crocodile snout – the smell of Eden at the dawn of time. A shadow came over his face. Darcy's eyes squinted, checking. This time, it wasn't the yelling man asking questions. Frances touched his cheek, placing a hand where she had struck him. Darcy opened his eyes wide, head pushing back into the hard pillow.

'No, I'm injured enough—'

She whispered in his ear. 'I read Eli Jenkins' prayer. I see your best side.'

'Really? I don't deserve—'

'Shush. Concentrate. We can sort this out later. Gino has no best side. He did it. He shot Pierce. Then he shot you.' She kissed his cheek. 'There's no God on this ward, but there are police. Gino did it. You know what to say.'

Further away, a door opened and curtains rustled. Darcy snapped his eyes shut, listening.

'Hi, detective,' said Frances. 'I was just dropping off flowers on behalf of the school staff. We're all so sorry Darcy was injured. Devastating too about Richard Pierce. We're organising flowers for his wife. What's the latest?'

'We need to detain your husband for ongoing questioning. Your husband hasn't been cooperative, but it's not looking good for him. I can't say much else at this stage.'

Frances replied loudly as if she wanted the entire ward to know. 'The insult to Isabella at the graduation must have triggered my husband. He was enraged. All night in his gun room.' Frances sniffled. 'Oh, detective, I should have tried to stop him, if… if… I knew… what he was capable of—'

'Oh, Mrs Russo, it's not your fault.'

'Call me Frances.'

Close-lidded, Darcy listened, but he only heard shoes shuffling and a sigh. He had the weird idea that Frances and the detective were hugging. Then he heard a door open, and Frances spoke again.

'Hi, Leo, you're here to see the detective?'

'Oh, yeah, Frances. Oh yeah, the detective, eh.'

There were murmurings that Darcy couldn't quite hear.

'Really? I need a statement,' the detective muttered.

A few minutes later, Darcy flexed his stiff hip again.

'Detective. He's rousing again.'

'No more painkillers!' the man yelled. More shoving. 'GRANT. WAKE UP!'

Darcy opened his eyes and tried to sit up, but he was a Hills Hoist clothesline, restrained by wires and cords. A balding man was in his face, asking about money and murder. He felt strands of hair falling on his face, like the web tresses at Dunk Island. Blinking, Darcy asked for water. He took a cup from his left hand, as his right was cuffed.

'Darcy Grant, I'm told Richard Pierce managed the cinema revenue. I have a theory you turned up wanting to discuss allegations of missing money. But Pierce was already down, and the killer blasted you, probably worried about being identified. Sound right?'

Darcy nodded. 'Yeah, that sounds right.'

'Did you see the killer?'

'Just out of the corner of my eye.'

'Hear anything?' The detective leaned in.

'Footsteps, but nothing much afterward. I must have hit my head and been out by then.'

'What about before?'

'He called out, "this is for my bella," or something like that. His voice was raspy and a bit hard to make out.'

'He? You're confirming the shooter was male?'

'Voice was male, yeah.'

'For Bella, huh?' The detective paused. 'Ah, maybe "for Isabella", the Russo daughter?'

He heard an echo. *You know what to say.*

'Yeah, that's what I heard.'

Darcy felt a pat on his shoulder.

'Voice was raspy, hey? Like a heavy smoker? My sources tell me you know Gino Russo. Was it his voice? Saying for Isabella?'

Gino had no best side. Frances and Isabella saw his. There was no God on the ward.

Darcy knew what to say.

ACKNOWLEDGEMENTS

Thanks to Carolyn and the entire Hawkeye team for your confidence in my writing and story, and your expert assistance readying the novel.

I often flick through tributes at the end of novels, wondering why a few thousand words involved so many people, when writing is a solitary exercise. Now I know. Across three years of drafting and redrafting, I was rewarded with excellent feedback related to story formation, content suitability, characterisation, through to edits. There are many people to recognise, starting with the inner circle.

Thanks to my family; Pauline, Helen, Carmel, and Kevin for advice and encouragement. Friends, JV, Toddy, Sandra, Danielle, and Bec provided input, especially about scenes and characterisation.

Thanks to my neighbour, Josie Caltabiano, a descendant of Sicilian immigrants. Josie helped with language and cultural descriptions.

Via the Queensland Writers' Centre (QWC), I was introduced to Dr Melanie Myers, an award-winning novelist and writing academic, who tackled a raw first draft, and many drafts thereafter. Her honesty and keen eye helped on many levels. Melanie is the main reason the book reached publication standard.

Thanks, too, to the QWC for early interest in the story, through the 'Adaptable' competition, for stories suited to the screen, and for curating excellent, practical writing courses, from which I benefited.

I was inspired by a photo of a cane scene and mountains, which later featured on the cover. It was a thrill to connect with the photographer, Alison Jones (www.amjphotocairns.com.au), a FNQ resident. I hope the story does the photo justice. Vikki Vaughan, a graphic designer, expertly added Frances' steely, watchful eyes into the background within her creative preparation of the book cover.

Thanks too, to Formula One and the Netflix series 'Drive to Survive'. I joke among friends that this is the book that Formula One wrote. While my partner, Stacey, found an obsession in prestige motor sport, I found the time to write. Then she had to share my passion, reviewing and editing many drafts. My final thanks to the many people who provided testimonials. The cheques are in the mail, or more likely a book, as in-kind payment.

ABOUT THE AUTHOR

Greg Bourke's career has focused on writing and expression, first as an English teacher, and later within corporate communications. Over many years, he has helped numerous families and people with their stories and memoirs. Greg was inspired to write a novel based in Far North Queensland, the scene of his first teaching post in the 1980s, when revisiting the region years later. His debut novel, *Under Silkwood*, was shortlisted for the Queensland Writers' Centre 2024 'Adaptable' program, and an excerpt from the novel was long-listed in the 2024 Sydney Hammond Memorial Short Story award.

Photo by: Stacey Hall

If you liked what you read today, please tell your friends or post a review
on Goodreads or your favourite forum about what you enjoyed.

Under Silkwood is available at hawkeyebooks.com.au
and all good bookstores and libraries.

. . . .

If you loved *Under Silkwood* you'll also enjoy:
The Ghost Train and the Scarlet Moon by Jack Roney
The Angels Wept by Jack Roney
Rosanna by Annie O'Moon-Browning
Forgotten by Casey Nott
Where There is a Will by Michel Vimal du Monteil